WHO INVITED THE DEMON TO TEA?

MARILU MOSER

First published in the United States of America On October 28 2024 by Tome Dragon Publishing LLC

ISBN- (Ebook) 979-8-9864261-8-1

ISBN-(Paperback) 979-8-9864261-7-4

Editing done by: K.F. Starfell

Cover by: Reina Diaz [@mytinybookshelfs]

Formatting done by: Tome Dragon Publishing LLC [tomedragonpublishing@gmail.com]

Foreword

Your mental health, emotional health, boundaries, and limits are important to me. Before you continue reading, please note this is an adult paranormal/monster romance with mature content. Recommended age is 18 years and older to enjoy this story. This book contains mature content and suggestive language.

Other elements include profanity, drinking, explicit sexual content, magical alcohol and pills, and strained/ unhealthy parental relationships

That being said, pleas keep in my mind, I am only human and do not intend any harm to any community. If there is anything harmful in this book, please feel free to reach out so that it can be addressed and/or corrected

For the most up to date list please visit my website

ALSO BY

Marilu Moser

The Reaper Tomes
Urban Fantasy
Fated Deals: The Reaper Tomes Novella 1
A New Era: The Reaper Tomes Book 1 https://mybook.to/xbLjj
Call of the Coven: The Reaper Tomes Book 2

Bound by Wing and Fang
Monster Romance
The Gargoyle's Gift https://mybook.to/aS4XYM
The Gargoyles Cupid https://mybook.to/RrVIR2

To all the book lovers who love a Gentleman in the streets but a Demon
in the sheets,
this one's for you.

Chapter 1
MENTAL NOTES
Davina

"WHAT A DUMP."

The thought slips through the holes of the Swiss cheese filter equipped in my mind. It's the only accurate way to describe my Uncle Alex's home. The old 3-story, 3-bedroom, 2-and-half-bath house sits on the corner lot of Trilley Road, shrouded by overgrown trees and shrubs.

Mounds of dirty, melting snow sit along the narrow road while drips of water from melting icicles plink onto parked cars. The snow fell early this year; Thanksgiving is still weeks away. Ironically, it works with the entire motif of the town of Earvil.

Good old Earvil. A sprawling town no one has ever heard of but claims to be known for its ghost stories. It's one of those towns where, when people ask where you're from, it's easier to name the closest and largest city. For this town, that would be Portland.

I close the car door and gaze at the unkempt house, wrinkles on my forehead growing deeper as my thick brows meet my hairline.

He'd had this house for years and never bothered to re-paint, install new windows, or clean the gutters.

Fingers crossed, the grey damp, weather is what makes the house seem worse for wear.

Ten visits, maybe, are all I can recall while growing up. My parents would say it was too far of a drive and would always invite him up for family functions. Visits from Uncle Alex were the highlights of my birthdays, summers, and holidays. I could always count on him to add some mischief and spoil me with all the things I shouldn't have.

How did I end up inheriting this? I was his only living relative he actually liked.

My parents brought me up in the Catholic faith. I'm talking Sunday school, bible summer camps, private all-girls academy. The whole she-bang. It was my mother's religion, and my father adopted it to marry her and appease my grandmother. Sometime after I graduated, we just stopped doing all the holy stuff, not that I'm complaining.

Uncle Alex did not follow that. He believed "to each their own" and practiced some variation of witchcraft. At least, that's what my dad, Rick, would say. Any time I wanted to know more, I was banned from asking and told to speak to the priest next Sunday. I stopped asking, like the good, obedient daughter that I am, because I didn't want to be rude.

The visits became fewer during my senior year at the academy—after my mother caught me 'attempting to summon demons' in my bedroom. My mother, Paloma, saw incense burning on my table next to a few vanilla and caramel-scented candles and crystals. She ran out of the room in hysterics and wouldn't listen to a word I said.

She failed to realize the incense was lit to mask the smell of cheap weed freely wafting around in my room while I attempted to make jewelry for the church craft fair. All I wanted was to relax while creating a side hustle to earn money for school snacks. Those cafeteria prices were atrocious.

Three dollars for a single sugar cookie? Freaking private school prices.

When I called my uncle and told him, he sputtered laughter through tears. He took the blame, even though there was none to take, telling my parents he had told me a silly incantation that would make a boy fall in love with me. He was a certified shit-stirrer. In actuality, it made it worse.

Paloma went on a tirade about how boys are a "distraction," and "my focus should be on school and family," and "practicing magic was a one-way ticket to hell."

She even threatened to take me out of soccer. Good thing she didn't. It would have cost me my full-ride scholarship.

Rick, however, wouldn't quit asking if I've been biblical with any boys because "he's too young to be a grandpa." That was followed by one helluva uncomfortable birds-and-the-bees talk. The only thing from that trauma-inducing conversation that stuck with me forever was that condoms are cheaper than college.

Thanks, Dad.

The awesome thing about the little fib was he didn't completely make it up. Uncle Alex would spout nonsense about magic spells to me all the time. Unfortunately, I never saw any results from these supposed spells. I always took them as fun stories and rhymes. All the horror movies I've seen so far in my life are enough to let me know demon summoning is a terrible idea.

After that, my parents banned me from visiting his place again during high school. Damn shame, too.

Uncle Alex believed being young meant I should be able to explore who I am and what makes me Davina. Even if it meant lighting a joint or two or having random hook-ups during college years.

He was fun. I miss him.

Looking back now, I should have come here during my college breaks, even if it meant risking tetanus. Instead, I always went back home because mom had galas and other events lined up. And apparently, the "family image" came first, especially since she owns a PR firm.

A smile curls up the corner of my lips at the memory and grows as I stare at my home.

Other than it being a complete dump, you won't find me complaining. Compared to college apartments, this place is the Ritz. I get extra points 'cause I only have to pay taxes once a year.

A win is a win.

Legally, this house is mine now. I get to do whatever I want with it. Nothing and no one can stop me. I'm moving in. If the ceiling collapses, I'll call it a skylight.

The taste of sweet freedom and the quiet sounds of birds chirping are welcoming.

Thank you, Uncle Alex, for freeing me of the sounds of my parents practicing positions depicted in the Kamasutra every single night. Man, they could go at it like rabbits.

Saving money was the only reason for still living with them. Which, mental note: I should call my therapist to cancel future appointments.

The commute from my new home to that crotchety therapist's office is one hundred percent not worth it. Seriously, that lady needed to get with the times and realize that it's totally normal for a woman like me, who's thirty years young, to be into and explore kinks. She damn near had a heart attack when I told her about the dark, wet dreams I had. What can I say? I read some very interesting fanfic.

"I should see if that vampire story has been updated yet," I say before inhaling the sharp, crisp, frigid air.

Looking at the chipped paint on the side of the house, I feel a tickling sensation on my nape. Not necessarily spooky, more like someone studying my every move.

It's probably some nosey neighbor. Nosey neighbors mean there is always someone to gossip with. Maybe I could even invite them over for tea.

I don't think I will, to be honest. Gotta see how creepy they are first.

I pop the trunk to my gray Honda Accord Coupe, lifting out the few pieces of luggage that had seen me through my college years.

As I take one suitcase, the one with the wobbly wheel, up the pavers, I make another mental note:

• Price new pavers or cement bags.

I can already see myself rolling an ankle from how wobbly and cracked these are.

As I near the door, a sudden surge of wind whips through the air, stinging my face with teal paint chips.

Mental note number three:

• Definitely need to hire painters 'cause I'm not skilled for this.

The sight of the snow-dusted rosemary bush surprises me. I helped plant it when I was six years old. It was the only thing that didn't look worn, tired, or dilapidated.

"You, my friend, can stay," I tell the bush, watching the plume of my breath float away.

I remember Uncle Alex telling me that talking helps the plants grow and brings peace to our inner selves. Rubbing feeling into my numb nose, a smile forms at the memory.

I quickly climb the two small, squeaky steps leading up to the homely porch.

Mental note number four:

• Put a bistro table and chairs here after power washing all the dirt and cobwebs undoubtedly hiding under the patches of slush.

The lonely rocker in the corner is not my style.

The brass key slides into the lock easily, unbolting the deadlock it greeted. I swing the door open and step into a flurry of dust.

"Home—" I sneeze.

"Sweet—" Sneeze.

"Home!"

Wait for it—sneeze—*there it is.*

If I don't sneeze in threes, I know I'm sick. Dad called it a cute quirk; Uncle Alex called it a witchy trait. I miss him.

A slam from the back of the house elicits a scream from me. There shouldn't be anyone else here.

I signed all the paperwork with the attorney last week and I have both sets of known keys.

Mental note five:

• Change the locks.

Two choices come to mind. I could call my dad and ask him to drive the two hours and twenty minutes here to check for hidden monsters in the closets. Or, option two: grab hold of the pepper gel dangling from my keychain and investigate my home.

Usually, in the movies, this is where the victim yells out something stupid like "Hello?" or "Is somebody there?" before they're murdered.

Not me. I'm not brainless. My finger is all set to tap my emergency app button. Right now, I am thankful mom installed it before I left for college and paid the subscription fee. Pretty sure she forgot about it and is still paying for it. I'll never tell her. She obviously would want me safe at all times, like now. If someone wants to break into my home, they're meeting me with the element of surprise. That surprise will be me blinding them with pepper gel while screaming profanities and hightailing it out of the house.

I walk the entire house, with the pepper gel leading the way, but I don't find anything out of place or any signs of intruders.

The lavender walls are covered in old ancestral photos so old, I couldn't even place all of them. The antique and ornate gold frames are a nice touch. The furniture is in decent condition; sure, the couch sags a bit, but I can live with it for the time being. My focus is on buying a new mattress and furniture for my new home office. Until then, the dark-stained table with six chairs in the dark floral wallpapered dining room will do just fine.

Somewhere between cleaning and ordering groceries and dinner, the day escaped me, and night crept up. Grumbling from my stomach sounds in tandem with the doorbell.

Digging my wallet out of my pink bag, I happy-dance towards the door.

"There's nothing like a Hawaiian pizza all to myself."

I don't care who you are. Pineapple belongs on pizza. It's sweet, and the ham is salty; it's the perfect combination. Just like fries and ice cream.

Too hungry to grab a plate out of a box, I set the pizza box on the couch next to me, turn on the TV, and scroll through every streaming service my parents have. All these streaming services and not a damn thing to watch.

"Why aren't there any good movies?"

Grabbing my phone, my thumb hovers over the pink and orange app I swore to delete several times.

"I'm a glutton for punishment."

I'm on left swipe 20, I think, and all these profiles and faces are blurring together.

"Why are they all wearing hats?" Another left swipe for the dude wearing a beer-brand trucker hat.

"Oh look, another guy holding a fish." I snort before grabbing another slice of cheesy goodness, "I swear they all fish in the same spot and just share the same fish for photos."

The next photo stops my rejection-happy digits.

"Well, hello, handsome." *His bio is actually good.*

"If you're into a bad boy, well, look no further. I'm so bad, I wink with both eyes…at the same time. I'm also not into multiple partners. If I wanted to disappoint multiple at once, I'd still visit for family dinners."

I swipe right on 33-year-old Grant, who is 20 miles away. Before I can swipe through another profile, I get an instant match.

"Well damn."

Grant

> Please don't be a bot

>> Promise I'm not

> Are you sure? Your photos are insanely attractive to be real

>> Last I checked I have all human lady parts

> Would you like some male parts in you

Frustration zips through me while staring at the dick pick that looks more along the lines of a blurry thumb.

"Oh for fucks sake! This is why I don't date."

Thank goodness I have a secret file in my phone of various penises. My penis vault is courtesy of a safe search filter I turned off for moments like these. For this occasion, I'll send an angry, veiny looking dick.

>> Mines bigger

>> Your moms a hoe.

Before he can respond, I unmatch with Grant.

Mental note:

• Delete this stupid dating app.

Usually to unwind, I'd game, but I don't want to get up. Tomorrow, I'll worry about connecting my gaming console. But tonight? Tonight, I eat my fill and pass out while watching a random movie. *I should get a mini Christmas tree.*

Chapter 2
Curtains
Davina

MORNING COMES FAR TOO soon. My pillow and mattress are whispering sweet nothings to me. It takes everything in me to peel my eyes open and kick the covers off, but I lay there counting the dots on my popcorn ceiling. The same routine I've done every morning for almost a month now.

My stomach cuts the embrace of memory foam short and announces it's time for breakfast.

"Being an adult is so stupid. God, I was stupid for fighting naptime when I was little," I grumble while slipping my feet into a fluffy pair of slippers.

There's still sleep in my eyes as I adjust my glasses and rummage around the shelves and fridge. With three eggs, ham, shredded cheese, and a pepper that has seen better days left in the fridge, an omelet it will be. The scrapping of the silver fork against the white ceramic bowl as I scramble the eggs fills the silence.

Mental note:

- Get a new charging cable for my phone. Cooking is not the same without music.

Standing at the small cement counter next to the bronze farmhouse sink, my eyes dance from the one window and around the hodgepodge kitchen. The bottom, midnight-black cabinets are a stark contrast to the open wooden shelves above them, putting all four of the plates and bowls on full display. The sage green wall is obscured by the fridge I mistakenly sized. Now, it takes up more than half of the wall and protrudes out to swallow up the kitchen floor.

"I knew I shouldn't have bought the scratch and dent model. I can't even return you," I huff my irritation at the stainless-steel appliance.

After making my breakfast on the wobbly copper pan which I found behind some other cookware that was left behind, I sit at the small round table. The white wood of the table takes up what is left of the kitchen floor space with its two mismatched metal and wood chairs. The only sounds are my small moans as I bite into my omelet—which I paired with a bowl of blueberries—and the clattering of my knife and fork against the wooden plate.

"I don't want to work today," I sigh hoping to convince myself I don't have to.

I only took one week off to move, and now I wish I had taken more. Dealing with clients and a work team via video chat is not what I want to be doing today. Unfortunately, being the senior lead risk assessor for the mega-corporation who has made more than a few questionable choices means I have numbers to crunch, and my team has a presentation to prepare.

There's still so much that needs to be done around the house. Luckily, the corporation is in Japan and that gives me a few extra hours. Maybe I'll start my workday after my morning workout.

The textured wallpaper brushes my arm as I stand. Drumming from my fingers against the plate accentuates my thoughts.

"Now, what do I do with you?" I ask the kitchen wall covered in black wallpaper with tiny peaches and leaves.

In all honesty, I find the wallpaper charming, but nothing in this kitchen matches. Who am I kidding? Nothing in this house matches.

Deep, satisfying cracks travel down my spine while doing my morning yoga in the living room. The musky odor of mothballs invades my nostrils as I fold myself into child's pose. Stiff piles from the faded, orange, shag carpet poke through the old yoga mat to scratch at my palms. The sensation is unsettling.

Trying to brush off the feeling, I force myself to concentrate on the peppy instructor on my iPad as she tells me to "breathe deeply and open your hips."

Fine strands of hair escape their bun confinement and sweep across my face. Two sneezes, and I pause for three whole breaths.

"Achoo!"

There's the third.

The rogue strands linger around my eyes, jolting me out of my meditative state. My nose scrunched as I brought my hand to my face.

"Why does it smell like that?" I asked myself.

I kept rubbing my fingers together in hopes of ridding myself of the stench.

Mental note:

- Price new flooring.

Gentle tickles down my spine catapult me off the ground.

"Spider! Spider! Get off me, get off me. Get. Off. Me!"

With every shriek, another article of clothing is stripped off, and the hair tie is tossed, never to be seen again. It isn't until the morning rays shine on my stark-naked body that I realize there was never a spider…it was sweat. Dragging my eyes from beads of sweat descending between my breasts to the open window, I lock eyes with the neighbor across the street. Adding insult to injury: it's not just any neighbor. It's the only hot, young, and very single neighbor on this street.

Blake Johnson, the middle school science teacher. He's classically handsome with his shaggy blonde hair, blue eyes, and dimples. Society would deem him the "female gaze."

We met the day after I moved in. Turns out that feeling of being watched was him.

He had no idea that my uncle passed or that he had any family. Apparently, my dearly departed uncle was labeled the town whacko. So, that was a nice conversation for all of 1 minute until I changed topics so fast that I gave us both whiplash.

Unfortunately, Blake doesn't like tea; he's a black-coffee-only kinda guy. Found that out when I asked if he could help me move the 50-pound box containing my new bed frame into the house and up the stairs. These pea shooters aren't made for heavy lifting. I offered him tea, and he'd wrinkled his nose with a laugh. He took the only other thing I had to offer: generic bottled water.

Snapping out of my deer-in-the-headlights state, unease hits me with the weight of an anchor, and I slink down to the ground in all my naked glory.

Smelly, orange-shag carpet seems like a cozy spot to die from embarrassment.

Crawling along the carpet, I send a silent prayer, hoping my nipples and mound don't chafe or get rug burn. Mid crawl, my limbs pause, and I groan; the smell from this carpet better not seep into the pores of my lady bits. I add yet another mental note:

- Get some freaking curtains.

Chapter 3

UNCOUTH

Mendax

BEING STUCK IN THIS dreary place for nearly four years is beginning to give me wrinkles. Mess up one time, and bam! Access denied to all other realms. No more gateways or quick trips to see what others are doing. No getting to do my job.

It wasn't my fault.

I had zero inclination that anyone other than that damn politician was interested in buying a witch's ladder. If I had, I would have entertained that offer, too, instead of being robbed. I wasn't even going to broker the deal. My brother was supposed to take the lead on that and then never showed up so, Mother called and frantically asked me to do it.

I was woefully unprepared. There were no notes on who I was meeting or the location.

I will never trust them again. But now, I have to watch the realms through our news networks. Not a single being I know enjoys watching Spawn at Dawn. The only ones who find that heap of trash informative and entertaining are grandparents. Even demons get boring with age I suppose.

It's all fine and dandy, I guess. The only realm I ever really frequented was the human realm, and that was for work. Humans suffer the ill fate of greed. All they ever do is whine and complain about not having enough of this or that. Wanting what someone else has. Whenever I've encountered a human, it's because they want to ask something of me.

Sure, it's part of my job, the grand ole family business: procurement, sales, brokering, and trades.

Hindsight has shown all those trips and deals were taken for granted. Boredom doesn't even begin to describe what I'm feeling.

I've tried to escape my home. I even attempted to bribe one of the gateway owners. All it did was extend my sentence. I get to leave my humble abode; I'm simply confined to this realm.

The only way to escape these dreadful grey walls is to be summoned. No one in the underworld has the power to stop a summoning. But that's a mere fantasy I will think of fondly. It has only ever happened once and I doubt all these years later, it'll ever happen again.

Thick black hair slips through my fingers as I massage my head, which reminds me I should schedule a haircut and horn polishing.

Clanging and chirping is a welcomed interruption to my brooding.

Gotha, my pet bat, rattles her cage in excitement; she's been pestering me all day since her cast was removed. Poor thing had a run-in with a stray dog.

Cold metal meets the blunt edge of my nails as I flick the lock open.

"Alright there. You haven't flown in three weeks, so don't go too far or too fast," I say sternly to Gotha. "Hunt your meal and come straight back."

A happy chirp sounds from her in agreement as she stretches her wings. Perhaps I'm a tad overprotective, but as I watch her fly from her perch and out my balcony door, the idea to follow her enters my mind.

"Why not?" I say to myself, slicking back my hair.

A quick glance in the mirror reveals how dull my ruby skin looks. Brushing my beard, I tug the sleeves on my navy suit jacket and make my way out.

Perhaps fresh air will do me good.

The jovial sounds of dancing and laughter float down the cobbled road. It's a stark contrast to the orange sky, grey clouds, and black rain pelting the ground. I do miss the bluish sky that held a tinge of green in the evening with puffy yellow clouds. But we're in a rainy year. Hopefully, next year I'll see that sky again.

Smashing glass rips me away from my longing for brighter years. Disgust curls my lip as I watch mead splash all over my cap-toe Oxford shoes. By human standards, these are vintage; by my world standards, they're a rarity.

"I spent three hours shining these last night," I grit out.

The amber mead streaks down my toe, eating away the shine.

Glancing up in the direction of where the bottle came from, the issue makes itself known. There stand the ruffians who are the cause of everything that has gone wrong in my life, also known as my brother and his friends.

"Sorry, Dax," my brother, Orroth, says with a sly smile. "I was supposed to catch that; it slipped."

Besides being bothers, we couldn't be more different. Orroth is a rabble-rouser; he has always lacked the tactful art of negotiating. His hair is grown out and unruly. He's constantly blowing it out of his pink-hued eyes. Quite frankly, he's annoying, but that's to be expected given our age gap. I'm a full 20 years older than him. Our parents just had to take that booze cruise to try and revive the marriage.

Shaking off the tip of my shoe and wiping it against his jeans, I sigh.

"Yes, yes. Well, you must be mindful of your surroundings. Like me." A smile paints itself on my face. "That's why my shoe hasn't slipped up your ass. See, mindful."

Our parents' golden boy swallows roughly as his scarlet face pales and his blush-colored eyes narrow.

"You talk a big game there, Dax."

"You know my talk is more than a game. You should watch how you speak to me. My memory may come back, and I may remember how you were drunk and skirt-chasing instead of simply forgetting you had a meeting that night."

His stubble tickles the pads of my fingers as I pinch his cheeks.

We both know the only reason why he gets to roam freely is because I shouldered the blame, like the good older brother I am. One of us had to clean up the mess while the other upheld the family name and business.

How unfortunate for me, I do one in public and the other behind closed doors: I tell him where to find our clients and the oddities they request. Fortunately for him, most requests are stored in one of our warehouses.

Hooting, hollowing, and hollering erupt from the bar, and the rest of Orroth's friends tumble out. There's one with both arms draped over two women, and another dragging a witch out over his shoulder.

"Yo, Orr! Let's go before your little lady tries to start any more fires." one of my brother's friends yells out.

I'm not sure if it's Dakolas or Rolvak. It's basically impossible to tell the identical twins apart from here. The only way to know for sure is their eyes. One has a small scar over his right eyelid from a street brawl. Other than that, they both have smooth, deep green skin, and brown hair styled in a fade. The three of them grew up together and are mischief, mayhem, and chaos.

My eyes roll involuntarily at the entire scene. The lot of them are uncouth. Only three more years and I can be done with my sentence.

A nice long vacation would do nicely after. I wonder how the sulfur pits are this time of the year, or maybe I'll venture back to the human realm and see some snow.

Nudging my brother in the direction of his merry little band of idiots, I issue a stern warning, "Behave yourself, Orroth. I mean it. It's all fun and games now, but eventually, you'll have to grow up, too."

There's more to life than being a trust-fund kid.

"Dax, while you're almost old enough to be my father, you're not. So, stop, okay?" he says, jogging off. "Oh, and Mom wants you over for dinner tomorrow, too."

I inwardly groan, knowing full well why she wants me over. Forever trying to play matchmaker so she can fulfill her desire to become a grandmother. Gotha swoops down from the sky, landing on my shoulder.

That's enough outdoors for the both of us today.

Chapter 4

COLD PILLOW

Davina

"Yes, Dad, I already changed the locks and put longer screws into the strike plate."

No, I haven't, but there's no need to worry the old man now. I already made a mental note to do it anyway; I just need to actually do it.

It's not like I don't have the right tools for the job. Me walking into the hardware store is the equivalent of chum being thrown in shark-infested waters. I hope the sweet old man who helped me never sits at a red light when he's in a hurry.

I've been in my humble abode for a full month now and this is the first time my dad has suggested changing the locks.

"Rick, did she get the toaster we ordered?" my mother yells in the background over slamming pots and pans.

Now we wait for the smoke alarm.

Hearing the heavy sigh from my dad, a soft chuckle escapes my lips.

"You didn't order it, did you?" I ask.

"No, I didn't," he whispers. "I completely forgot. Sorry, Pumpkin."

His answer makes me laugh harder because I wouldn't expect anything else. Dad is the person who asks where his glasses are while wearing them.

"Ugh, Dad. Please stop calling me "Pumpkin.'"

I still cringe at the nickname neither of them will ever let go of.

"Tell her I got it but haven't opened it yet. I'm still—"

Rustling on the other end cuts off my words, and I wince hearing my mother. She always speaks—or rather yells—into the phone while nearly swallowing the receiver end of it.

"Mom? I have no idea what you said. The blood in my ear canal muffled it," I grumble, pulling the phone away.

"I don't appreciate your attitude, Missy. I can tell by looking at your father he didn't order it, so don't bother covering for him. Did you get the email I sent you with the contractor's information?" she asks in between clinks of her spoon on a tea saucer.

It's the one thing we can bond over, me and my mother—our love for tea. If we didn't have that, we would be at a loss.

"Mom, I replied and texted you. I'm not using him. He's an uninsured, 75-year-old handyman. What if he has a heart attack pulling up these carpets? I'm not getting sued by his family or living with that on my conscience. I appreciate your help, I really do, but I'm going to pass on this one," I reply as I slip a freshly charged battery into the red power drill.

The warm glass of my phone presses against the pad of my thumb, turning on the speaker. My mother's voice startles me as I place my new phone on the top of the ladder.

"You know, your father and I have been meaning to visit since you moved. The house is too quiet without you now."

"Here, I thought you and Dad would enjoy the alone time," I say before climbing the silver ladder to hang my new blackout curtains.

My fingers tug the bike shorts that have risen higher on my inner thigh than comfortable.

Maybe I should have bought these in an extra-large instead of a large.

After several minutes of listening to my mother gossip about Mrs. Johnson, who lives down the street from them, and how she has been letting her dogs poo freely on everyone's yard, my dad starts yelling in the background.

"I'm going to spray those ankle biters with the hose, Polly! So, help me God! I'm going to hose them down and that walking corpse, too. I'll do the entire neighborhood a favor."

His rant is cut off by the slam of the front door.

"Oh God. I have to go, Pumpkin. Your father has gone off the deep end, and we don't need an HOA complaint… again. I can only do so much damage control."

Again, with the 'Pumpkin.'

"You go wrangle Dad in. I have to put these curtains up so my neighbors don't get any more free peep shows." My eyes widen at my own words, dreading to hear what she'll say.

"Peep show? Davina Nicole Myles—" My mother is inhaling and growing louder. I can tell she's torn about whether it makes more sense to have a conversation with me about being decent or chase my dad around the neighborhood.

I'll throw her a bone and make the decision for her. The drill whirs, cutting her off her next words. "I gotta go, Mom. Have fun with Dad. Love you guys."

Twenty minutes and 24 holes in the wall later, my bronze curtain rod hangs with floor-length champagne-colored curtains. The curtains stay parted at just the right amount to let enough sunlight in, but the many holes in the wall beckon for my gaze. I'm making a quick mental note to buy spackle when a ripping sound and specks of dust float around the room as I drag the ladder across the dingy and worn carpet and away from the bay window.

"Please don't be expensive, please, please, don't be an expensive repair," I chant and brace myself.

I have never been happier to see something break before in my life. Under the rank, orange carpet is beautiful wood flooring. Sweet, glorious, natural hardwood flooring. Gathering my long brown hair into a messy bun, I march into the kitchen and scour the junk drawer. I'm sure this rusty box cutter has seen better days, but the edge still seems sharp.

"Let's do this."

Music blares while a tie-dye bandana around my face muffles the badly sung and probably wrong lyrics I belt out. My fingers brush the underside of the carpet just as the beat drops, and I drop it low like I did back in college—except my knees don't really move that way anymore.

A rapt against the bay window of the living room has me shrieking, dropping the box cutter, and clutching my chest. Focusing on my breathing, my attention is pulled away from the ratty carpet.

Looking over my shoulder from my crouched position on the floor, I see none other than Blake giving me an awkward wave before pointing to a box in his hand. My now chipped, manicured finger points to the door before I stand and close out my music app.

"Hey, Davina," Blake says. "Sorry to interrupt your remodel; I swear I'm not creeping on you. I tried ringing your doorbell, but I don't think you heard me. Your package got delivered to my house, and I didn't want to leave it out here in the open."

His fingers drum on the box while a giant grin spreads across his thin pink lips.

"The kids in this neighborhood are the local porch pirates."

"Well, at least you didn't see me naked again, right?"

Why am I like this?

Blakes eyes dart to my chest before he clears his throat and looks me in my eyes again. I take that second of eye contact to regain control over my blunder.

"Anywho, thanks for bringing this by. It was so thoughtful and nice of you."

I offer a smile before grabbing the small box from him. Scanning the label, a small thrum of giddiness erupts when I see it's the first box of my Tea of the Month yearly subscription.

"What can I say," Blake cards his fingers through his thick blonde hair while he rocks on his heels. "I'm a nice guy."

I watch as his mouth opens and closes before he takes a step off my porch.

"Hey, Davina?"

I hum in response.

"Can I take you out sometime? There's a great Italian restaurant not too far from here."

He seems almost shy, but there's something about the way he asks that also screams confidence in those baby-blue eyes. Ringing from my phone buys me a few seconds to think.

"Uh, sure. That'd be nice. Let me double-check my work schedule so we can figure out a time?"

"Well, how about a weekend?" he asks with a smirk. "I know I don't work on weekends, do you?"

"Unfortunately, sometimes I do." The ringing stops before starting back again. "I really have to get that. Thanks for dropping this off. I'll let you know my schedule."

I smile before closing the door. I hope I didn't come off as rude. He really does seem like a nice guy, and bonus points for being easy on the eyes.

Walking back into the living room, my phone slides across the newly exposed flooring, showcasing my coworker, Tony, calling…on a Sunday.

"Well, this can't be good."

If one day, I ever get the balls to do it, I'll start my own consulting and marketing firm and put a strict no-working weekends policy in place.

"Tony, what can I do for you this beautiful Sunday morning?" I answer, turning to see where I left the box cutter, I catch sight of a lingering Blake on my porch.

Stuffing the box under my arm, I quickly walk over with the phone in my hand and pull the curtains closed the rest of the way.

"What do you mean, Tony?"

One of my coworkers working on this project begins to stutter on the other end.

"Crap," I mumble as I trip over discarded plastic from the curtain rod packaging. "Tony, you better explain how you forgot to send me three entire spreadsheets of data. This impacts all the numbers and our presentation."

I longingly stare at the unopened box of tea, knowing that instead of a relaxing night reading unhinged fanfic and sipping the mystery tea of the month, I'll be hunched over my computer, crunching numbers, spewing profanities, and wishing Tony's pillow is never cold.

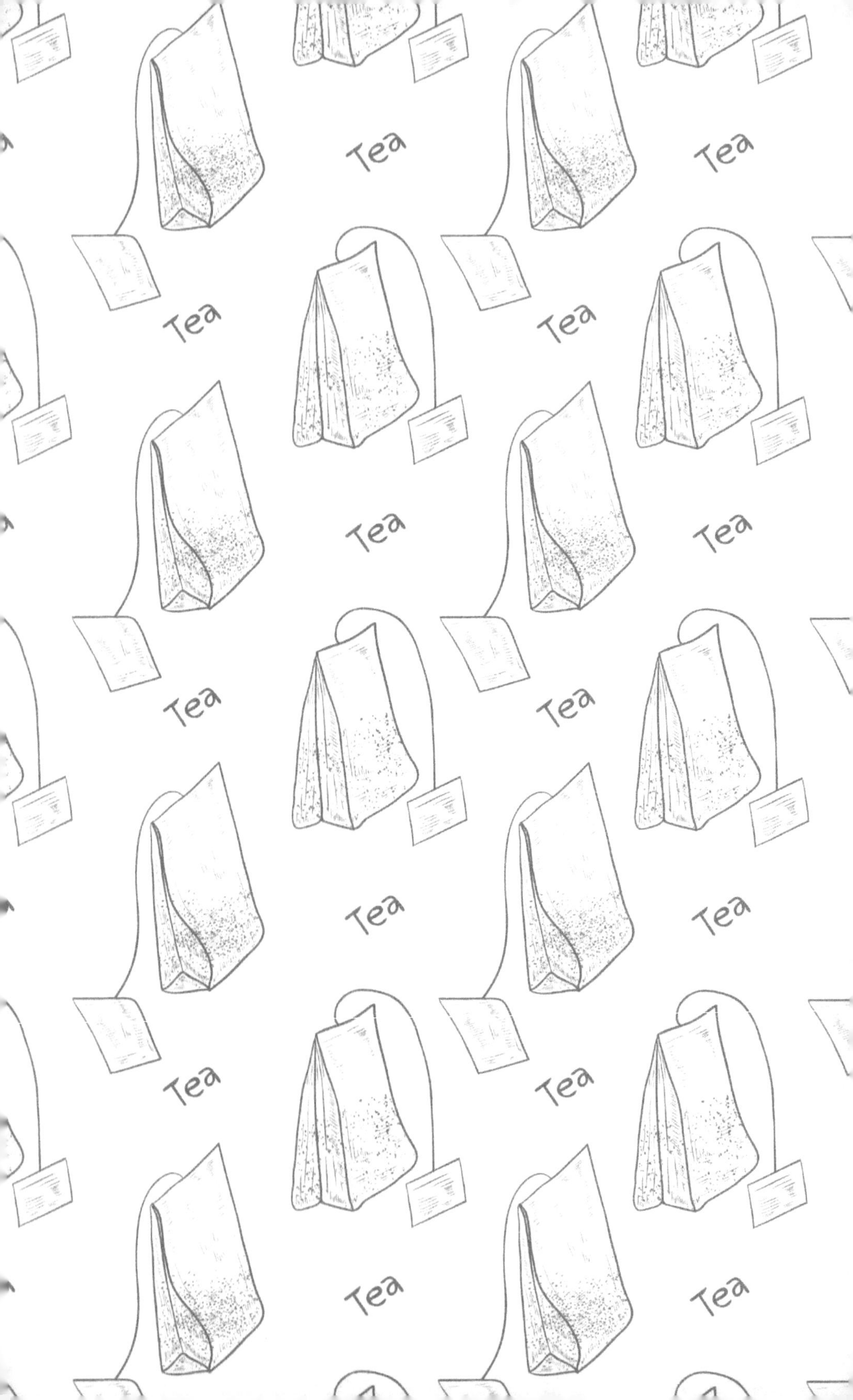
Tea
Tea
Tea
Tea
Tea
Tea
Tea
Tea
Tea

Chapter 5
JAILBREAK
Mendax

S HE SET ME UP—MY OWN mother set me up on a blind date, last night, at her house, no less. To say I'm shocked would be a lie. I wouldn't put anything like this stunt past her. Her desire for grandchildren is beyond wild. There's more to it, though. She also wants a societal marriage. Something that would bring prestige and restore our image.

"Gotha, why can't mother count you as a grandchild?" I ask as I watch her fastidiously groom herself. Her tongue pauses from licking the tip of her wing and offers me a wide-eyed expression while cocking her head to the right.

The white sheets slide down my green silk pajamas as I stand and stretch. A series of pops and cracks roll down my body.

"I'm too old to have children. Not that I want any."

At least, I don't think I do. Having offspring always seemed more like a checklist item than anything. One thing I do know for certain: It is highly unlikely for me to do it.

The poor woman my mother set up thought I had agreed to the date with the intention of marriage. How Mother convinced her of that is anyone's guess.

I had asked why such an upstanding demon as herself would want to date a convicted demon like me. The twitch in her lip as she painted on a fake smile and cleared her throat made me chuckle. I will say her ability to change subjects was uncanny. No doubt, she was certainly taught how to be the perfect wife. In other words, how to have a boring, dull, and empty marriage.

Eventually, with a little prodding here and there, letting my charm do its own thing, along with a few glasses of wine, her loose lips let slip the financial ruin her family is in. Someone always wants something.

Perhaps it was in poor fashion to stay and get her hopes up, but I had no intention of ever seeing her again. There was zero chemistry. Everything about her and the date screamed forced and fake.

No, thank you. I'm happy on my own, living the bachelor lifestyle.

With a yawn, I dispel any further thought on the matter. Ringing from the white marble-faced rotary phone halts my motion to the bathroom. The corners of my mouth tug down in a frown.

"It's too early for this."

Carding my fingers through the mess of tangled black hair, I sigh as the ringing stops and starts again. The sound of my feet padding against the black stone floor swallows the gaps of the high-pitched ringing. I glare at he phone once the ringing stops then glare harder when it commences.

"Mendax," I grit out as I eye my pillow and contemplate crawling back in.

"Yo, Dax. My favorite brother from the same mother. You aren't planning on going anywhere, are you?" Orroth chuckles. "We have an object that needs to be dated. One of Father's friends found it and may want to sell it if it's valuable enough."

It *really* is too early for this.

"Unfortunately, for you and him, I do have plans today. I'll be busy all day."

My plans? Simple really. Do nothing. At all. All day.

"Perhaps you can learn to do it for once, hmm?"

The line goes quiet for a few minutes only the sound of his breathing can be heard.

"I'm talking to him now, Mother." There's an inflection of unease in Orroth's voice. "Trust me, *Mendax*. You really, *really* want to take a look at this item. I can't *date* it."

Something about his phrasing puts me on edge. Especially since he always calls me by the nickname he gave me when he was two.

"Come over now, then."

"On my way!"

His shout is overdramatic. Mother must be listening. The call disconnects.

Staring out the windows of my bedroom, it dawns on me.

"Gotha, the sun is fully up."

I guess it isn't early.

I was always an early riser with a carefully constructed and full schedule.

"Is this what I've amounted to?"

With a yawn and stretch, my knees pop, and my back cracks.

I'm not really that old. Am I?

Looking at myself in the oval bathroom mirror, I can't shake the uneasy feeling growing in the pit of my stomach, but I refuse to give in to anxiety before I've had a cup of tea. Maybe a hot shower will ease the tension. I would soak in the giant clawfoot tub but knowing my brother, he'll be here sooner rather than later. With the idea in mind, I turn the brass knob all the way to the left and wait while the steam billows in the room.

"Don't you dare," I point my blunt black nail at Gotha.

With the shower being wide open with rock tiling, she usually takes it as an open invitation to a group bathe. Her chest puffs out as if I offended her. Barely five steps into the shower, and her undeniable weight is on my shoulder. I really should just accept it; in the seven years of having her, it's always the same.

The day is already utter crap, and I haven't even had lunch yet. My horns are dull and beginning to crack. The wax I normally use on them is dried out, rendering it useless. Not to mention, the length of my hair is grating my nerves. I continue to blow the unruly strand from my eyes as I place the left pearl cufflink into the wrist of my button-down shirt.

The banging on my front door rattles the delicate artwork on my living room wall. Pressing my lips into a thin line, I watch the handcrafted gold frame crash to the ground.

That was a never-seen eighteenth-century original by Giovanni Batista Tiepolo.

It was never sold because he feared a witch cursed it. He was correct. It had been passed down through generations of my family since no one could ever find a buyer. The painting is gorgeous, so curse or no, it's mine.

It takes every ounce of restraint I had not to pull the door off the hinges.

"Orroth, could you not knock like you're a guardsman?"

My brother pushes past me and tosses a small glass jar towards me. Snatching the jar with one hand and using the other to close the door, I hold the jar up to the light.

"Please, do come in."

He whistles, and Gotha swoops from one of her perches towards him. As she climbs all over him, I frown.

"Orroth," I begin as I shake out a sliver of a crystal from the jar, "why in all the realms have you brought me a Red Beryl?"

Sure, the crystal is extremely rare, but I can't think of any buyer who is willing to drop tens of thousands of human dollars for one carrot. At least not this very instant.

"Yeah, I don't really care about those. It was just an excuse to get here," he says. "I just grabbed it off the shelf on my way out of the warehouse. There was never an item."

He laughs when Gotha chirps excitedly after finding the earthly berries in his pockets. Those are always a rare treat for her now.

There's an odd tingling sensation ruminating throughout my body. I've only ever felt something like this once before, but that couldn't be possible now. Rolling my shoulders, I set the jar on the entry table, walk towards my kitchen, and past Orroth, who is now playing with my bat.

"Care to explain why you were in such a hurry to get here, then?" I ask, setting a copper kettle on the stove to heat up.

He tosses a berry into the air and watches as Gotha darts up to catch it.

"Well, I figured I owed you after you took the fall for everything."

The couch rustles beneath him as Orroth begins to bounce his knee. Now, I'm beyond curious about where this is going. I raise a brow, waiting for him to continue, when that tingle shoots up my arm.

"Remember what's-her-face that mother set you up with last night?" He waits for my response.

Waving my hand and nodding for him to continue, because it was last night. Of course I remember her. Arching a brow, the counter digs into my hip holding my weight as I lean against it crossing my ankles.

"She's already drawing up the marriage agreement with the family. Listen, if I can't stand her, I know you can't. We may not always get along, but I can't let her do that behind your back."

He stands and paces the room.

A fissure emerges from the bottom of the floral teacup due to me slamming it down.

"Why is she hell-bent on marrying me off? I've suffered enough for this family." My hand rubs circles on my chest. "I want to live my life in peace."

"Are you okay? You look a little pale there."

Orroth inches closer to me, squinting his eyes trying to figure out what has my lip curling into a grin.

"Really, Dax? You're the easiest one to do this, too. Lucky for me, I'm fully committed and in love with Wren. Who just so happens to run in the same circles we do. The bachelor life came back to bite you in the ass."

This cannot be happening.

"We have to stop her madness. There is no way I would ever marry that woman. There has to be a way to get her to back off."

Orroth stood there staring at me with empty eyes. He shrugged his shoulders before scratching his pointed ear.

"Have you met your mother?"

"Oh, I see. When she's ruining my life, she's *my* mother. When she gives you everything on a silver platter, she's *our* mother?" I clip out before pressing my lips into a thin line.

Nervous laughter bubbles up from my brother.

"What if we fake your death?"

I'm not going to lie; it's a tempting idea but not exactly feasible.

"You know full well I can't do that. If I did, I'd have to leave Gotha so as not to raise suspicions. Who would care for her?" Even though I refute the idea, it tosses around my mind.

No, no. It isn't going to happen. Well…no, no, I can't.

"I can take Gotha," Orroth replies as my bat lands on his shoulder.

I smirk, knowing what she's about to do.

"Ow!"

She bit his cheek. That's my girl.

"Shoo."

He pushes her off his shoulder with a huff. *I'm definitely not leaving her with him.*

That familiar tingle is back and begins to feel like a hot poker prodding into my chest.

"Do you think it would be wise for me to step away for a bit? Perhaps collect my thoughts away from our family?" I ask with excitement.

Turning around, I swing open the large walk-in pantry door. Glass jars bump under my finger before I turn with a grin.

Gotha lands back on Orroth's shoulder, rubbing her face against his cheek as an apology. They sport identical confused expressions.

"I guess so? But where would you go? In case you forgot…" Orroth motions around the room. "You're kind of stuck here, man."

He leans over the counter, squinting. "Why are you smiling like that? That's a creepy smile, Dax. I don't like it. Stop smiling like that! It's creeping me out."

A deep, rumbling chuckle leaves me as I run a conspiratorial hand down my beard.

"Perhaps I need a jailbreak."

The shrill whistle of the kettle cuts off my laughter as I'm yanked out of my realm.

Oh, this is going to be fun.

Chapter 6
Tetanus and Tea Cups
Davina

"**M**r. Hayashi, I understand this would be a notable opportunity for you and your company. But the numbers don't lie." *This has been the longest post-presentation call to date.*

"You hired us to run the risk analysis for you, and I have done that. If you decide to go forward with this new avenue of business, you only have a thirteen percent chance of succeeding."

Mr. Hayashi gives me a polite smile on screen.

"One moment, please." His camera blacks out, and the audio mutes.

I take this moment to also black and mute my screen. It's seven at night here in Oregon, which is midday overseas, and I'm already exhausted.

I'm currently the captain of Team No Sleep. I had to run all the numbers for this presentation several times last night and help rework the presentation this morning. If he decides to go through with this, we'll move on to phase two, which is marketing.

I'm not ready to tackle that beast yet.

There was a pocket where I could have taken a nap, but try as I might, sleep evaded me like a dog running away with something it shouldn't have in its mouth. A yawn leaves me as I slide the oversized gray, square glasses down the bridge of my nose. My fingers find the imprint of the nose pads quickly and massage them. My right butt cheek has fallen asleep, and I can feel the numbness spreading down my leg.

Several minutes of silence have come and gone, and I'm left wondering if this meeting is still ongoing. My hip knocks into the corner of my dining table as I stand to refill my water. Just as I do, the screen comes back on, and I scramble to turn my camera and audio on, too.

Mr. Hayashi began to speak but paused and leaned into the camera. Heat flushed my cheeks as I realized he probably noticed the cupcake pajama bottoms I was sporting. I was currently rocking the signature work-from-home mullet. Business on top and party on the bottom—or, at least in my case, sleepwear on the bottom.

Clearing my throat, I pulled our focus back to the task at hand.

"As I mentioned before, I am not going to tell you how to run your business because that's not my job. I am only here to provide you with numbers and options, which I have done. You wanted to know what I would do in your situation, and it would be advisable to not go forward. If you wish to do so, it will be at your own discretion. However, my marketing team is willing and able to do the research to best market this new venture if you so choose."

"Will you, Ms. Myles, be a part of that team?"

Pushing my glasses back up the bridge of my nose, I take a moment to word this carefully because the answer is yes and no.

"I will be there to support the portion of my team who handles marketing."

He nods his head and thanks me and my team for our time and efforts. We exchange more words as we discuss items to be emailed before concluding our meeting.

Pulling the hair tie out, I'm flooded with relief. The slicked-back high ponytail was beginning to give me a migraine.

"How does mom wear her hair like this all time and still have a thick hairline?"

Right now, there is only one thing that can cure this…tea. The cardboard box is still waiting for me on my kitchen table. My blue sock booties grip the floor as I discard the black blazer and white blouse leaving, me in my cupcake bottoms and white bralette.

A satisfying rip fills the room as I finally get to open the mystery tea from Steeped in Surprise; the first package from my tea of the month.

"Oh, this seems nice," I mutter to myself. The smooth metal black tin warms in my hand as I read the label, "Ceylon Tea with hints of honey and citrus. This should be lovely."

The cord to the kettle isn't long enough to reach the outlet. I frown and try again. The damn prongs refuse to enter the slots. Setting the tin down, I force the cord into the outlet, and it finally slides in. One quick and powerful sneeze flees me.

"Ow, mother fuuu—" My forehead collides with the thick wooden shelf.

The throbbing is immediate, and there will be, without a doubt, a knot the size of Jupiter on my forehead by morning, given the fact that I bruise like a peach. A shattering sound pulls my eyes to the floor, and I let out another sigh. With one hand on my forehead, I bend to pick up the broken pieces of my shattered teacup.

"Well, this stinks."

It was the only one I had left. I've waited too long for this tea, and I refuse to drink it out of anything else other than a teacup. It wouldn't be right. This tea deserves respect, plus it's part of the tea experience.

Nibbling on my bottom lip, I look around the kitchen. I can remember one beautiful set my uncle had ages ago and wonder if it's been stashed away somewhere. If it is, it's most likely in the attic with everything else of his that has been boxed and put away.

Blake had volunteered to move a few boxes out of the bedroom and into the attic when he helped to drag in my new bed frame.

"I really should get back to him about setting a date."

Walking past the powder room, I catch a glimpse of my face in the mirrored wall. That's right, an entire wall of square mirrors in the tiny powder room. If I wasn't such a scaredy-cat, I'd bust them all down, but I don't need seven years of bad luck multiplied by however many mirrors this is. As I watch the bump turn an angry shade of red and purple, I make a mental note to find someone else to break these mirrors.

Stale air greets my nostrils as the old wooden door to the attic creaks open. A wad of spit is stuck between my tongue and my throat. The darkness swallows my hand as I swallow my childish fear. This was the one place I wasn't allowed to go to when we visited my Uncle Alex. It's childish of me to feel that now, this is my house, and I can go wherever I please.

Blindly, my fingers find the antique blackened button light switch. I hiss as part of my skin gets pricked by the corner of the jagged face plate.

Once again, I add yet another mental note—this one moves up the priority list:

- Get a tetanus shot.

The stairs groan under each light footstep as if announcing my arrival to whatever childhood fear lurks in the shadows.

Imagine my surprise upon seeing a neat row of boxes off to my right and old luggage discarded to the left. Everything is left wide open. A circular shutter-style window is closed off on the back wall, adorned with cobwebs. A red and gold area rug is forgotten in the middle of the floor, and it has certainly seen better days.

"Maybe I should make this my office instead of a spare bedroom."

I fist my hips and survey my surroundings.

With a sigh, I rub my forehead and wince when I meet the growing planet on my skull.

"I'm definitely getting an ice pack."

What time is it? How many items have distracted me on my side quest for my uncle's teacups? And the answer is: yes, my ass has fallen asleep on this floor, but I'm in it to win it now.

Finally, after the seventh or maybe the tenth box, I find what I'm looking for—two vintage black and white china teacups with gold trim and matching saucers.

My thumb brushes over the top half, which features a thick black stripe with gold filigree. It all feels so delicate and just right. It's like it was meant for me. As I fish the second saucer out of the box, an emerald-green velvet book beckons for my attention. The smile that blossoms on my face is one I wouldn't even try to hide.

"I remember you," I greet the book, readjusting my seating.

Tossing off the top hat I found in box four off my head, I thumb the pages of the book and inhale the scent of old ink and yellowed paper.

"This smell should be made into air fresheners and candles."

Focusing back on the book, memories dance around my brain. This was the book Uncle Alex would read and teach me "spells" from. I chuckle, remembering how cool I felt thinking I was casting spells. In actuality, these are nothing more than silly nursery rhymes.

Fancy tea, fancy cups, a trip down memory lane, and a possible side of tetanus sounds like a marvelous night. With my mind made up, I collect my newfound treasures, top hat included, and make my way downstairs to the kitchen.

"Damn. I'm gonna have to reheat the kettle again."

Chapter 7
The Devil Wears a Suit

Davina

THE WARM, SOFT LIGHT from the pink lamp on my nightstand is the perfect ambiance for tonight. Giddiness erupts in my chest while the grey, weighted blanket settles across my legs and stomach. Tossing the ice pack on the far end of my king-sized bed, I grab the velvet book and my steaming cup of tea.

Each ink-filled page is marked with scrawling's of sketches or silly nursery rhymes. After passing the page of the woman who found her soulmate by baking a meat pie, I come across one I don't remember at all. The page has yellowed more than others and isn't even attached to the binding. It's wrinkled as if someone shoved it in between the pages randomly.

Setting the book on my lap, I study the picture to the left of the rhyme. It's a delicate drawing of a little girl wandering the forest with an unlit lantern in her hand. There's some kind of horned creature standing in front of her who possesses a bright light in their palm.

Pursing my lips, I blow on the hot amber liquid, savoring the earthy scent as the steam wafts around my nose. Taking a long sip, warmth coats my throat while the soft briskness and full body flavors of honey and citrus notes explode on my tongue. This tea was definitely worth the wait. Taking one more sip, my lips begin to murmur the words on the page:

> *Searching for your heart's desire,*
> *In the dark, beware the liar.*
> *Listen closely for whispers in the night,*
> *Follow the path towards the tempting light.*
> *Through twisted trees and misty haze,*
> *You'll find the object of your gaze.*
> *Heed my warning, don't lose sight,*
> *Danger lurks in shadowed night.*
> *With steady steps and heart held strong*
> *You'll reach the place where you belong.*
> *Be brave and face your fear*
> *What you seek will soon be near.*
> *In the darkness lies a prize,*
> *With this rhyme, I shall rise.*

"What kind of rhyme is that?" I snort before taking another sip of tea and realizing my cup is empty.

When did I drink it all?

My eyes flutter closed, and I shake my head in a poor attempt to rouse myself. Placing the cup on the saucer, I snap the hefty book shut. Eerie silence encompasses my once tranquil space.

"Leave it to me to be creeped out by a nursery rhyme," I huff out before shoving the heavy blanket off. Swinging my feet over the side of the bed, I jerk them back up. That silly childhood feeling of some monster grabbing my ankles begins to overtake me. Before I can let this anxiety monster claw further into my mind, my feet thud against floor. Blowing out a breath. I'm darting to the bathroom.

Movement from the corner of my eye stops me dead in my tracks. My heart hammers in my chest so hard I'm afraid it'll rupture on pure impact.

Turning my head, I glance at the suddenly darker corner of my room…the corner right behind my door. The same door that always creaks a little too loud whenever I open or close it.

"You're a grown-ass woman, Davina. Too grown to be scared senseless by a children's book," I scold myself while never peeling my eyes away from the door.

Pushing my glasses up the bridge of my nose, I laugh at myself. *There's nothing there; it's just an overactive imagination at work.*

"What was in that tea?"

It's well past my bedtime when I finish my nightly routine. The sheets billow around me while I toss and turn, trying to find the most comfortable spot on my bed. There's a loud ringing in my ears, drilling into my brain. Rolling from my stomach onto my back, I groan.

"Why is the silence so loud?"

The room is dark, and I can't see a single thing without my glasses or contacts. But even in my squinting state, I can make out a figure by the beige swivel accent chair.

Snatching my glasses and phone off the nightstand, I poke my eye while sliding the frames onto my face. Tapping the flashlight option on my phone, I scan the room and really laugh at myself. "It's just a robe. Good God, woman, get a hold of yourself."

My fingers slide under the lenses before rubbing my overly tired eyes. A heavy sigh releases from my mouth, and I toss the phone and glasses back on the nightstand.

Let's try this sleep thing again.

Pulling the weighted blanket higher to cover my shoulders, I fight the urge to wake up. That weird feeling of being watched tickles my nape, and I slowly blink away the sleep. My hand reaches for my glasses while I yawn. Judging by the lack of light in my room, it's still early dawn.

In the middle of a lazy stretch, my entire body freezes as my arm bumps into something, or rather someone. My fingers tap up and down what feels like an arm. An arm covered in some kind of expensive fabric.

Taking in multiple shallow breaths, I think, *"Hey, God, it's me, Davina. Haven't done this in decades, but if this is how I die, please don't let someone say my smile lit up the room. We both know that's a lie. Amen."*

Stealing myself, I decide to roll, however ungraceful it may be. If I roll to my other side any slower, I would roll in reverse. Reverse doesn't sound half bad right about now. As if my body is at war with my mind, I continue to roll, or at least try. The sheets rumple beneath shoulder while the mattress dips with my new position. Warmth from the pillow against my cheek coaxing me to open my eyes.

There sitting leisurely on the edge of my bed, studying me, is the Goddamn Devil stroking his beard.

My eyes go from squinting to growing wider than the china saucer on my nightstand as he leans in a bit closer, and his blurred face comes into focus. Crimson skin, horns, and a perplexed expression make up the devil on the side of my bed.

"Excuse me, but who are you?" he asks.

The devil is asking me who *I am*? The devil certainly didn't go down to Georgia tonight; he came to Oregon.

Panic and fear finally catch up to my lungs, and I scream. I scream like my life depends on it and bolt up. Except in my haste to sit up, and true Davina fashion, my forehead smashes into his horn as he tries to back away. It's the same spot from last night, but the pain doesn't fully register. The devil's eyes widen as he takes in my screams and the unfolding scene.

All the oxygen I had in my lungs has vanished, and I'm gasping for air. The noose of fear tightens around my neck, further dulling the ache on my forehead. The covers get tangled in my legs as I scramble for safety. Landing firmly on my ass, I struggle to free myself from the vice grip known as jersey cotton and jump back up.

Where would I go for safety? Clearly, the bedsheet isn't the answer, and hiding under the bed seems stupid now. He stands next to my bed and puts his open hands out in front of himself like I'm the one who can do some damage in this situation. He takes one tiny shuffle towards my oak nightstand, and I scream again, hightailing it to my closet.

Slamming the door closed, I curse at the sudden darkness.

"Why does the light switch have to be outside?"

Mustering up what little courage I have, I crack open the door. He's still in the same spot, staring back at me.

"Satan?" My voice cracks over the word.

From what I can tell, his hands go up in the air before slapping down to his legs.

"No," he huffs like *I'm* the offending party. "I see we've gotten off to the wrong start. My name is Mendax Draxton. Pleasure to meet you." The blurred figure of his arm reaches out to his side. "Do you need these?"

The sound of my frames scraping against the nightstand lets me know he has my glasses in hand. I offer no verbal response, only a wide-eyed stare. What seems like hours tick by when Mendax clears his throat.

"Okay. This is clearly a lot to take in—or a misunderstanding. I'll leave the glasses here, and um—well, I'll go wait in that chair."

A strangled whimper is all I can manage.

"I promise, I mean you no harm. You should know you summoned me," he says.

I summoned him?

"What the frick is happening?"

My hand meets my cheek as I slap myself.

This has to be a dream. This doesn't happen in real life. I'm dreaming. I know I am.

"Come on, Davina, wake up!" I slap myself harder.

"Oh my. Please, stop that."

This Mendax sounds either worried or horrified at my behavior. Which I honestly can't be bothered to care about.

"How about I make myself scarce elsewhere around here while you freshen up, hmm?"

The question, I think, is meant to appease me and settle my nerves.

With that, I shrink back and watch him slowly stride out of the room as if he owns my house.

A bubble of laughter surfaces as one single thought enters my mind.

The devil wears a suit.

Chapter 8
BeD-AND-BreakFAST
Davina

WITH REDDENED AND STINGING cheeks, I come to the conclusion that I am, in fact, not dreaming. Hearing the confident steps one floor below me helps to solidify the conclusion as well.

How the hell do I get this devil out of my house?

Every logical thought was pushed out when fear took up residence in my mind and set roots in my feet, planting me in the same spot I have yet to move from.

Time to woman up and meet this creature downstairs.

Any false bravado I had deflates as my hands run down my cupcake-patterned fleece pajama bottoms.

There's no way I can look cool, calm, collected in these.

Rapid knocking from my front door filters up through the floor.

"Now what?"

The knocking doesn't let up, and I'm afraid whoever that is will break my door down. Blindly reaching behind me, I knock an oversized sapphire blue sweater off the hanger and onto the floor next to a pair of gray shorts. I don't want to waste any more time, so I quickly strip off the pajamas and put on the new clothes.

With the first two steps out of the closet, I wince, remembering why I never wear these shorts anymore. Every stride leads to my ass eating up the shorts like a hungry hungry hippo. Again, there is no time to waste. Besides the scarlet-horned man wandering around downstairs, I'm pretty sure an entire swat team is trying to break my door down. There is no protocol on how to handle this, and right now, I'm really wishing I watched more paranormal or supernatural shows. I am so out of my element here. My cheeks puff up as I blow out my nerves.

"Here goes nothing."

The second to the bottom step creaks despite my delicate, shaky tip-toeing. Seeing this man with horns in a perfectly tailored suit standing in the middle of my semi-remodeled living room is quite the juxtaposition. With the traitorous step alerting him to my presence, he turns and tugs on the cuffs of his jacket. There's a charming smile, and if I were sane, I wouldn't notice how handsome he looks. But I never claimed to be sane, and the grin does nothing to put me at ease.

I wonder if the beam I exchanged looks as forced as it feels.

I probably look like the Cheshire Cat right now. *Way to be calm, Davina. Way. To. Be. Calm.*

The knocking has turned into pounding, and I watch as the amusement falls from his face, and he gives me a questioning look.

"Davina!" Blake yells from the other side of the door. "Davina? Open the door, please."

"Do you need to get that?" Mendax scratches his eyelid before speaking. "I don't mind waiting."

His lip twitch, rocking on his heels and shoving his hands in his pockets.

I probably should, and my body agrees because it moves on its own accord. Before I can register what is happening, I gently push the door ajar, the hinges creaking softly as the gap widens. I force my lips into an artificial grin, feeling the strain tugging at the corners of my mouth.

"Blake, hey. Everything okay?" I ask, noticing how my voice went up an octave towards the end.

"I should be asking you that." Blake's eyes search my face before trying to peer behind me. "I heard you screaming from across the street, then it went quiet again."

Doing my best to hide the tremor in my hand, I push my glasses up my nose.

"Well, aren't you a knight in shining armor?" I laugh.

There's no way I can tell him there's a demon in my house. No one would ever believe that. Soft steps filter from behind me. With every step this Mendax dude takes, my eyes widen. He's nearing the door, but he turns away with a deep chuckle.

I need to think of something to get rid of him so I can get a grip on my current situation.

"Blake, it's very sweet of you to come and check on little ol' me, but I have to apologize," I say, leaning against the door frame and closing the door a little tighter around me. "Scary movies are a horrible thing to watch before bed without a classic Disney movie for a chaser. I had a nightmare and scared myself awake." The lie rolls effortlessly off my tongue. "Sometimes, I scare a little too easily. Honestly, I scared myself the other night reading a book. Granted, I was exhausted from work, so that probably played a part in it. Did you know the amygdala is responsible for controlling fear? It's an almond-shaped part of the brain, and well, yeah, pretty sure that was the first thing in my brain to fully develop."

Gosh dammit, woman, shut up!

Why do I ramble when I lie? Because lying is rude. Being rude makes me uncomfortable. This entire situation is uncomfortable.

A deep chuckle emanates from further in the house; it carries across the awkward silence like an opening riff at a rock concert that gets the audience screaming. I cough, trying to play off the sound.

This handsome neighbor of mine puts his hand on the door, trying to open it wider. He means well, but I can't get him involved in whatever the hell this is. Quickly, I place my barefoot behind it, stopping it from being opened anymore. All I can do is stare and smile so wide I'm at risk of getting premature wrinkles.

Blake leans closer to the door, his voice hardly above a whisper, "Scratch your nose if you need help."

He holds his large, calloused palm up, ready to pull me out of the house the moment I slip my hand in his. It's sweet, but something won't let me do that.

Licking my suddenly dry lips, I give a wider smile.

"Like I said, I'm sorry for waking and alarming you."

I put my hand on his chest, feeling how steady his heart beats under the plain white shirt. Patting him lightly before pushing him back a little.

"I promise I'm okay."

He doesn't seem satisfied with my answer, but I don't have the capacity to deal with him right now.

"Good night, Blake, or is it good morning? Either way, you should go back to sleep or whatever it is you do at this time of day. It's probably sleep or maybe breakfast. I don't know." *Why am I still talking?*

I give him one last tight-lipped smile before closing the door.

Was I really that loud? Pressing my face to the peephole, I watch Blake stand there, looking around my property. A heavy sigh leaves me as he walks away, glancing over his shoulder.

He's nice. I should set up a date with him.

Scurrying over towards the window I watch him walk into his house. Within seconds the lights in Blakes' home flick on. The soft curtains rustle as I clutch them tighter and draw them even closer, so each panel overlaps.

"Is there somewhere you would feel comfortable to hold our discussion?" Mendax asks with a raised eyebrow, leaning against the banister.

Clearing my throat, I nod. For someone who normally has the gift of gab, forming a single sentence is a struggle right now. Wordlessly, he follows me through the dining room and into the kitchen.

I motion to the chair at my small table.

"Please, sit."

Standing in front of the sink, I finally take him in completely. He moves in such silence that not even a whisper accompanies his steps. His every motion is as silent as a ghost. Thank God my ceilings are high because if I account for his horns, Mendax easily closes in on seven feet. Talk about "holy height Batman."

He isn't broad or packed with large muscle; the well-fitting suit shows his lean build. With a single hand, he unbuttons his jacket before sitting.

His eyes scan up and down my body but hold no judgment, which is fantastic because I'm currently sporting the mother of all wedgies, and it'd be a bit weird to pick it out right now.

If anything, he looks confused. *I'm right there with ya buddy.*

His smooth, silky voice interrupts my thoughts, "How is your head?"

When he poses his question, I realize I'm standing twiddling, my fingers staring at him.

"It's fine." I wince when my fingers brush against the small bump. "I honestly forgot about it until you brought it up."

"My apologies," he says, lacing his fingers together. "Not exactly the best first impression I let someone have of me."

For someone who looks so terrifying, he has the manners of a gentleman. All he's missing is a posh accent, and he could be royalty in a novel. Pacing my kitchen like the swing of a pendulum, I stop in the corner with the kettle.

"Can I get you anything? Water, tea, I'm plum outta blood of a virgin."

My hand shoots up to cover my lips.

There's a smirk Mendax tries to fight off and shakes his head.

"Tea would be lovely. Any kind you have is fine."

No words are spoken between me racing back upstairs to grab the forgotten teacup and saucer, washing it, and brewing the tea to now. I've come to a few conclusions:

1. This is not a dream

2. If I had my Ouija board, I'd be summoning Uncle Alex for questions—Mom would probably kill me if she knew I actually bought and played with one.

3. My house looks like a hovel with this sophisticated demon in it.

Mendax sits calmly across from me, pouring milk into his black tea. I'm still trying to wrap my mind around everything and figure out what led me here.

Is this how Alice felt during her first tea party in Wonderland? Because I feel like this is my own tea party while tripping on acid. A nervous laugh bubbles out of me again.

Who invited the demon to tea? Oh, right. Me.

"So, Davina," Mendax breaks the silence first. His gaze holds me in place as he studies me. A small tug at the corners of his lips leaves as quickly as it came. "How did a witchling such as yourself manage to summon me? I don't sense any kind of notable magical energy from you."

He brings the teacup to his lips, inhaling the aroma.

"What is it you require?"

Dumbfounded isn't a strong enough adjective to describe myself right now.

"Re-require? I-I don't require anything. Well, at least not from you; I don't even know you. I honestly don't even know why or how you're here." I blurt out. "I'm also not a witchling. I'm just me."

"Well, no one and nothing is ever 'just.'" He takes a long sip of tea. "Let's start over."

He begins by sitting up a little straighter. Which, how is that possible?

"Mendax Draxton, at your service. A demon, not Satan." He winks with a playful smirk.

The air grows a bit hazy after that, and a calmness washes over me. Why am I leaning in more intently?

Flattening his tie, he continues, "My specialty is in the business of procuring oddities and their sales—with the occasional brokering. You want it or need it, you name it, I get it," he says with a charming smile. "All for a price, of course."

"Why did everything get fuzzy around you? One minute, anxiety is ripping through me like the express train, and the next, I'm hanging on your every word."

His head cocks to the left, studying me more intently.

"Apologies, sometimes it just comes out. It's a pheromone I release to help others relax around me. It makes negotiations easier."

"Please don't do that again."

The tea I had built up anticipation for, which I savored just last night and brewed once more for this impromptu tea party, has gone cold in front of me.

Mendax's nostrils flare a bit before taking in a deep breath. When I blink, the haze is gone and I'm grateful for that.

How is this my life? My hot breath brushes my knuckles as I bite my thumb nail.

"Well, Mr. Draxton—"

"Please, call me Mendax. Mr. Draxton is my father." He interjects before continuing to sip his tea.

"Right."

Running the pad of my finger around the rim of my cup, my mouth opens and closes before deciding to release the words in queue on my tongue.

"Mendax," my tongue taps my top lip. "While I do appreciate you divulging your line of work. Um…the fact remains, I don't need anything." My nail picks away at the chipped paint on the edge of the table. "I especially don't have a need for any kind of *oddity*. This situation is odd enough," I say with a laugh.

"I honestly don't know how you got here, but you're free to go after your tea."

Holy crap, I'm kicking a demon out of my house.

A soft click from the cup onto the saucer from across the table grabs my attention.

"I think you do know how I got here. I also can't leave," he says it so casually, leaning back in his chair.

Why does this tea party feel like it's turning into a bed-and-breakfast situation?

Chapter 9
DEVIL ON YOUR SHOULDER
Mendax

I LIED. I COMPLETELY, one hundred percent lied. I mean, liar is my name. Of course, I can leave; I just don't want to. At least not yet.

The portal she opened in her room is a direct door between her home and mine. It is wide open; I can waltz in and out of here at any given time. In all my years of business, there hasn't been anyone like this. Honestly, who invites a demon they just met to tea?

Truth be told, it's rather refreshing.

I'm used to meetings with high-powered individuals in cigar lounges, or a chic office sipping a single malt scotch, or barreled age whiskey. At least that was something I was used to.

Sitting in a small kitchen drinking exquisite tea is a breath of fresh air. This human perplexes me, and it isn't that I couldn't use my full pheromone on her which *always* works on *everyone*. There's something about her mind I couldn't wrap my ability around.

What gets me even more is how she truly believes there is nothing she wants or needs. The conviction behind Davina's words almost has me believing her. But that can't be true. Every single human being I have ever met always wants *something*. They're never content with what they have. Then again, is anyone?

Stretching my legs out in front of me, Davina pulls hers in and up towards her chest. She's practically perched on her chair. It reminds me of how Gotha perches on the back of the couch at night.

Oh goodness, I really hope Orroth is taking care of my girl.

Shoving the idea to the recesses of my mind, I focus on the woman hugging her knees. If I were to wager, I'd say she's a little above average height, thanks to her long, toned legs. The shorts showcase her beige olive skin is marked with some kind of tattoo on her thigh. When I really stare at her face, I can't help but smile; her tawny hair is highlighted with strands of pure yellow. The same yellow that reminds me of my favorite clouds from my realm.

"I don't know why you think *I* know how you're here." Her voice pulls me back to the conversation. "But more importantly, what do you mean you can't leave?"

There's an undertone of frustration in her voice. Poor thing. I do feel bad for lying…well, not *bad*, perhaps a little guilty, but this is the perfect opportunity to bide my time away from my mother's plan.

Skirting her question, I pose one of my own, "Well then, shall we solve the mystery of the summoning together?"

Davina's dark brows rise above her glasses as her deep brown eyes rapidly blink. The way her chin inclines towards her chest is stiff, but I'll take it as a form of agreement.

"Walk me through the events of the day leading up to my arrival."

The amount of detail and derailing Davina has managed with her retelling is truly awe-inspiring. There must have been at least five side stories woven into this conversation. It's not entirely her fault though, I'm guilty of asking question after question, which she happily answers every time. One thing is certain, she's gotten more comfortable with my presence.

"So, yeah, I closed the book and went about my business. Woke up. saw everything was fine, and when I woke up again, well, here we are."

As she spoons the loose-leaf tea into the steeper while talking, one detail digs its claws into my brain.

"Excuse me, but would you show me this book? It's the second time you've mentioned it."

Her face scrunched up for a few seconds before shuffling away from the counter and back to it. Grabbing the kettle, she pours water into the teacups once more and nods.

"I'll be right back."

Her footsteps pad softly up the stairs, followed by the creek of her door. Taking this time to stretch, I glance out the small kitchen window where the sun has fully risen, greeting the early birds. There's one circular archway leading towards overgrown lush grass covering pavers. Random terracotta pots are packed with white and pink flowers, while others have one I know to be lavender.

"Eventually, I'll get to the backyard," Davina sighs behind me. "No, I don't need or require your help for that. Not selling my soul for that, at least." She chuckles while handing me a hefty velvet book.

Grasping the book, I can't help but laugh, which catches her off guard as she cocks her head to the right.

"People don't pay me with their souls. I have no need for those. If a demon ever asks for your soul, they're downright criminal, and you should run the other way."

I glance at her before beginning to study the tome in my hands.

"Listen, my ass is going to bruise if I sit on my chair any longer. How about you bring the book into the living room? I'll meet you there for our tea," she offers.

I only nod in agreement, too entranced by what I'm holding. This is a rare oddity. Getting the opportunity to even lay my eyes on, let alone my hands on, this kind of book is a privilege.

"Where did you get this?" I ask, my fingers skimming the spine.

I frown a bit as the tiny lines from the cracked spine brush the pads of my fingers. That certainly doesn't bode well for the integrity of the pages. It also decreases the value.

The couch dips on the other end before the clattering of ceramic fills the lull of spoken words.

"Oh, from my uncle, along with everything else here. He found me reading it one time, and he would let me read it every so often," she states matter-of-factly. "My favorite was always the woman and the pie."

"Do you realize what this is?" I ask while riffling through the pages and finding the one she mentioned.

"Yeah, it's a silly story book," Davina snorts before sipping her tea.

Skimming a few pages, I find a tattered page and my heart rate quickens.

These were all supposed to be destroyed. Unless…looking around the room, realization crashes into me like a tidal wave. *Perhaps it's best not mentioned right now.*

"My dear, Davina, this isn't a storybook." I turn the book on the cushion and point to the picture.

My crimson finger is a stark contrast to the ink-clad page. I watch in fascination as her eyes dance between me and the book.

"This is a spell book unlike others out there. What's curious is how this spell about yours truly managed to get in here."

"Unless…" I mumble. My words trail off, as I try to find the missing component.

Her lithe fingers grip the book, flipping through every page and studying every word.

"I don't understand. Why did my Uncle Alex have this story about you?"

We don't have to worry about the *why* for right now.

"Are you looking to sell the book? I could find a buyer for you." The couch groans and squeaks underneath me.

The book slams shut before she clutches it to her chest.

"Absolutely not. I don't want to sell this, and I really don't want anything from you."

"Everyone wants *something*."

I narrow my eyes, studying her. How does this human not want anything? Silence shrouds us like a wool blanket until the growl from her stomach surfaces. My eyes widen at the sound. It's reminiscent of the growls I was told came from ancient demons. The demons that would venture into the human to defile and possess. Growing up, we were told that if we did too many misdeeds, we would devolve into such demons.

Obviously, it was all tales to keep us children in line.

Her cheeks flush.

"Sorry, I'm hungry," Davina says with a tight-lipped smile. "I don't want you getting me food either. I'm fully capable of cooking and ordering."

I hold zero interest in going home now even more. There are matters to be discovered. Stretching my arms over my horns, I smile and try to get comfortable despite a spring threatening to prod in an area I have no interest in being explored.

With a giant grin, I ask, "What's for lunch?" Her smile drops, and I bark a laugh. "I told you; I can't go back. For the time being, I'm going to be the devil on your shoulder."

She slumps on the couch and groans. It's a vast improvement from screaming, so I'll consider it a win.

"What do demons even eat?" she wonders out loud.

"I'm sure anything is fine. The food from here is very similar to my own realm. Sometimes, we have food imported from here to there," I tell her before standing. "Oh, good heavens."

A cord that has been tossed and long forgotten has made an assassination attempt on my life. I came inches away from cracking a horn against a ladder. My silk shirt glides under my palm as I press my hand to my heart. Looking around, there are half-done or half-started projects.

"Are you sure there isn't anything you require?"

"If you don't like *my* home, you can leave," she says, almost challenging me with her tone. "Now, I hope you like Thai because I didn't go grocery shopping. But don't worry, I've made a mental note to go soon."

What did I just get myself into?

Chapter 10
Friend Shaped
Mendax

D AVINA IS ONE INTERESTING woman. I often find myself simply watching her work. When she's working, it's like a production has been put on. Her focus is laser sharp, notes in order; it's like she's a completely different person. There also seems to be a "Tony" who can never do his job correctly, like now.

"Tony, I swear to God, if I could have you pulled from this account, I would do it so fast you'd get whiplash."

The crunching of papers fills the silence on her end while there's stuttering on the other.

"No, Tony."

The glittery pink pen in her hand wobbles precariously in between her fingers as she tosses her hand in the air.

"A semiparametric statistical model is not the same as a parametric; the name is different for a reason. You can't just up and decide to forego one for the other without informing the team or getting *my* approval."

Bare feet slap against the floor as her pacing quickens. Unruly strands of yellow hair blow freely around her glasses as she fans her face. Spreadsheets are fanned out across the table with a tablet and a laptop open on top of them.

It's been close to four weeks since I've popped up here, and she's slowly becoming more comfortable around me. Every once in a while, her large, doe eyes land on me like a spotlight, and I feel as though I'm back to playing the childhood game of "escape the guardsman."

The 'guardsman' would have their eyes closed and walk around while the 'captured' would try their best to sneak about and get past the guard to capture the key to freedom—usually a stick. When Davina's gaze lands on me, I freeze, just like I did playing the game and when I was spotted. My hands lift to show I'm innocent. When she takes her gaze away, I go back to reading files of clients she has and taking peeks at her.

This line of work seems like it could be useful in my line of work. I wonder if mother and father have ever heard of a risk analyst before. It would save us from future mishaps like the one I was caught in. The clatter of a phone against the table draws my attention. Looking upward, I notice the glasses that usually slide down the bridge of her petite nose are pushed up on her head.

"You know," I begin. "If you keep rubbing your eyes that hard, you might push them all the way to the back of your skull."

"I wonder if I could claim that as workers comp," Davina replies, sitting down and blowing out a harsh breath.

She hardly ever sits with both feet on the ground. Like now, she's angled sideways, right leg curled underneath her, while her left foot brushes back and forth.

I arch my brow in question.

"Don't worry about it," she says while her fingers move across the keyboard, click-clacking away on obnoxiously loud multi-colored keys. "I'm just seriously wondering how my coworker got the job he did. To be honest I don't know how we keep landing these major clients, either.

"Am I thankful? Yes, and I know I should never look a gifted horse in the mouth, but—"

The doorbell rings, cutting her off.

Fixing her glasses, she stands and adjusts the waistband on her maroon joggers. For the first time today, she looks excited as she bounces on her toes, trotting towards the door.

She's only gone for a few seconds, but I take this opportunity to look at her computer. Her company's website, Catalyst Consultant Group, is up, where employees go and log in, and I can't help but laugh at the picture of a middle-aged man with red hair, pale skin, and eyes that would make a serial killer nervous.

"The new tea of the month is here!" The deep rich purple box with creamy white lettering is clutched to her chest, as she returns to the room.

Her chin tips in my direction. "Why are you laughing?"

"How about I tell you over tea?"

"Deal."

My clear glass teacup swirls with grass and a thick slice of lemon. I convinced Davina to buy new cups since I didn't want to risk using the same fine china every day.

"What are you making me drink?"

"It's rosemary tea," she says while sliding a plate of croissants between us. "Don't give me that look, Mendax. That's what this tea is supposed to look like. It all came in the box in separate tins."

"It looks like lawn clippings."

Tea in the kitchen has become our rendition of having high tea.

"Is that ginger in the picture on the computer your boss?"

She nods. Her lips blow into her cup, sending a tiny plume of steam in my direction.

"Yep, Jason Walker. He's pretty hands-off, has tons of visits from the idea fairy, and lets everyone else figure it out. There's zero personality in his voice, almost robotic. I'm talking *super* monotone—which makes how he lands these mega clients even stranger."

Stroking my beard, I brushed my finger in circles over the table. "I know how he lands those clients."

"How?" The croissant hovers just in front of her lips.

Warmth of the mug caresses my hand while the earthy aroma wafts up towards my nose. I hide the grin on my face as an impatient groan comes from Davina. The small sip I swallow and lingers on my tastebuds is enough to boycott this tea.

"It's like licking a pine tree."

"It can't be that bad." Davina eyes her tea while shoving a ripped piece of pastry into her mouth.

"Mendax, tell me what you know. Pleeease. This is what you always do, you know that. You start a story, and then you pause halfway, building it up. I can't take it, Mendax. You're edging me with gossip."

"I'm what?" I laugh, grabbing my own buttery snack.

She meets my gaze under her dark lashes.

"That's not important. Tell me about Jason." She bites back a smile while taking a sip. "This tastes like a Christmas tree farm."

I sit back victoriously but say nothing.

"You forgot to turn the subtitles off on your face." Davina scowls, and it pulls a laugh from me.

"Anyway, back to Mr. Walker." I lean in, and she mimics my movements without even thinking. "He has a charmed ring."

If her jaw dropped any further it would smack against the little table.

"Shut the front door! How do you know? How does it work? Where did he get it? Are there more?"

Tearing the corner of my pastry, I toss it into her open mouth before she can spout another question. I choke down another laugh while she angry chews.

"I know because it came from my family's warehouse of oddities. Twenty years ago, I procured that particular ring from two witches who decided to close up their little shop and retire early. What they got for the ring was enough for a fun kickstart week in Vegas." Biting into the pastry I stare at her, waiting how long until—

"Mendax," she pouts, "don't you dare stop. I know there's more." Taking another sip of the horrid tea, she winces.

Reaching across the table, I pull the cup away from her. Drinking this is pure punishment.

"All he has to do is wear it and make sure the person he is trying to get, touches it. There are more…but I'm not sure how many."

I can see the gears working in her head as she brings both legs onto the chair to sit crisscross.

"Twenty years ago? How old are you?"

Sliding my chair back, I stand and make my way to the fridge. Pushing past the milk and yogurt grabbing the bowl of strawberries.

"I'm 50."

She snorts in amusement. "And not a grey hair in sight. What a shame; you could have been a silver fox."

Time seems to fly around here, and I wonder if it's because I'm enjoying being here rather than my own home or if there is a hex built into the walls that causes time blindness. Before I know it, we're back in the kitchen with a new tea steeping in the teapot. This time, it's a loose-leaf Assam.

"So, you obviously know more about me than I do you. Tell me about your home, Mendax. What's it called?" Davina asks from the counter she's sitting on, swinging her legs.

Resting my elbows next to her, I spot the iPad she's been tapping and swiping on.

"Hey! Give that back," she protests as I pluck it from her fingers and hold it just out of reach.

"What is this?"

"It's a dating app. I swore to delete it, but it's my guilty pleasure. It's also why I'm still single."

All those profiles are why I haven't had a real relationship in years."

Just looking at these pictures and reading their bios, I can understand why.

"How do you get to the next one?"

She folds her arms under her chest, narrowing her eyes. "Swipe left for no, swipe right for yes."

"Excellent." I've never had this much fun swiping a screen before.

"Whoa, slow down; some of those guys are cute!"

Try as she might, I'm not giving this back.

"Cute? Davina, there's problem number one. Cute is for teenage boys who haven't reached puberty yet. You don't want cute; you want handsome, rugged, charming, distinguished; I'll even allow beautiful."

I gaze at her with smug satisfaction, and she laughs.

"Are you trying to describe yourself right now?"

"Why do you find me handsome, Davina?" I chuckle and she rolls her eyes before I resume swiping and reading bios. "I hope there's no limit to rejections because you can do better."

I look at the screen, wishing I had my reading glasses now.

"Allen, 36, who loves dogs, beaches, and a female who isn't afraid of an alpha male."

What the hell is an alpha?

She barks out a laugh.

"Wait don't swipe yet, I wanna see what he looks like. I promise I won't swipe right."

I hand it back to her and pull it away once more before she snatches it.

"That's not Allen! That's dick-pick-Grant. He made a different profile with the same pictures. Again, this is why I don't date." She tosses the tablet aside and stares at me.

"You were about to tell me about your home before you became my love guru," she says as she smiles and bats her lashes.

"You're ridiculous."

Pulling the milk out from the fridge, I ponder what to share with her. I've never had to have a conversation with anyone about my realm before.

"My realm is called Alegos; Struk would be your version of a state."

Helping Davina off the counter, I place the teacups, teapot, and milk on a serving tray while she rummages through her cabinets for snacks. Once she's gathered everything and has not allowed me to look, I follow her out of the kitchen and towards the mudroom that leads to the patio.

The rain stopped yesterday; it was nothing but downpours for one week straight. Luckily, the patio is covered and completely dry. Setting the tray on the wicker table I continue sharing my world with her.

"The city is called Piros. It's beautiful when it's not the rainy year like it is now. Lots of skyscrapers and high-rise apartments. It's an affluent society and holds what would be known as Wall Street and Rodeo Drive mixed."

"Sounds fancy." Davina places a plate filled with yellow cakes on the table.

I go around her, pulling her chair out for her.

"It was mostly old money, but now, there's an influx of new."

I unbutton my gray suit jacket and adjust the gold collar pin bar before sitting. I should have worn the suit with the matching vest and brown wooden buttons. The fabric is more suitable for today.

"I'm guessing your family is the former?" Davina asks.

I'm about to reply when her actions take me off guard.

"Did you just pour milk into your cup first?"

She gives me a smirk. "Yeah. You don't?"

"What are you, a heathen? It's tea first, then milk. How else do you ensure your level of teaness?"

"I trust my instincts," she giggles. "Twinkie?"

"Twinkie? Good God, woman." I scratch my jaw, feeling how thick my beard has gotten. "A *Twinkie?*"

"It's a cake," she says like it just makes sense. "Friends don't judge, Mendax."

"Are we friends?" I'm not known to have friends. Only associates.

She pours the tea into her milk, *like a heathen,* and buys her time for a response.

"Well…" three cubes of sugar drop into her cup. "I'm friend-shaped; your friend-shaped. So?"

What is she going on about?

"Friend-shaped?" I parrot back.

There's no hiding the smile growing on my face while I pour the strongly brewed tea.

"Yes, we are both friend-shaped, get along, and enjoy each other's company. So, we can be friend-shaped together."

She smooths her hands down her white crop top and down her peasant-style yellow skirt before pushing the sleeves of her oversized gray cardigan up her forearms.

"I'll be friend-shaped with you only if you tell me that you don't pour milk in before the cereal."

Her front teeth bite into her plump bottom lip. Thick brows rise above her frames while her eyes give me an apology before a smile creeps up on her face.

"I mean, it's the right way to do it."

Her fingers tuck her locks behind her ear, showing off dangling mushroom earrings.

"You monster!"

She tosses her head back, and a cascade of brown and neon yellow hair tumbles off her shoulder. A warm, full-belly laughter wraps around instead of the cool breeze. The laugh is so pure and filled with so much amusement I can't help but join her.

"To friend-shapedness," I say, holding up my cup.

She gives me a dazzling smile that could guide a lost ship home. And just like that, I have a friend.

Chapter 11
Tea, party of one
Davina

FIVE MONTHS, SIX DAYS, and ten hours have passed since Mendax popped up in my life. Let's say it's been…eventful.

The first night, sleep did not come easy. How could it? Despite sharing a cup or two of tea and a few meals, I was a fish out of water. No sane person can act natural when a demon is roaming around their house. Luckily, the rhyming book from hell kept him occupied. Mendax, had asked me for a notebook and a pen before I headed off to bed that night. I found a thin notebook in my knock-off designer bag and gave that one to him.

Which, mental note:

- Get a new notebook for my bag.

I also gave him my favorite pen, the ten-color retractable ballpoint pen. Pretty sure Mendax stuffed it in his pocket, and I'll never get it back. He won't admit to it, but there was a sound similar to giggles coming from the attic.

When I took a peek at his notes, which were written in a language I've never seen before, I caught a quick glimpse at rainbow swirls and scribbles before he folded the paper. Every single day, we drink tea and read the same rhyme that brought him here, trying to figure out if there was a hidden word in somewhere in there that could send him back.

I can recite it in my sleep.

By month two, I had asked him how he was changing clothes after noticing his different suits. His reply was simply "magic". Not sure I buy that. If it were magic, why couldn't he teleport himself back to his home?

I know he showers here because just about every single bath product I own is damn near empty, and his skin is glowing like a ripe cherry now. It seems he favors coconut-scented products.

A few weeks back, during a break in the traditional Pac Northwest spring rain, Mendax went to pull the curtains open to let some sun in, and I tackled him to the ground, or at least attempted to.

The last thing I need is to have a seven-foot-tall horned demon spotted in my living room. There's a snowball's chance in hell for me to explain that one to anyone who walks by. One thing I don't want inherited from my uncle is his reputation as the town weirdo.

Now, I need a break from my own house and desperately need to feel the sun on my skin. Tugging my shoelaces a little too tight, I've decided to go for a run. Maybe I should get a dog to go running with.

Mental note:

- Look up local animal shelters and rescues.

A slight rustling draws my attention toward the living room while I bound down the stairs, skipping the squeaky step. Watching Mendax meander through my house is something I'm not sure I'll ever get used to. As usual, he's dressed in a suit. Today, it's a midnight blue two-piece slim fit with a black silk shirt. Compared to most days, he looks casual with no tie and the top three buttons undone.

"Oh, are you heading out?" he asks before digging into a white bag.

A throaty laugh leaves me.

"Are you snacking on the leftover croutons from last night?" I ask before taking my glasses off to wipe the lenses. "And yes, I'm going for a run. It shouldn't take me long; I have a ton of work to catch up on."

There was an influx of new clients that need a deep-dive analysis, and I haven't even started working on those yet. It's a bit difficult to create my SWOT analysis charts, which is only the first step, with Mendax asking me a new question every five minutes about my work. Not that I mind the questions, but answering them always gets me off topic, and before I know it, I'm researching something else or asking him questions about his line of work.

"I'm also thinking about getting a dog. Maybe an older one."

"I like these croutons, thank you very much. I didn't say anything to you when you ate a bag of mini marshmallows two nights ago while watching a horror movie," he quips before tossing a single crouton into his mouth.

"I was stress-eating. That nun running down the hall was scary. It was either scream or shove something into my mouth," I say while finding my running playlists, which help me keep my heart rate at 185 bpm.

"Shove something into your mouth?" His brow quirks with amusement.

I *really* need to stop and focus on filtering my words more. "You shush."

"Well, go for your run. I promise to be a well-behaved demon and stay away from windows and not answer the door if anyone were to knock." He offers me a smile that's a little too large. "You should get a dog. I know a few breeders. Or I can find you the perfect dog if you get me a list of requirements."

Putting one earbud in place and only one because if those murder shows have taught me anything, it's that a girl can't be too careful. While adjusting the earbud, I can't help but let a thought escape through my hole-filled filter.

"You're up to something." I wait for him to say something as I slip the earbud case and my phone into the thigh pockets of my shorts. "Like I've said before. I don't want anything from you. I can find a dog on my own, plus I'm going to adopt. There are too many furry friends in the shelter that need a home. One day, if I hit the lottery or become mega-rich from my imaginary company," I begin stretching my legs, letting all the cracks and pop settle. "I'm getting a ranch or large open space somewhere so I can save all the dogs, especially the ones with frosted faces."

Mendax simply continues to smile in my direction as he makes his way to the couch and grabs the remote. The crouton bag sits next to his hip while he crosses one ankle over his knee and scrolls through one of the streaming apps I'm still logged in to.

"I'll be sure to remember you want a ranch."

"Mendax, don't you dare. I don't want to owe anyone anything. I'll do it on my own."

"Davina, go for your run." He settles in further choosing a documentary on Sharks.

For some reason, there's a nagging feeling I can't seem to shake.

The pavement relentlessly pounds under my feet, my lungs flare with fire, and my tongue is coated in metallic taste. Wiping my face with the bottom of my old UCLA t-shirt, I suck in air greedily. "Holy fuck. When did I get so out of shape?"

The weather is finally warming up, with summer looming right around the corner. It'll be the perfect opportunity to do something other than yoga again. Conversations and ambient music float out from the mom-and-pop shop on the back streets of downtown. I hadn't even realized I had run this far when a honk and a voice called out to me.

"Davina?" A male voice floats from a black Toyota pickup truck.

Squinting, I try to ignore the sting of sweat in my eyes. Thank God I didn't wear my contacts today.

Mental note:
- Get prescription sunglasses.

"Blake?" I say his name trying not to sound breathy but end up panting it anyway.

Double parking his truck, Blake leans over towards the passenger window.

"I thought that was you." He gives me a warm smile. "You look like you ran a marathon. Do you want a ride back?"

Didn't think I looked that bad, but okay.

"Shouldn't you be teaching today? Last I checked, school is Monday through Friday and today is only Wednesday."

"Usually it is," Blake laughs. "I'm enjoying spring break instead of getting my lesson plans together."

The truck locks click. "How about that ride? I'm heading home anyway."

Something in my gut tells me to say no, but the cramp in my calf is yelling "Yes please."

"That'd be nice," I say. "Hope you don't mind the sweat."

"Don't worry about that. This interior can handle sweat. You haven't seen me after a gym session." My hand hovers over the door handle, but I push away my doubt and climb into his truck.

He slowly puts the truck in drive and starts down the street.

"I just need to make a quick stop at the cafe here. I put in an order."

He smoothly parallel parks one-handed, which I'll admit is impressive. Before I can say anything, he's hoping out, but he leaves his keys. Blake gives me a wink before jogging into the little coffee shop with an orange awning.

Pulling my phone out of my thigh pocket, I close out of my music and put the single earbud back in its case to charge.

Would it be rude to go through the glove box? Yes, it would. Am I still tempted? One hundred percent. The last thing I need, though, is for Blake to come out and catch me snooping.

To distract myself I check emails on my phone. Most of the emails are from my team. They have single-handedly inundated my inbox. Thirteen from Gina, asking about reference materials and a change in trajectory, twelve from Mitch regarding a blind study and how we need to do more research, eight from Tina going over new marketing concepts and needing a possible PR collaboration and suggestions for possible companies.

"Oh look, top of the list is my mom's company. Shocker."

I roll my eyes. Tony has the most shocking amount, thirty. A full thirty with him going into melt down over missing reports and new client schedules, a knock on the window has me clutching my phone to my chest. He does know this is email and not Slack right?

"Be professional, Davina. Be. Professional." We really need to use Slack more.

The driver door opens.

"Sorry, didn't mean to scare you," Blake says, holding up a bag and drink carrier.

I offer a tight smile. "No worries, you're fine." I wave my phone. "I was in work mode."

The white bag rustles on the center console.

"This is for you." Blake then brandishes the drink carrier like it's some kind of magic trick. "So is this."

I take the bag, which has a bran muffin in it, and the large brown paper cup.

"Thank you. You really didn't need to get me anything. The ride is more than enough."

He waves me off and stares at me with a grin on his face. *This is uncomfortable.* My eyes dart between his face and the steering wheel in silent question.

Why aren't we moving?

"I hope you like what I got you." He nods to the cup and muffin.

Didn't I say thank you? I could have sworn I said thank you already.

Unless he's expecting me to eat this right now, I don't know about him, but personally, after a long run and feeling hot and sweaty, food and a hot drink aren't exactly my go-to. But I suppose it'd be rude to not at least sip and nibble.

I pick off the top of the muffin since that's always the best part. I cough, nearly choking at how dry it is. Swooping the cup towards my lips, a gush of hot liquid coats my tongue. Bitterness explodes across my tastebuds.

Awe, hell, it's coffee. I can't stand the taste of it. But I don't want to sound mean or ungrateful.

"Do you not like it?" Blake asks. A frown contorting his face.

Well, shit. I placed my mouth on mute but didn't turn the closed captions off on my face.

My phone pings loudly, buying me some time. Glancing down I see a message from my mom. Saved by the grace of my mother.

"No, no. This is fine and much appreciated. It was hot. I think I burnt my tongue. Should probably let it cool huh?"

He laughs and nods in agreement before starting the truck and driving down the winding roads back to our street.

"I'm surprised I still have tastebuds from how often I do that."

The drive back to our respective houses seems to stretch longer than usual, even though I know it isn't. It doesn't help mom's text has become the backdrop for all my thoughts.

Your father and I are coming down for a visit this weekend. I won't take no for an answer.

Why? Simply why?

When my mother says she won't take 'no' there is no way to convince her otherwise. Getting her to change her mind is like trying to get a mountain to move.

Where am I supposed to keep my parents? My house is a borderline hovel. How do I explain Mendax? *Oh, this is bad.*

"You know, we still haven't picked a day for our date." Blake turns down the music and gives me a side glance. "How about this weekend?"

"Huh?" I blink at him even though I heard him clearly, for some reason, my brain buffers randomly when I'm asked a question. "Oh, um, sorry, I can't this weekend. I'm working overtime, and my parents are visiting."

"Well, I guess we'll have to pick another weekend." Blowing heavily out of his nose, he hums. "Can I get your number? I'll give you mine."

When did he park? Was I that lost in my own thoughts? This is how people get murdered; they get charmed by the conventionally attractive man, get in his car, and before they know it, bam. They're the topic of a murder show.

Blake is staring at me again with a hopeful expression.

"Huh?"

He laughs before asking for my number again. I quickly give it to him before hopping out of the truck and walking across the street to my house. Halfway across the street, my feet skid to a stop and backtrack to Blake. He's still in the driver's seat, grinning at his phone. My knuckles rapt against the slightly warm window. I wince, watching his phone fly into the air and crash onto the dashboard.

"Sorry," I laugh awkwardly.

His jovial laugh filters out as he lowers the window. "No, no. You're fine. I was lost in thought." Blake's eyes flicker between mine.

Rocking on my heels, my teeth find the inside of my cheek. We stay there like a pair of idiots staring at each other until I clear my throat.

"I left the muffin and coffee."

Does it taste good? No. But he did something nice for me that he didn't have to, and I don't want to be rude.

Carding his fingers in his hair, he smiles and nods. Hoping out of the truck with the drink and bag in his hand, he walks around the back of the truck, even though the front would be faster. "Here you go. I'll message you later?"

Picking the bag from his fingers, I nod my head in agreement.

"That's why I gave you my number."

I shrug with a smile before jogging back to my home.

It's quiet…too quiet.

"Mendax?" I call out while scanning the living room.

Walking through the house it's as if he was never here. Slowly going up the attic stairs I see how tidy he made it. Artwork is hung, cobwebs have been cleared, the rug vacuumed, and I don't even know where those two desks came from. There's even a stack of files of my work along with different items from the dining table on the larger navy-blue distressed secretary desk with a hutch. In a copper container sitting on the edge of the desk are some of my favorite things. Like the dual bold and fine tip, pastel, highlighters, with smear guard in 12 shades. I thought I was out of those; when did I get them?

Oh my god, there's even another cup full of the 0.20mm archival ink pens I love. *Where did he find those? I searched everywhere for them.*

The second desk is outfitted with his things and matches mine, without the hutch.

"Awe, he's making me an office."

Tricky demon. He's giving me something I never asked for. Everything is neat and organized, a stark contrast to the rest of the home.

Walking back down to my kitchen, I notice a new cardboard box sitting on the table. So much for not answering the door.

"Liar."

I chuckle to myself. It's a new tea shipment from Steeped in Surprise. Looking up at a shelf, I see the now-empty tin of black tea sitting on it. The lid is still off. I smile, remembering how Mendax basically called me uncivilized for not having any coasters. He took the tin lid and told me to use that for a coaster. It's still on the living room coffee table.

Perhaps the spell I used to summon Mendax had an expiration date, and he's gone back to his realm. The thought of enjoying the new mystery tea by myself seems odd now. Maybe I'll save this cup for another day; drinking tea alone doesn't seem as appealing, and I don't know why. No, that's not right. It's because my friend is gone. Mendax isn't here.

Chapter 12

DATING CONUNDRUM

Mendax

FIVE, FOUR, THREE, TWO, one. The last few seconds of the extra ten minutes I always wait whenever Davina leaves or falls asleep finally pass. There have been a few close calls of her almost catching me sneaking through the portal. Those were difficult to play off; I've learned to carry a duster with me when I go to leave—it's easier for me to say I'm getting all the high places she can't reach.

Does part of me feel bad that I've been lying to her about not being able to go back? At first, no. But now? A little, but not enough to stop me because I'm doing it again.

Once she was out the door for her run and my time buffer was over, my feet scurry up the stairs and into her bedroom. Knowing how easily distracted she can get, I'll have about one hour and twenty-two minutes before she sets foot on the front porch. Sunbeams touch every piece of furniture and corner of Davina's bedroom. Every corner, except for one that is. The corner behind her door is a touch darker than anywhere else.

Portal magic flits in the shadowed corner. Reaching my hand out, I pause briefly, listening to the houses settle. Truly convinced she is gone; my fingers wrap around a thread of magic. A burn fills my chest as I'm yanked back into my realm and home. It now takes only seconds, but the feeling is always the same. It leaves my head spinning and my stomach in knots. Dots dance behind my eyelids as I squeeze my eyes shut, trying to steady my mind. Swinging the pantry open, the sight before me has me nearly running to vomit in the kitchen sink.

"Orroth!" I scold my brother.

His witch is riding him on *my couch*. This isn't the situation anyone would want to be caught in or witness, especially with family. This is uncomfortable all around.

"You are defiling my home!"

I slap my hand over my eyes while smacking the other down on the counter. Shrieks and gasps from the couch are followed by thumps before someone lets out a pained "ow." I couldn't care less who was hurt. The disrespect for my home and my furniture is what matters. The gall my brother seems to have never ceases to amaze me.

I drum my fingers so hard on the counter while waiting to hear the door open and close that I'm afraid they've permanently bruised and blistered.

"I'm sorry, I had no idea he would be here today. I'll call you, okay?" Orroth tells his girlfriend before what sounds like kissing.

"The coast is clear, Dax." He has the audacity to sound irritated.

"Oh, forgive me, Brother, I didn't mean to intrude in my own home. I'm going to have to burn that couch now." I look at him before eyeing the couch and shivering.

Orroth walks over to the couch and flips the cushions over.

"See, like nothing ever happened."

His actions only prove to me this isn't the first time it's happened.

"Where's Gotha?"

Raising an expectant brow, he saunters into my room. The clicking of a cage echoes in the space before he returns with my pet.

"She was sleeping off a big meal of mixed berries." He smiles while stroking a finger over her ears.

I can't help the frown that forms on my face. She looks rather cozy with him. The little traitor. "Why, Orroth?" I ask.

It doesn't matter how many times my knuckles press into my eyes; the image of the transgression on my couch seems to have assaulted my brain and transformed into an unwanted core memory.

His full belly laugh surrounds me as he trots into the kitchen.

"Chill, Dax." Orroth rummages around the refrigerator. "You know we're part incubus. We need to be satiated. You should try it sometime. Draining your balls every once in a while might help to get rid of the stick up your ass."

My hand meets the back of his head the moment he stands and closes the refrigerator door.

"We're *one-tenth* incubus. That's hardly anything at all. Don't be that demon. Simply don't. It's unbecoming."

As for the second offense, I never had any issues getting my needs met. There are plenty of women here that I could meet for sex, and I have. Never at my place, though; that's what their home or hotels are for. However, I haven't had the urge to have sex in months. There just hasn't been a need or even a thought, which normally comes from stress or boredom.

Gotha, my traitorous little bat, chirps and flies over to me. She hangs upside from my left horn, and I know she'll be, as the humans say, full of piss and vinegar today.

"So…" My brother stands at the counter making himself a sandwich. "How's your vacation going? Figure out how to get out of mother's contract yet or what?"

His question hits me like a bucket of ice water. I've been sneaking off to Davina's house daily, and I still haven't figured out how to get out of the situation my mother has put me in. To be honest, I've been focused on simply relaxing and enjoying my time with Davina.

"Where are you staying anyway? I know you have the family credit card for that realm. I think I should know, in case our parents start asking questions."

Sighing, I open the balcony door and watch Gotha fly out.

"Why do you care if they ask questions?"

Orroth raises a finger and points to his mouth. He's taken such a massive bite out of his sandwich his cheeks look rather comical.

"Listen," he begins, almost choking on his food before sitting on the counter, "we both know I'm a little shit. Not exactly winning brother of the year here after leaving you high and dry and still skating through life. But I'm self-aware." He chews another bite of the sandwich. "This is me trying to make amends. If they ask about any charges on the card, I can say I did it. Buy you some more time to figure something out."

Shocked isn't the correct word or expression. Orroth has left me flabbergasted.

"Thank you." It's all I can manage to utter. Never in all these years has my brother ever done anything like this for me. "As of right now, it'll probably be just restaurant and delivery charges. I'm staying in a house, not a hotel." *Perhaps he is maturing.* "It's also, from my own account, not directly from the business accounts. So, unless mother is snooping on my personal finances, it shouldn't even be a problem."

He narrows his eyes while taking another large bite of the sandwich. *I swear, he inhales his food.*

"Whose house?" His face scrunches up, and I can almost hear the gears whirring in his mind, trying to figure out which one of my contacts would open their home to me.

The first day I came back through the portal was the second day after being summoned. I couldn't stand not changing my clothes. Reluctantly, I told the truth about being summoned, the detail of who and where was left out. My mother has a way of prying out information out of just about anyone.

"A friend of mine."

The term rolled off my tongue effortlessly. So effortlessly, I had to pause and appreciate that's who Davina is to me. After months of sharing meals, watching horrid murder shows and horror movies, learning about her job, and our near-daily tea conversations, she is my friend. In fact, my only friend. I know she considers me the same.

We're friend-shaped.

We really do fit well together. Why does that make me nervous? I'm never nervous.

"Oh," Orroth snorts. "It's a lady friend."

"I beg your pardon?" I stammer out.

Placing his hand on his chest, a fit of laughter consumes him. "You zoned out for a solid two minutes. It's cool. Maybe she can be your 'out' from the arrangement."

The front door swings open, slamming against the wall. Turning on my heels, I'm met with a sight made from nightmares.

"Mendax Alistair Draxton," my mother's peeved voice booms from the entryway.

How long has she been waiting outside the door? *Did she hear anything?* I turn back to my brother, and find he's frozen in fear, that or he choked on the last bite of crust and is too afraid to make a sound.

"Where have you been?! Why are you avoiding me and your responsibilities?" She stalks into my apartment, waving a well-manicured hand in every direction. "I call, you don't answer. I send your brother, you ignore him. I send your father, you're not home."

Peering over my shoulder, I see my brother giving me a remorseful look accompanied by a shrug. Of course, he never told me she was looking for me. I've only been here daily to collect clothing and spend time with Gotha.

"Mother, I'm sorry. Truly, I am. However, being the adult I am, I do have my own life and personal matters." I can't very well say I've been avoiding her.

She's unaware I know about her rogue marriage contract. Tugging the sleeve of my shirt, I notice the time, and my heart nearly lodges in my throat. It stopped. My watch has stopped ticking, and I don't know how long I've been here. Davina could be back at any second…or worse, she already is. How do I sneak back and explain my absence?

My mother fixes her skirt before sitting on the couch in a regal manner. Meanwhile, I'm struggling to maintain my composure. She sniffs the air, and her brows furrow. The couch probably smells like Orroth's ass and sex.

Digging into her bag, she pulls out her perfume and sprays it before giving herself a satisfied nod.

"Oh yes, personal."

Her face pinches. My eyes roll at her assumption of me while my brother laughs.

"You're not getting any younger, Mendax. I've done you a favor and found you a wife. I won't lie to you; you'll be doing her family a favor, too. It's Elara, you remember her. The lovely demon from your date," she rambles while picking imaginary lint off her skirt. "She really is wonderful, smart, sweet, single."

"Mother," If I grind my teeth any harder, they might crack.

Ever the picture of grace and elegance, she places her hands neatly clasped on her knees. "Her father sits on the board of judiciaries. He can call your sentence complete after the marriage instead of waiting another three years."

"Mendax already has a girlfriend!" my brother blurts out from the kitchen.

Oh, I'm going to murder him.

The look in my eyes must portray my violent thoughts because in the time it takes me to blink, he's by our mother's side.

"Who is it? And why wouldn't you tell me?" There's a tinge of panic in her voice, and it throws me for a loop.

"Why did you make a marriage contract and not even ask me?" I counter.

There go her fingers, soothing the throbbing vein on her forehead.

"Is it serious?"

Orroth pats her knee. "Of course, it is. He's been seeing her every night."

I will show him no mercy.

"I've been getting to know her. Nothing more."

Standing, my brother looks dumbfounded. There is no chance I'm going to involve Davina in this. It simply wouldn't work.

"You'll have to stop seeing whoever this is. According to the contract, you are obligated to another three dates with Elara, followed immediately by an engagement, then the binding ceremony." My mother's voice pitches towards the end.

A humorless laugh escapes me watching, her massage her temples. She got herself into this; I will not help her get out.

"This was done of your own accord, Mother. Figure out how to end it."

She stands from the couch and treads lightly in both steps and voice. "You don't understand, son. There is a clause: if this marriage contract is voided by you, me, your father, or anyone in our family," her ruby fingers rub the hollow of her slim neck. "Your sentence will have more years tacked on. Ten to be exact." Her sharp nails begin to pick at her cuticles until she hisses. "Unless he decides to go the other route in which he gains full control over our business, cutting us completely out."

All the air has been sucked out from my lungs and apartment. My knees shake, and it's either from shock or anger. Probably both.

"Megai," calling my mother by name, draws a gasp from both her and Orroth, but the situation she has put me in is drawing out the worst in me. "You will figure this out because I refuse to be chained to a woman whom I find intolerable." I've paced so many times; at this point, I'd like to dig a trench with my feet.

"What does he have on you or our family? This can't be legal."

Megai's mouth opens and shuts several times. Refusing to shed light on whatever dark secret she's clinging to. Her mind is still unable to wrap around her own flesh and blood, disrespecting her. Orroth takes this as a prime opportunity to nudge her out the door.

"It's a binding contract, so it makes it legal."

"Mom, this is a lot. You dropped a major bomb on Dax here. Give him some time to think. He should probably talk this over with," Orroth turns to look towards me with imploring eyes, "his *girlfriend*."

I may receive additional years in my sentence or lose the business I will inherit because I am seriously considering harming my brother and mother. It is the sound of the door locking that rips me out of my murderous thoughts. Shuffling towards the couch, I plop down and exhaled the deepest breath.

"I believe this what's known as being 'up a creek with no paddle.'"

Orroth sports a shit-eating grin on his face as he squats before me.

"Oh, I'm about to be your favorite brother, because I got your paddle."

"You're my only brother." Emotionally and physically exhausted, I wait for him to continue because faking my death seems even more tempting now.

"You just have to get Elara to hate you and try to convince your friend to act like your girlfriend, just in case," he says it like it's simple.

It's anything but simple.

"Sure, Orroth. Date one woman so she breaks the contract, and convince another to act like she loves me as a backup plan. On what world does that make sense? Why would Davina need to involve herself?"

Shit. I let her name slip, and Orroth's grin grows.

"If you get *Davina*," he wiggles his eyebrows while saying her name, "to pretend to love you, you can get Elara to hate the idea of being a homewrecker. Like I said, *she's* your out."

I now find myself in a dating conundrum.

Chapter 13
Left on Read
Davina

FIVE FULL DAYS HAVE passed, and Mendax hasn't returned. I keep looking over my shoulder, expecting him to stroll around the corner and ask me a question about my work or try to convince me to sell the rhyming book. It's amusing how he bristles when I tell him no or that I don't need him to get me anything.

Besides the clicking of the keyboard, my house is quiet. Normally, there would have been music or a show playing in the background, but, I don't feel like it for some reason. Cold white light flickers to life on my phone before it dings, and my eye twitches.

My father created a group chat for our family because he was tired of playing Messenger. I'm seriously thinking about ditching this chat because of all the videos he finds funny, the winky faces between them, and my mom's plans.

I save the spreadsheet I'm currently working on for an Influencer who is shifting their brand from bottle service and fast fashion to vegan health and ethical fashion; the perpetual midnight oil has burned out. I've never been gladder to end a workday.

I wasn't kidding when I said my work was a mountain, barely a dent has been made even working all night. My parents were supposed to show up tonight, but they got "sidetracked," as my father put it. I'm pretty sure they forgot it was a group chat; the text with the eggplant emoji is something I should discuss in therapy.

Mental note:

- Seriously find a new therapist.

Yawning, my hand wanders the table in search of my phone.

"Please don't be my parents." I don't think I can handle any more of their flirtatious texts to each other.

To my relief, it's Blake. Since exchanging numbers, we've texted here and there but if someone were to ask me what the conversations entailed... well, let's just say I'm glad my life wouldn't depend on it.

Blake

> I noticed your lights on. You're not watching scary movies again, are you

> Why are you being a creeper? JK. I'm working late. Why are you spying on me?

Blake

> Not spying, just looked out the window... I was thinking

"Oh hell."

This man. It's too late to be scheming.

My eyes burn from leaving the contacts in for longer than I should have, and my ass is sore from that old dining chair. Three dots dance on the screen, and I take this as my cue to get ready for bed.

The first task of the night will be to remove the shards of glass from my eyes, shower, laundry, tea, and bed.

"Do I really want to do laundry tonight? Should I start it now? If I start it now, it'll affect my hot water for my shower. Wait, do I even have clean towels for after my shower?"

Suddenly, I'm rooted to the spot, and a tiny sense of doom is taking over. Closing my eyes, I take a deep breath and smell the lavender and cedar oil wafting out of the air diffuser.

"One thing at a time, Davina. One thing at a time."

Trudging across the downstairs, a little sense of satisfaction blossoms in my chest. I don't know what got into me yesterday, but I was actually able to clean up my entire living room. For once, I willingly woke up before the ass crack of dawn with energy and motivation. The carpet was ripped up; the floors were swept, mopped, and polished. I put every pillow in place, wrapped up every cord, and dusted every crevice. Was I drained after? Absolutely. Am I proud of what I got done? Hell yes.

Buzzing from the phone in my hand vibrates up my arm while I pass the attic stairs.

Part of me wants to call Mendax's name to see if he's there, but that's silly. He would be nagging me about drinking more water while trying to organize my mail if he was here.

Walking into my room, I click the small lamp on before heading into the bathroom to take out my contacts. Cool glass presses against the pad of my thumb as I swipe away the Lock Screen.

Oh yeah, Blake was texting me.

Going to spend time in his house seems a little too intimate. *What if he's secretly a murderer and his kill layer in the basement?* I don't care how attractive he is; we're going on a public date first.

I wonder what Mendax would say if I told him about Blake. Why would he even care?

The question pulls a soft laugh from me as the fluffy yellow bathrobe slides off my shoulders.

"It's none of his business if I date anyone." My bare feet tap against the cold tile floor while I contemplate if Mendax would care.

"Do I want him to care?"

My right hand reaches for the shower, and I stills as I notice the phone. *Oh yeah, Blake.* He wanted me to come over. *It's ten at night.*

"Who goes out this late?" I begin typing but delete it several times.

Turning the shower on, I shift towards the counter and toss my phone on it. It's at that moment my dryer-than-the-desert eyeballs gain my full attention.

"Holy crap. That's better," I say with a sigh of relief.

Steam starts to billow in my tiny bathroom and the smell of the eucalyptus hanging from the shower head assails my nose.

I'm shucking my worn-out black t-shirt with bleach stains into the hamper when a creaking in my bedroom snaps my attention. Sliding my glasses on, I grab the closest thing I can find. My fingers wrap around the handle of the three-inch curling iron. Nothing says intimidating more than a woman in hot pink yoga shorts, a bra with sprinkle print, and a curling iron. As I hype myself up to face whatever it is this time, I make a mental note:

- Get an alarm system, and a dog…or two.

The sight of Mendax emerging from yellowish light and blue smoke brings mixed emotions roaring through me. He strolls out casually like he's done this a million times, and the act causes my jaw to drop.

Right as I'm about to come out of the bathroom, a freaking bat pops out of the orb.

"Gotha, not now," Mendax sighs. "I can't exactly let Davina meet you yet when I still have to explain how I'm back." He stops for a second, and his pointed ear twitches, and I hold my breath.

"Lucky for the two of us, she's in the shower. You scurry back home, and I'll go hide somewhere."

Stomping out of my hiding place, I toss the curling iron on the bed and hear it thump to the floor before whirling around to my demon friend.

"You!" I point a finger at Mendax.

I watch as the color drains from his face. The bat flies around me, and the shriek that leaves me is one I didn't know I was capable of.

"Gotha! Get back here," Mendax huffs while trying to corral this bat. "This is a horrible first impression!"

The bat, Gotha, is swooping down on me over and over, and I'm close to the brink of tears. With every tactical swoop a new scratch appears on my arm, leaving a stinging sensation and blood beading on the surface. I run, swatting the air like a mad woman.

Mendax strips off his suit jacket, catches me, and covers me with it. Gotha swoops down once more, and before I can fully regain composure, the curling iron rolls under my foot, causing me to tumble on my bed with Mendax on top of me.

"Yo, Dax," an unfamiliar voice calls out, "Oh, sorry to intrude."

If my heart could fall into my ass, it would. In the dark corner, where Mendax and Gotha emerged, is a floating head. It looks like a "young rocker" version of Mendax.

"Mendax," my chest heaves against his while I attempt to calm my clambering heart, "…What the hell is happening?"

Violet eyes graze my face before he huffs out a murmured curse in a language I've never heard before. Gotha takes this moment to perch on Mendax's back and stare at me.

"Orroth, come here and take Gotha."

Orroth chuckles. "Say, please."

The fanning of Mendax's breath across my cheek makes reality bitch slap me. Here I am, pinned under a handsome demon in my bra and shorts, while a talking floating head that sasses us. Oh, and I can't forget the judgmental gaze from Gotha.

The silk of Mendax's white shirt slides under my palm as I push him, or at least *attempt* to push him, off me. My grunt gives him a hint, and he murmurs an apology while helping me up.

Carefully, he adjusts his jacket to cover me completely while guiding me closer to him. The warm jacket almost touches my knees, and like the weirdo I am, I inhale his scent. A spurt of giggles escapes me as I think about not only how ridiculous I must look, but also how my life is turning out.

Somewhere during my fit of giggles, Mendax manages to get rid of Orroth and Gotha and move away from me. Now, he's leaning against the doorframe with his legs crossed at the ankles. As his fingers stroke his beard. *He looks tired.*

"I guess I owe you an explanation," he sighs, pushing off the doorframe. "Why don't you shower first and then maybe join me for tea?"

There are constantly a minimum of one thousand questions swirling around in my brain, and that number has gone up exponentially, yet not a single one wants to make a debut on my tongue. All I can do is narrow my eyes and nod.

"A new Tea of the Month came in. I haven't tried it yet."

The sight of his fingers effortlessly gliding through his hair is a mesmerizing display of confidence and self-assurance. Each strand obeying his touch, falling into place perfectly. As his fingers move, his shoulders relax and his posture straightens. A cool, calm, subtle wave of relaxation washing over him.

With a flash of pearly white teeth, his lips curve upwards, exuding warmth and charisma. The corners of his eyes crinkle slightly, revealing a hint of mischief and playfulness, adding an irresistible allure to his already magnetic presence.

This smile, it's not just a mere expression, but a potent tool that effortlessly navigates the intricate web of human emotions. It possesses the uncanny ability to melt away apprehension and doubts, replacing them with a sense of trust and comfort. It is a smile that persuades, convinces, and seduces if you stare for too long. *I think I'm starting to stare for too long.*

"Then we'll try it together."

There's nothing quite like the water going frigid halfway through your shower. At least the cold shock wakes me enough for this impromptu tea session. I slip into a green, ribbed tank top and matching shorts. Sliding on the fluffy gray slippers, a dull ache pinches my brows.

"Why does my ankle hurt?"

Bounding down the stairs, I push past the pain, wincing with every step, and focus on braiding my damp locks.

Soon, it's just me and Mendax, sitting on my lumpy couch: me staring at him and him avoiding my eyes.

"Who decided sleepy-time tea was a good idea?" he asks, yawning after one sip.

"Mendax," I say flatly.

He clears his throat in visible discomfort but doesn't lift his eyes to meet mine.

I sigh while tucking a piece of damp hair behind my ear.

The clatter of his teacup on the saucer fills the conversational void.

"I lied."

He dares to glance my way, but my stare is blank because I'm genuinely curious about which part was a lie. I won't say it, though; there's a bit of twisted satisfaction and mirth in seeing Mr. Charm-and-Elegance squirm a little.

"The entire time I was here," Mendax crosses one ankle over the opposite knee and begins folding the sleeves of his shirt. "I was able to travel to and from my home."

He winces, bracing himself for the bomb to go off.

"You, lying son of a bitch," I laugh. Mendax looks taken aback by my reaction. "All the countless hours we spent together reciting the stupid rhyme."

"I had to make sure the portal stayed open. It's also why I had you recite it while drinking tea from that fine china."

Mendax scratches his leg just above the ankle, still avoiding eye contact.

Realization washes over me like a bucket of ice water. All those times sharing tea feel somewhat tainted.

"So, you didn't want to just have tea with me?"

His eyes widen. "No, no. That's not it at all. Notice how these cups are different? The others were magical cups, offering cups. We only used *those* when reciting the summoning spell. All the other times were honestly the highlight of my day. I truly do enjoy our teatime. I would never intentionally hurt a friend." He turns his piercing gaze on me and grasps my hand in his. "I—I am. I'm sorry."

"Awe, that looked painful for you to say. I feel so special." I playfully bat my lashes at him, causing him to chuckle and the tip of his pointed ears to flush a darker hue.

"I'll forgive you on one condition," I inform him, leaning over towards the table and grabbing my cooled tea. "Explain to me why."

It's two o'clock in the morning, and I feel like I've been sucked into a binge-watching session of a soap opera. Except that the soap opera happens to be Mendax's entire life—or at least part of it.

According to him, it was important to start from when his brother began working alongside him to now in order to see the picture. Me being me, I had to ask several questions, which led to more than a few offshoot stories. Which eventually circled back around to the main story.

All my focus is on how, this entire time, I've harbored a fugitive, and he ate all my good snacks.

He owes me new snacks. I only had one limited edition Oreo out of the entire pack. I wish I had a snack right now.

"Okay, let me recap so I can make sure I'm following. Your brother, Orroth—the floating head from my room—is covering for you while you hide out from your insane and overbearing mother," I say in between bites of borderline-stale graham crackers, "while you seek sanctuary from your arranged marriage in my humble abode?"

The Mendax sitting next to me is a completely different person from the Mendax of four hours ago. His shirt is untucked, his shoes are kicked off, and to my delight, he is *slouching.*

"What if you tell Elara you're a habitual womanizer and have, like, twelve children out of wedlock?"

The deep, rumbling laugh that leaves him takes me by surprise. "You're just as bad as Orroth; he suggested I fake my death."

"Too many risk factors in his scenario. Honestly, in mine too. Want me to run the risk numbers for you? I can totally do it." I shove a powder cinnamon donut hole into my mouth. "I still don't understand why you have such a long sentence. Here, theft is around two years for first offenses and maybe a fine."

His breath fans across my face as he leans closer, releasing a heavy sigh. With a gentle swipe of his thumb, he removes the crumbs from the corner of my lips, and I'm mesmerized as I see him lick his thumb clean. Are swallowing and breathing considered normal bodily functions? Juggling both functions is proving to be a challenge.

"Our laws aren't the same as yours. There are different sets of rules and regulations based on business and law. Draxton Procureurs and Purveyors did not own the item in question: the witch's ladder."

A series of cracks ripple down his back as he rolls his neck and shoulders.

"We were acting as a broker for this particular transaction. Since it was already appraised as a high-value item we had tried to purchase beforehand, it seemed to the authorities like we wanted to obtain it.

"I was accused of faking the theft. Warehouses were raided, we were audited, and so many more things. Clients pulled business from us; we lost contracts. It was a mess.

"And the unknown buyer demanded their pound of flesh—through their lawyers, naturally.

"I had no idea who this item belonged to, and it was either this sentence or we lose everything."

"That's some bullshit. I thought our laws were bad."

I offer him the last extra-large, extra-thick s'mores gourmet cookie.

"And now you're in this predicament. How are you going to get out of it?"

Fixing his hair and beard, Mendax slowly sits straighter. He slings his arm over the back of the couch and gives me a dazzling smile that would probably charm the pants off anyone else. Unfortunately for him, it leaves me feeling suspicious.

"I know you said you have no need for anything. But I have a favor to ask that could prove beneficial to you."

Oh, this is going to be good.

"Go on."

Do I get to harbor a fugitive forever? What would I do when someone visits me? I can't exactly say, 'Oh, don't mind my demon roommate.' Who am I kidding? I never have visitors.

Maybe I should charge him rent.

"Be my girlfriend."

"What?" I cackle. Never in my life had I cackled, but today was the day it happened. "Mendax, you can't be serious."

He releases a huff and pouts as he crosses his arms.

"It would be pretend, of course. I just need someone to pretend to be in love with me to get Elara to break the contract first."

Oh, he's serious.

"Let's say I agree to this insanely high-risk endeavor of yours: what about it is beneficial to me?"

Mendax leans forward and stretches my legs across his lap.

"You, Davina, my darling, my love, my princess," he grins, and I can't help but laugh. "You get one favor from yours truly. Anything you want will be yours. Name it and it's granted no matter what; no matter big or small."

Scrubbing a hand down across my forehead, I groan.

"Mendax, I don't want anything."

"*Yet.* You don't want anything *yet.* This favor has no expiration date," he says while massaging my feet.

He's trying to butter me up, and I'm gonna to let him. I'll sit here until he does both feet 'thinking it over.' His thumb digs into the arch of my foot with the perfect amount of pressure. Clamping my lips tightly, I cage a deep moan that is trying desperately to escape into the world.

Are his hands magical?

I didn't realize how sore my feet were until now. Several minutes pass, and I finally take pity on him. Plus if he goes on any longer I'm not sure I can keep these moans to myself.

"Alright, Shnookums, you've got yourself a girlfriend." I stick out my hand.

"Please, anything but 'Shnookums.'" He laughs, shaking my hand.

"You've got *no* say in what I call you, babe. Want me to dress borderline scandalous and hang off your arm while pouting and batting my lashes?" I bounce on the couch. "Oh, how clingy can I act? Can I be a stage-five clinger?"

"I already regret this," he rolls his eyes but can't keep the humor out of his voice.

Tossing a cookie wrapper at his face, I let out my best villain laugh. "I don't!"

The sun is going to be up soon, so I stand and stretch my body. Through a gap in my curtains, I notice all the lights in Blake's house are off.

"Oh, crap. I forgot to reply."

Mendax shuffles around the couch, folding the giant fuzzy blankets we used.

"I'm pretty sure you gave me your answer."

"Not you. Blake. He texted, and I didn't reply. That's so rude."

A wafting breeze from a blanket being shaken hits my skin.

"Is he from the dating app? Let me guess: Blake, 28, likes fishing. Will let you borrow my hoodies. I'm not looking for anyone to make babies with, but the practice is fun."

Turning on my tiptoes, I grin. "Listen, you had me at hoodies."

The outrage on his face is clear as day, and I'm living for it.

"I'm kidding." *Sorta.* "Blake lives across the street," I say, hooking my thumb over my shoulder.

"So he's always around then?" There's a tone in Mendax's voice that my tired brain can't compute.

Patting his shoulder, I make my way to the stairs, where I can hear the siren's call of my bed.

"I guess. We've trying to set a day for a date. I feel bad because I left him on read."

Chapter 14
Razzle Dazzle

Mendax

Davina went to bed not long after agreeing to help me with my situation. Her swift decision caught me off guard. Never in my life have I groveled, but I was prepared to give it my best go if I had to.

It seems she saved me from that, as well. Davina has saved me more than she knows and is slowly becoming my hero. So much, in fact, if she saves me anymore, I'll owe her not only a favor but an ode, too. All I have to do now is figure out how to get her to my realm and make our meeting and relationship believable. Being friends is one thing, but faking love is another.

Sure, I could exude some charm pheromone, but that can only get us so far.

Surveying the space, little "doom piles" –as Davina likes to call them—dot my vision like a game of Connect the Dots. The last time I was here, she had work piled up to her eyeballs. For that I do feel guilty; I wasted a lot of her time pretending to be stuck here. To make up for it, I've spent all morning cleaning the house while Davina sleeps. Starting with the random piles of laundry.

"I don't understand these sizes."

One pair of shorts says 'medium' the other says '6', another says 'large', and another says 'twenty-seven.' *Is this a secret code?*

The undergarments are another puzzle; some are "XL" while others have numbers and letters. Delicate white lace slips between my fingers while I read "34 DD."

This is confusing.

Either way, it goes into a separate pile, like the directions say, with a sense of satisfaction. Watching Davina do laundry is a nightmare; everything goes in together with no separation and it all gets washed on the same setting.

And she wonders why some of her shirts feel tighter than others.

"She's never touching my suits."

I chuckle at the thought and gather our dishes from last night. When did we get donuts, and why didn't I have one?

Water sprays everywhere as the hot stream hits the curve of the back of the spoon. After drying my arms and hands, the yellow checkered kitchen towel slaps over my shoulder. A soft knock sounds from the door.

Curiosity has taken hold of me and is leading me towards the front door. The cool surface of the door presses against my cheek while I peer out of the peephole.

On the other side stands a relatively tall man with salt and pepper hair, heavy on the salt, and glasses. His fingers pick away flecks of paint from the banister on the porch. The woman, who is much shorter than the man, lifts her fist to aptly rapt on the door again. She appears to have deep brown hair and a shock of pure white hair framing her face. There is something familiar about her.

"Who are these people?" I whisper.

The scratching of my beard fills the morning silence before I trot up the stairs. Skipping the fourth step that creaks in the middle, I continue up and then turn down the hall to Davina's room. Her bedroom door groans in protest to opening. The room is dim except for the ray of sunlight that dares peek through the lavender curtains. Light snoring seeps through the heavy gray blanket. Laughing to myself, I make my way over to the bed.

"Davina." I poke the small lump under the covers. "Davina, there's someone knocking."

The knocking from downstairs grows louder, yet Davina sleeps like the dead. My body stretches luxuriously across the bed, sinking into the plushness beneath me, a contented smile spreading across my face as I rest my head on my hand. Observing the room while lying next to her brings a sense of tranquility. The feeling is undeniable, which is why I act on it with no hesitation or prior thinking.

"Oh, dear," I chuckle, pulling the cover down a bit to expose brown hair splaying across the pillow. Her mouth is slightly parted while a small pool of drool collects beside her cheek. Leaning closer, the pad of my finger pokes her nose.

Her eyes shoot open.

"Fucking hell, Mendax." Her lithe fingers rub sleep away from her eyes. "You gotta stop waking me up like that."

"Like what?" I ask, stretching my legs further down the bed and dragging the sheet. "Waking you with a dazzling smile and charm?"

Davina's lips twist in a tragic attempt to hide a growing smile. The next second, there's a soft thud against my face, and the world turns black for a few seconds.

"Did you really smack me with a pillow?"

Just as the cool Egyptian cotton is in my clutch, and I'm ready to smack the pillow back towards her, knocking floats up the stairs.

"Nooooo!" Davina gapes, cutting her eyes towards her bedroom door and then back at me. "I forgot my parents are coming today for the weekend."

In a state of panic, she quickly removes the sheets and jumps out of bed, leaving her pajamas crumpled and forgotten in her haste. Appearing out from under the seam of her shorts are a pair of cotton panties with purple hearts. As she paces back and forth, my eyes are drawn to the delicate floral tattoo on her thigh, its intricate design peeking out from under her shirt and gracefully crawling up her ribs.

"Your parents? How did you forget your parents are visiting?" I sit up higher on her bed, leaning my head against the sapphire-colored tufted headboard.

"Davina, I can't believe you're flashing me your underwear."

A grin splits my lips as she clutches invisible pearls before fixing her shorts.

"You, my fugitive friend, can't judge me. That's, like, the number one rule of friendship. Everyone knows that." Her steps are quick and barely make a sound as she scurries into the bathroom.

"Fugitive?" I bark out a laugh. I guess, technically, I *am* a fugitive of my realm, but no one outside of Orroth and Davina knows about it. Flushing, followed by the sound of the faucet running, seeps from under the door.

The hinges squeak as the door opens. Waving a hand, she dismisses my fake outrage.

"First, have you met me?" she says, sliding her glasses on. "I forget to feed myself, so obviously, I forgot about their visit. To be fair, she never sent a follow-up calendar invite via her assistant or my dad's. So, I didn't think they would show up. Third, remind me to spray something on those." She points to the squeaky doors.

Turning slightly, I watch her march towards the new vanity tucked in the corner of the room. According to her, this exact spot has the best natural light. The bottles click together while she selects the correct jar. Swinging my legs over the edge of the bed, my forearms rest on my thighs while I observe as she scrubs her face and applies three different serums and two types of lotion before returning to the bathroom to brush her teeth.

How is she this beautiful first thing in the morning?

The thought catches me off guard, and while I'm shaking my head to get rid of the thought, she's tossing clothes in her closet and holding up dresses in front of me. It's odd seeing her hold them up because, in the time I've known her, she's only ever worn baggy t-shirts and athletic shorts. Plus, the occasional fluffy pajama bottoms or matching pajama sets. There's a brown corduroy dress in her left hand and a long, pink dress with a white floral pattern in her right. Her eyes bore into mine waiting for a response while she lifts them up and down like a judgment scale. I point to the pink dress and her phone rings on the bedside table.

"Mother dearest?" I question the name scrolling across her screen.

Tossing the dress on the bed she stomps over towards me and plucks the phone from my hands. "Hello, Mom."

A muffled voice from the other end has Davina pulling the phone away and wincing. She's pacing again, sliding her fingers under her glasses to cover her eye. A heavy sigh escapes her before her soft voice floats around the room.

"Mom, if you stop for a second, I can explain. I was up late working and slept in. I'm getting dressed now."

There's no "goodbye" or "I'll be right down." Just a disconnected call.

For some reason, there's a tinge of discomfort in my chest when she doesn't mention she was up late helping me.

Why does that bother me?

Shuffling off her bed, I stroll towards her, the plush carpet swallowing my footsteps. Gently, my hands grab her bare shoulders, and I notice how her breath hitches. Perhaps my hands are cold? The phone is discarded on the bed as I guide her back towards her closet, not before snatching the dress off the bed.

"Get dressed, Davina."

With an exasperated sigh, she turns around in my embrace, forehead pressed tightly against my chest, seeking solace and refuge from the overwhelming chaos of her thoughts. As I watch her rest against my body, an unfamiliar warmth blossoms within me, accompanied by a powerful surge of protectiveness, making me desperately wish I could solve all her problems.

"Are you going back to your home?"

It would be rather difficult to explain a demon to her parents. But there's something in her tone of questioning that gives me pause. It's almost as if she doesn't want me to go.

"Want to introduce me to your parents? See if we can be a convincing couple?"

Mischief sparkles in her eyes, and our gazes lock. Her eyes are so captivating, I struggle to breathe.

"Oh yeah, let's show off this fake relationship with a little razzle-dazzle and a side of heart palpitations," she snorts before taking the dress from my grasp and heading into the closet, leaving the door slightly ajar.

"I'll introduce you as my 'Pookie Bear.'"

"You're not calling me 'Pookie Bear.'"

"Whatever you say, Pookie Bear."

She's going to keep calling me Pookie Bear, I just know it.

Walking towards her bathroom, I pose a question, "You don't think I can charm them into liking me?"

On the counter is an assortment of perfumes. Most have never been touched except the large circle glass bottle with a flower cap. Opening it, I inhale the scent I have come to associate with Davina. It's a smell so familiar that it almost gives me a nostalgic feeling of home.

"My dad, maybe."

Her response startles me. I didn't even hear her follow me into the bathroom.

"My mom? I'll bet two hundred dollars she'd try to douse you in holy water," she muses. "Unless you do that thing where you ooze charm. But that's cheating."

I watch as she grabs the wooden paddle brush and sleeks her hair into a high ponytail, showing off her elegant, long neck. With the back of my thighs resting against the counter, I hand her the perfume and observe how she places it in each spot with fascination.

"Turn around, I have to spray my lady bits."

Chuckling, I turn and cover my eyes.

"To answer your question, no. I'm not going back to my home. It's still too early. There are set times I go back when I know only my brother is there."

She taps my shoulder, signaling me to turn back around.

Panic etches on her face; all I can do is run a hand through my hair. I really should get a haircut. "Not to worry, princess. I'll stay in the attic like a good little demon. You can keep me your dirty secret for now." I wink at her.

Davina goes uncharacteristically quiet. Her mouth opens, but whatever words she has are stolen by the sound of incessant ringing.

"Mother dearest?"

She nods and rolls her eyes.

"Mother dearest."

I've never minded the attic before. There were plenty of objects and books to keep me occupied—even client files for Davina. She had no idea most of the items packed away in these boxes are magical.

Spinning in a circle, I release an uneven breath. I can't decide if I'm lonely or bored. It wouldn't be so bad if Gotha were here to keep me company, but she had to misbehave upon her stowaway arrival. The creaking of the house settling gets drowned out with two sets of new voices.

"Hey, Pumpkin."

"Dad, you gotta stop with that nickname. It's embarrassing," Davina replies. Even though its muffled, I can still hear the humor in her voice. "Mom, thanks for knocking like you're SWAT. Pretty sure you woke up the neighbors."

Pumpkin? I wonder why she doesn't like that name. If Davina calls me "Pookie Bear" one more time, I'll use pumpkin against her. I did notice how her lips curled when I called her princess. Maybe I'll call her that more often. *That wouldn't be weird, right?*

Moving to the bottom of the attic stairs, I keep my footing towards the outside of the steps to avoid the creaking. The cold, hard, wooden step lets out a small groan as I sit towards the edge and nudge the door open. It's just enough to hear their conversations more clearly.

Sounds of clicking heels echo before a voice, who I assume is Mother Dearest, starts, "Honestly, Davina, you stay up too late. You always have. That's why I always had to remind you to set five alarms. Plus, you can't blame me for trying to get you to open the door."

I don't care much for the way she speaks to Davina. The tone reminds me of too much of my own mother and her 'holier than thou' persona.

"Your father drank two Big Gulps on the drive here."

"Two? Dad, no one should drink two of those."

"Your mother's ice was melting. What was I supposed to do? She wasn't going to drink it while she was drinking mine. I paid for it, and I'm not letting a good Coke get watered down," he huffs out. "That's wasted money in my book. Now, if you ladies will excuse me, I need to take a leak."

Heavy thuds scamper up the steps, and I hold my breath. Moving from the stairs or closing the door would make too much noise.

"Oh God, this was a horrible idea," I mutter to myself.

"Dad, there's a bathroom down here!" Davina calls up frantically.

Her bare feet pound against the stairs in chase of her father.

"All those mirrors have always creeped me out. I'll just be—" The words are cut short, and a strangled sound leaves her father as he spots me from the crack in the door.

The door rips open and the man standing before me looks like his brain has quit functioning.

"Oh, hello there." I offer a grin and stand dusting off my pants.

It's only now that I realize my unkempt state. My shirt is untucked, sleeves rolled up, a few buttons undone, and I have no shoes. It's not the best first impression, which seems to be a growing trend with this family.

His chest heaves up and down. I've seen that look before. It's the same Davina gave me on our first encounter.

"Please, don't scream. There really is a wonderful and lovely explanation for my being here."

Darkness engulfs me as the door is slammed in my face, and the sound of rushed footsteps followed by a yelp enters my ears.

Adjusting my clothing, I decide it's time to meet Davina's parents. I won't let her fend for herself and try to explain this mess—time to razzle-dazzle indeed.

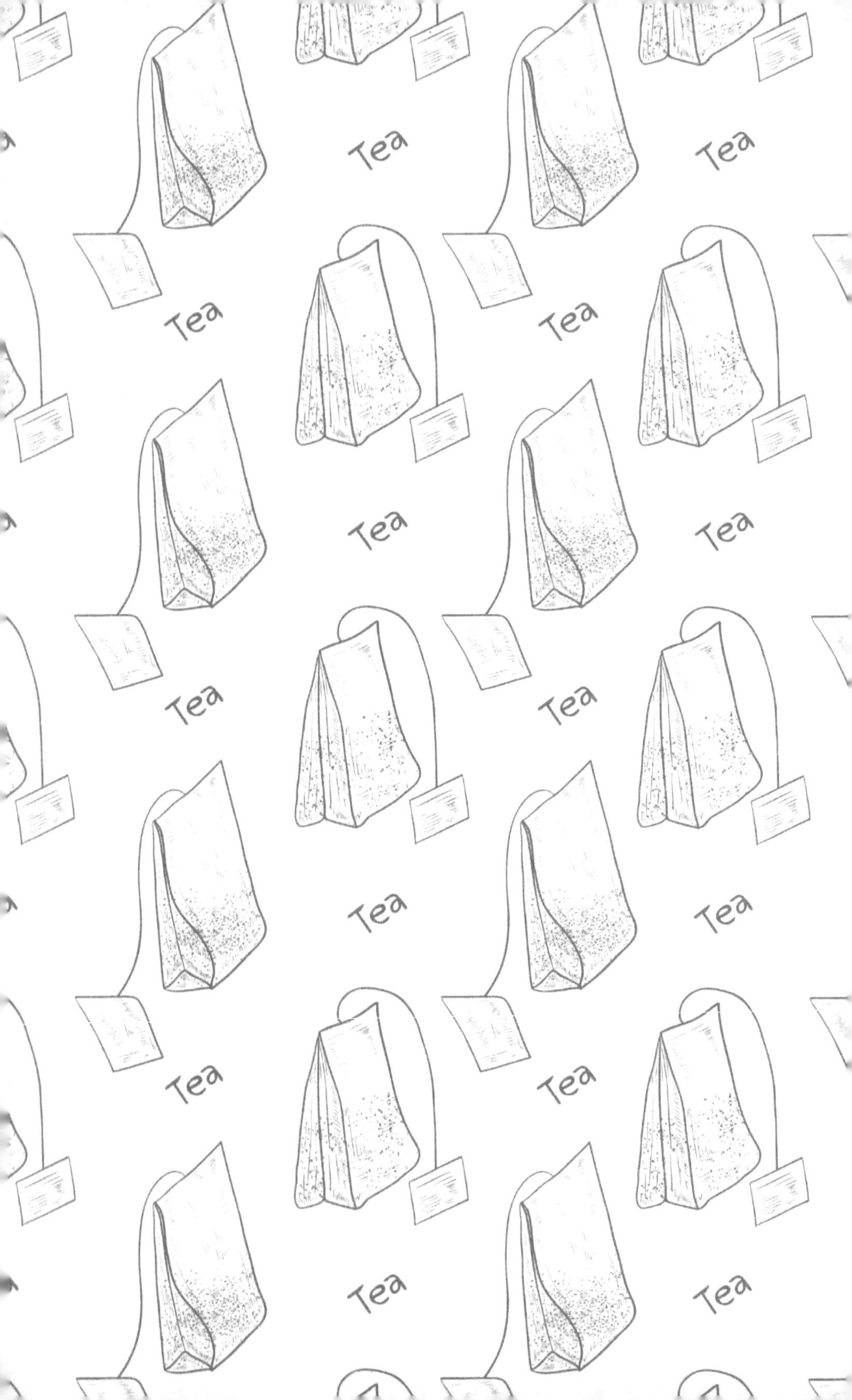

Chapter 15
MOTHER DEAREST
Davina

First, there was thudding, then the smooth and casually cool voice I've come to associate with Mendax. One loud and determined slam entered my ears before the sight of my father skidding and bumping down the stairs on his heels while the banister slid between his palms with one long squeal.

Before I knew it, my world is turned upside down again, only literally this time. I didn't realize the squeal of surprise is from me as my dad doesn't bother to stop. Instead, his shoulder digs into my stomach as he tosses me on his shoulder.

Is it necessary? No. Is it impressive? Yes. I had no idea my father could still pick me up like I am a toddler having a tantrum in the middle of the grocery store.

"Rick, what are you doing?" my mother's question pitches towards the end. With every step, Dad's shoulder digs deeper into my stomach. *That's going to bruise by morning.*

Mental note:

- Buy some arnica gel.

The scraping on my hardwood flooring from my mother's heels makes me want to cry, but I groan instead. Thank God I do yoga or else my neck would hurt from craning it.

All I can do is roll my eyes while Mendax strolls down the stairs. I'm not sure if it's the sheepish wave, the rumpled clothing, or the angle

I'm watching from, but he looks extremely handsome. Almost painfully handsome. Handsome enough to make my heart flutter a bit. My vote is it's from the blood rushing to my head.

"Rick! Stop this right now." My mother's spiked heel digs into the ground.

"Mom," I wheeze. "I just waxed the floor."

Her designer Chanel bag thuds to the hardwood as she tries and fails to rip her arm out of my dad's grip.

A spike of irritation surges through me. I worked hard on these floors!

"Mom, you're still scuffing my floor. Dad, I'm going to pass out."

The pounding in my ears is a soundtrack to the chaos in my home. Colored dots take hold of my eyes like a little light show accompanying the soundtrack.

"Put me down."

The tips of my blunt nails scratch his sides. The ticklish reaction causes him to drop me like a sack of potatoes.

"Davina," worry laces Mendax's voice, "are you alright?"

He squats to my level, checking me over.

"I have at least twenty-four hours before a bruise forms on my ass," I reply, wincing.

A stuttered beating from my heart starts as Mendax helps me to stand. Giving him a grateful smile, I smooth my hair back, readjust my glasses, and fix the nonexistent wrinkles from my dress. Finally, the moment my mother notices the seven-foot-tall demon has arrived. To say I'm disappointed would be a slight understatement.

Turns out the stuttered humming was coming from a frozen Mother Dearest. I expected her to scream. Instead, there is only a thud as her knees buckle, and the floors she scuffed welcome her for a nap.

That's right, my mother fainted.

"What happened to being a 'good little demon,' Mendax?" I ask while spooning loose-leaf tea into the gold steeper.

Measured steps come from behind me.

"Davina, I promise it wasn't my fault. I was being good." Ceramic mugs slide across the counter next to the teapot. "I was bored. How was I supposed to know your father would come upstairs?"

Mendax's beard scratches my shoulder as he hugs me from behind. The moment he hugs me, my body freezes. We've never hugged like this before. It's… cozy. He smells like coconut and campfires. It's an odd combination, but for some strange reason, it's right for him.

Before I can dwell any longer on the hug, he pulls away and clears his throat. Rustling from the bottom cabinet draws my attention. Sighing while looking over my shoulder, I spot him rummaging around the bottom cabinet for snacks. He stands, and for reasons beyond my comprehension, my heart beats a fraction faster with every step he takes closer to me.

"Oh stroopels! I forgot we had these." The smooth gloss of the cardboard slides into my palm while I examine the ingredients. Thank you, glucose syrup, wheat flour, and vanilla pods, for becoming so fascinating and giving me time to slow my heart rate.

"Stroopels?" A black, blunt nail enters my line of sight and points to a name. "It says '*Stroopwafels.*'"

A throat clears from the kitchen doorway.

"She's always called them stroopels, even as a little kid."

My dad taps the doorframe with his knuckle. His eyes are filled with caution and confusion.

If we stood side by side, we wouldn't look related at all. He's on the taller side, with a fair complexion, light blue eyes, and the salt and pepper hair was once jet black. Now our behaviors, mannerisms, well, that's how you'd know he's my dad.

"Pumpkin, what's going on? You seem…how do I put this?" His mouth opens and closes several times, trying to string a coherent thought into words.

My teeth bite into my button lip, caging back my grin. It was fine for me to find humor in this, especially since I experienced the same level of shock. Maybe one day we'll look back at this and laugh. Or maybe we'll use it as a trauma-bonding experience; only time will tell.

A nudge on my arm pulls me from my thoughts. The world comes back into focus and my gaze lifts up to meet Mendax staring at me while giving a slight nod towards my father.

Oh, I zoned out for real this time because, looking at my dad, he is waiting for a response.

Mendax comes to my rescue like a knight in shining armor.

"Perhaps it's for the best if we take this conversation to the living room?" He turns and grabs a serving tray. "Tea always helps ease a conversation. Plus, it sounds like your mother is waking."

Pausing in the doorframe, I retrace my steps into the kitchen to grab an ice pack, just in case.

The sweet and nutty flavor, with notes of honey and caramel from the rooibos tea is the only thing making me believe the scenario playing out right now. What started as a conversation that was less awkward than the time I asked my parents how babies were made has turned into something out of the twilight zone.

Why couldn't I have met Mendax sooner in life? He could have saved me some trouble and premature forehead wrinkles.

All it took was two hours, a teapot filled to the brim, cookies, and the razzle-dazzle that seems to ooze out of Mendax naturally. That, along with a few well-placed compliments, a disarming smile, and one sentence: "I can understand how alarming it must be to see your wonderful and precious daughter in the company of a demon." *This is probably what makes him—or rather made him—so great in his line of work*. And now my parents are talking to him as if we've been lifelong friends.

Mental note:

- Ask Mendax if he'll show me some of these oddities.

"Cheater, you did that thing," I whisper, hiding my lips behind my cup.

He brushes a stray strand of hair from his forehead and whispers back, "All's fair." He doesn't bother finishing the saying. We both know this isn't love or war.

An airy laugh lures me back into the ongoing conversation I know I have missed almost all of.

Is my mother blushing?

I narrow my eyes at Mendax as he slings an arm behind me and on the couch. The fake laugh he pulls from her makes me want to punch him in his handsome, angular face. A side glance at my dad shows me we're sharing the same thought.

"Take it easy on the charm," I grit out low enough that only he can hear through my forced smile.

"I know this probably sounds ridiculous, but I could have sworn I've seen you before," my dad says, mimicking Mendax's leisurely sitting.

Okay, maybe we're not thinking the same thing.

Mendax solemnly nods and sighs, "Unless you were here—or rather in the attic—years ago when there were rock posters everywhere, I doubt you have."

What? That wasn't what I expected to hear.

That timeline would place my dad at twenty-two, just before he met Mom. Anyone would be mad at this revelation, anyone but me. I'm more fascinated by why he was here and why he never mentioned it.

"Davina," My mother chastises, "why didn't you tell us your *friend* knew your Uncle Alex?"

All I can do is stare at her. It's uncanny how much we look alike. I'm basically a carbon copy of her. Maybe that's why I decided to color my hair with streaks of neon yellow and get tattooed.

I should get a new tattoo.

"I'm not sure, Mom." I smile sweetly and stare up at Mendax, who refuses to look at me now. "It probably slipped my mind."

The cushion lifts as my wonderful demon friend shuffles away from me. *He's not getting away that easy.*

"Mendax, why don't you tell them how you knew Uncle Alex."

I shuffle closer, grabbing his hand, anchoring him to me.

This is going to be good. That trademark charming smile drops so fast that if I blinked, I'd have missed it. The struggle to cage my laugh behind my lips is a battle I wasn't ready for.

"Well, hold on, now." Mendax pulls his hand out of mine, and his fingers curl around a yellow lock of hair, and I don't think he even notices my struggle to keep a straight face. "It probably slipped Davina's mind because," he playfully tugs my hair. "For starters, she's been terribly busy with work and making this lovely house a home."

The fingers leave my hair and skim my shoulder. Heat erupts in my veins and I turn my head to hide the blush on my cheeks. *Maybe I have late onset asthma, because this breathing thing sure is hard.*

"Secondly, I didn't spend much time with Alex. Years ago, I was summoned here, and yes, apparently, by the same summons Davina used. I was a teenager then. Just started working with my parents."

He looks me in my eyes, then past my shoulders. The lack of warmth as he removes his hand kisses my skin like the first frost of winter.

"There were two men in the attic, one named Daniel and the other, I presume, Alex. They were looking to buy a certain artifact. If memory serves me correctly, it was a green flame candle. Very rare and hard to come by." He said before leaning over to pick up his cup. "But I don't remember seeing you during that meeting."

My dad pulls at the collar of his polo shirt. Mom probably made him wear it; he hates collars. If my dad could purge and restock his closet, it'd be nothing but jeans, sneakers, and old band t-shirts.

"Well, I wasn't in the room," he admits, stretching before standing.

Even though his feet carry him around the room, his eyes wander to the past, revisiting the memories hidden in these walls.

"I came over here to borrow the keys to his car. He had the nice candy apple red vintage convertible, and I had to pull out all the stops for a hot date."

I raise a brow at the statement. They never told me about their first date. I want to interrupt and ask every question currently playing leapfrog in my brain, but this is not the time. I'll put a pin on that for now.

"The front door was open; he always did that," my dad chuckles. "I heard voices from upstairs and followed them. Alex was convinced he could do magic and would always tell me about spells he was working on. I humored him because it was brother, ya know? Well, turns out the son of a bitch *could.* I was hiding just at the top of the steps; it was dark, so no one could see me. There was a plume of yellow smoke, and out came, well, out came you." My dad turns away from the bottom of the stairs and looks at Mendax.

"I didn't want to believe it. I blamed it on possible lead poisoning, giving me hallucinations. Anything sounded more credible than admitting my brother conjured a demon. But now? Well, I'll be damned."

Adjusting my dress, I turn towards Mendax.

"Did my uncle get the candle? What was he using it for? How often did he summon you?" Questions pour out faster than I can breathe. By the time I am done rattling off questions, my mother is rubbing her temples, and Mendax looks at me with a glint of humor.

The soft pad of his finger pressed against my lips, stifling any further commentary. This earned a chuckle from my dad.

"That was the only time I met him; I did find the candle, but my mother handled the rest. What someone uses their purchase for is none of my business because that would be *bad* for business. I've only ever been summoned via magic twice now. Luckily for me, it was within the same family."

He keeps his finger over my lips during his explanation. Heat crept up my chest and cheeks.

Why is it so hot in here all of a sudden?

"Anyone want more tea? Mom? Dad? Where are your bags? I can set you up in one of the spare rooms."

Why do I feel flustered?

"I think we've had enough tea for now. Thank you, Mendax." My mom smiles at him rather than me.

What am I, chopped liver?

My dad grabs hold of my mom's hand, bringing it up to his lips to kiss her knuckles.

"Oh, don't worry about our bags, Pumpkin. We didn't want to intrude, so we're staying at a hotel. Plus, your mom wants to visit Salem."

Try as I might, I can't hide the fraction of a sag in my shoulders. You can always count on Mother Dearest to demand a visit and then change her mind. This visit was probably her version of a wellness check. Breathing out my frustration and mild hurt, I put on a practiced smile.

"Well, maybe dinner tonight?"

"We have dinner plans with Mr. and Mrs. Lutz. You remember them, right?" my mother says, scrolling through her phone.

Oh yeah, I remember them. Their daughter, Justine, is a real peach. We were friends until we started college. She changed after a few frat parties: Body shots became more important than studying and hanging out with me in the library.

During sophomore year, she stole my boyfriend. But hey, it's fine; if a miniskirt and a box-dyed blonde can take him, they can keep him. Senior year, Justine flunked almost all her classes because she didn't have me to cheat off of, and my ex cheated on her. Karma is a beautiful thing.

Come to think of it, that was the last time I was in a serious relationship. After him, I swore off boys and focused on my career with the occasional hookup and a hopeful, every once-in-a-while date.

The brightness of a screen is shoved in my face, and I'm staring at a photo of Justine in a wedding dress with none other than my ex. The venue, the colors, and even the dress are everything I had shown her I wanted when I eventually got married.

It's fine; trash deserves a dumpster.

I hope she falls down and scrapes both of her knees.

"How about breakfast? I'll make my famous birthday cake flapjacks."

Oh, my poor dad, always playing peacemaker between mom and me.

The same flapjacks he would make when mom was too busy with work. Don't get me wrong, I'm proud of her for owning and managing one of the biggest PR firms on this side of the country. It's what made me want to go into a similar field.

After graduation as Cum Laude, did I think my mom's firm would hire me? Yes, yes, I did. But there was zero chance of it happening when she told them no. If there's one thing Paloma Myles believes, it's that we get what we work for…on our own. No nepo-babies in this family.

Anywho, I'm just saying that it would have been nice to have had more memories of her being at recitals or talking to me about my period. Dad was as lost as I was.

"Only if you have time. I'm sure you'll manage to find some time on your way back."

Mendax stands up next to me and holds his hand out. My hand slips into his palm like it is something we do all the time. After he helps me stand and places a hand on my lower back, he addresses my parents.

"It was so lovely to meet you, Mr. and Mrs. Myles, however unconventional this may have been," he chuckles. "I would hate for you to be late for your plans because of us keeping you against your will."

Holy crap, did he just tactfully tell my parents to pound pavement? Why is that oddly satisfying?

A single sharp intake of breath from my mother, and I can tell she's itching for a fight with words. Let's just say, if word fighting was a sport, she'd be heavyweight champion of the world. It's also what makes her good at her job; my mother can make anyone look like a golden nugget rather than a turd.

"Polly, sweetheart," my dad redirects her attention to him, "this is your itinerary, and I doubt you want to miss any part of it. Plus, there's traffic and my sciatica is going to act up if we idle in traffic."

A surge of laughter flows from me. "Dad, you sound like you're ninety."

"Just you wait until you get to be my age, Pumpkin."

"Mendax is close to your age, and he doesn't act like that."

The groan of leather enters my ears while Mendax rocks on his heel.

"Different species." He winks at me before going to retrieve my mother's forgotten purse my mother from the floor.

Warm, slender fingers wrap around my wrist, bringing my focus back to my mom.

"I'm saying this because you're my daughter, and I love you…"

Oh, boy. Here we go.

"What are you doing with a demon? Did he trick you somehow? Did—" Her voice drops to a whisper, and I'm left no choice but to lean in closer. "—Did you sell your soul?"

Her hand wraps around her neck, and the countdown has begun for her to devolve into hysterics.

How she manages to calm other people and spin a crisis amazes me because she is horrible at calming herself. It's a good thing her dad is great at it. Me trying to calm her is the equivalent to a toddler raking their hand down an elevator panel.

"Oh my God, Rick. Our daughter sold herself!" Cue the tears.

"Calm down. I'm sure that's not it," my dad says reassuringly to her, but his questioning eyes land on me.

"I didn't sell him anything, so calm your ti—titillating imagination." *Ew, why did I use that word?* "He's my friend and kind of lives here now." Let's see how well they believe it. "Plus, we're sorta dating. We're still working on the details."

Mom goes to open her mouth, and I can only imagine what she's about to say. I kind of want to hear it because it's been a while since she's shown any kind of concern for my well-being. Unfortunately, a throat clearing derails her train of thought.

"Well, this has been a fun family gathering," Dad chuckles.

I know for a fact, he hasn't missed the tension between us. If anything, their home life is probably much more enjoyable with mom still working but more scaled back and dad retired from being a trauma nurse.

I smile while the lie seeps between my teeth. *This gathering is for the fucking birds.*

"I'm glad you got to meet my best friend, Mom, you seem to approve."

I happily walk over to where Mendax waits by the stairs holding my mother's purse. I'm at the point in my life where I shouldn't care if she approves of my life choices.

"Anyway, dad," I take the purse from Mendax, "I don't want you getting stuck in traffic."

"Oh, Pumpkin, don't worry."

He wraps me in a giant bear hug. It's a hug that sends me back to a time where I'm a kid in pigtails and life was simple.

"If anything, I'll be here for flapjacks. You know I can't stand shopping," Dad chuckles and kisses my forehead.

Mom's fingers grasp her purse, and we stand there while she scans me from head to toe, forcing me to shuffle from foot to foot. No matter how old I get, there will always be a part of me that feels the need to stand up straighter and do what I can to get her to say I've done well. Her eyes leave my face and land on Mendax. There's a fire in her eyes; it's that trademark Paloma Myles gaze that can make anyone spill their deepest, darkest secrets. I'm waiting for step two, and I don't have to wait long.

Her rosy lips stretch into a smile so sweet it's scary.

"Mendax, there's no denying you're sweet, smart, and charming." Mom reaches her hand out and picks off imaginary lint from his shoulder. "But sometimes, poison is sweet and undetectable."

"Mom!"

Shoot me now.

She ignores my protest and continues, "Davina is my daughter, my only child who I love more than life itself." Her eyes cut to mine and soften for a fraction of a second. "I don't care where you come from, what you do, or who you know. You so much as hurt her or put her in a situation that could harm her in any shape or form. I will make it my life's mission to ruin you."

Words and breath are tangled knots lodged in my throat, but I swallow it down.

"Mom, we're more friends than anything."

"Friends don't look at each other the way you two look at each other, Pumpkin." She grabs my shoulders and places a kiss on my cheek.

The way dad is looking at her, I'm glad they aren't staying here now. I want someone to look at *me* like that, for real, and not pretend. Maybe I should give dating another serious try.

They say goodbye one more time before I close the door behind them. The click of the deadbolt is like a curtain closing on a scene in a play. Mendax exhales while I lick my lips and inhale.

"I guess we make a convincing couple, huh?" I let out a nervous laugh.

Intense violet eyes stare back at me. He doesn't say anything, but the way he moves towards me sends my heart racing. Our breathing drowns out the hum of silence. I have to crane my neck back to force my eyes away from his lips and towards his eyes. As his mouth opens, a voice smashes us back into reality.

"Yo, Dax. Oh…hello again, Beautiful."

Mendax shuts his eyes, and when they open, the heat is gone, and I'm left feeling cold and exposed.

Chapter 16
Practice Makes Perfect
Mendax

W HAT WAS I THINKING? What was I going to do? Paloma's words play on a loop in my brain.

"Friends don't look at each other the way you two look at each other."

I can convince myself I wasn't going to do anything; I was going to give her a pat on the back and tell her job well done. But, deep down, I know differently.

I wanted to wrap that ponytail around my hand, tug her hair, and tilt her head up just enough so I could lean down and kiss her. I want to know if the natural pink of her lips can deepen after a kiss. Does she taste as sweet as she sounds? I never thought I would be so relieved for Orroth to show up unannounced. He saved me from making a terrible mistake. Kissing her would have destroyed our friendship.

"Orroth, you can't come here unannounced."

"You do," he counters.

Heavy boots thud down the stairs and land next to us. Orroth, smirks and leans against the wall next to me.

"So, you're Davina."

He lifts her hand, kissing her dainty knuckles. Davina seems to be at a loss for words. Her large eyes scan him up and down and again. The soles of her shoes shuffle across the floor as she scoots closer towards me.

"He doesn't look like the floating head from room or like rocker you. He looks human," she whispers, before leaning closer to my brother.

"What happened to—" She waves her free hand over his face.

"Magic." He winks.

Her lips pucker to the left for a moment.

"Bullshit. Last time a demon told me something was magic, it was when Mendax kept changing clothes. That was a lie."

"More of a slight alteration of the truth," I say.

"Straight-up lies," Orroth laughs, pointing an accusatory finger towards me.

Davina's eyes cut to my brother with a glint of mischief.

"I'll let you raid my good snack stash if you tell me the truth. Mendax doesn't even know where those snacks are."

"We're supposed to be friend-shaped and dating, and you're withholding snacks from me?"

All she does is grin. Her skirt billows and twirls as Orroth spins her into his arms. I'd be a liar if I said I didn't feel a surge of jealously.

Where is all this coming from?

"Transformation pill," he explains, gliding her around the room effortlessly.

Their feet come to a sudden stop, causing her to wobble on her heels.

"We swallow one pill, and it lasts for either two realm visits or three months." His arm drapes around her shoulders as she leads him towards the mudroom.

"When we cross a realm gate, it activates the magic powder in each tablet, and we can blend into whichever realm we're visiting."

Davina looks over her shoulder in my direction with furrowed brows. Surely, she's comparing how my brother now looks, with his long black hair, shaved on the right side of his head, eyebrow and septum piercing and sun-kissed, tattooed, and tan skin looks compared to my natural state. I can see the question is on the tip of her tongue. She's trying her best to find a nice way to ask. It's one of the things I admire most about her, she never wants to be rude.

"Part of my punishment," I sigh while carding my fingers through my hair, "I won't have access to any of those until my punishment is fully served."

"Speaking of which," Orroth interrupts, his arm is still around her shoulders and she's focused on the rose tattoo on his hand, admiring how it sparkles every time the sun hits it, "Mom wants you over to her house tonight. Probably got another date planned for you."

He rolls his eyes, but that's not what catches my attention; it's how Davina's body went rigid and how her eyes slowly lift to land on me.

"She's also planning another family dinner with guests, it might be a good time to show off your beautiful girlfriend, if you know what I'm saying."

Panic. Sheer panic sets into Davina's face.

"We never came up with a cover story. Mendax, if they ask how we started dating, what are we going to say? No one else is supposed to know that you can leave! This is horrible. I'm a terrible liar. I'm a rambler when I lie. I'll ramble so much that I forget what I was saying and what the hell I said."

"No! You?" I say, feigning shock.

A beautiful blush covers her cheeks, and she averts her eyes to the shimmering tattoos.

"You gotta go, bro. It's almost time to meet mom. I'll work on a cover story with your girl," he grins. "And enjoy some of her special secret snacks. Don't worry, I'll tell you how delicious they are." He wanders over to Davina, dipping her low before setting her upright again.

"My eyes aren't that low, buddy," Davina scolds before extricating herself from his hold.

In true Orroth fashion, he simply smiles, showing off those dimples that have always either gotten him out of trouble or into someone's bed. *Pretty sure that's how he met his now-girlfriend.*

Leaning against the back of the couch, Davina slides her shoes off and rolls her ankle with a sigh.

"Those heels are torture devices."

"I'll be back soon," I assure her. "We'll sort it out, I promise."

Something Rick said rings in my head.

"Davina?"

"Hmm?" She looks up at me while cleaning her glasses.

Leaning closer, I ask, "Birthday flapjacks?"

The oversized frames seem small in my hand as I pluck them from her fingers to wipe the lenses on a handkerchief for her. A soft pink blush paints her cheeks as I slide them back on her face and allow my eyes to study her. There's a small smattering of freckles across her nose and cheeks that I never noticed before.

"Oh, those."

She clears her throat and glides away from me to the other side of the couch. The clinking of cups on the serving tray is almost louder than her dismissive tone. "Dad would make those every year for my birthday since I never really liked birthday cake. It's not a big deal. My birthday feels like just another day."

"When's your birthday?" I ask, ignoring an amused snicker from my brother.

She turns, holding the tray low at her hips, and shrugs. "Tomorrow."

A bark of laughter from the dining room carries into the living room. "You forgot your girlfriend's birthday?"

"I can't forget something she never told me," I huff.

Davina's hair whips behind her as she shakes her head.

"*Pretend* girlfriend, Orroth. *Pretend.* Like I said, it doesn't matter. It's just another day. I haven't celebrated my birthday for a while besides the birthday flapjacks. No presents, no parties, just me, tea, and a good show."

"Have you two even kissed yet? You almost seem believable," Orroth asks, examining the color-coded calendar Davina has hanging on the dining room wall.

"Orroth, we're not talking about kissing, and no, we haven't. It's not like we need to kiss in front of guests," I say as my nails scrape against the rough hairs of my beard.

"Agree to disagree." The smirk on his face matches his nonchalant attitude.

Davina sighs and pushes the tray into Orroth's hands. He arches a brow in return. Spinning on her heels, she sashays my way with a look of determination.

"First, forget about my birthday. I never told you, so there's no reason for you to feel bad or guilty. Second, he's right. Your parents and whoever else is at the party will expect some form of affection from us."

There is determination in her stride as she walks to me, but time slows the moment her slender fingers slide up the silk fibers of my shirt. She clutches the collar and jerks me towards her.

The afternoon sun glitters in her eyes, giving life to the flecks of gold normally hidden in the deep brown. Small creaks from the wooden floor seep between the pounding pulse in my ears as she lifts herself onto her toes. Her lips land on mine in an almost bruising kiss.

The searing heat from my rising blush is camouflaged perfectly beneath my already reddened ears. Just when my eyes close, it's over. *I want a redo.* It wasn't nearly long enough to savor, or fully register how soft and plump her lips feel. I don't even know if I kissed her back. One thing I do know is, my hands stayed by my side, and I didn't get to feel the dip of her waist.

I'm not counting as a *real* first kiss.

"That was so fucking awkward!" Orroth laughs at us.

The clinking from the cups on the tray sound with every shake of his stupid shoulders.

"Forget I said anything. Just say you don't do PDA. Everyone will believe that from Mendax."

With three short steps, Davina backs away from me and scratches her nose.

"Well, it isn't a real *'in love kiss.'* Those kisses should have everyone saying how adorable the couple is or to get a room. Those kinds of kisses should give you fireworks."

"Fireworks?" I ask like an idiot.

She bites her lip, the same lip I have the sudden urge to kiss and bite.

"Yeah. At least, to me a real meaningful kiss should give you fireworks. Mom told me when she first kissed dad, she got tingles down to her toes. Dad told me he felt fireworks. I want to see and feel fireworks," she mumbles the last part.

The flush from Davina's cheeks earlier deepens in hue and spreads towards her chest.

"Maybe we should practice?" Her fingertips brush her lips stifling a giggle. "Practice makes perfect. I'm just kidding."

I'm not.

"We don't have to kiss again."

Yes, we do.

She's right, practice does make perfect, and I want to practice again…right now. Unfortunately for me, she pushes me towards the stairs before going to find my brother.

"Now, go before you're late."

My feet feel heavier than wet cement as I walk up towards the bedroom. My heart stops for a second as I overhear their conversation.

"You know Mom is probably going to keep him for a few days, right? She's been hounding him to visit her."

"It's fine. Plus, he has a date obligation. Which reminds me, I left a certain guy on read and he's been trying to get me to go out with him. Maybe I'll take him up on it. But first, our cover story."

The clattering of dishes follows before I hear her sweet voice again.

"Why are your tattoos shiny? I want shiny tattoos."

"Maybe one day I'll take you to get one of these tattoos from my artists. It's a special ink he has and it kinda burns at first. But after a few minutes, it just feels warm. Oh, I know, we can get matching tattoos."

His laugh is pure joy. He's already grown to like her in a matter of minutes.

"Maybe he can start a new piece on me."

"You seem nervous."

I try my best to stay as still as possible so I can listen a little longer.

Her voice is soft, but the worry in her tone is hard to miss. "How can I not be?"

"Don't worry, Davina, stick with me, and I'll have you believing the lie yourself. I'm a seasoned pro when it comes to lying to our mother."

He's not wrong; he can talk his way out of anything when it comes to Megai. If he told her the clouds were made from cotton candy, she wouldn't question him.

"Like you said to Mendax, practice makes perfect. Now, let's talk about that kiss. You look rusty, maybe I could help."

"Shut up, Orroth. You're not kissing me."

Good girl, Davina, good girl.

If she's going to practice anything to perfection, it's going to be with me. Also, I'm not too fond with the idea of her going on a date. She hates dating, she said so herself. Look at me being hypocritical now. This woman makes me feel and behave in ways I never have before. When did I become so possessive of my friend?

Chapter 17

Love?

Mendax

DARK RAIN DROPS PELT the ground, enhancing the dampness of my mood. Luckily, I can always count on Gotha to keep me company. We haven't spent much quality time together. Gotha must take after me when it comes to making less than stellar first impressions with Davina. I'll have to try and introduce them properly. Gotha just needs to warm up to Davina first.

My mother seems to have already stopped by my apartment. There's a note along with a garment bag.

"Gotha, you should have chased her out of here."

She simply chirps from her cage before flying towards me and perching on my horn.

"Your little talons are going to ruin my horns." I really should have them polished again. "Let's see what mother wants now."

MENDAX,

PLEASE COME PROMPTLY TO THE MANOR TONIGHT AT SEVEN. DO NOT BE LATE.

THERE IS A MATTER WE NEED TO DISCUSS AND HANDLE. I'VE ALREADY PICKED OUT SOMETHING APPROPRIATE FOR YOU TO WEAR. THERE IS NO GETTING OUT OF THIS. SHOW UP ON TIME.

–MOTHER

"So charming. Doesn't she just give you warm fuzzy feelings, too, Gotha?"

It's adorable how she believes snapping her fingers will make me jump. I'm far too old for that.

Also, picking out my clothes? Sometimes I truly do believe she forgets I'm not Orroth. But curiosity seems to get the better of me because before I know it I've already pinched the cold zipper between my fingers to tug the garment bag open.

"Gotha. Are you seeing what I'm seeing?" I can't help the amusement in my voice.

There's not even a snowball's chance in hell I'm wearing a full tuxedo. She's not even trying to hide the planned date, and if she is, she's doing a terrible job. The bag crumples on the bed as I drop it unceremoniously.

"I'm not wearing that."

Gotha's wing smacks my eye as she stretches before flying off to land on my bed. Her talons catch in the fabric of the tuxedo, snagging threads in their wake.

"No. Please. Stop," I drone, examining my nails.

After several circles a tiny shiver wracks her body; she flies back into her cage and doses off like it's her job. If she wasn't already sleeping, I would kiss her. There's a piddle puddle smack dab in the center of the shirt and more spots on the jacket. She's the best bat ever.

"What are you wearing?" Megai, my mother, hisses at me from the grand foyer. "This is not what I left out for you."

"No, Mother Dearest, it is not."

I can't help the smirk growing on my face. Davina's mother would make a formidable foe to my mother.

"Unfortunately—or fortunately depending on how you look at it." I step further into my childhood home and place a kiss on my mother's warm cheek. "Gotha had a little accident on the clothes you left. It was my fault, I had opened it and left it on the bed while I showered. And well, I don't know about you, but I didn't want to wear soiled clothes. Plus, your note said not to be late and I was already running late. I grabbed the first thing I could." The lies slide off my tongue like butter on warm toast. Her gasp as I remove my wool coat has me fighting against the chuckle creeping up my throat.

Her tone is clipped as she begins to scold me, "This? *This* is the best you can do? You're going on a date with the daughter of a man who could end your sentence."

"Oh, is that what I'm doing here?" I roll my eyes with my response. "I never asked for Elara or for her father's help. I've come to terms with everything. I thought you did, too."

She's left scurrying behind me as I make my way past the sitting room, the long hall with framed paintings and sculptures. All this art and not a one family picture. Not even a single photo of her favorite son. Around the corner, past my mother's office, down one more hall, and past a bathroom, is the dining room. The low candlelight from the table and the chandelier above the table illuminate the figure standing off in the far corner. Before greeting Elara, I turn to my mother.

"I'll have dinner because I'm hungry. Not because I plan to see this through. I have Davina and she's all I want." I leave Megai opening and closing her mouth like a fish, and shut the door behind me.

Floor-to-ceiling windows only aid in making the already large dining room more cavernous. The black walls and dark flooring swallow any light or happiness that dared to enter. My nails scratch into the already ornately set dining table with each passing second, I want to be anywhere other than here. Well, that's not exactly true. I'd rather be home, with Davina sipping tea, hearing her prattle about work or some town gossip she overheard. Hell, I'd even enjoy sitting on that couch while she attempts to teach me how to play another war game. I still can't figure out how to move my soldier at the same time as my camera.

"Mendax?" a honeyed voice calls from across me.

I'm acutely aware of my rudeness of zoning out on Elara. My mother, yet again, set up another dinner with the woman she wants me to marry. She wasn't even ashamed, since according to her it's all contractual. I should ask to see the contract. Then, I could make a mad dash towards a fireplace and watch it burn to ashes.

"I feel like I'm boring you," Elara states with a slight nervousness. "I don't blame you. Not many people find accounting exciting."

The involuntary sigh leaves my lips before I can cage it and I can feel words of protest coating my tongue. Instead, I grasp the delicate wine glass and sip the Cabernet to wash the unpleasant words away.

"It's not you. Well, it is, but it isn't." *Maybe I should have gulped the glass down.*

The gold fork stills at her lips as her yellow gaze locks on me. I'd probably be willing to give Elara a decent effort if I had never met Davina. I don't think Davina has the same sprouting feelings for me that I'm still attempting to deny I have for her. Elara is almost my height, with her forehead reaching my nose, whereas Davina's only reaches my chest.

How would it even work with Davina? I've never been involved with a human before in any kind of capacity. Would she want to try a real relationship with me?

"Then, what is it?" Elara asks, pulling me back into our awkward dinner.

"I'm sure you're lovely. However, I have zero interest whatsoever in marrying or having any kind of romantic relationship, contractual or not, with you."

The clattering of the fork against the matching gold plate echoes in the room. Her blue fingers tuck a lock of pink hair behind her ear, showing off a gold hoop earring. I've barely noticed what Elara is wearing until now. It's a tight-fitting black dress with a scoop neck, the hem ends just above her ankles. Matching black strappy heels, making her long legs appear even longer. It's a stark contrast to me. I threw on the first thing I found in my closet.

Normally, I'd grab a *minimum* of a two-piece suit to just relax with Davina. For this evening? I went wayward with my selection of clothing: Khaki pants, with a brown belt and a simple white button-down shirt that hasn't been steamed or pressed in months, a casual navy performance blazer with the sleeves rolled and unbuttoned complete my outfit. I don't even feel like myself. These are all pieces Orroth bought me for my birthday last year, saying I needed to relax my style more. He and his girlfriend are itching to restyle my wardrobe.

"I'm not saying we have to walk down the aisle tomorrow. This is only our second date, Mendax."

She offers me an easy smile, but her posture is stiff. I'd expect nothing less from someone trying to be the perfect society wife.

I wonder if Davina is really going to plan a date.

"And we won't ever be walking down the aisle. I'll only have one more date with you because I'm obligated to do so. Unfortunately, that obligation comes at the expense of my girlfriend." I decide to drop the fake girlfriend bomb and see where it leads me. I can't believe I'm missing her birthday.

The velvet high-back dining chair scratches across the floor and nearly topples over as she abruptly stands.

"Girlfriend?" she hisses. "How long have you been with her? Why would my father agree to marry me off to a man already in a relationship?! Does your mother know? Oh my God, your poor girlfriend, she must be miserable right now."

Sure, so miserable she's planning a date of her own. The more I think about it, the more my mood worsens.

"Wow, with a look that sour, you could curdle milk," Elara says.

"So, now what?" Her hands swipe her thighs before fixing her pin-straight hair. "I'm guessing you want to call this entire thing off."

The wine swirls in my glass as I twirl it delicately before taking one last sip and standing.

"I would appreciate it if you told your father you didn't want to go through with this." I should have worn a jacket, my fingers need something to do and normally, I'd button my suit while standing.

"What if I don't want to do that? We have a lot in common, you know. At least according to your mother." Elara's heels click tightly against the wood flooring while she fists her hips. "You appreciate art; I have an art collection. We're both busy professionals, for the most part. My line of work could help you and your business. We both want a large family."

For the most part? Oh, that jab was unnecessary.

Her "helping' is laughable considering her father is in a financial crisis. A large family, though?

I'm still uncertain if I even want any children at all. I wonder if Davina wants children. What would our children look like? *Holy hell, where did that thought come from?*

"And I'm sure you enjoy Piña Coladas." A hint of smile ghosts my face, remembering Davina singing and dancing in the living room while she cleaned to that song. She started it over because, apparently, she missed the good part.

My stride slows as I walk out of the room to look over my shoulder.

"My mind is made up. I have a girlfriend, who I adore and look forward to seeing and spending time with from sunrise to sunset." Everything rolls off my tongue so effortlessly that I have to stop and consider if it's a lie or the truth.

"Mendax?" Elara's steps click hurriedly behind me. "Where are you going?"

Sighing, I stop to turn towards her. My shoes squeak against the newly polished floors.

"Shopping. I need to get her a birthday present for the birthday I'm missing to be here. With you." There was a snowball's chance in hell in trying to hide the scowl on my face.

Rounding the corner, my mother emerges from her home office with a box of items tucked under one arm. With her free hand, she delicately pushes her reading glasses back up her nose. No doubt, she's behind updating our inventory due to her meddling in my life.

"You're done with dinner so soon?"

"We're going shopping." Elara wraps her hand around my arm, and my mother smiles.

As soon as my mother continues down the hall, I pluck the hand off me as if an old banana peel has landed on me.

"I don't appreciate being touched by another woman. Only my girl-friend touches me."

"Well, I can't have her reporting to my father the date ended early and horribly."

"I don't care what she tells him. I've already told you how I feel. It's up to you to catch up and tell your father."

"What gift are you going to get her?" It's almost like she's gauging how well I know my supposed other half.

"That's a great question. What do you get the woman who says she doesn't want or need anything? I would have gladly spent the day with her on the couch eating all her favorite food and watching all the shows she loves."

Just the thought makes me smile because it isn't a lie. I used to hate spending my time around others. I always thought humans were greedy and selfish; then, I met her. A strange sensation settles in my chest.

"So, is it a birthday present or an I'm-sorry-I-missed-it-and-you pre-sent?" There's a longing in Elara's eyes as she tries to read my face.

"Why not all of the above."

"Do you love her?"

Do I love Davina?

I know I've grown *fond* of her and enjoy spending every day with her. Then there's the urge to kiss her again. Is that what love is? Finding enjoyment and comfort in the presence of another no matter what you're doing?

All I can do is smile because I don't know how to answer. I help Elara put her coat on because I still have manners, and this situation isn't her fault. She's merely a pawn in our parent's game.

"If you don't love her, then this arrangement between you and I could work, Mendax."

"I won't tell anyone I love her before I tell her first."

I quickly grab my coat and rush out the door with Elara hot on my heels.

Is this love?

Chapter 18

Burritos

Davina

I T's TEN IN THE morning, and I'm ready to throat-punch Orroth. While I appreciate him coming up with a cover story for me and Mendax, he needs to relax.

We were up so late that I was beginning to laugh deliriously. The words from the cover story haunted me in my sleep, which was a restless sleep because I passed out on the couch. Now, there's a kink in my neck, my stomach is about to devour my spine, and I have the sudden urge to either fight someone or cry. *I need a burrito.*

Across from me, on the other leather couch, is the bane of my existence for today. While I was fighting sleep last night, Orroth was wide awake, talking shit in a game lobby while I ordered us burgers and fries. I had to triple-check his order. I was so used to ordering my bacon avocado burger and Mendax's usual grass-fed truffle aioli, Swiss cheese, and arugula burger that Orroth threw me for a loop. Turns out he eats like a toddler. One single patty burger with ketchup and mustard … that's it. At least we both agreed steak fries are the supreme fry, unlike Mendax who swears by onion rings.

Honestly, that's apples and oranges. Pulling the waistband of my one-size-too-big joggers up a little higher, I trudge into the kitchen to fight the beast in my stomach that is determined to devour my spine.

Somewhere between the fridge and the stove, I zoned out. When the hell did I decide to make a dozen eggs, two packs of sausage, shred a block of cheese, and cook peppers?

"I'm a one-woman breakfast burrito assembly machine." Setting the last two ingredients on plates, I hear Orroth's heavy steps.

"Morning, Vi." He started calling me Vi two hours after his brother left to go on that date.

Maybe I should have gone with Mendax. I should really start selling this whole relationship thing. It's not right that he's being forced into a marriage with someone else. God, what if he can't get out of it or changes his mind? Would he ever want to see me again? Who would I have my daily tea with? The refrigerator door slams harder than I intended.

"Morning."

"You're just a ray of sunshine today," Orroth chuckles, pointing to a plate and then to himself.

I nod and watch as he carelessly grabs the plate at an angle, and the burrito tumbles to the floor. "It's all part of my sunny disposition," I huff. It doesn't help that my uterus is about to rip down the wallpaper in the empty nursery.

The disgust on my face couldn't be more obvious as I watch him bend, blow off the burrito, and take two large bites.

"Twenty-second rule."

"It's a *five*-second rule," I say, leaning past him to grab my own tortilla of culinary perfection.

"Whatever, still tastes good. Tell me the story again."

On the way to the living room, I snatch my phone from the charger and see the notification for a work email. Opening it, I don't make it past the first line, before anger starts to simmer beneath my skin.

"You have got to be freaking kidding me!" My words are garbled with half-eaten food.

"Damn, alright." Orroth holds his hands up defensively.

What a terrific start to my birthday. Before I open the email from Tony, another message comes in, and that familiar sting strikes again.

Dad

> Hey, Pumpkin. Runnin' behind schedule. Rain check on flapjacks?

I already knew Mom and Dad weren't coming; if they were, they would have been knocking on my door before sunrise, singing Happy Birthday.

"You okay?"

My eyes drift from the small, cold screen and up to a concerned Orroth, clutching the last three bites of his burrito like his life depended on it.

"Peachy. Fantastic. Never better," I reply before taking another bite of my breakfast. "I met Mendax through you, Dakolas, and Rolvak."

I make sure to get his friends right and not say *Declan and Rolex,* even though giving people nicknames is the easiest way to remember their actual names for me.

"I tagged along with you and your group of friends after one night at a bar, even though I hate going to bars," the last part mumbled, earning a side-eyed glance from Orroth.

I sigh and continue, "While doing a pub crawl, we stumbled across Mendax during his evening stroll, and he saw how I was having a less-than-stellar time. He joined us to keep me company, and we got to talking, and one thing led to another."

I take another bite of food, now wishing I had bacon instead of sausage.

"Since he can't come to visit me, I visit him. You generously escort me through the gates, and here we are."

Wiping his mouth on the back of his hand, his eyes narrow. "You missed a few details, but I'll let it slide. Last time, you kept rambling beer facts when you stumbled. Maybe the simpler, the better."

I give a noncommittal shrug because he's right, and I don't want to admit it.

"Don't you have anywhere else to go? You can't possibly want to spend all day with me."

Orroth is already grabbing a controller from the TV stand.

"There's a lobby filled with overconfident guys and twelve-year-olds who act like they're grown; I'm going to kick their asses for a bit. It brings me joy."

Shaking my head, the amusement is short-lived as I open the email. I knew I should have waited for normal working hours, but me, being me, would have simply forgotten it, and it would have been left in the graveyard of unopened messages.

"Per! He per'd me!"

My hands clutch the phone and burrito tighter. Grease dripping onto the softest joggers I own.

"I don't know what that means but you sound mad." Orroth quickly glances my way before sniping three enemies in the game. "Who are we mad at?"

"Fucking Tony. *Per my last email.* He never sent me that email. How about "per these hands," Tony? Per. These. Hands."

"You should write that and send it," Orroth laughs before roasting someone online.

I absolutely will not write that. Even though I *really* want to, I won't. Normally, I would ask myself how Mom would address and handle the situation. But now I'm wondering how Mendax would respond to this.

He'd probably be extremely charming and diffuse the entire thing in a few words.

Me? I'll wait for normal working hours, because that's a boundary I'm not going to cross, and I might say something I'll regret. So far, I'm going on a spotless HR record, and I plan to keep it that way.

The groan of the leather couch muffles my own while I lean over the arm and stare at my home. Cabinets are left open in the kitchen, making it look like a poltergeist visited; little doom piles are nestled in places I don't remember creating.

When did I get all this new furniture? Oh crap, did I blackout buy? Was it a fix-the-sadness-by-adding-to-cart moment?

I should shower. But I have to do laundry because I'm out of underwear and towels. My feet freeze as I pass the kitchen to the laundry room. There's also the garbage that needs to be put on the curb.

Fuck. There's going to be more garbage after cleaning up my cooking spree. Maybe I should do the dishes first? But then, if I do that, there will be no hot water for my shower. A sense of paralysis begins to overtake me, and all I can do is surrender to it with a sigh. That is, until a knock on the door pulls the paralysis from me like a ripcord.

The afternoon sun is shining like a spotlight on me, and I would have stayed on the porch, but Orroth is nosey and I couldn't stand the tapping on the window.

"I feel like maybe we've been beating around the bush," Blake starts. He's got a determined look in his eye.

I cock my head to the right trying to focus on what Blake is saying, but all I can focus on are his faded jeans and simple blue cotton t-shirt.

What would Mendax look like wearing something so simple? He'd probably have a conniption if I asked if he owned a pair of jeans. *Shit, I should pay attention.*

"Would you like to go for a quick walk with me? There's that shady park just down the street."

A slam from a window cuts off my response, thankfully.

"Yo, Vi," Orroth calls out from the living room window. "I forgot to ask if you were saving these burritos. I ate three more."

"Don't you dare eat any more! I only had one."

"Who is that?" Blake asks with a tinge of jealously.

Well fiddlesticks, how do I explain this particular demon? Thank God this one *looks* human. "Family friend," I say. "He came by with my parents. We were neighbors growing up, him being a few grades behind me. Orr—" I pause at saying Orroth's name because, well, Orroth isn't exactly a normal name, and it would probably raise more questions. "Orr would hang around my group of older girls."

My tongue darts out to lick my lips while my eyes focus on that stupid spot of grease ruining my white joggers. *Why did I decide to wear white?*

"Anywho, they sprung a visit on me; that's why I kinda left you on read. I totally didn't mean to. Here I was, late at night, speed cleaning and getting rooms ready. But you know how these things can get; one thing leads to another. Did you know 70% of dust particles are dead skin flakes and cleaning in general burns around 100 calories per hour?"

Davina, woman, shut up.

Blake chuckles and tucks a lock of hair behind my ear. Or at least he tries, because I swat his hand and my hair with it.

"A walk sounds nice," I say quickly with a smile.

His eyes travel across my face, and suddenly, I'm aware that I still have a nub of a burrito in my hand. There are choices every woman has to make in life. Some are life-altering, others can be pushed for a later date, and you cross that bridge when you get there. Me? I'm always at *that* bridge.

I've never detoured away from decision bridge. There are two choices right now for dealing with my burrito. Either I shove it in my mouth or, option B: toss it aside into the rosemary bush. I opted for the former. So, with cheeks as puffed out like a chipmunk, I flourish my hand down the walkway. I'm not wasting food; my dad raised me better than that.

"Stranger danger, Vi! Stranger danger."

Then the window slams shut.

Pastel chalk lines the sidewalk in hopscotch scribbles and random shapes. A handful of teenagers are racing down the streets on electric bikes and scooters. Earvil is a weird little town that wants to grow and be modern, but still clings to its quaint town charm.

"Nice weather for once, huh?" Blake says, squinting up at the sky.

I inwardly groan. I loathe small talk. I would rather not talk if small talk was the only option.

"Yup, it usually rains on my birthday." I let that nugget of information slip and it has me groaning out loud.

His solid shoulder bumps into mine.

"Today's your birthday? Well, happy birthday."

He flashes me a smile and all I can do is give a mid-western smile and nod.

"What kind of trouble do you have planned for celebrating? Are you celebrating with your friend back there?" Blake turns and starts to walk backwards so he can fully face me.

"Nope, no plans."

I stop and turn, resting my hip against the old black iron fence surrounding the cemetery across from the park. Not my first choice for a park placement. Whoever planned this layout said, 'fuck it' and plopped a playground where it would fit.

"I never do anything for my birthday."

A shrill scream followed by an uproar of laughter catches both of our attention. There's a group of moms working out together while their kids either busy themselves on blankets or run around playing tag. I startle a bit as Blake's calloused hand engulfs mine before tugging me across the street.

The chirp of birds fills the crisp afternoon air. We find a shaded wooden bench close to the swings that has seen better days. His index finger rubbed across his bottom lip before he slings his arm over the back of the bench.

"I can't, in good conscience, let you not celebrate your birthday. Have dinner with me." He flashes me a smile. "My treat."

"Well, that sounds nice."

"I'm a nice guy." He winks.

I bristle. "I just don't celebrate my birthday. I'm okay with that. Plus, Orr is here and I can't abandon my friend while he's visiting." I press my fingers to my eyes under the rim of my glasses. "It would be rude."

"That would be rude, and I can tell you don't like being rude. I appreciate how thoughtful you are. I like that about you," he sighs, sliding a little closer while I slide back. "Let's do another day then. Wednesday work for you? We can have drinks or dinner."

I need to pee, and my stomach is cramping. I'm still hungry. I want to go back home and have some ginger tea.

"Wednesday." I nod. "Dinner is good. As long as it's not a ten-at-night dinner." I give an awkward laugh.

He tosses his head back and laughs.

"I promise it won't be that late. I have class the next day, and I'm sure you have work to do, too."

"I sure do; I have more spreadsheets to create and market research to review. Along with a new batch of data."

His face scrunches up before speaking. "Sounds… fun?"

Resting my elbows on my knees, I give him a quick sideways glance before looking back at the yoga-pant-clad moms.

"Well, I would say, for me, it's more enjoyable than teaching a room full of hormonal preteens the anatomy of a cell."

"Touché." His voice carries over the laughter of children running wild.

"Do you want any little Davina's running around one day?"

What the hell? That question came out of left field. I had never considered myself the maternal type especially seeing as I forget to feed myself—less so these days, thanks to Mendax shoving plates of food and glasses filled with water in front of me.

"Maybe if I found the right person. But it isn't a necessity."

Could demons have babies with humans? I couldn't imagine pushing horns out of my vagina. Wait, do the horns grow later?

Mental note:

- Ask Orroth or Mendax about it later. Much, much later.

"I would like at least two. We can talk more about life plans along with likes and dislikes on Wednesday. I don't want to keep too long from your friend."

Blake stands with a slight stretch and holds his hand out for me.

My eyes danced between his open hand and his face. I'm being a bitch for no reason other than the fact that I'm hangry.

Pushing my glasses back up my nose, I let him pull me up. He keeps my hand tucked in his while he walks me back to my porch.

His teeth sink into his bottom lip before winking at me. I don't miss the way his eyes trail quickly over my body, either.

"I'll pick you up at seven."

The calluses on Blake's hand scrape over my fingers as he raises my hand to his lips. He sends me another smile before whistling and walking across the street.

Why do I feel like this is a mistake?

Pushing the thought aside, I turn and hop up the first few steps and spot the lonely rocking chair still there. Maybe I should get a second chair instead of a table. Swinging the door open, I'm immediately bombarded by Mendax's brother.

"You should gouge his eyes out the next time he eye fucks you," Orroth greets me with a scowl.

Cold wetness across my hand has me recoiling until I look down and see the streak of hand sanitizer gliding across the back of my hand.

"What are you doing, Orroth."

"No, no. You can call me Orr. All my friends do. And I'm simply saving you from germs. That guy was basically slobbering on you. Don't you know you shouldn't walk with strange guys, Vi?"

"First, I literally let a strange demon live with me out the gate, followed by his brother. Second, he's not a stranger; he's Blake. He's the science teacher at the only middle school in the district and my neighbor. He also runs every morning and goes to the gym. And why do you care?" I can't help but ask as I rub the hand sanitizer around my hands and up my arms.

Sorting through the pile of junk mail that has collected in a metal bin on the wall, I toss Orr a curious glance.

The gaming console turns off with a beep. Heavy, booted steps filter into my ears before he swings around the banister as if he's Fred Astaire.

"Just being a good brother and looking out for my brother's girl," he says with an all too casual smile.

"I'm not really *his girl*." Even though, I say it out loud, it doesn't sound right. The thought has my head reeling.

"Sure, let's go with that," Orroth laughs. "I'll be back. I'm going to check on things at home."

I wave him off with a stack of sales fliers in my hand. Right as I get to the recycling bin to toss the mail, I notice the now-empty plate of burritos.

"Those were my burritos!"

Warmth stings the back of my eyes. I wanted birthday flapjacks and for my parents to care about my birthday again. I wanted more than those burritos. I wanted Mendax here and not on a date with some other woman.

"Oh, sweet Mother of Cheesus," I speak out loud as realization dawns on me.

I want Mendax.

Chapter 19

BITTER

Davina

HOW DID MY LIFE suddenly get filled with so much damn testosterone? I really need to make more friends who are women. That becomes even more clear as Orr and his group of friends play soccer in my backyard. Luckily, he brought his girlfriend, Wren, who I learned is a witch by birth with an affinity for fire. She's absolutely stunning. With her mauve-colored hair styled in a sharp, angular bob and deep ocean-blue eyes, she could be a supermodel. I'm five feet seven inches tall, but next to her, I look short. Wren is close to six foot even, with legs for days and more curves than a back country road.

The flames she conjured for the fire pit flicker between us, warming the chilled spring night air.

"Okay, explain to me how this works again," I say, eyeing the pearlescent pill pinched between Wren's chipped, manicured fingers.

She pokes her pierced tongue out at Orr, who made a comment I missed because I'm too transfixed on this pill they want me to take.

"I promise it's not some kind of trippy drug. This is like the anti-transformation pill. This one strips the transformation. For you, though," She grabs my hand and plops the pill down. "It'll let you see past the magic. It's a side effect. My father owns the pharmaceutical company that creates these. I'm still not sure how to get rid of the side effects. It's also not a priority for me to figure out."

Right, because why wouldn't there be a pharmaceutical company in another realm that creates magic pills?

Not only am I suddenly surrounded by demons and a witch, but they're also a lively bunch, each set to inherit empires. It isn't regular nepotism, though. According to each of them—well, except for Orroth—they all started at the equivalent of a mail room. Wren started out at Neurosynth Labs as a part-time receptionist, working her way through the company until she got her degree in magica chema engineering. Now, she's set to inherit the company that makes these nifty pills once her dad decides it's time to retire.

"Come on, Davina. You can do it. We're even better looking after the fact," Rolvak calls out before the ball thuds against his forehead.

He's the twin set to inherit their mother's tech corporation while his brother Dakolas is taking over the security company.

"Hey, Orr?" My gaze darts from the pill to the twins, to Wren, and then finally to Orr. "Are you and Mendax splitting the family business?"

He's in the middle of attempting the Cruyff turn and lands hard on his ass after losing his balance.

"No way, that's all him. I'm happy to be a trophy husband." He winks at Wren, who simply pinches the bridge of her nose and shakes her head. "I do have my own little pet project. But it's a secret."

Orroth stands, wiping grass and dirt off the seat of his black jeans. "Stop changing the subject, Vi. Down the hatch, it goes. Then you can tell Dax I'm the better-looking one," he laughs while dribbling the ball like a pendulum.

Taking a bolstering breath, I place it on my tongue. This reminds me of college. Instead of shotgunning a beer and "chug it" chants, it's a shiny pill followed by "one of us" chants.

I wonder if this goes against the D.A.R.E pledge I made back in elementary school. It's already fizzing on my taste buds before I can wash away the burnt taste with a cup of lukewarm lemon tea. Even in the evening light, the sun seems too bright now. Halos surround every little source of light in my backyard while Orr and his friends begin to shift appearance mid-chant.

"Holy fuck."

Where there were once three human men kicking a soccer ball are now three demons. Colorful dots line my vision as I squeeze my eyes shut before opening again.

"Yo, Vi! Told you I'm the better-looking brother."

Wren's head tilts, and her eyes squint.

"Mmm, 'better looking' is subjective." She tosses me a conspiratorial smirk. "Mendax has that melt-your-panties-off-and-have-you-calling-him-'sir'-or-'daddy' attractiveness."

The lemon tea turns bitter on my tongue, and I choke.

"What?" The question comes out a little high-pitched. It is perfectly timed with Orr's gasp of outrage.

Wren scrunches her nose and blows a kiss to Orr. "I prefer your brand of attractive, babe."

My head is still reeling from the sight before me. Two green demons, one ruby and horned demon, one runway ready witch, stare back at me. Now thoughts of Mendax being called 'sir' or 'daddy' plague my brain. *How is this my life?* There's no statistical data I can use to comfort me and regain control over these thoughts.

A snap followed by a crackle of a twig being thrown into the fire snaps my thoughts from going back to the 'sir' and 'daddy' comment a third time.

Dakolas smirks, eyeing me over the fire. He always has an assessing look on his face.

"You got her thinking about Mendax, now," he says.

Slinking down in the chair, I pry my gaze away from Dakolas, gnawing on my bottom lip. Normally, I'm better at masking my emotions.

Maybe if I close my eyes and stay really still they'll forget about me and move on to something else.

"Vi and Mendax kissing along the Styx," Orroth begins singing. His friends join in on my embarrassment.

"K-I-S-S-I-N-G. First comes—"

So much for moving on.

"Summoning!" Wren belts out, joining in on their fun at my expense.

Heat creeps up my cheeks thinking about kissing Mendax again. He didn't seem to enjoy it, though. A girl can dream, right? *Right?*

I wasn't convinced Mendax would be okay with Orroth telling his band of buddies everything. Despite my protesting, Orr did anyway, insisting they were crucial to our cover story. They've been here since Sunday night. Somehow, my house has turned into a hostel for wayward demons and witches.

By the time they finished singing, they're all making kissy faces at me. *I really need to figure out how to not blush so easily.*

Sighing and taking another sip of my almost-cold and almost-gone tea, I send a secret prayer to whoever might be listening that it'll help cool the embarrassment burning my face.

Stretching my legs under the table, I can't help the smile growing on my face. Despite being twins, it's easy to tell that Rolvak is jumping on Dakolas' back; Rolvak has a squarer jaw, and Dakolas has a nose that's crooked—a little to the right. Wren is slow dancing with Orr to a song playing through my outdoor speaker, lost in their own world.

All I'm missing is Mendax. It's been days since I've seen him, and I can't believe I miss him this much.

Sure, Monday was filled with HR meetings, thanks to Tony. That drama *still* isn't over, and Nancy, the HR rep, is breathing down my neck, checking every 't' that's crossed and 'i' dotted between *all* correspondence sent to team members. Tuesday was designing a new algorithm because Orr wanted to see how it worked. Now, he has a rudimentary risk analysis program for his family business. It's not foolproof since I don't really understand how to value certain artifacts, but overall, for a work in progress, it's pretty good. This morning was filled with training, and now—

"Oh crap!"

The merriment in my backyard stops like the scratch of a vinyl record. Snatching my phone off the table and tapping the screen, the red battery and nine percent catch my eye. I honestly thought I had charged it. The second thing that sounds alarms in my brain is the time.

"I'm supposed to have a date with Blake in thirty minutes."

Orroth walks closer to the patio and pulls a face. "Ew, why are you still going with him?"

He leans past me, grabbing a lemon square off the plate. Powder sugar covers his mouth; all I can stare at are the crumbles of lemon and sugar.

Tossing a cloth napkin at his face, I turn and stomp into my home.

"I don't know. Because he's a nice guy, and I said I would."

I bend and start sifting through the dryer, trying to find something clean, but it's only towels. Turning to the folding table, at least four loads of clean laundry pass my hands before I snag a pair of dark-wash jeans and a white, long-sleeve bodysuit. Orroth and gang tumble into the small laundry room.

"Where is he taking you?" Rolvak asks.

His gaze narrows on the clothes as green fingers pluck the push-up bra and cotton thong from the bundle. The underwear goes flying back to the folding table, leaving me fuming and slack-jawed. Orr plops a t-shirt-style bra that has seen better days into the mix, along with granny panties that are reserved for when Aunt Flow visits.

"I'm not sure which restaurant, but we agreed on dinner," I huff, pushing past them and picking up the underwear I had already selected.

This is the only kind of bra that won't dig into my shoulders, and I refuse to be uncomfortable tonight.

Dakolas chimes in, adding a chunky knit sweater that would cover me to my knees. "What time's this Blake guy bringing you back?"

Giving up on the overbearing brothers I seem to suddenly have, I sigh, resting the back of my head against a wall.

"Not sure, but I won't be out super late. We both have work in the morning."

Orroth leans against the doorway, his entire body blocking my path. "Is he picking you up?"

"You should definitely drive yourself, Davina. Never let a man drive you anywhere. That way, you can hightail it out of there if the date goes sideways," Wren chimes in, walking past everyone and further into the house.

Clutching the clothes tighter to my chest, I barrel past the wall of muscle the three guys have constructed around me.

"I'm going on a date; it's not a big deal. Mendax had his date and still isn't back. So, for all I, or any of us, knows, he changed his mind and wants to be with *her* now instead of me."

My feet halt at the lurch of embarrassment.

"You know what I mean. The entire fake dating and him kind of living here and our tea time." They all give me the same look that has heat rising to my cheeks.

"Shut up."

"You sound bitter," Rolvak teases as he saunters into the living room, firing up the gaming console. His free hand digs around in a box of cereal.

Dakolas stops next to him and frowns. "There are bowls in this house. You should know you were at Target with us."

"Yeah, I know. I picked this box out, Doofus. I'm looking for the temporary tattoo; that's why I picked it out."

There's no way I'm bitter. Bitter would mean I'm jealous. And to be jealous of another woman would mean I have to be in love with Mendax.

Sure, I enjoy his company, and I love being around him. But that doesn't mean I'm in love with him, right?

"You won't find the shimmery pink and yellow butterfly tattoo," Orr teases.

"What did you do with it? Davina! He stole my tattoo."

"Not my problem."

Dragging my feet, clothes, and thoughts, I slowly make my way up to my room. The idea of a date with anyone else suddenly doesn't seem appealing anymore.

Stern voices carry up the stairs, and I stop to listen. The rapid-fire questions from my newly founded inquisitorial squad make my jaw drop.

"Where are you taking her?"

"You're going to have her back by ten, right? She's a good and decent woman and better be treated like it."

"What are your intentions with her? And you better not tell me it's a pump-a-dump situation."

"Fucking hell," I whisper.

The last question/statement Wren threw down has me running down the stairs. Blake is seated on the couch with one twin on either side. Orroth and Wren sit across from them, like stand-in parents for me.

"Hey. Hi. Hello," I speak up with an awkward wave. "Sorry. Hope you weren't waiting too long."

I don't know why I apologized; I'm not even late. In fact, he's early.

Awkwardness settles over me as his eyes rake over my body, settling at my chest for a beat too long before meeting my eyes.

"You look…wow." Blake stands and walks closer. "You look great, Davina."

He moves to give me a hug, but before he can, Orroth shoots out of his seat and over to me.

"Don't touch her unless she says you can," Orr scolds over his shoulder.

He then proceeds to look me directly in the pupils before speaking. "You charged your phone, right? Nod yes. And you have the pepper gel and switchblade I gave you? Nod yes."

I nod and giggle after each time he has me agree with him. We both know damn well there is no switchblade.

"Good. Don't stay out too late. We'll be here if you need us."

I can't help but laugh and wrap him in a big hug.

"Thanks, Orr. There's plenty of food in the kitchen. Oh, and give those gaming assholes hell for me," I say with a wink, knowing it's his new favorite pastime. "Especially you, Wren."

She smiles and cracks her knuckles. "With pleasure."

While the guys and I have a tally going with rounds won, Wren keeps tally of how many guys she makes have an aneurysm.

The couch rustles in tandem with Dakolas' moan as he stretches his legs across the cushions. Shimmering pink against a deep green ankle snags my attention.

Rolvak jolts up from the floor, knocking the cereal box over. "You gave my brother the tattoo?"

Dakolas and Wren devolve into a fit of laughter. Shouts filter from the living room to the small porch as the door clicks behind me.

"They seem like a lively bunch," Blake comments as I fish out my keys.

If he only knew how lively they really are.

I just laugh and nod in agreement.

"So, I'll follow you there? Or you can send me the address, and I'll meet you there."

His face contorts in something akin to confusion or maybe offense. "Why would you do that? We live across from each other, so it makes more sense for me to drive. It's the nice thing to do, right?"

Right…because he's a nice guy.

"Because this is what makes me comfortable. If you're such a nice guy, you'd understand that," I say with a playful tone, but I have my fingers crossed he actually takes the hint.

His large hands land on his hips, eyes dancing between his truck and me.

"Alright, I get it. Your car is the escape plan," he says, it with an easy-going smile. "I promise you won't need it though."

Was I expecting some kind of swanky restaurant? No. Was I expecting something with some kind of semblance of a dress code? Yes. Was I expecting an Italian spot like what was mentioned, even though it was a while ago? Possibly. And that is exactly everything this karaoke dive bar is missing.

If I knew I was going here and two towns over, I wouldn't have bothered rushing to get changed. I even shaved … past the knee.

This is the bar that caters to those who want to live in the city without actually living in the city *and* have never actually left their hometown.

"This is my favorite place to unwind after work. Especially after a stressful day or week." Blake drums his fingers on the tall, sticky tabletop before he sits down. "No chance of running into parents here. At least, I haven't yet."

Every meal and teatime, Mendax has pulled out my chair. Either I've grown accustomed to it, or a new bar has been set. My eyes flick from the chair to where Blake happily sits, not even paying attention to me but rather to the large screen hanging on the sidewall displaying an interview with a baseball player involved in a scandal. I recognize his face and name since he's been a long-time client of my mom's. *This douche canoe is probably the reason my parents didn't come back for my birthday.*

"You like baseball?" Blake asks once he notices me frowning at the ruggedly handsome man on the screen.

The scraping of the chair fills our little conversational bubble as I drag it out and sit down with a heavy sigh.

"Not really. I enjoy hockey and soccer."

He laughs. "Soccer is hardly a real sport, though. It's just filled with a bunch of dramatic crybabies faking an injury."

My tongue swipes my teeth before I suck in the rudeness that's ready to seep from my lips.

"I played soccer in college. It was actually a full-ride scholarship. There were a few scouts who wanted me to go pro, too. We'll have to disagree on it 'not being a real sport.'"

I remember breaking the news to my parents about the scouts. Mom was thrilled and was already thinking about how to put forth my best image to get the best offer. Dad gave me a wry smile; he knew sports was my independent way to pay for college. Never once did I claim to want to be an athlete growing up. Mom was a bit heartbroken but said, "If you think it's best, I support you." My trophies and medals are still proudly displayed in the basement next to all of Dad's sports memorabilia.

The tips of his fingers stop the drumming on the table, and he clears his throat. "I'm going to get us some beers."

Before I can tell him that I don't drink beer, he's already pushing through the crowd and headed towards the bar.

Maybe he'll come back and ask what I want.

"So, Samantha is mad at Trey because he's been texting Avril. But Avril isn't interested because she's been texting his friend, Kyle. Kyle is dodging Avril's texts because he doesn't want to talk to her; he's been trying to get Samantha's number from Avril because Avril and Samantha are friends." Blake takes another sip from the brown glass bottle. "Then they all confronted each other at the same time while Chelsea was presenting her project, and her project ended up in the crossfire and got demolished."

"Wow, that's crazy."

In the two hours we've been here, I've only smiled, nodded, or hummed in agreement. Blake hasn't even bothered to notice that I'm still nursing the same beer from when we first arrived. Beads of moisture collect on my thumb as I trace the curve of the opaque glass neck. My stomach growls like an angry, caged beast. All we had for dinner was a basket of pretzel nuggets and cheese sauce. And when I say 'we,' I mean him. I had *maybe* two before he inhaled the rest.

I wonder if Mendax's date went this rough. Who am I kidding? Mendax probably had her laughing at his effortless charm while she gave him bedroom eyes. She's probably thinking of running her fingers through his thick hair. Hair so black that it has streaks of midnight blue in it when the light is dimmed just right. Or maybe, she's thinking about how his horns would feel pressed between her thighs and in the palm of her hands—

"Earth to Davina," Blake laughs nervously.

Holy hellfire, where did those thoughts come from?

A lick of white-hot heat uncoils in my stomach and works its way up to paint my chest and cheeks in embarrassment.

"Are you hot? Because I'm hot." Readjusting myself in the seat, I can feel the dampness pooled in the gusset of my panty.

Chessus, Davina, get a hold of yourself and your lady bits.

Blake finally takes note of the now-warm and still full beer bottle on my side of the table and the empty basket of pretzels over on his.

"So, on birthday celebrations," he diverts his eyes from me and on to the karaoke stage where a young woman holding a shot a glass butchers a rendition of "Used to be Young" by Miley Cyrus. "Where does this outing land?" He gives me a side glance.

My fingers clasp on my lap, eyes set on the stage, but my mind takes me back to every disappointing birthday. All the years mom missed because she was putting out a celebrity fire or the years dad missed because of night shifts in the ER are "where the money and action is." His words, not mine. Then, the years at college when my boyfriend was too tired to do anything, and my friend had conveniently forgotten, and really, they were off together.

This year, when I was brave enough to hope I had a friend to celebrate with, it was doused in flames because he had to go on a date. Now I'm here with Blake, a guy who is conventionally attractive, and I'm sure some girl out there would find his down-to-earth attitude appealing. But I'm not that girl.

"I don't have enough empirical or quantitative data to answer that question," I say with a forced laugh. Sighing, I dig my wallet out of my purse and slap a twenty on the table.

"It's getting late, and I have an ever-growing list of numbers to crunch and presentations to review and approve. Thanks for the night out."

Thank God, I listened to Wren and drove myself despite Blake insisting he drive together.

Dashing my way through the crowded bar, I can hear Blake asking me to wait up. Did I ruin his favorite escape? He took me somewhere special to him, and I'm probably being rude with my exit. Maybe it's because

I'm thirsty and hungry, but I can't seem to bring myself to care about bailing.

The crisp air that rushes in from the open door is welcoming and refreshing. My stomach grumbles again, reminding me I barely ate anything and solidifying the reasons why I swore off dating to begin with. Unlocking my car and sliding into the worn-in seat, I start the engine and begin the long drive home, hitting every single red light.

Lights dance past my window while my thoughts drown out my shuffled playlist. Did I really give Blake a fair chance? I kept thinking about Mendax, in ways a friend shouldn't think of another friend.

Mendax. He should have been back by now. Damnit, I *am* bitter, and I have no right to be. Mendax doesn't see me that way. He only thinks of me as a means to an end, and a vacation getaway from his imprisonment.

That's not right either. While I do give him a getaway from his current predicament, I'm also his friend. We're friend-shaped; he even called me his best friend. So why do I feel this way? I should be content with being only his friend. Am I being a pick-me? *God, I hope not.*

Before I know it, muscle memory has me pulling into my driveway and throwing the car in park. The last few words of my favorite song ring out through the speakers. I missed my favorite part of the song. I could restart it, but I just don't have it in me to appreciate it right now.

With a heavy sigh, I rest my head on the gelled cushion steering wheel cover. Tiny lights dot behind my eyelids as I squeeze them tighter, willing myself to get out of the car. My head slips, bumping my forehead into the horn, sending a rapt blare into the night air.

"Shit."

I pop up straight in my seat like some kind of prairie dog. Pushing the car door open, I lean over to the passenger seat to grab my purse before exiting.

"Fuuuu——"

My teeth bite into my bottom lip like little gravestones for every cuss word that has just died on my tongue. *If I could murder a door, I would.*

My heel connects with the door that slammed back on my shin. Slamming it closed, I trek across my lawn, twisting my ankle on a paving stone.

"I really need to replace those." I make a quick mental note before entering my home.

I had expected—and secretly hoped—for a rowdy welcome. Maybe someone I could eat a pint of ice cream with, but all that welcomes me is a dead plant, long forgotten in a corner and the warm glow of a table lamp. I'm starting to hate this house and the way my adulthood is unfolding.

I'm a bitter Betty.

Chapter 20
cake

Mendax

I DON'T KNOW HOW I ever let my mother convince me to stay this long, but here I am. Well, that's not entirely true. I do know; she guilted me into staying to help inventory the *largest* warehouse we have.

Inventory is a tedious task. One I never enjoyed but, it has to be done. Normally, my father is the king of the warehouse domain, but he's procuring more trinkets and oddities in another realm. How convenient. At least we aren't doing appraisals and acquisitions today.

What I *do* know for certain is I have been gone for longer than I wanted. A deep groan makes its escape from me as my finger ticks yet another box on the never-ending list.

"Why do we suddenly have eleven time-halter pocket watches?" This precious item is so rare that despite the dings and scratches, my father refuses to sell it for anything under mint pricing. The soles of my black loafers echo against the highly waxed tile floor as I count the aisles and bays that will eventually lead me to the watch.

"Dax!" Orroth huffs from around the corner with a mouth full of cake.

There's a box wrapped in gold paper and an ivory bow with a cake tray balancing on top. Gotha is swaying side-to-side on his horn, attempting to reach the cake. He hasn't been back to Davina's since her date with *Blake*, the neighbor.

It's wrong to feel jealous, given why I left her on her birthday—that and the fact this is all pretend. But there is some horrible part of me I never knew existed that hopes her date went horribly.

My dear brother decided to fill me in on the cover story he created in between ticking boxes on the inventory list. However, I'm not thrilled knowing his friends are in on the charade.

My eyes close to near slits as I eye him and the tablet with inventory.

"Orroth, first, why is Gotha here? Last time, you lost her for a full month. Second, why do we suddenly have *eleven* time-halters?"

Rolling my teeth over my lips, I send a little prayer for patience to anything in these boxes that might be listening and willing to grant my wish.

"Where did you get that cake from?"

He snorts in amusement while tossing Gotha a raspberry.

"Let's see…" His face scrunches so hard I'm not sure if he's about to choke on the new mouthful of chocolate frosting or if all the sugar is about to cause a total system flush. "One, she was restless and needed extra love. B, she was a baby when she got lost, and we knew she was in this vicinity, so not *totally* lost." One more berry gets tossed to my bat. "We don't have eleven; we have one. I fat-fingered that and forgot to change it. Oh, and Elara had someone from her staff drop this off for you at Mom's house. I grabbed it before getting the present Wren enchanted for you."

It's been a whole month, and the box wobbling in Orroth's hand is weighing down the lead ball of guilt in my stomach. Elara followed me around that night, clearly not getting the hint our date was over. She had the audacity to ridicule the gift I picked for my Davina. According to her, "a woman would never want something so simple and mundane. A dazzling necklace would be better."

The thing is, I know Davina would adore what I picked for her, but a small seed of doubt was planted, so I ended up picking out a luminescence pendant necklace.

The leather case from the tablet thumps on the metal shelf before I grab the gold box and velvet pouch resting on top. Doing my own inventory, I open the pouch, and a frown takes over my face as the light from the stone fades. The magic of stone is tied into another realm. When the three suns set, the pendant shines; as each sun rises, the light dims. Sinching the bag closed, I safely tuck it into my breast pocket. Fixing my cufflinks, I clear my throat.

"What if she's angry? You haven't seen an *angry* Davina. Her anger can contend with Mother."

"*If* she's angry—and I doubt she is: grovel. Then, show her the shiny necklace. Have you noticed how distracted she gets with shiny things?"

He's not wrong, but it isn't that shiny things distract her. She appreciates the beauty in little things, which is something I admire.

Admire? Friends can admire each other, right? I'm sure they can. Putting a pin in the thought, my leather case scrapes across the shelf before I sit on top of the box.

"Don't worry, I'll fix the inventory error for you."

"Oh, we're changing subjects because you're uncomfortable. Got it. No worries, Bro. I won't remind you how effortlessly beautiful Davina looked for her date. Or how Blake couldn't stop looking at her like she was the best thing since—what do humans say again? Oh yeah, since sliced bread."

The pad of my finger stills, poised over a new list item. Suddenly, the cavernous stone walls of the warehouse shrink closer around me, and the fluorescent overhead lighting spotlights the uneasy emotion playing out on my face. Tucking the tablet under my arm, I snatch the cake platter from his fingers and set it on a shelf.

"Here, you take over the list. I'm going to see Davina and inform her of the dinner," I say, shoving the tablet to his chest.

All I get from Orroth is an impish grin and a little wave of his fingers. Gotha leaves her perch and flies to rest on my shoulder.

"If you're coming with me, you best behave. I don't need you attacking Davina again."

Quiet engulfs the apartment that, once upon a time, I found comforting. Now, it's lacking … everything. Even with artwork, throw pillows, and warm lighting from lamps, it all feels…not like my home anymore.

Checking my reflection one last time, I smooth my beard and fix a few rouge strands from the top of my head. It's useless, though; they always fall over my brow.

I don't know why I'm so nervous; It's only Davina.

"It's only Davina," I chant my new mantra while picking up the carefully wrapped box.

"Okay, Gotha. I need this to go well. Please behave. The two of you getting along would mean the world to me, especially because I l—"

I what?

"I like Davina a lot. She means a great deal to me."

A single flap of her wings is all I get in acknowledgment; I'll take it.

Turning the lights off in the apartment, the gold paper rubs between my palms as I fix the bow. Gotha snags the velvet bag before perching on my horn. The magic portal hums behind the pantry door. Excitement—with a side of nerves sprouts in my chest before the magic engulfs me in a yellow light and matching plume.

Tingles and sparks dance down my spine as I step out of the portal. The familiar scent of lavender and eucalyptus greets my nose while darkness welcomes my eyes. Sounds float around the bedroom, seep into my ears, and jolt my heart into a frenzy.

"Mmm. Yes. Uh—" Her voice is seductive, and those moans are enough to drive any man mad.

Man.

A man.

Any man.

Blake is a man.

There's something ugly and feral clawing at my chest and ensnaring my throat. A cool breeze from the slightly open window whips my head in the direction of the bed, where I can make out a slight movement under the bedsheets.

What Davina does in her own free time is her business. It's not mine. She's not mine. I should be leaving.

"Oh God," she pants. "Men—oh—-da!"

Her plea of pleasure, right on the cusp, has my fingers itching and my throat swallowing roughly. I could have misheard it. I should go back and re-enter with a grand entrance. But my feet and hands have other plans. Before I can figure out what I'm doing, my fingers find the light switch just as she releases a deep moan.

She screams.

I scream.

Gotha shrieks.

We're all screaming. A vibrating wand circles around her legs as she pulls the sheets up and tighter around her chest. The sheet clings to her skin, her nipples poking just behind it, calling for my attention.

"Get the fuck out!" Her voice is breathy and shrill.

"I didn't see anything! I swear!"

I don't know what to do. Her moaning my name is playing on a loop in my brain, and my trousers feel tighter than ever. So, I do the next logical thing. The gold box flies across the room as I chuck it toward her as if it'll sprout a wall of privacy, and I hightail it downstairs.

My body is on autopilot, which leads me to my least favorite room at home, that bathroom of mirrors.

Where the hell is Gotha?

"Gotha? Gotha?"

I peek out of the bathroom and spot her flying into the laundry room. The wooden bathroom door shuts with a soft click before supporting my sagging frame.

"She moaned my name."

I stare at myself in the reflective wall. A notable bulge pressed firmly against the zipper of tailor-made trousers stares back at me.

"No, she didn't. I'm hearing things. There's no way—well, there is a way, but there's no logical reason she would. Right?"

A twitch in my pants tells me otherwise. Peering down to the fully pitched tent in my pants, I groan.

"*You* need to relax and behave yourself." I point to my crotch before readjusting my cock.

Turning the faucet on, I focus on the sounds of running water and not the pacing footsteps above me. Cold water trickles over my fingers before splashing on my face and through my hair.

A new scent invades my nostrils as I take a deep breath. She would leave a candle on, and I would always trail behind her every night, blowing them out. Every inhale and exhale evens out with each flicker of flame. My breath fogs one of the square mirrors as I inspect myself again.

I really do need to make a horn shine appointment. There's a slight scratch on my left horn, and if left untreated, it could turn into a crack. If it cracks, it could break, and horn reconstruction is not on my to-do list.

Eyeing the melted wax gives me an idea I will never be able to speak out loud. The warm glass presses against my fingers as I inspect the label.

"Vanilla frosting." *Delightful.*

Careful not to singe my hair, I let the wax drip over my horn. Here goes nothing.

It's been about a full hour since, well…since the bedroom, and Davina hasn't come down. Her continued pacing lets me know she's far removed from sleep, and occupying myself downstairs seems like a better option than checking on her because I'd rather not make her more uncomfortable. The thought of my Davina feeling uncomfortable because of me churns my stomach.

First, to occupy and distract me, was finishing the snack pantry clean out that she had started and clearly been distracted away from. Clear containers covered any available counter space. Behind each glass canister was a snack. She had started organizing them but it looked like by the time she made it to the sea-salt dark chocolates, she lost focus and turned to the pots and pans, which were pulled out, too.

After each jar was filled and organized by height, the next task was moving a load of laundry into the dryer. Now, I'm staring at the tin can of Pu'er tea. The safety seal is still on it, and it's already well into the month. I've already read the label several times, which explains how Pu'er tea has a savory notes with umami and woody sweetness. It pairs with sweet and savory food and is closer to black tea rather than green or white.

"You're back?" Davina's voice is soft and uncertain.

The white tin clangs against the counter as it slips from my fingers.

"Sorry," the apology lodges in my throat as I take in her appearance.

Her hair is in soft, tousled waves, and her glasses sit just a little further down her nose than normal. Her creamy skin carries a hue of flush. She looks absolutely breathtaking in an oversized shirt. The only thing I can think, is how it should be my shirt.

"I didn't mean to be gone that long." It's the lamest thing for me to say.

Her lips press in a firm line. A heavy exhale and rough swallow follow before a silent nod of acceptance of my stupid apology. She deserves a better apology.

My gaze falls from her face. She looks anywhere but my direction. Rhythmic fingers drum on the box I threw at her.

"What's this?" She finally glances at me.

How have I never noticed how long and thick her lashes are?

"It's for you." Resting my hip against the counter, I look down at my shoes unable to fully meet her captivating stare. "That wasn't …. It was meant to … What I wanted…" Damn, this is difficult. "About upstairs."

She forces a laugh before shuffling to the small table.

"Upstairs? Never happened. We're going to pretend that never happened. You walked in as I was waking up. That's all that happened."

Right, we're going to pretend what happened up there isn't going to be the greatest fantasy for the rest of my life. We'll pretend I never heard her and how everything in me is dying to see what she looks like, moaning beneath me and writhing on top of me.

Rubbing the back of neck, I clear my throat.

"It's a late birthday gift."

Gotha takes that moment to fly back into the kitchen from outside. Davina stiffens as my pet lands on the box and stares. It's a silent battle of wills until Gotha flaps her wings and flies into the air before landing on Davina's shoulder.

She shuffles from foot to foot eyeing my bat. "Are we cool?"

Gotha flies to me and nestles her way into my jacket before coming out with the velvet bag. She drops it on the box before taking off and landing on the spice rack.

"How about some tea?" Things are awkward between us, and tea seems like the solution. No matter what happens, we'll always have tea.

"Tea sounds perfect."

Moving around the kitchen, getting everything ready, the minutes painfully tick by. The kettle is on, the cups are placed on the table, unicorn and shark silicone tea infusers at the ready.

Poking the golden unicorn horn, the corner of my lips curls up. "These are new."

Those perfectly white, straight teeth dig into her plump bottom lip with a grin. "The platypus and axolotl steepers needed some friends."

My shoulders shake in silent laughter. "Makes sense."

The chair scrapes across the floor. There's a small creek from the floorboards as she settles into her seat. It's always the one that faces out of the kitchen.

"Which should I open first?"

"Whichever you like, I suppose." *What if she dislikes both of them?*

Before I can register the thought, a small gasp grabs my attention. She's holding the necklace, watching the light from the luminescence stone slowly fade.

"Did I break it?"

Sliding into the chair opposite her, I chuckle and explain the origin of the stone.

"It's lovely. Thank you."

She doesn't seem thrilled, but I can tell she does appreciate it as she carefully slips it back into the bag.

"I was thinking you could wear it for dinner in two days."

"Two days?" Her fingers still over the ivory ribbon. "Oh, right, the date thing. I'd love to."

Those warm brown eyes go back to the box.

I'm a firm believer that there are two kinds of people when it comes to gifts. Camp A: tears wrapped presents like wild animals hopped up on triple shots of espresso and sugar. Camp B: savors the feel of the tape running under the pad of their finger as they carefully undo each fold as if they're unveiling a precious artifact. Davina falls firmly into "camp A" and I absolutely love it.

"You got me a teapot."

Her fingers skim the outer edges of the open wooden box before they dip into the black velvet lining. Aside from her soft breathing, the room is silent. She lifts the green, gooseneck teapot from the box, the pads of her fingers brushing over the gold filigree inlay and pearlescent lid.

It isn't a question. She says it as a fact, but the tone has me on edge. That is until I notice the shimmering tears brimming her eyes.

"No one has ever gotten me something for something I actually enjoy. Hell, it's been *years* since I've gotten a birthday present."

Oh hell, now I want to hold her and kiss those tears away. I didn't mean to open any wounds or make her emotional.

"I asked Wren to enchant it so it'll always keep the tea warm until it's empty. Then, it instantly cools. I know it isn't much—oof!"

Air whooshes out of my lungs as Davina launches herself into me. There is zero hesitation in my arms wrapping tightly around her. Hugging her might very well be my new favorite thing.

"It's perfect. I love it."

She peers up at me, and now my heart is beating so fast I think she might feel it against her chest.

"Thank you, Mendax." Her lips brush my cheek in a quick kiss, but her face lingers near mine.

She inhales and pulls back slightly. Her face scrunched in confusion.

"Two things. One: can we try the kettle now? Two: Why do you smell like cake?"

Just like that, any awkwardness is long gone.

"We absolutely need to try it out now, and I have no idea why you're smelling cake. Maybe you're having a stroke."

Her laugh fills the kitchen, and all is right with the world again.

Chapter 21

Trouble

Davina

DAD ALWAYS SAID, "PATIENCE is a virtue." Mom always said, "Grab life by the horns." Me? I've always believed in being patient enough to grab the *right* horns. It just so happens that the horns I want to grab are attached to one particularly painfully handsome demon sitting across from me. It was those exact horns I envisioned pressed between my thighs last night while having some much-needed "me time."

Did I remember there was a portal in my bedroom? Nope. I sure as shit did not. That baby wasn't being used, so it was outta sight, outta mind. Does knowing Mendax could catch me in the act again bother me or excite me? Well, no more than it should.

Sitting near the handsome devil now while we eat lunch and play Scrabble in my backyard, the amount I've missed him is finally registering. I've missed his deep, silky voice, the way he makes sure I have everything I need before he sits down, and the campfire smell of him, which now has a tinge of cake.

I've missed how attentive he is when I'm telling him about some client or celebrity gossip with several stories in between. Overall, I missed him more than I probably should have. It was only one month, and I can already tell if he told me he polished the stars at night, I'd believe him. Oh, this smells like trouble for me.

Warm fingers grasp mine from across the table, pulling back into a conversation I missed. I really should stop doing that.

"What was the last thing you heard?" Mendax asks, his thumb stroking my knuckles.

There isn't a single ounce of judgment or annoyance on his face. His hand stays on mine while he casually scoops the Mediterranean Couscous salad we made to place more on my plate before adding another serving for himself. While his hand is searing emotions in me, that I have no right to feel, his beautiful eyes scan the Scrabble tiles.

All I can do is turn my face to hide the blush coating my cheeks. The urge to flip my hand palm side up and lace our fingers together is otherworldly.

"You said your mother is going to have guests, and even though it's a dinner, there is hardly an actual dinner. Which is asinine to me. Please remind me to eat before we go."

The click of lettered titles settles between us. "Oh, asinine, thanks for that."

The food tastes like ash in my mouth as I say the last part I heard, "The very last thing I heard was your mother's choice of future daughter-in-law will be there, and neither of them have any idea I'm party crashing."

"It's not crashing, Davina. You're coming to play the role of my girlfriend. If we play our parts convincingly enough, it'll get me out of this contract. I really don't want to marry...*her*."

Would it be considered creepy if I entwined our fingers together now under the guise of playing pretend? Because I'm doing exactly that. There's a furious flutter in my chest from the stampede of butterflies in my stomach. Even though Mendax's hand engulfs mine, I can't deny how perfect it feels. I'm turning into a creeper. *Oh, sweet mama, this is trouble.*

"Don't you worry, Snookums, I'll be the world's best loving and doting girlfriend," I say, batting lashes. "There will be no doubt in anyone's mind that you're my Sweetie Pie. The Mac to my Cheese, the PB to my J. I'll have them knowing I love you so much I'd willingly talk on the phone with someone instead of text."

There's nothing but silence until he tosses his back, and a rumble of laughter thunders past his lips.

"Of that, I have no doubt, princess." He winks before lifting my hand and kissing the tips of my fingers.

Setting my hand back on the table, his fingers wrap around the green glass bottle of sparkling water.

The heat in my cheeks reached an infernal level hearing that term of endearment, and his effortless intimacy with me made it feel like I was standing in the fires of hell. To calm the newly formed butterfly rave in the pit of my stomach, I chant in my mind, *This is all pretend, this is all pretend, this is all pretend. This is all—"*

When did this all start to feel so real?

After chugging most of the bottled water, Mendax refuses to meet my eyes.

"I promise, you only have to be yourself. You're charming enough and don't need to do anything you're not comfortable with."

I don't know how to respond to that. *Distraction.* I—no—we need a distraction.

Looking at the board and my tiles, there's one word I can lay. It's worth twelve points. Sure, I have other options, but twelve points is twelve points, and it would put me ahead of him in the game. It also just so happens to be all I can think of, so I play C-O-R-N-U-A.

God, I hope he doesn't know it's Latin for 'horns.'

I know for a fact he can literally exude charm. But now I'm questioning if he can make time stand still. Everything seems to stop, except for my racing heart, as his pants rustle against the cushion of the chair while he leans forward, scanning the board and squinting at the tiles I put down.

"What word did you play?"

Time still isn't moving as his hand engulfs his drink.

I can't bring myself to say it, and I feel like a dunce for even playing the word now. Scrunching my brows and biting my lip, I point to the row of letters.

He looks at the board and chokes on the water.

"Wrong pipe," he coughs. Mendax looks at the tiles and back to me. "I've got nothing."

His Adam's apple bobs as he downs the rest of the water. Never in my life have I found a man's *throat* sexy before, but I guess there's a first time for everything.

"Good game," I manage to squeak out.

Tiles clatter into the box as I sweep them in with one hand. I swear there's a smile trying to break free on Mendax's face, and he won't even look at me as he folds the board.

I made this pleasant time awkward as fuck.

Sitting here in silence, since lunch is done and the game is put away, I let the rays of the afternoon sun, the song from the birds, and the warm breeze float around us.

"We don't have any pictures together." The statement is so far out of left field, but it feels safer than the thought brewing deeper down. "Couples have pictures together. Wait…do you have a phone? Shouldn't I have your number?"

Sucking in a sharp breath, I ready my next set of questions, but every single syllable wraps around my tongue, making my lips lame. I'm ensnared by violet eyes. Violet eyes with a swirl of pink around the pupil and flecks of fuchsia.

Mendax tugs on his cuff links and stares at me.

"We don't have any pictures, do we?"

The scratching of his beard enters my ears first before the scraping of his chair against the cement patio. I want to ask where he's going, but there's a cluster of emotions having an all-out brawl between the ropes of my heart and brain.

"This is all pretend," I mutter, grabbing my glass of lemonade.

The early summer rays brush along the blades of grass, reminding me I really need to mow.

Mental note:

- Get a lawn mower and learn how to get those sharp lines in the grass.

This is all pretend. We're only friends.

Those warm rays cover my face, and my eyes flutter closed. Hopefully, the sun can sear my new mantra into my mind. Breathing in the warmth of the day and the gentle breeze, my next breath hitches as strong arms wrap around my shoulders and the scent of campfire engulfs me.

Peeling my eyes open, the image of Mendax with his arms wrapped around my upper body stares back at me from my phone.

"Smile." His breath fans over my ear while his beard treks forward, caressing my cheek.

I can see the blush painting my cheeks, and it only grows deeper in hue. With a smile, one thought flits through my mind: *Trouble has a name, and its name is Mendax.*

"There's something about him, Gotha." The comment bypasses my filter while I'm busy scrubbing the pot with a burnt bottom of Couscous.

After a few scratches and bribes, this bat is my new best friend. All it took was a pint of strawberries. She tilts her furry head in my direction, her talons digging into the wooden spice rack while she hangs upside down, grooming her wings.

The only reason I'm even saying any of this out loud is because the man who currently occupies every corner of my mind is up in the attic. Probably researching that book again.

To be completely honest, I had forgotten about it until he mentioned it again. Apparently, there's a similar one at his family's warehouse that no one had any idea of. The cover was hanging on by frayed threads, and the pages were so damaged from element exposure and time they crumbled at the barest of touches.

Soapy water splashes on my face and splotches my glasses. Gotha is happily bathing herself with my spoons.

"You know that's dirty water, right?" The damn bat doesn't even care. "You do you, Gotha. You. Do. You."

Sighing, I wipe my lenses with the bottom of my cotton shirt. I probably should have used the jersey skirt instead because now the glasses are all streaky.

Is it safe to leave her in the sink alone?

"I'll be right back."

Running out of the kitchen and skidding into the laundry, a slew of cuss words tumble free just as I clip my shoulder on the door frame. Speaking of tumbling, swinging the dryer door open, I snag a towel out. A shiver wracks through my body.

"Good God."

The feel of microfiber towels, especially dry microfiber towels, is enough to make my skin crawl. If anyone needed to torture me for information, all they'd have to do is rub dry microfiber across my skin.

Back in the kitchen, I cradle Gotha in my hand before rinsing off the soapy water with a warm running stream from the faucet.

"Okay, let's go find our guy," I whisper, wrapping her like a baby bat burrito.

"Mendax?" My voice carries up the darkened stairway. All that greets me is silence.

The boxes once shoved against the far wall, half unpacked on my long-ago quest for teacups, are emptied and gone. Cobwebs are a thing of the past, and apparently, so is dust. The smooth grain of the dark-stained shelves glides under the pad of my index finger. Rows of alphabetically sorted books line my vision. Neat, handwritten labels are placed carefully on a variety of jars.

This room feels so foreign and yet oddly familiar. I still haven't used the desk he set in here. It didn't feel right to be in this space without him.

The warm glow of the desk light lures me towards the desk.

"What do we have here?"

The corner of my lips quirk into a smile, looking at the book that started all this. Emotions I haven't felt in a long time try to surface, but I'm quick to push them away. These feelings are misplaced and pretend. *This is pretend.*

A rainbow of sticky notes jut out of the notebook I gave him. That was one of my favorite notebooks.

"Oh, I forgot I gave him my favorite pen, too." It suddenly occurs to me I've been giving Mendax all my favorite and prized possessions.

Gotha dozed off during my perusal of the shelf, leaving me to talk to me, myself, and I. The day after he disappeared was the last time I was up here, and it was only to get some files he moved.

"Unfortunately for you, Miss Myles, that is now my favorite pen."

With my heart leaping into my throat from the jump scare, my little bat burrito tucks closer to my chest.

"Didn't mean to scare you," Mendax chuckles.

It should be illegal in every state, country, and realm for him to look as handsome as he does right now. We can add the chuckle to illegalities, too.

Leaning against the door jamb, ankles crossed, hands in his pockets, he looks right at home. The first few buttons of his white dress shirt are undone, and I get a glimpse of the hair on his chest. The suspenders are only adding fuel to the fire burning in me.

Look away, Davina. Look. Away.

But nope. My brain has turned into soup, and my tongue is savoring every delicious morsel of the thought.

Clearing my throat and trying to figure out why Mendax is staring at me with a puzzled expression, I swallow the last of my tantalizing thoughts.

"I was looking for you."

"I was looking for you, too. Looks like we finally found each other."

Is his voice always this deep? Man, I should put an air conditioner up here.

"A call from Mother Dearest came in while I was plugging your phone in."

"Oh, okay. I'll go call her back."

Even though my words say I'm going to complete that task right now, my feet stay rooted to the area rug.

"I've been meaning to talk to her."

One.

Two.

Three.

Four.

Five.

Five even, casual, and assured steps is what it takes for Mendax to close the distance between us.

"I have to go back to my apartment for a bit," he says. "There's something I need to get for the party."

He leans further down, tipping my chin up with one finger.

I can keep track of values in an analysis, I can count the number of times Mendax has called me 'Miss Myles'—one, and I can count the five steps he took to get to me. Yet I can't count the number of seconds my eyes stay closed or how long his warm lips are on my forehead.

Back when I was fifteen, Dad warned me about forehead kisses. He said, and I quote, "When a boy gives you a forehead kiss, he sucks all the common sense out of you."

Except Mendax isn't a boy, he's a handsome devil, and his forehead kiss took every last thought I have ever thought or dared to think.

"I promise I'll be back soon. We have more to prep for the dinner." He leans away. "We're going to give one hell of a performance."

I can't move, breathe, or form words. All I can do is watch him walk down the creaky attic stairs. *"One hell of a performance."*

I almost forgot; this isn't real. It's Mendax, the charming salesman and procurer of oddities. The man who can get and give me anything I want and/or need. What if my heart is set on wanting him?

This is pretend. *This* is pretend. This *is* pretend. This is *pretend.*

This.

Is.

Pretend?

Oh, I'm falling deeper and deeper into trouble.

Chapter 22
Mine

HAVING A FAKE GIRLFRIEND should means it's a no-hearts-involved, everyone-comes-out-unscathed situation.

Why did I pick *this* situation to listen to Orroth? I never listen to him.

How much convincing did it really take to ask Davina to play pretend with me?

A sensation blooms in my chest whenever I'm near or think of her. I still haven't admitted to myself what it is, even though I'm *fully* aware of what it is. Once I do admit to the feeling, it's real. And this perfect, casually-effortless, intimate friendship could be ruined.

Seeing Davina in the attic, holding Gotha like a baby, put ideas and images in my brain I'm not sure how to get rid of, or if I want them gone at all.

Would she want a family with me? I never thought of myself as a family man, until she came along. For her, I can be, if that's what she wants. I was firmly in the camp of "pets can be grandchildren for my parents."

Now, here I stand, ready to risk everything.

Orroth is back at the warehouse, keeping mother busy while Wren meets me in the sitting area of Enchanté Couture. Only the who's who of Piros shop here. If I'm going to walk my sweet Davina into the lion's den, I'm going to give her the best armor there is. There will be no question that she not only will look amazing, but that she belongs with me.

According to Wren, if I want Davina to dazzle and wow, this is the place to get her a dress. Apparently, Syn, the owner of Enchanté, is 'cool people.'

"You know her size right?" Wren asks, pulling dresses off chrome racks and yanking me back to the present.

A chime from the front door catches my attention. Dakolas and Rolvak saunter in, the later grinning more than the former.

"I finished it!" Rolvak shouts across the room.

Wren's squeal of excitement makes me suspicious. "What did you finish?"

Hangers rattled as Dakolas runs a finger over them.

"It's a secret," he says with an impish grin.

Both twins are closer to Orroth's height putting them closer to chin level with me, but they have more width and mass than I do. So, seeing them shoulder their way through the racks, fighting to see who gets closer first is comical.

Rolvak wins out with an elbow to his brother's ribs.

"Alright, let's find something for our favorite human. She has to look hot and sexy, right, Mendax?"

I roll my eyes, running a hand across my mouth and down my beard. "You're not picking her dress, Rolvak."

Wren steps between us, fisting her hands on her hips. "Size, Mendax. What is her size?"

Swiping through a few gowns behind me, a frown finds its way to my face.

"I know she's a 34DD, and there's a lot of M's and L's." Plucking a white shimmery gown, I hold it to the light. "There was a 28 in a pair of jeans too."

This dress is too transparent, and I'll end up with an assault charge at best or murder charge at worst if she wears this. With possessiveness burning in my veins, I place the offending dress back.

"There was also a 6 in a pair of shorts."

If Wren sighed any heavier, she'd blow every dress off the rack.

"Well, it's a start." Every dress draped over her arm is placed back on racks. "It's fine. I can do this." A crack rolls from her neck. "I got this."

"We've got this, Wren." The determination in my voice is set as I pluck an onyx long sleeve, high neck gown and contemplate it.

"*We* don't got this." Wren's face scrunches with disgust. "I'm not going to let her go out there looking like someone's widowed grandmother." She goes back to wandering around grabbing and pulling fabric before putting it back.

Rustling from another side of the store drags my attention as Dakolas snags a mini tube dress in green. The same shade of green as him and his brother. Speaking of his brother, he's holding a cerulean blue garment that shouldn't be classified as a dress at all. It's nothing but straps and buckles. Where did they even get those?

"Those are not dinner attire. Those are club dresses. Put them back," I speak slowly and firmly. Emphasizing the last part.

Rolvak looks at the contraption he's holding and then at me, wiggling it in the air. "What kind of clubs are you going to and why haven't you invited me?"

Dakolas chuckles and points to a sign above where they stand. *Of course.* They're in the lingerie section.

"You're not picking out lingerie for her."

I'm so glad we're the only ones in this store right now. I can't believe I'm having this conversation. I go back to scanning dresses, playing with the pink lace on one. Davina would find this itchy, so I place this option back.

Measured footsteps sidle up to me.

"If you don't pick any lingerie out, and won't let us," Dakolas points between himself and his brother, "maybe someone else will."

Rolvak nods a grave frown marring his face. "Someone like Blake."

Pinching my eyes shut I focus on my breathing. Wren walks back over and notices the brown dress currently in my hand. It's nice enough with its simple elegance. Thin straps, square neck and floor length, there's no further embellishments to it.

Ring clad fingers drum on her lips. "Syn! I need a favor."

A young, shorter woman with orange eyes and pure white hair skimming her hips strolls out from a back room, clutching a bolt of yellow wool.

"Always happy to help you." Syn gives a large smile showing off a set of dimples.

If it weren't for her eyes and sharper than average nose, Syn could pass for a human. Her eyes lock onto Dakolas, and he stares at her with a brooding look, causing his brother to smirk.

I'll have to see if Davina can get the story about this out of him because there is certainly something there.

Wren and Syn link arms, talking in hushed tones away from me and the twins, moving away toward the room Syn came out of.

With only couture dresses and the brothers to keep me company, my mind wanders to what Davina would say if she were here now. Would she like anything in this store?

"Yo, Mendax. What about this one?" Rolvak holds a lace nightgown to his body. "Oh, and it's so soft."

I shake my head and chuckle. "I don't think it's your color or size."

Dakolas pops out from behind another rack. "No, no. Get these."

He holds up a bra and matching thong. "She's going to need something under her dress. Show her you thought of everything. Plus, it's her size, or at least *one* of the sizes you mentioned." His fingers skim the bra. "Her boobs are huge."

Snatching it from Dakolas, I look over to Rolvak, who has put on a silk pink robe to model as if he was Davina. I feel like I'm babysitting these two all over again. All I'm missing is Orroth's commentary.

Dakolas leans against a table, watching his brother, and picking through more underwear. "Please, stop, that's nightmare fuel."

With his best model walk and spin Rolvak stares at his brother. "You're jealous I have the legs for this, and you don't," he deadpans.

"We're twins, you idiot."

While they're busy arguing I put the bra and thong next to the register and go back to looking at more dresses.

There really should be chairs in here.

Between the chiffon, tulle, lace, and silk I've lost track all time, but I know I've been away from Davina and Gotha longer than I wanted to be. Boisterous laughter grabs my attention as Wren and Syn saunter from the back room with a black garment bag in one hand and a small silver wrapped box in another.

"These are for you." Wren hands me the small box while Syn drapes the bag over my arm.

Rolvak walks up to us, shoving his brother into Syn, forcing Dakolas to dart his hands out and steady her. His smile is too large, and he looks far too pleased with himself. Meanwhile, Dakolas is ripping his hands off Syn's shoulders like she's made of pure lava. I *definitely need* to ask Davina now.

"Give her the box first, when you see her," Rolvak says. He's still wearing a smug smile.

Before I can protest the fact that I didn't even get to see the dress, Wren is already slipping her hand into my jacket pocket with a grin and walking away with my wallet. *How am I paying for a dress I didn't even get to see?*

Before she can get far, I lightly nudge her. Leaning in, I whisper, "There're two other items at the register, too."

Rolvak is dragging a reluctant Dakolas closer to Syn and the register.

"Smart man," Wren laughs.

Dakolas leans his forearms on the counter. "Hey, it's the set I picked!"

Fucking hell. It's not lost on me, the scowl Syn is now wearing at his statement.

"Don't you dare peek!" she calls from the register. "It's a wonderful surprise for both of you."

My fingers stay poised over the black zipper, itching with curiosity, but then my mind races with all kinds of images on what Davina could be wearing tonight. Just as a vivid image of her in bed with nothing on begins to form, it slips away like sand through fingers at Wren's voice.

"Okay. All set." The wallet is slipped back in place. "You're going to love it!" Wren gushes.

"Don't you mean she'll love it?"

Dakolas swipes the garment bag from me, shielding it from my view while Rolvak stuffs the added underwear into the bottom of the bag.

Syn is watching the suddenly grumpy twin closely. Her mouth opens and closes several times until she huffs and stomps away, and the whirring of a sewing machine eats away at the tension.

"Well, her too." Wren gives me a wink, nudging me back into our conversation. "Now, go get your girl, Mendax. We'll see you both at the dinner."

"She's not my girl. Well, she is. But not exactly—"

"You keep telling yourself that, buddy," Wren says, linking her arms with the twins walking towards the door.

Dakolas turns to me. "You two belong together. Eventually you'll both realize you're as much hers as she's yours."

Rolvak mutters the word 'hypocrite' under his breath.

"Do you two have to go back to work right away?" Wren asks.

"Unfortunately. New security protocols to review for a new client at a high-profile event. I need to look at schematics and figure out where to place security," Dakolas states.

Rolvak is bouncing like a puppy. "I have a 3D-model that needs to be approved by Mom before phase two starts. Then I get to tinker around."

"Drop me off on the way?" Wren asks with a large smile. A smile that, much like my brother, gets her just about everything. "I have to see about a new enchantment pill. Someone added something they weren't supposed to, and now we have a boner pill."

They all wave their goodbyes while I'm running everything over in my head. I bought her a dress; I noticed the shoes Wren added along with the bra and panties.

This is going to work.

The sound of the city competes with my thrumming of my heart as I'm left on the sidewalk rethinking Dakolas' words.

The bedroom is quiet, the late afternoon sun is morphing into the evening glow. Gotha is laying in the middle of the bed surrounded by pillows. Davina is spoiling this bat, and I can't say I mind. Leaving Gotha to snore, I hang the garment bag in the closet and set on a mission to find Davina.

It doesn't take long. Sitting crossed legged on the couch, controller in hand, and headset on, she's spewing more profanities than I've ever heard her say before.

"You cock-sucking little shit! I'm on your damn team. Why would you shoot me? Someone revive me."

Leaning against the banister, I watch the entire thing unfold and the smile on my face grows wider and wider. While she's busy sniping treacherous teammates, I'm busy wondering if we could make this work, for real.

Before Davina, I was fine being alone. I didn't want or need anyone. I was content aside from the house arrest. But now? Now that I've spent time with her, fine doesn't seem fine anymore. I want to always feel as great as I do when she looks at me. I want that stutter in my heart when I hear her laugh. The wrinkles on her nose when her face scrunches in concentration while working on a new spreadsheet or trying to decide if a presentation is ready causes the corners of my eyes to crinkle. Davina makes my life better than great, she's the reason it's fantastic right now.

"I need to start putting a bell on you." Her voice drags me back to reality. "When did you get back?"

She stretches, placing the controller and headset back on the charging stand. The polka-dot yoga shorts cling to her thick thighs and round hips like a second skin, while the cropped loose-fitting green shirt plays a game of peek-a-boo with her tight stomach and my eyes. It's getting more and more difficult to ignore how beautiful and perfect she is.

Even though the sun is out, the curtains are closed. The curtains are always closed, because of me. I don't exactly fit in this world, at least not right now. How long could she keep the curtains closed? She deserves to bathe in the light of the sun and stars.

"Just as you started destroying those teammates of yours."

Sauntering over to her, I dare myself to give this a try and see what it would feel like. Dropping the small box Wren gave me on the coffee table, I engulf her soft, delicate hand in mine and pull her towards my chest. Orange light seeps through the seams of the curtain and the small stained-glass window at the staircase, showering us in a soft rainbow. Our bodies swaying side to side, my right hand curled around her left. My left hand placed on her lower back pulling closer. I'm too tall for her hand to reach my shoulder comfortably so she rests her free hand on my chest, staring up at me. Now I'm trapped in pools of honey.

"Mendax, there isn't any music." She offers me a self-conscious smile. "Are we practicing for the dinner party?" There's something in the way she says it that squeezes my heart. Does she want this to be practice?

Instead of answering, I hum a familiar tune. It's the same song my heart sings whenever I'm close to her. Her breath warms a patch on my chest as she sighs and rests her cheek against me. Now I find myself fighting to slow my heart rate, so she doesn't feel it thump against my ribs. If I could freeze this moment, I'd live in it forever.

Removing my hand from her back, I place it behind my own and twirl her around. We continue gliding around the living room, I bring her hand to my lips and leave a chaste kiss on her knuckles. Her skin is so soft and warm it singes my lips with the need to kiss her more. With every hum, step, glide, and sway the flame of desire for Davina grows. I want her to be mine.

Davina stares up at me from under her lashes, and my body is reacting on its own. I'm leaning down, slowly closing the distance between us. There's a smile quaking at the corners of my lips at the sheer thought of tasting her lips properly this time.

"Mendax?" Her voice barely above a whisper.

It's only my name, but the question in it is loaded with other questions. The only answer I have to offer is a kiss. I don't dare to speak; any sound would be screaming over silence. Our lips are a breath away, my hand pulls her tighter against me. I watch the rainbows dance over her brown and yellow locks before they caress her high cheekbones and pert nose.

Knock. Knock. Knock.

The knocking on the door might as well be a sledgehammer. Davina jumps away from me and back to her senses.

"Sorry," she swallows as heat rushes her cheeks and neck.

Why is she apologizing? Before I can say anything she swats my arm playfully.

"If we act like that tomorrow night, everyone will believe this is real."

She fiddles with her fingers at her hips while biting her plump lower lip.

Right, because this is pretend. For her.

Smoothing down my beard, I walk away, further into the living room, watching as she opens the door. I should man up and tell her how I feel, but it'll ruin everything. For now, I'll enjoy what I can. Even if it is stolen, interrupted moments.

Her phone vibrates across the table next to the forgotten gift.

"New tea for us to try," Davina says in a sing-song voice. "I hope it's something fruity, we haven't had one of those yet."

"Why don't I take that, and you can open up this one. Wren said it's for you."

Instead of grabbing the small present, after passing the tea box to me, Davina reaches for her phone.

"Oh, she didn't tell me you guys were meeting today. Neither did Orr."

The crinkle of the wrapping draws my attention to her as she settles herself in her favorite spot on the couch. My eyes travel down her long, toned, tan legs that she curls under herself. Gone is the aqua that covered her toenails. While I was gone, she painted them a barely-there pink that matches her fingernails.

This is also the same couch that Davina still hasn't realized I ordered to replace that old lumpy couch. I swear, she was one wiggle and bounce away from a spring poking out and getting a tetanus shot.

The confusion on her face was priceless, she spent a full two hours talking to the furniture store customer service because it was sitting in her cart, but she never purchased it. I still can't tell her I bought it.

Last time I offered to buy one she liked, she said, and I quote, "I'm not asking you to get me a new couch, Mendax. I don't want you to get me anything. I'm perfectly capable of buying my own things…when it goes on sale."

I'm still feigning ignorance.

"How would they tell you?" I ask, searching for something to open the box.

She wiggles the phone in the air. "Group chat."

My hand stills, poised over a pair of scissors. "How are you in a group chat with Wren and my brother? And why?"

Her laugh floats around the room. "First, it's not just Orr and Wren. Dakolas, and Rolvak are in it, too. I'm pretty sure that group of extroverts adopted me. They're my friends now"

Confusion must still be evident on my face, because she laughs even more.

"They're a fun group…in small doses. While they were all here, Rolvak took my phone and fiddled with it, and now I guess I can text them from this realm to yours. I still need to add your number."

"When I get one, you'll be the first person I give the number to." Her jaw drops, but I continue, "Before you say anything, I enjoyed not having one. I have a home phone."

Now she's in a full-blown fit of laughter. "You're such an old man."

I narrow my eyes at her, but try as I might, the smile still spreads on my face.

"Just open the box then we can try this." I hold up the dark cardboard box containing the mystery tea.

Her fingers fly over the wrapping paper, and the lid of the box is tossed to one side of the couch, sliding across the leather.

"It's an earring. Like, just *one* earring."

Settling next to her, I grab her legs and place them over my thighs before looking at the single gold cuff chain earring. It looks familiar, but I can't place it.

"Orr has terrible handwriting." Her eyes squint trying to decipher the note my brother placed in the box.

"Make sure you wear this on your left during the dinner party. I promise you'll Love what it does."

-Orr

P.s. Wren says it doesn't matter if it's the left or right ear. But I say left because That's your good side.

"Your brother is ridiculous," she says with pure mirth filtered into every word. "Both my sides are equally good."

I'm glad she's friends with my brother.

"You're beautiful, Davina."

I watched the blush rise from her neck to her cheeks. She tries to pull her legs off my lap, but instead, I gave her a grin and hold her ankle.

"But the right side is the best."

Her right heel connected with my ribs playfully. "Jackass."

It's decided, Davina is mine. Now to make her believe it.

Chapter 23
Monster

Davina

I'M GOING TO VOMIT. First, I'm going to panic; second, will be to cry; and *then* I'm going to vomit.

Memories of every gala, charity event, and dinner from my adolescence that had been buried under the childhood bed in my mind are being dragged out by the monster of anxiety.

Mendax left to get ready at his place, just in case his mother hounds him. The plan is for him to come back and take me through the portal in my room. That alone is enough to ensure a nice fat panic attack. If, for whatever reason, he can't get me, we move down the line of escorts, starting with Orroth and ending with Dakolas.

One way or another, I'm going to that dinner.

"I can't believe I'm going to crash a dinner party."

The phone bounces across the soft sheets of my bed. I just know I'm going to forget something or screw something up. It's times like these when I often wonder if quitting my ADHD medication was a good choice because it gave me laser focus. But it also made me feel weird—like I wasn't myself.

"Get a grip, woman. You can do this." I point to myself during my horrible pep talk in the bathroom mirror.

The tremors in my hand won't still, and every thought I had ever conjured is now surfacing. *What is the food like there? Will there be dancing? Do I have to act prim and proper? Do I remember which fork is the salad fork?*

What if I can't win them over? Should I focus on making the contract-girlfriend feel bad? What am I going to do if Mendax changes his mind? Will I be able to accept being only friends with him if that's the case? Why does my right tit hurt?

There's one surefire way I know to relax…but last time I did that, Mendax walked in on me. Eyeing the shower in the mirror and then my reflection, I nod.

"I should shower first anyway."

Discarding all my clothes, the cool shower handle meets my palm before steam fills up the room. Rivets of hot water cascade down my body. It doesn't take long until images of Mendax fill my mind. My fingers skate down my breasts. A small moan leaves me as I tweak and pull my nipples, hardening them to stiff peaks.

Continuing the trek down my stomach, even the hot water can't stop the goosebumps rising on my skin as I think of his fingers making the same journey while he stands behind me, nipping at my neck. My palm slaps against the cool tile as I find my lower lips slick with my arousal from the sheer thought of Mendax.

"Fuck," I moan, bucking my hips against my fingers.

Even with the tight circles against my sensitive nub, it's not enough.

"Tell me what you need, Davina," he whispers in my ear—his beard scratches against my neck and cheek. Long, thick fingers work their magic.

I know exactly what I need now.

I only allow seconds to break the fantasy, so I can reach the detachable shower head. With a simple twist, the shower mode changes, and I'm thrown back into the fantasy of Mendax's fingers exploring me.

"Taste me. Please. Taste me."

"How can I say no when you beg so pretty?" His voice is deep and filled with a sinful promise.

His fingers curl around my hips, turning me so water sprays my back. The sight of him on his knees for me is almost orgasmic by itself. His horn tickles my thigh as he hitches one of my legs over his shoulder. Soft lips leave a trail of admiration as he plants open mouth kisses up and down my thigh, always nearing where I need him but just out of reach.

"Please, Mendax. Please, please."

I should be embarrassed by how needy I sound, but embarrassment is the last thing I feel. I need his attention, fingers, mouth, and cock. I need him.

He lets out a dark chuckle before kissing my engorged nub. A wicked swipe of his tongue in between my seams begins my unraveling. The attention to my clit leaves me breathless. Thick fingers push into me in slow, torturous movements while his free hand massages my breast.

Cold tile shocks my back, sending an eruption of goosebumps over me. The chill of the wall only heightens the intensity of the pulsing warm water pushing against my pussy as my hand shakes.

I tug at my nipple almost painfully, and with a moan, my hand wanders down, meeting the water. Ravenously, my fingers work my clit in tight, quick circles.

"Oh, God."

I'm lost in shameless pleasure.

"Yes."

The edge of ecstasy is right there, and I'm running, ready to jump. Even the water can't camouflage how I'm dripping for the charming demon. I press harder against myself, forcing my feet to stand on tiptoes. The shower handle that's set to hot presses against my ass. The heat and the hardness of it against that tight ring of muscles. Pressing against it more, the sensations drown me, and I shatter.

"Mendax."

My hair is blown out, skin care is done, and contacts are in. Yet, even wrapped in a fluffy robe, I feel exposed and nervous. Wren texted me a guest list and a quick rundown of who is who and what circles they travel in. Thank God she did because that's something Mendax and I forgot to go over. But my stomach is in knots, and I don't know if I can sell this. I mean, Mendax's sentence could be extended if this all goes wrong. Picking up the phone, I call the one person who I know won't bullshit me and talk some sense into me.

On the second ring, the voice of reason enters my ear, "Hey, Pumpkin."

If I wanted to be coddled, I'd call my dad. But I need someone who won't sugar coat anything like a candy factory.

"Hey, mom."

"Rick, stop revving the lawnmower. I'm trying to hear our daughter!"

"Why is Dad revving the lawnmower?" As soon as the question leaves my mouth, I regret it because I know my parents.

"It's a great show, plus there's music. Better than Magic Mike." Mom laughs. "He's doing it in cutoff shorts and a muscle shirt."

"Oh, ew. There are some things I don't ever need to know, Mom." There isn't enough bleach in the world to burn that image out of my mind.

"You asked the question, Pumpkin." Her voice filled with amusement.

Even though they gross me out at times, a little voice tells me I want a relationship like the one my parents have. I need something like this.

The ugly monster of anxiety is clawing at my stomach again, threatening to erupt. Its lethal claws pierce my lungs, depriving me of oxygen.

Seconds take on the disguise of minutes until I remember to breathe with a gasp.

"Davina?"

"I'm meeting Mendax's mom, and she already hates the idea of me. It's a dinner party with other guests, too. The worst part is that there's another lady there, who his mom wants him to be with and actually marry. And this lady wants Mendax. Mom, I don't know if I can do this."

The damn anxiety monster tore me open, and the floodgates of insecurity and truth have been breached.

"What if I mess up? What if Mendax realizes that I'm not the right choice? What happens—" There's no stopping the flow of my words now.

At least, there wasn't any stopping until my mom's voice becomes a life raft.

"Whose daughter are you, Davina?"

"Is this where you tell me I'm adopted, and that's why you sent me to all those fancy private schools and etiquette classes? Because you didn't want to be ashamed of me, and I still turned into a disappointment?"

I can hear a door close on the other end of the line.

"Davina, I love you. Stop talking and listen. You're going to give yourself another stress rash." Her sharp, no-bullshit tone comes through loud and clear, and I clamp my lips shut into a thin line.

Oh yes, a stress rash. Because why wouldn't I literally be allergic to stress? I'm so allergic that if I get too stressed, hives make an unwanted appearance, like a fruitcake at a potluck. There's already small patches of splotching around my neck and chest.

The last time I got one of those was before my Uncle's funeral. It wasn't pretty and made me even sadder and bitchier. Maybe I have time to disassociate for a bit because that always solves everything.

"You came from me and your father. You have never once disappointed either of us. The private schools and etiquette classes were to give you the advantages I never had growing up.

"I know I wasn't always the best at being around when you needed me because I was busy building my firm. All I wanted was to leave a legacy for you one day. For that, I'm sorry, Pumpkin. I really am. I thought I was doing what was best for you."

She takes a shuddering breath. "You are my daughter, and you are beautiful, smart, and capable. You will not let anyone, and I mean anyone, make you feel less than. Do you understand me? You are the same Davina who refused to let us pay for your college education in an Ivy League school because you wanted to earn it yourself. And you know what? You did earn it. A full ride.

"Then, you turned down the opportunity to play professional soccer because it wasn't the career you wanted. You know your worth, but now you need to understand the value of your worth. I had hoped, by not hiring you at my firm, you would learn that value."

The back of my eyes sting with unshed tears, and my throat feels tight from holding in the sobs. I push myself off my bed and make my way down the stairs.

"Mom, there's more. If she doesn't approve of us, she's going to force Mendax to marry this other woman."

It isn't *exactly* a lie. She would lose her ever-loving mind if I told her the entire truth.

"Listen, I still don't know how I feel about you being with a demon and how it all works or how it'll end up working. But I can tell you, he looks at you the way your father looks at me. If you actually want Mendax, then act like it. You will go to that dinner party with her head held high and charm the *fuck* out of everyone. You will show them that they need to measure up to you. Mendax should be proving how worthy *he* is of *you*, not the other way around. Remember what I taught you: manners. Manners and tact, do you remember?"

I can't help but laugh. "Anyone can tell someone to go to hell. Manners and tact will have them wanting a timeshare there. So, I win the crowd first, then the mom?"

"Not at all. You're going to behave like you belong there because you do. Everyone will have their attention on you. It's an opportunity to sell yourself. Don't you dare downplay your job or talents. Show the other woman who she's messing with, and she doesn't stand a snowball's chance in hell. Now tell me what you're wearing to this event."

Shit. Shit. Shitty shit, shit.

"I haven't picked it out. Mom, I haven't picked out my dress!"

"Breath, Davina. You have tons of dresses."

She's right; I need to breathe. But I don't have tons of dresses. I have *four* work/dinner–appropriate dresses, all of which have never seen the light of day. Right as panic is setting in again, a yellow sticky note written in neat, masculine, blocky letters catches my eye.

DAVINA,

FIRST, THERE'S A BOTTLE OF WATER AND A PLATE OF SNACKS IN THE FRIDGE. SECOND, THERE'S A SURPRISE FOR YOU IN YOUR CLOSET. DON'T FORGET THE NECKLACE TOO. I'LL SEE YOU SOON.

YOURS,

MENDAX

"Davina, Pumpkin? Can I call you right back? Your father is about to spray some kid with the hose. I can't leave this man unattended anywhere."

"Yeah, that's fine. Oh, Mom?" I wait as she hums in reply. "Thank you."

"I love you, Davina, more than you know. Now, go grab life by the horns."

Oh, I'm going to grab horns, alright.

The only way to sell this is to finally admit to myself I want Mendax for keeps. There is no way in hell I'm going to let anyone take him from me. Once I sell this relationship, I'll tell him how I really feel. It could ruin everything or be the start of everything.

A slight gust of cool air meets my freshly shaven legs while I peer inside the fridge. As the note promised, a giant bottle of water stands next to a cling-wrapped plate of olives, cheese, blueberries, and chocolate from my secret stash. A laugh bubbles up when I read another note on the plate.

THIS DOESN'T COUNT AS A MEAL, DAVINA. GIRL DINNER SHOULD NOT BE A THING.

When in the fresh hell, did Mendax put this in my closet, and how did I miss it? Plopping a square of salted caramel chocolate in my mouth I carry the garment bag out.

"This is almost too light to have anything in it." The zipper sounds like a chainsaw in the stillness of my room. "Whoa."

The word is an understatement. The dress consists of a structured corset bodice with delicate chains draping loosely around the chest and weaving down. Each chain drips with tiny crystals. The skirt seems formfitting, with a long slit up the side to allow for movement. A heavy thunk echoed in the room as the bag fell to the ground.

Curiosity always gets the better of me and has me reaching back into the bag. I find strappy, high-heeled sandals, but it's the sexy underwear that appear like a rabbit out of a hat that leave me truly stunned.

"Can't say the man doesn't think of everything."

Holy cannoli , it's the right sizes too.

Moving to the dresser, my fingers clasp the necklace and the single earring. Slowly, my nerves disappear. Mendax picked out a stunning dress, and the jewelry pairs perfectly.

"I can do this," I whisper to my monster, and shove his ugly face back under my childhood bed.

Chapter 24
so wrong
Mendax

THE MOST INTENSE GAME of tug-of-war is being played in the pit of my stomach. Tugging on one end, excitement; yanking on the other, nervousness. At this point, it's a coin toss on which side will be declared the victor.

This entire dinner party feels off. Mother is barking orders to every hired staff member while she wrings her hands raw. Candles have been enchanted to float around the lower level of the family estate creating the illusion of intimacy.

"Mother, is all this," I wave my hands at our surroundings, "necessary? It's a bit over the top."

A humorless laugh flees her lips, amid a smile that never quite reaches her eyes.

"Of course, it's not over the top. Tonight is a big night. We have friends and possible investors coming. Plus, you can consider this a date with Elara and show off how wonderful you two are together."

I should tell her that I'm bringing Davina here, but I can't. Megai will only make sure to separate us the entire night. Dakolas asked if he could bring a plus one—being one of the sons and next in line to inherit a billion-dollar company, he got his request. Luckily that plus one is for Davina and will ensure she gets a seat at the table.

"Why aren't you dressed yet?" My mother eyes my wrinkled pants and shirt.

Blowing the errant strand of hair out of my eye, I meticulously choose my words. "Between helping to set up for the party, finishing up the inventory backlog, and having you send me out every ten minutes to run errands." I pick invisible lint off my sleeve. "Where would I find the time? All of my things are back at the apartment."

The apartment, not home because it's not home. Home is wherever Davina is. Her eyes, smile, laughter, company, she is home.

Megai's fingers stroke back and forth across her collar bone, the one fidget she can never hide when she's extremely nervous.

"Well, go get changed and hurry back." She smooths the nonexistent wrinkles from her gown. "Our guests will be arriving soon."

My eyes dart to the figures scurrying out of the dining room. Wren, Orroth, Dakolas, and Rolvak all give me a quick thumbs up while trying to contain their laughter, all but Rolvak. He is busy pouting and plucking leaves and twigs out of his hair. No doubt he got the hard part of my request. I saw the two out of three rounds he lost of Rock, Paper, Scissors, with the guys.

Knowing they succeeded in their tasks for tonight eases the tension in my shoulders. Tonight is going to be a great night. Nothing can go wrong.

As I turn to leave my mother's home, I hear her clipped tone, "Why are you four here? Go home and get changed. Orroth, Sweetheart, your suit is upstairs already."

The smooth taupe silk tie slips into place with one final adjustment. I've never worn this cappuccino brown, tweed, vintage suit. I never found a good reason for it, but tonight seems appropriate. Because tonight is the night I tell Davina exactly what I feel for her. Setting the pocket square in place, I readjust the solid gold monogram cufflinks before stealing a glance at Gotha.

"Are you ready to get our lady?"

She answers me with a stretch of her wings, beads of water still clinging to her from our shower. She zooms out into the kitchen faster than I've ever seen her fly. The soles of my highly polished Oxfords tap lightly with each step. A blip of yellow light and smoke fills the kitchen.

"She couldn't even wait for me."

Nerves try to settle in, but I force them away and out of my mind grabbing a large, plush teddy bear.

"It's just Davina. Nothing to be nervous about."

Knowing she's waiting for me, I enter the kitchen and pass through the silver of magic that separates and connects us.

I was wrong. I was so very wrong. My feet refuse to move while my eyes forgot how to blink.

Standing in the middle of the lush green grass surrounded by over-flowing terracotta pots of pink flowers is a sculpture come to life. Davina looks as though she was dipped in liquid bronze and it's dripping down her body. Each crystal sparkles in the waning orange light appearing like drops of dew. Her hair is in soft waves pinned off to one side showcasing her long, elegant neck where the necklace I bought her teases the valley just above her breast.

Who is this creature? Where did my loungewear loving Davina go?

I am woefully unprepared for a night of Davina on my arm.

"Gotha, those marionberries aren't ready yet." Her soft and teasing admonishment jolts my feet to move again.

"I must say," I prowl closer to her conjuring the white teddy bear out from thin air, "You are enchanting, Davina."

She gasps, "How did you do that?"

It didn't really come from thin air. I had left in the kitchen and did a simple demon magic spell. Orroth is the best at it, between the two of us, he can pull items from across the manor, while I can manage them a few feet apart. *There so much more I can do.*

I remember her saying one time over our daily tea, "flowers are overrated and presumptuous. The guy is assuming she doesn't have allergies. Assuming she even *likes* flowers. Plus, she has to find a vase, if she even has one, cut the flowers, and arrange them. That's if she doesn't have to lug them around all night or risk them wilting in the car." Her hands waved animatedly around her, and I had a sneaking suspicion all those had happened to her in the past.

She needs to see I'm not like those *boys*. I'm a *man* who pays attention to her and will do anything to make her happy.

"And you, Mendax." She looks at me from under her lashes, snuggling the bear closer to her chest.

I'm jealous of a stuffed bear. I want to be pressed against her inhaling her perfume, enjoying the softness of her skin.

"You are quite the charmer." Her hand presses against my chest. "You know, you'll have to show me whatever else you can do, right? This entire time you've been holding out on me."

The solar lanterns begin to flicker on, casting shadows of moons and stars along the grass.

"I have a lifetime of things to show you." Instinctively, my fingers wrap around hers before the soft smooth sink of her knuckles press against my lips. "Are you ready?"

"As ready as I'll ever be, Hunny Buns." Davina's hand taps my chest twice before walking toward the backdoor with an extra swing in her hips.

There was no way I could fight the incredulous laughter flying from my lips. "Hunny buns?"

A playful smile quirks her lips as she gazes at me from over her shoulder.

"Get used to it. I have more, too."

She laughs as Gotha flies from the potted bush she was picking clean, and around her head before flying into the house.

Jogging closer, my hands itch to feel her creamy skin. Giving into temptation, my fingers curl around her shoulders. The delightful and heady scent of lavender and eucalyptus I inhale from her neck caused my mouth to water.

"I think I prefer Pookie or Pookie Bear." I smile against her neck before placing a lingering kiss on her pulse point.

Her body stiffens, and the spot I kissed beats faster.

"Are you coming?" The tone is huskier than I intend, but it conveys my feelings all the same. My brow arches while my outstretched hand waits for hers.

"Mmmhmm."

Her high-pitched hum of agreement draws a dark chuckle from my chest.

With that, I lace our fingers together and escort her up to her room, where the portal awaits.

"You promise this isn't going to screw up my body, right?" Davina's fingers constrict on mine.

"Like," Her tongue darts out to lick her bottom lip, "will my tits, pits, and naughty bits be where they're supposed to be after I step through?"

I force myself to swallow down the laughter because she doesn't need to feel like I am belittling her because I'm not. Her scrunched-up, worried face is adorable, and she's about to do something she has never done before.

Placing my index finger under her chin, I tilt her face up and wait for her eyes to drag from the corner of the room where she placed the bear on the chair to my eyes.

"I promise every single wonderful part will be exactly where it belongs. I won't let anything bad happen to you."

Her chest rises and falls as she took in a deep breath.

"Okay, Zaddy, let's do this."

I snort. "Never 'Zaddy,' please."

Gotha flies ahead of us, and I give Davina's hand a reassuring squeeze before stepping through first and tugging her behind me.

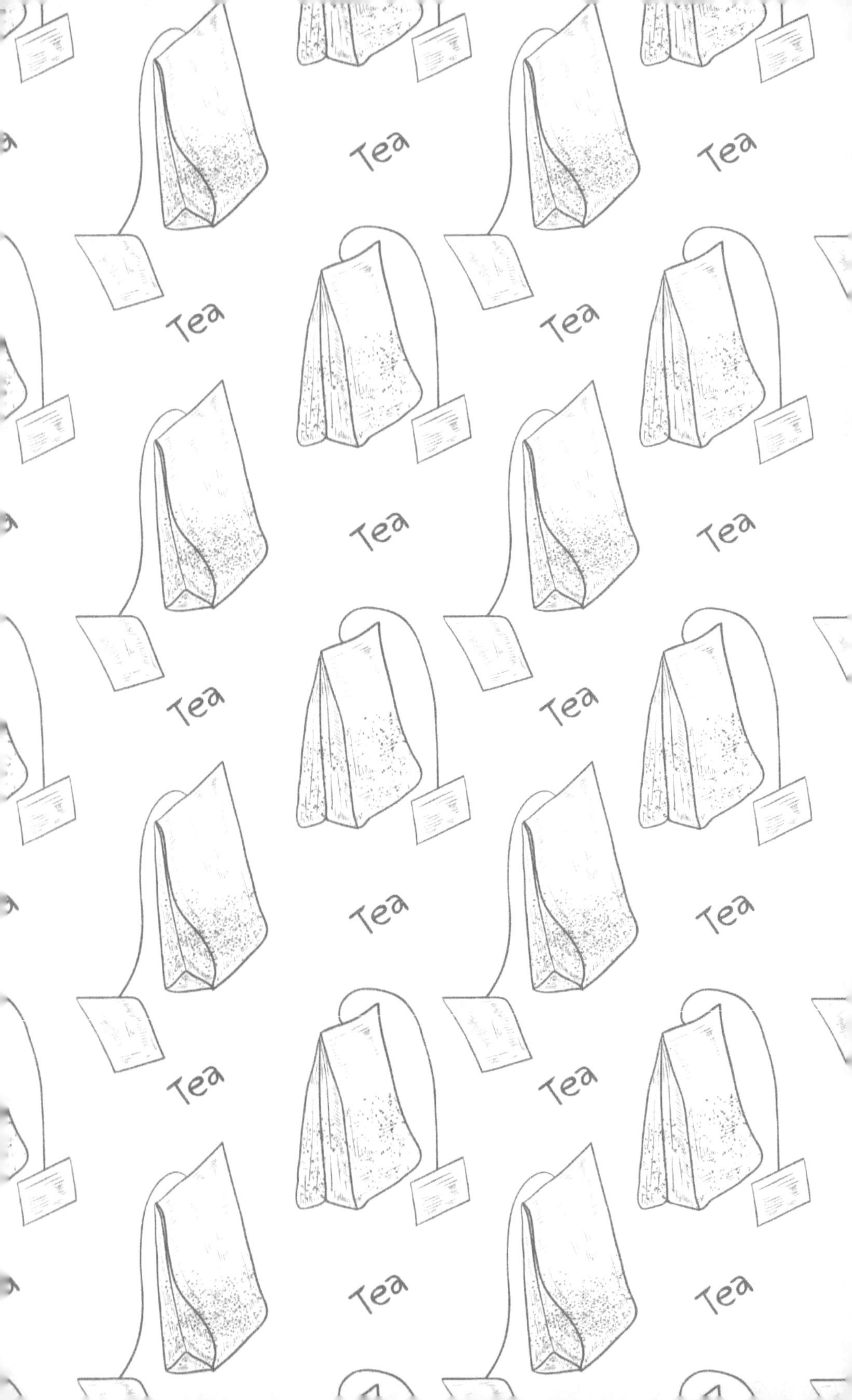

Chapter 25
AWKWARD

WHAT.

The.

Ever.

Loving.

Frick.

Was that?

This must be what every Star Trek character felt when they were beamed up. I thought my lungs were going to burst while feeling shocks and tingles in every nook and cranny in and *on* my body. Doing a cursory pat down, I inventory every limb, boob, and butt cheek.

"All accounted for?" Mendax grins, his eyes roving my body in a languid caress.

An involuntary, delicious shiver rolls down my spine in the wake of his gaze.

There are times, like now, when I wish I didn't blush so easily. It's honestly embarrassing. But to be fair, no man has ever made me blush constantly like Mendax. I just haven't built up much of an immunity to his charm yet. I should work on that.

"Yup." My fingers toy with the necklace that's beginning to glow. "You have a nice place. It's very... You"

Sharp clicking from my heels echoes against the floor as I walk out of the pantry—that's bigger than my upstairs bathroom—and into his apartment. Everything screams "masculine" and "sophistication."

How does Mendax stand to be in our—no—my home? Even *that* doesn't sound right. Our home sounds accurate, given the amount of time he spends there. There once was a time when my uncle's house resembled a mismatched hovel, but ever since Mendax came along, all the little pieces are beginning to paint a beautiful picture.

Meandering from the kitchen to the living room, I can pick out all the little pieces of art and furniture that mimic what mysteriously shows up on the front porch of the house.

It should bother me, shouldn't it? Him, embedding pieces of himself into my life. But all it does is bring comfort. All those things he's added—art, trinkets, lamps—while they all scream 'Mendax,' it's all things I love. Each piece is unique, colorful, and a bit odd, but it still carries a hint of charm and sophistication.

This man just gets me. I've never had that before.

Somehow, I've lost myself in thought and ended up in his bedroom. More precisely, the large floor-to-ceiling windows that take up the entire wall. A city of silver, gold, and bronze towers glittering with yellow and orange lights becomes a haze behind the opaque raindrops. Gotha flies out of her golden cage, and I hold my arm out for her to rest on.

"Gotha, you should have warned me I was in Mendax's room. I shouldn't be in here."

"I don't mind the sight of you in here at all." *Speak of the devil.* "This, at one point, was my sanctuary. But it hasn't been that way for a while now."

The intensity of his violet gaze causes me to squirm. If I stand this close to him any longer, he's sure to hear my heart beating against my ribs like a battering ram.

"You know what the hardest part of all this is going to be?"

He steps closer to me, so close the damp coolness of the glass wafts over my chest.

"What's that?" His voice is low enough to vibrate through me.

I roughly swallow. "Pretending that not only I've seen all there is in your world, but pretending I belong in it."

When did it become so hard to focus when he stands this close to me?

A panty melting grin pulls at his lips. Normally, I see the charming or playful grins and smiles from Mendax, but never this kind.

"Oh, Davina. I'll keep waiting until you see it."

"See what?"

"Where it is you truly belong."

Without saying another word, he takes a place behind me with his hand resting lightly on my hip. It isn't curled in possessiveness or anything of the sort. The way his hand fits on my hip, well, I don't think there's a word for it. Until I can understand what it is, I'll just enjoy it. Whatever this is, it feels right.

"The car should be here in a few minutes. Do you have everything you need?" Mendax asks.

I'm digging out my eye drops and cursing at myself about making the stupid choice of contacts for tonight. As I tilt my head back, Gotha flies right into my hair. Her small, sharp talons hook into the crystal hairpins, yanking one out.

"You're a menace, Gotha. You're lucky you're cute." I have to remind myself to take deep breaths. "Do you have a brush I can borrow?"

"For heaven's sake, Gotha, she'll be back tonight."

He snatches the pin back from her, trying to control his laughter.

"It's her insurance policy to make sure you come back. She hasn't done that in ages." Mendax passes me the hairpin. "There's a brush and some hair products on my bathroom counter. Use whatever you need."

He presses his lips to my forehead, and I say goodbye to a few brain cells.

Heading into the bathroom, I hear the doorbell ring.

"Shit, the car service is here early."

The stiff bristle brush tames the last of my yellow waves back in place.

"Mendax," a breathy female voice flits in from the living room, "you look incredibly handsome."

"Elara. You look…You're here. What are you doing here?"

Was he going to compliment her? That shouldn't bother me. I'm a grown woman who has never been the jealous, territorial, or insecure type in my life. Why do I feel that way now?

Mental note:

- I *really* need to find a new therapist.

Slowly, I tiptoe out of the bathroom and wait just inside the bedroom.

"God, why am I being so weird right now?"

"Well, it's one of our dates, isn't it? Megai said you would be here. I had my driver leave me here so we can arrive together."

Damn, that's bold. If I wasn't dating—*fake* dating—Mendax, I would applaud the boss move. But this ain't that.

Nerves were beginning to dog pile on each other. For the first time in a long while, I was feeling out of my depth. My mind plays every risk variable equation and comes up with negative results. This is either going to go astoundingly well or so wrong it'll be a legend. But Mother Dearest didn't raise no bitch, so I'm going to do my damnedest and make sure it goes well.

Over my dead body, will another woman get Mendax.

My fingers find my phone in the small clutch. I quickly find the group chat and start typing.

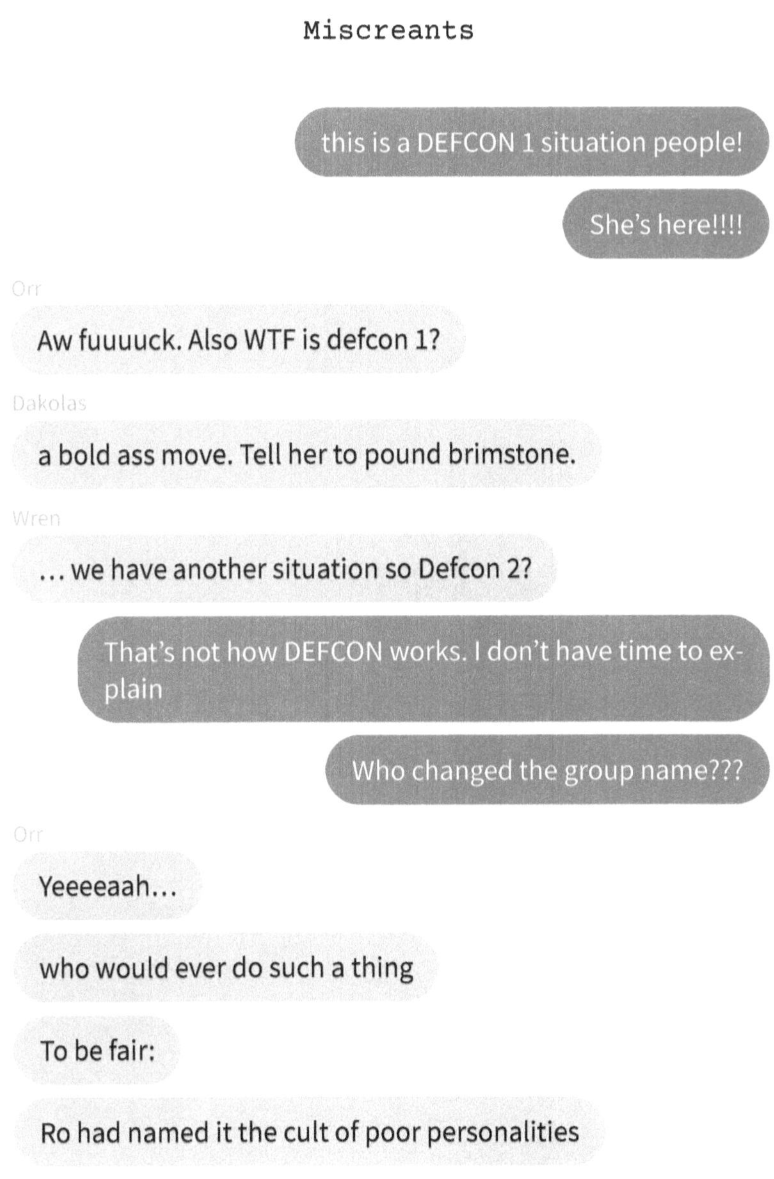

Dak named it Chucklefuckers

Wren had reasons I drink

You still havent renamed it

If you ever see "Assholes Anonymous" as the group name, it's me

Rolvak

...umm any way

.... Wren and I found some shit out. But don't worry.

Dakolas

Don't say don't worry.

she's going to worry even more

Orr

how did you two find stuff out before me? I'm still at home.

Wren

I added some stuff to really amp up the special request

What special request?

Orr

Not important

Dakolas

I'll intercept the lady.

Rolvak

Yeah do that and I'll help play interference for the night

cause woo mama!!! you're gonna need it.

You guys aren't helping my nerves.

I can feel the stress hives trying to take center stage of chest

*on my chest. I hate auto correct. it wasn't even correct.

Orr

LOL

Rolvak

Don't blame auto correct. You're nervous and fat fingered

Dakolas

Duys leave her alone. Davina breathe

*Guys.

Shut up both of you

Wren

BACK TO DAVINA

Think of the toughest bitch you know Davina. And pretend to be her or act like her. You got this!

yeah, i got this

I don't got this, and I can feel the itch of the stress rash looming under my skin.

The toughest bitch? Like mean bitch or bad bitch? I'm horrible at playing a bitch.

Shoving my phone back into my purse, I try to push aside whatever situation lies ahead. The toughest bitch I know? Pulling my shoulders back and raising my chin, I pull up every memory of etiquette and pageant classes that taught me how to walk in heels like I was made for the runway. Time to channel, Mother Dearest. *Fake it til I make it, right?*

"Mendax, I'm all sorted again," I say with a giggle, stopping as I reach him. His back is ramrod straight; Elara is standing to his left.

"I don't think we've met before. I'm Davina. Who are you?" I ask, putting on my best smile.

Chessus, this woman is gorgeous. I can't help but notice how they look good together, and it pisses me off. She's not nearly as tall, but certainly taller than my 5'7" self. I am glad for one thing. The floor-length black dress she's wearing, with long billow sleeves and a high neckline, covers all her curves, which is saying something because I can still see how she has an hourglass figure to die for.

"You're Davina?" Her eyes bounce all around me, scanning me, looking for an imperfection.

If she looks any harder, she'll see the tiny scar on my forehead from when I fell from my tree house in 3rd grade. Or maybe she'll notice the raised, faded scar under my right knee from when I got kicked with metal cleats during the championship game in 12th grade.

Clearing my throat, I offer a small laugh before looping my arm through Mendax's and giving him a soft squeeze that drains the tension from his shoulders. He looks down at me, and a slow smile grows on his face before he pulls me closer.

"Davina, this is Elara," Mendax finishes the introduction.

My mouth forms a little "o" like I'm just now putting the pieces together.

"Elara, you remember me telling you about my beautiful girlfriend." He drives the point home with a kiss on my forehead.

Well, there goes some more common sense because I actually believe him. He's going to leave me stupid and heartbroken. I just know it.

"Elara was stopping by, hoping to get a ride to the party tonight. It seems her driver left without confirmation."

"That's terrible," I say, looking right at her.

I feel like a total bitch right now, but I have to keep reminding myself that I'm doing this for Mendax. There is zero selfishness involved. *Nope, there's not an iota of selfishness in this right now.*

"It was actually meant to be our date night," she says, pulling at her collar. "This is a rather uncomfortable situation."

"'Uncomfortable' is thinking you can date a man who's spoken for." I have no idea when I sharpened my claws and tongue, but I'm rolling with it.

"But, still, *we* have manners. I don't see why we can't all pile into the car."

I stare up at Mendax with a loving smile and gaze. There's a different look on his entire face now. If I didn't know any better, I'd say he was turned on.

"Now we can all be uncomfortable and awkward together."

Chapter 26
Surprise
Mendax

I DON'T KNOW WHO this new Davina is, but it would be a lie if I said I wasn't extremely turned on.

Unfortunately, the car ride to my mother's house snuffed out any flames of desire. Elara did try to play a power move and slid into the back seat, offering Davina the passenger seat next to the driver. Before I could say or do anything, Davina waved off the thought, stating it was a good thing she was tiny so she could fit in the middle of the seat. And that's exactly what she did.

I slide in next to her. There was obviously no chance she was going to allow Elara to sit anywhere near me. There was also zero chance I would miss an opportunity to have Davina pressed against me.

Skyscrapers and high-rises whiz by the car window as we get further out of the city. Davina's knee knocks into my thigh as her leg bounces a mile a minute. Stealing a glance at her, it isn't nerves that have her leg going; she's trying her hardest to contain her excitement. Her eyes are wide with wonder as she takes in all that is my world. I'm not sure how long we are into the drive, but I've abandoned all sight of the window, leaning back more so Davina can witness it all. The true wonder and sight to behold is her and the joy glinting in her eyes.

Elara's body is angled and crammed into the corner seat. Her fingers fly furiously over her phone, barely allowing it to buzz in response.

"So, how does this work now?" Her yellow eyes glance over towards me.

My eyes go back to Davina who is now staring at me. Those eyes say so much without giving much away. She's basically tagging me in to handle this one since she rescued me from the blunder of an introduction earlier.

"Care to elaborate?"

"Well, we—you and I," her eyes darted to Davina, then back to me, "should be walking in together." Elara's voice is raised in pitch and the car is beginning to slow.

The cobblestone noise of the city shifts to the crunch of onyx brimstone beneath the tires. Home sweet hellish-home is around the corner.

One of Davina's unfiltered thoughts makes its appearance. "Really laying the awkward and uncomfy vibes on thick, huh?"

Her teeth dig into her bottom lip in an attempt to cage more thoughts that are undoubtedly tumbling free.

Her fingers press into my leg before rubbing up and down. My body responds immediately and in the best possible way, but in the worst possible situation. She's so focused on fighting her thoughts she inadvertently skims the side of my balls and cock, which causes him to stir to life. To make matters worse, Elara is still imploring me to give her an answer with her gaze.

If someone had told me months ago, this would be life: fake dating the woman of my dreams to get out of an arranged marriage with a woman I have no interest in while being stuck in a car together; well, I would have laughed until my sides hurt.

Gently, I curl my hand around Davina's and bring the tip of her fingers up to my lips. I watch her breath hitch, and she's pulled back into the present next to me. Kissing each of her individual fingertips not only gives me an excuse to show more affection but also buys me time to think.

I could do the gentlemanly thing and escort both of them in, one on each arm. But, as I toss the idea around, I swear Davina knows exactly what I'm about to say because if looks could kill, I'd be as good as dead right now.

She sheaths her daggered stare before morphing it into a pleasant smile and turning towards Elara. "Lucky for you, part of my job is thinking up worse-case scenarios. I have already sorted out someone to escort you. You don't want the gossip and unflattering comments of walking in on the arm of someone else's boyfriend, am I right?"

When the hell did she sort this out? Before I can ask *who* she picked, the car comes to a gentle stop. The door swings open automatically before Elara can get a word out. Never in my life have I been happier to see Dakolas standing on the bottom step. He looks put together in a tailored all-black suit, enhancing his deep green skin tone and light brown hair. His strides are long, sure, but the way he pushes his glasses twice up the bridge of his nose seems more like a tick than a necessity considering they aren't even sliding down. *I didn't even know he wore glasses.*

I step out first, holding my hand out for Davina. Her hand slips into mine perfectly. A low whistle from Dakolas clenches my jaw.

"Woo, Da-vi-na! You look—" He bites his lip and wags his thick brows, which causes her to purse her lips. "You gotta admit, that was a better reaction than that Blake dude."

I had almost, almost forgotten about him. Almost.

"Where are your glasses? I wore mine so we could match."

"Rolvak, I didn't spend hours doing my eye makeup to hide it behind my giant glasses." Her arm waves away his comment but there's a small grin on her face.

"Why are you here? I thought your brother was escorting Elara?"

Rolvak? How does she tell them apart so easily?

"Dad called him some kind of last-minute business contract. All I know is I'm happy I get the tech company from Mom." His low, gravelly voice rumbles as he whispers the last part.

It's amusing how Davina thinks she doesn't belong here; she was made to be here. She looks like she's always been here.

"Let me introduce you to Elara." Davina's flawless segue back to why he's here draws all eyes to the woman who, despite being born here, looks more out of place than anyone.

Rolvak shifts from foot to foot while rubbing the back of his neck. "Just so we're clear. My money is on Menvina."

Confusion paints Davina's face. "Who or what is Menvina?"

Fixing his tie, he smirks. "Mendax plus Davina equals Menvina. It's your guys' couple name." With a hearty laugh he walks between us and offers his hand to Elara.

"You look uncomfortable. Allow me to show you to the open bar."

Tucking her hand in his elbow, he drags her away while she steals backward glances at me.

"We're not being called 'Menvina,'" I state with finality.

"What's wrong with Menvina?" Davina's laugh is a balm for my soul. "We could put it on t-shirts and stickers."

"Did you hear the way it sounded? It's terrible and hardly creative."

Her hand rests in the crook of my arm. "Naming babies with you is going to be interesting."

The statement takes us both by surprise. While her face is burning with embarrassment, there's a flutter of hope and excitement in me. There's no way in hell she meant to say that out loud and the way her teeth embed into her lip tells me I'm right.

I smile at her and hook my finger under her chin, forcing her to look at me. "As long as it's not *Menvina*, I can be reasonable."

"Okay." It's all the response she manages to squeak out.

Bending, I kiss her temple, and she releases a sigh. We don't say anything else as we walk up the path. The *carpeted* path. *That's new. There wasn't any carpet when I left.*

Stepping through the entryway, everything has been transformed into something grander than a simple business dinner.

"Mendax, this isn't a simple dinner." Davina's nails digging into my arm emphasizes her statement and our shared shock. "This is a full-blown party."

"I promise, I had no idea about this. I'm as surprised as you are."

A sharp voice I know all too well, cuts in from behind. "Well, it's a night full of surprises then, isn't it?"

Oh hell. It's my mother.

Gripping Davina and pulling her tighter towards me, I lead her away from Megai and into the crowd of mingling guests. *So much for a networking dinner.* Mother's voice fades with every step not only because we're further into the fray, but mostly because of the white noise rushing in my ears. The stares we get as we walk fill me with pride making me want to pound my chest like some kind of uncultured little boy.

"Mendax, that was rude," Davina whispers. "Can you slow down? I have little legs compared to you."

Shit, I'm messing this up already.

There's a server with a platter filled with drinks. My hand plucks two off, handing one to Davina, whose beautiful face tilts up, pinning me with a narrowed gaze.

The cool glass presses under each pad of my thumb as I try to collect myself.

"You know those final boss battles in those games you play?"

She nods, her lips quirking up in the corners.

"My mother is the final boss."

I look back toward where I think she's lying in wait like a jaguar waiting to pounce. A gentle hand rests on my biceps before her fingers rub back and forth against my jacket.

"Okay, mini bosses first." She clinks her glass against mine with a smile. "Let's down some mana then."

The glass tilts up and I watch in horror as Davina downs it in one gulp.

"God, it's like I swallowed the entire Macy's perfume department."

Oh, I fucked up. I fucked up big time.

The drink I gave her wasn't meant for humans; it's only meant for demons. Oh hell. Giggles erupt from her perfectly painted red lips. Her eyes widen as she slaps a hand over her mouth.

More giggles erupted and a breathtaking smile broke across her face.

"Oh, look at the butterflies. The neon streaks behind them are amazing."

Food, I need to get her food. *Damnit, why is there only tiny food here?*

"Davina, my darling, princess. Don't tell anyone you see those wonderful butterflies."

Snagging the first food item I can find, I push the tiny meat skewer to her lips and watch her chew. If feeding her is what my night entails until it is time for my surprise, I'll call tonight a success. Unfortunately, an older couple is approaching us. I recognized them as the Lyraeths. If old money had a picture in a dictionary, it would be theirs.

Mrs. Lyraeth is a short, portly old woman who wears jewelry like it is going out of style. Her teal skin turning ruddy gives away how many glasses of the same drink Davina drank she has already downed. I shake one of her husband's four hands while Davina looks on wide-eyed. I can practically hear the thoughts buzzing in her head, and I can't even blame her. I would probably have the same reaction if it was the first time seven eyes were staring back at me from only two faces. I should have prepped her more. But leave it to Davina to do exactly what I asked of her: Pretend to be my girlfriend.

She smiles and nods and clings to my arm like a dotting girlfriend. She even laughs at the horrible jokes Mr. Lyraeth tells—that could be the alcohol still in her system. This older couple prattle on, and Davina shoves more meat skewers in her mouth to stop anything she feels as an unfiltered thought from breaking free.

"I remember the first time Valen here brought me to one of these. It seems like eons ago. I was a nervous wreck and drank entirely too much to calm the nerves."

Looks like *that* hasn't changed. In that moment, Davina hiccups three times in a row. The drink is finally wearing off.

"Sorry about that; I hiccup when I get hungry. This bite-size food, while delicious, doesn't seem to be enough." She hiccups again. "Did you know in human folklore, it's said when you hiccup someone is talking about you or missing you? Then, to get rid of the offending hiccup, you should go through a mental list of everyone you know. When the hiccups stop, whoever you thought of last is the person responsible. Of course, now we know they go away when you aren't focused on them because our breathing goes back to normal." Her brows furrowed, and her teeth once again cage her bottom lip.

The elderly couple glance at each other and laugh before Mrs. Lyraeth speaks, "Mendax, she's absolutely the opposite of you, which means she's perfect. It's so wonderful. Maybe Davina will finally liven you up some. You were always such a serious boy growing up." She pats my cheek, at least she tries to. It is more of her fingertips skimming my jaw through my beard.

Her husband presses his hand to the small of his wife's back and clears his throat.

"Here comes your mother. We'll leave you to it."

"There you are." The sharpness of my mother's tone cuts through what was a pleasant atmosphere.

I turn to look at her, pulling Davina even closer. My hand wraps possessively around her hip. The surprises don't stop coming.

Chapter 27
MINGLE & MAGIC
Davina

WELL, THIS KEEPS GETTING better and better. My emotions are running a marathon, and I'm not sure who will win. Will the gold medal go to embarrassment, jealousy, guilt, nervousness? My head is still a bit foggy from the drink, too. It's cool, though, I can push past it. I just need to channel my 22-year-old self who could ace a test with a hangover the next morning and win a soccer match that night.

One thing for sure is that the bronze is going to go to happiness. I feel like a steaming pile of dog crap for how I treated Elara because that was *not* female solidarity. But I have to remind myself I'm doing this for Mendax. He doesn't want to be with her. That's why I agreed to pretend. This is pretend.

Even I don't believe the lie anymore. This is very much real. I don't want Mendax with her; I want Mendax with me. *Apparently, I wanted to have his babies, too.* I'm still dying inside from that blunder. Now I'm facing the full fury that is Mendax's mother and the angry, throbbing vein in her forehead. All I have to do to survive this night is remember what Wren said: be the toughest bitch I know. So, I'm going to be a mini-Paloma; too bad she isn't here to witness it. She would be thrilled.

"Mother, I'd like you to meet Davina," Mendax begins, "my girlfriend. Also, the love of my life."

He's staring down at me with a look I don't dare define because it's giving me mixed signals. He either actually means that, or this demon deserves an Oscar.

"Davina, meet my mother Megai."

Her baby-pink eyes scan me from head to toe. Yearly gynecologist visits don't leave me feeling this exposed. Putting on my best smile, the same one worn during initial client meetings, I acknowledge her.

"It's a pleasure to meet you. You did an exceptional job raising this gentleman." I stare up at Mendax with a smile that grows a little wider as has hand skims from my lower back to rest on the curve of my hip.

"Of course, I did. I taught him to be exceptional." Her leer switches from my face down to his hand and back to Mendax. There's a sudden stiffness in her upper lip. "I also taught him to strive for more than mediocrity."

Wooooow. Okay. She wants gloves off? Fine by me.

"Well, isn't it wonderful he knows what he wants and isn't forced to settle for less than exceptional?"

Round one of what now feels like a cage match is a split decision. We've both drawn blood.

"Don't pull your punches, Vi!"

What the fuck?! Why am I hearing Orroth? I must be going crazy if my inner hype-women sounds like Orr.

A series of different laughters fill my head, and I know those voices, but they aren't anywhere near me.

"Don't take it personally. She likes me even less."

Now I'm hearing Wren. I knew going through that portal was going to mess something up.

"My brains are scrambled eggs now, but at least my tits and bits are in place."

A bark of laughter and snorts whips my head to the right, where my group of friends are gathered around a large abstract painting.

"You guys are asshats," Wren chides, fighting the laughter in her voice. *"The earring."*

A perfectly manicured finger taps her ear, showing another earring that looks like what I am wearing.

"We can hear what you think, and you can hear us. Pretty cool, right?"

They all turn their heads, showing off the earrings.

Rolvak quirks his brow. *"My latest gadget."*

"You could have told me earlier, you asshole."

"That's no fun, Davina. Oh, and Megai is looking at you weird," Dakolas says full of amusement.

I'm going to kick to their shins when I get a chance.

"I'm sorry, Orroth was trying to get my attention. You were saying?"

Megai runs her fingers across the string of pearls, trying her best not to look flustered.

"Mendax, I need to speak with you now. In private."

With a quick kiss on my cheek, he excuses himself from my side, promising to be back soon. This must be what those gazelles feel that I always cheer for on nature documentaries before the lion's attack.

"Safety in numbers?" I look over to my group of friends.

Orr opens his arms to me with a slight tilt of his chin. *"We got you, Vi."*

I don't know how long I've been here, and I've lost track of where Mendax is. What I do know is that there have been eighteen nods in agreement and a few "Oh, really" and "Wow, that's fascinating" thrown into the conversation between myself, Dakolas, Rolvak, and a portly man with grey iridescent skin and deep brown hair. I really can't remember his name for the life of me, and I know it's rude.

"You look like you need to use the bathroom, Davina," chuckles Dakolas in my head.

"You try standing in these heels. I'm also starving," I think back. It's best not to say I'm still seeing the occasional neon butterfly.

The portly man speaks, interrupting our mental discussion. "So, tell me, Davina. What is it you said you do in the human realm again?" His deep timbre booms with curiosity.

Rolvak snatches what looks like a finger sandwich from a passing silver tray and passes it to me with a wink.

"You get hangry and then you get scary. We need a nice Davina tonight."

Taking the food graciously, I smile at the man. "Risk analysis. It's woven into the consulting firm. I basically run programs with different values and variables, with a few other statistics thrown in to determine if something would be worth the risk or not, given various factors and trends. At least that's the *main* function of my role at the consulting and marketing firm."

"I'm assuming this only works for a certain type of clientele?"

Stifling a laugh, I bring up a childhood memory. "You know, my father, Rick, would always say, 'Davina, when you assume you make an ass out of you and me.'"

Silence hangs heavy around us. I think I might have put my foot in my mouth. Laughter explodes the stillness.

"I'll have to use that line. My grandchildren will detest it." He downs a pink drink, which has a plume of steam swirling around the glass.

"So, this can be used for any kind of decision?" He pushes a similar drink towards me.

Chuckling awkwardly, my fingers wrap around the warm tumbler. There's not a chance in hell I'm drinking this but to keep up appearances and not be rude, I'll hold it.

"To answer your question," I begin hoping to make a good impression on the now-forming crowd around us, "any and all can benefit from my line of work. I've worked with celebrities, companies both big and small, influencers, charities, and the list goes on. It can be used to weigh out the risk factors and help make decisions. Numbers aren't yes-men; they're pure facts."

It's times like now when my mother's favorite saying comes to mind. *"Just when I think everything is going well, the devil knocks me down a peg or two."*

The devil, this time, isn't wearing a suit and tie, no, no. That would be a welcomed sight.

"Where is Mendax?"

This time, it's a pair of she-devils known as Megai and Elara. I swear I saw the duo emerge from a haze of sulfur fog.

"I swear I'm looking, Vi!"

"Orr, I can already tell you he isn't in the tray of food you've been guarding." Dakolas chimes in.

The sharp clicking of heels abruptly stopped next to me. An eerie sensation creeps over me as the hairs on the back of my neck stand up and a chilling shiver courses through my spine. With a swift turn of my head to the left, I come face to face with the dream-crushing duo, and it's Mendax's mother who greets me with a snide look. I appraise her with a critical gaze, scrutinizing her from head to toe as she aimes her disapproval in my direction.

"Tell me, Davina, did you run a risk analysis for dating Mendax, considering how different the two of you are?"

This is one of those moments where I'm self-aware enough to catch the jailbreaking thoughts.

"This is not the time to roll my eyes. This is not the time to roll my eyes. This is not the time to roll my eyes."

"I dare you to roll your eyes," Dakolas chuckles, slipping the warm glass tumbler out of my hand. He winks before sipping it.

Plastering on a pageant smile I wave her insinuation away. "Why would I do that? Risk analysis is mainly for things you aren't certain of. For starters, Mendax isn't a *thing* to be played around with; he's a *man* who is important to *me* and who has *feelings* that aren't meant to be toyed with. Secondly,—" Elara squirms, pulling the collar to her dress, "there are many things in my life I'm hesitant or unsure about, but being with Mendax is not one. If anything, he helps my world make sense. So no, Megai, I didn't run an analysis on our relationship."

"You can feel free to call me 'Mrs. Draxton.'"

"And you can call me 'Ms. Myles.' I love to address people with the same of level of respect awarded to me."

"Ms. Myles for now," Rolvak whispers leaning closer to me.

At the mere suggestion that there might be a future together with Mendax, my breath catches in my throat.

"Go Menvina!"

Dakolas clears his throat, thrumming his fingers on the side of the crystal tumbler, now filled with shimmering blue liquid. "I can't wait till you force him to write vows because that was beautiful."

The small crowd around us chuckles and whispers words of weddings and which realm it would be in—everyone except for a pissed-off Megai and Elara, who looks like she wants the ground to swallow her whole.

Maybe I'm selling this relationship *too* well because marriage is a big step from a pretend girlfriend.

The iridescent man speaks again, addressing Megai, "I must say if this is who Mendax has his eye on, he's one lucky man."

"Can I record you saying that so I can play it back and remind him?" I laugh, trying to ease the tension around us.

"I won't make any official statements just yet, not when there could be a risk involved." He eyes me curiously, and a smile forms on his face. "Well, if you happen to take on new clients—" His hand flourished around, and a cloud of fuchsia floats above his palm before a business card surfaces, "I know myself and a few other corporations who could use your services."

"Magic is so freaking cool."

More laughter follows, and my cheeks grow five degrees hotter.

"Was that meant to be an inside thought?"

"Shut up, Rolvak."

I've been passed around like a hot potato for about two hours between my friends, and I still haven't seen Mendax. Seeing all these beautiful people makes me feel like I'm lacking in appearance. I'd rather be anywhere else than here—anywhere, like my couch in a pair of comfy pajamas. It's late; I'm getting too old for this. On the bright side, I've managed to mingle with the elite and build up a healthy potential clientele if I ever want to start my own consulting firm in this realm.

There also has been no shortage of magic to entertain me once word got out that Mendax's girlfriend loves seeing it.

One woman, who was closing in on 400 years old, affectionately patted my hand and said, "It's so nice and refreshing to see authentic people enjoying the little things."

She then proceeded to conjure a champagne flute for me and waltz off. I'm still not entirely convinced her feet touched the ground.

"DEFCON 3! DEFCON 3 IS HAPPENING!" Wren screeches, causing me to wince.

"That's not how DEFCON works. But what's happening? Orr, where's your brother? I can't exactly keep selling 'us' when 'we' aren't together."

"Don't freak out," Orr mumbles.

"Dude, that's how you get ladies to freak out," Dakolas chimes in with his casually cool wisdom.

I gotta say, he isn't wrong. I am very much freaking out right now.

"I swear I tried running interference. Megai is fast, scary, and on the warpath. She grabbed Elara, and they're locked up in the office where Mendax has been all night," Rolvak sounds defeated, which causes my heart to clench. *"Oh yeah, I found Mendax, by the way."*

"Your timing is impeccable." I groan before picking up what I think is a mini quiche.

A rumbling sound from the flaky pastry surfaces before a plume of hot steam puffs in my face.

"Oh God. The quiche farted in my face."

Orroth, Rolvak, and Dakolas erupt in a fit of laughter from across the room. Each leaning on the other, they draw attention to themselves, but they couldn't care less. They are lost in laughter at my expense.

Wren whispers, *"Babes, DEFCON 1 was Elara showing up at Mendax's place. DEFCON 2 was the sudden change from a small dinner to a giant party. Davina, DEFCON 3 is now. This is an engagement party. Their engagement party. She's forcing Mendax to put the family ring on Elara."*

Oh. Hell. No.

My hand flies to the necklace he gave me, pushing it into my skin. Maybe if I press hard enough, I can keep my heart from breaking.

Chapter 28
caT BurGLar
Mendax

M Y FATHER WOULD TELL me, "A man is only as good as his word," which, right now, would mean I'm less than honorable. I promised Davina I wouldn't be long, but my mother made a liar out of me.

When had she found the time to enchant the room so I couldn't escape or muffle it from the outside?

The tie around my neck feels like a noose. No matter how much I loosen it, it seems to only get tighter. My frustration is at a fever pitch. The material coils around my fist, strangling my fingers before I yank the silk noose out of my collar. It flits across the room before landing in a puddle next to an armchair. The top two wooden buttons are the next to be undone. A lock of hair falls into my eyes as I pace the length of the bookcase wall. I've lost track of how many times I have run my fingers through my hair.

What was happening out there? Did she notice I was gone? Was she alone? Are our friends keeping the wolves of our society at bay?

I don't trust Orroth to do much; knowing him, he's probably shoving his face full of food. Wren, I can trust, I like her but she's probably busy wrangling the man-child I know as my brother. Dakolas and Rolvak, I'm still undecided about, but I can only give them the benefit of the doubt, seeing as one of them came to her rescue after the car fiasco.

As more thoughts begin to spiral, the door chimes with magic warnings and swings open. My mother and Elara saunter in. Dakolas…wait, no, Rolvak, notices me and races for the door before it slams shut in his face.

"Keeping your own son prisoner is not a good look, Mother."

Megai smooths her dove-grey dress and drops a small wooden box on the table. The thud of it sinks my heart like a stone.

I know that box; I have avoided that tiny box my entire life.

"You're not a prisoner. Think of it more like timeout while you come to your senses," my mother says as she sinks into a high-back white leather chair. "I mean honestly, Mendax. After all your father and I have done for you and this family, I understand you took the fall and the brunt of the punishment, but you are the eldest, and it's your responsibility to take care of your brother."

She raises her hand sharply, stopping me from interrupting. "Now let me do my job as a mother. I can help you out of this mess and restore your image before the damage is permanent. How do you expect to take over the business if your reputation is tarnished. It'll be completely ruined if you keep parading around that, that, human."

"Davina." My voice comes out low and sharp. "Her name is Davina."

Elara is busy fidgeting off to the side of the desk. In a way, I feel bad for her. She's stuck in the crosshairs of this situation, but a larger part of me feels no mercy towards her. She could have said no and let it go, and we both would have been on our merry way. Elara may not be as horrible as my mother, but she can stand there being uncomfortable and compliant to this madness.

Megai slowly stands; the desk creaks under the weight of her palms.

"Elara is good for you and your image. Her father has connections and can have your sentence revoked and removed from all records. Think about it logically. You both are adults, from the same realm, both enjoy art, and are both sensible. You never gave her a fair chance! Arrangements aren't a bad thing. It happens all the time with families like ours."

This is what humans must mean when they say a person is batshit crazy.

"Honestly mother, you've gone off the deep end here. You and father are an arrangement."

"Exactly my point. Look at how long we've been together!"

"That's my point exactly!" I'd have better luck getting a brick wall to understand me. "Where is he for all the events you throw, hmm? He's always off somewhere procuring another antique or oddity. You went on a cruise to try and salvage the shamble of a marriage you two have and ended up no better than before. The only good thing to come from that was Orroth. Anyone with a single eyeball can see father loves you but he isn't *in love* with you." I regret the words as soon as they fly out of my mouth, but forge on. "I need to be with someone who I am in love with and is in love with me. Wholly, eternally, maddeningly in love."

"Love doesn't happen overnight, Mendax. This isn't a fairytale, but we could work. We could grow to be in love," Elara whispers with hope gleaming in her eyes. "I'm … I'm willing to let you keep Davina as a mistress. You can see her within reason; I just don't want to know the details."

My stomach is in knots. "Would you have a lover in secret, too? That's how you want your life to look?"

"It's not like you would care. I would still expect everything out of our marriage: some intimacy, children, outings, all that. You can't have any children with her though."

I eye the damn wooden box. My mother's fingers come into view as she flicks it open. The Trielle cut alexandrite stone is nestled in the white gold prong claws of the white gold band encrusted in tiny diamonds. It is an old, ornate, and tacky ring. The family engagement ring. It looks like something Elara would wear daily, but I can't, for the life of me, picture this heavy ring on Davina's dainty hand.

I can't believe this is happening.

"Well?" My mother's voice pulls me back to the current situation.

I look at her and then at Elara. A sigh that could move mountains leaves my lungs.

There is laughter floating through the air of the party. Everyone but me seems to be in high spirits. A large meaty hand clasps my shoulder.

"Mendax! There you are," booms Alecton. His skin seems even more iridescent under this light. He swears the sheen was natural, but we all know it's cosmetic and let him have his open secret.

"I must say, Davina is absolutely marvelous. I've been keeping a very close eye on her tonight. Everyone is buzzing about her. It's awful how this isn't a party for her."

I stiffened at his tone. I shouldn't be surprised Alecton knows: he's in the business of knowing everyone's dirty secrets; it's how he's managed to run his corporation so successfully. Blackmail is business's best friend.

"If you aren't going to marry her, I'll introduce her to my son O'yan. She's the kind that would keep him on his toes. Anyway, lovely party." With that, he leaves me standing in the crowded room, and I have never felt more alone.

I need to find Davina. Cutting through the crowd and saying "hello's" and dodging small talk, I finally find Orroth and Wren.

"Dax! What happened?! Davina has been holding her own out here for hours. Why didn't you tell Mom to shove the proposal? You didn't propose did you?"

I couldn't bring myself to face the one-man inquisitorial squad.

"Wren, where is Davina?"

The glimmering gown rustles around her arms as she crosses them over her chest. "Well, after you abandoned her. I had to break the news to her that this is an engagement party. After putting in hours of work to win over the crowd, she was near tears. She felt she let you down. After helping her fix her face, I showed her out to where the surprise you wanted us to set up is. Don't worry, she still doesn't know anything."

Fuck. Me.

"Why did you tell her that? You know what? It's fine. I'll fix this. I can fix this. I have to fix this."

The pitter-patter of freshly fallen rain drips off the teal leaves of the red bark trees. Small lights have been strung about each branch and flicker to life one by one. Once the entire courtyard is lit, all the lights blinked in time with the distinct beat of my heart. It wasn't an easy enchantment, but Orroth, Wren, Dakolas, and Rolvak had pulled it off. I will forever be in their debt for this.

The sound of a soft gasp catches my attention, leading my gaze to the pond where fish glide through the water, leaving behind enchanting rainbow ripples. Davina's fingers lightly brush against the fading colors, causing her to burst into a fit of giggles.

This woman—she must be a cat burglar. Not only has she stolen my breath and heart, but she's also stolen the motion of time.

Chapter 29
Crisis and Kisses

B EING OUT HERE SURROUNDED by all these mystical-looking plants and creatures feels like what Uncle Alex described as his one and only acid trip.

"Holy Sugar Honey Iced Tea." *Was it really an acid trip or did he come here?* Maybe he came here for an early mid-life crisis.

Tonight certainly feels like the start of a midlife crisis for me, so I'm right there with ya, Uncle Alex.

It all feels like one day I was swiping left on profiles of dudes in group pictures so you couldn't tell which one was the actual guy, and the next I'm falling apart because my fake demon boyfriend is getting engaged. What the hell happened to my life?

The small fish in the pond jump in and out of the water, causing the surface to shine in rainbow ripples. Running my fingers over the water, a small giggle surfaces at the way the fish nibble each pad on my hand. Lights on the trees flicker on.

It really is beautiful here.

The burning in my eyes and the tickle on my face let me know I am beginning to cry before a tear splashes in the water. I shouldn't be crying over this. This was pretend. I was stupid to let my heart get involved. He asked me to do this as a friend. Mendax never promised me anything.

Buzzing in my crystal-encrusted clutch pulls me out of my one-woman pity party. *Damn, I get service here? Thanks Rolvak.* There are several missed texts from my family group chat that begin with encouragement and end up with Dad and Mom arguing over whether it's polite or not to call everyone here demons or not.

I want something like they have.

The newest texts are from Blake.

Blake

> I'm crossing my fingers that you haven't blocked me.

> I knocked on your door but you weren't home and I called but you didn't answer. I should probably take a hint but I want to say this before I lose my nerve.

> I'm sorry.

> Our date was super self centered on me and I was an ass. I should have paid more attention to you.

> To be honest, I haven't been on a date in close to a year.

If I stare any longer at the message, the apology will probably imprint on my retinas. Do I reply? I can't leave him on read…again. It's sweet of him to admit to his part of the date being bad.

"Damn it, Blake, your timing is crap."

> I promise you're not blocked.

> I'm out of town for the day. Maybe two. Reception sucks where I'm at. I appreciate you apologizing.

> I'm also sorry, I shouldn't have just walked out without an explanation.

Before I can put my phone away, it buzzes in my palm.

Blake

> I swear, all on me. But I appreciate you trying to make me feel better.

> If you're willing, I'd love a second date. Another chance to win you over.

Before I can reply, the bubble on the screen reappears.

Blake

> Before you say no, there's an afternoon tea type place in Portland.

> I don't know shit about tea but there's food there and I know you like tea.

> I'll give it a try if you'll give me another try.

More tears fall and I couldn't feel more idiotic than I do now. There was a research article I read once in college about how more negative decisions are made when emotionally charged. This has to be one of those moments. I'm too worked up to answer Blake.

Blowing out a hot breath and sliding the phone back into the clutch, the aqua-colored grass crunches beneath my stilettos as I shakily stand. A large shadow looms over me, drowning out the steady pulsing lights.

"Hello, Davina," Mendax's whisper feels like a scream over the silence.

Dabbing my eyes with the back of my hand, I force a smile and turn to face him.

His thick brows furrow and the grin on his lips drops. "Why are you crying?"

"Because beautiful things make me cry." I try to sound as nonchalant as possible while flourishing my hand at the teal trees with pulsing lights. The night sky shimmers while a melodic tune hums in the light, cool breeze.

"I'm glad I don't suffer the same affliction. I'd be a weeping disaster every time I look at you." The pad of his thumb wipes a lone tear before his palm rests on my neck.

I know he can feel the quickening thump of my pulse.

"Open your mouth, I want to see if you have forked tongue," I say with a teasing smile.

Mendax takes a step closer to me. The lights in the trees flashed a little brighter.

"Why are you crying, Davina?"

The hand on my neck grows hotter—or maybe that's just me.

Oh goodness, if this weren't his engagement party, tonight, right here and now, would be absolutely perfect.

"I want him to kiss me. I want Mendax."

"Then kiss him, Babes," Wren speaks in my mind.

"Menvina. Menvina. Menvina," Rolvak and Dakolas chant.

"Get your man, Vi." Orr chuckles.

I snort with laughter, hearing my friends, but this moment is something between Mendax and me. Taking the earring out and placing it in my clutch, I looked at my handsome demon from under my lashes.

"I'm crying because I have delusions of grandeur." I step away from him, instantly missing his warmth. "Anyway. This place is beautiful."

The sound of his suit and measured steps match the lights, and the sight of the trees captivates me. "It pales in comparison to you."

"Don't do that, Mendax."

"Do what?"

"Make me feel like this. I let you down." The familiar feeling of failure and uncertainty begins to coil around my heart like an angry snake. "You're getting engaged."

"You have never let me down. Every day with you, I feel like I'm on cloud nine. But you're right."

I watch intently as his fingers card through his hair, skim down to smooth his beard, and finally fix his cufflinks.

"I will be getting engaged. One day."

The steady pulse of the lights flickers faster and unsteadily. Is there a power outage happening? "What does that mean?"

Mendax holds my hand like I am the most precious item he has ever held and walks me to the courtyard with a clearing in the middle of a dense circle of trees. Spinning me in a circle, we dance while he hums a song. It sounds like the same one he hummed when we danced in the living room. His intense gaze, framed by thick lashes, bounces between my eyes and lips as he places my hand over his heart. *The lights are in rhythm with his heartbeat.*

"Mendax?" My own pulse quickens.

"I can't do this anymore, Davina."

We stop mid-sway. My lungs seized in my chest.

"I will wait an eternity for you, but I can't live a lie that long. My mother wants me to marry Elara. She wants me to give her the family ring, too."

The blood rushes in my ears, drowning out pieces of what he is saying. I force myself to listen to his retelling of Elara's offer to keep me as his dirty little secret. His violet eyes bore into mine as if he can see into my soul.

My mouth opens and closes several times, but words refused to surface. For once in my life, there isn't a single thought. Dread murdered every word I have ever learned.

His fingers trailed up and down my arms.

"Breathe, Davina."

His right hand is playing with the fingers of my left hand.

I have never wished for much with birthday candles; never had a chance to make a wish on a shooting star, but if I could make a wish now, it would be for this to be real.

"I only want you. I don't know when it happened, but somewhere during our friendship, I fell for you. I love you. I'm in love with you, my Davina." His thumb brushes back and forth across my knuckles. "When I do get engaged, it'll be to you."

The lights in the tree grow frenzied as his heart quickens. Air rushes back into me.

"We're not playing pretend anymore, are we?" My voice is barely a whisper.

He shakes his head.

"Thank God, because I'm in love with you too, Mendax."

The lights pulse faster. He closes the distance between our bodies, pulling me in. Gooseflesh erupts over my body as Mendax cups my jaw with the other hand on my waist. There is a look of adoration gleaming in his eye, I only hope I'm returning it. My fingers cling to his lapels. Our breaths mingle, each waiting to see if the other will back away.

I brush my lips hesitantly against his.

His nose nuzzles mine, and our eyes lock, sharing a small, nervous smile. Firm, plump lips press against mine, coaxing them into a heart-stopping kiss. I match his lips and moan, losing myself in him, this kiss, this moment. The lights explode into fireworks, and swirls of magic spin around them. We break apart breathless, lips swollen, cheeks flushed.

"Fireworks?"

"You said you wanted them. I was trying to be romantic. It's probably over the top, though. In my defense, I want to give you everything you desire. It can't be helped."

"You gave me fireworks," I say with a growing smile. "It's perfect."

My cheeks will surely hurt from grinning so hard. Before he can utter another word, I tug him down for another kiss.

He breaks away for a second to take his jacket off and drape it over my shoulders before he lifts me. My legs wasted no time in wrapping around his trim waist.

My Mendax, ever the gentleman. The jacket covers what would be my exposed ass and his wandering hands. It also acts as a buffer against the rough tree bark of the tree he pushes me against. His lips trails down my jaw and neck while my fingers wind in the short strands of his hair.

"Oh, Mendax," I moan.

His lips smile against my skin. "You have no idea how long I've wanted to hear my name on your lips." A hot, open-mouth kiss is placed on my throat. "It's better than I imagined."

His lips drag up my throat, chin, and land on my lips, stealing every ounce of breath in my lungs.

This moment. This kiss is absolutely everything.

Chapter 30
concede
Mendax

T HIS IS REALLY HAPPENING. The indecision to savor every inch or to rip her clothes off here and now is a battle within me.

Hearing her moan and sigh my name is better than any opera, play, or sonnet written and performed. Her soft, sweet lips glide against mine, deepening our kiss. Ripping her face away, Davina inhales a much-needed breath. I've successfully kissed off any lipstick she had, and seeing her swollen lips further aids the swelling in my pants.

My eyes travel across her face and down to her chest, where the necklace beams between us.

"Tell me what you want, Davina."

"Mendax." My name is a broken whisper, but it's not from Davina.

Looking over my shoulder, I find a crestfallen Elara interrupting a private moment. My brother and his friends run into the courtyard, all with giant apologetic smiles on their faces.

"We tried to stop her, Dax." Orr begins rubbing the back of his neck. "Fireworks drew a crowd. It's cool, though. We got everyone to see them from the front of the house."

Wren rolls her eyes. "She wouldn't listen. Already telling everyone she needs to find her fiancé, flashing that rock around."

"Wait." Davina squirms in my arms. "You gave her the ring?"

"I didn't give it to her. I swear."

Elara is still standing, rooted to the spot, while I set Davina down, helping to right her clothes. *This is not how I envisioned any of this going.* There should be no Elara or any audience. I'm glad I didn't rip the dress off like I craved.

"Elara," Davina calls her attention.

Daggers are all she gets in response.

"Don't you dare give me that look." There's a fire in my princess' eyes. "You're the one trying to take the man I love. Why? Don't you value yourself more than that? Why settle for something that isn't real? Why are you pretending to be happy being option B?" Davina's voice cracks a little towards the end. I wonder if that's how she felt during this entire charade.

There was a small tick in Elara's jaw as she looks at the family ring on her finger. She and my mother could compete for who has more audacity.

"It doesn't matter what I want," Elara bites out. "I'm doing this because I have to. I've already been passed over to take over my father's accounting firm for my step-brother. If I don't do this, I lose my inheritance, and if you don't remember," she looks directly at me. "You get a longer sentence or lose your family business, which would destroy your family image."

Orroth chuckles, wrapping his arm around Wren. "I always thought our family could use some rebranding."

Wren is another woman my mother never approved of. Even though her family is wealthy, smart, and prominent, no one would ever be good enough for her baby boy. It was some weird attachment I couldn't for the life of me understand.

"I'm not going anywhere, so I'll wait for Mendax for however long it takes," Davina's voice cuts through my thoughts. "You deserve your own happy ending. Stealing one isn't the move you think it is."

Elara eyes Davina with suspicion. "Why are you being so nice and calm about all this?"

"Being a bitch is exhausting. I could cuss you out from here to Timbuktu and back a hundred times over." Davina shrugs before walking back to me and lacing our fingers together. "But you seem like a determined woman, and maybe logic suits you better. Don't be that woman. It's so cliché. Because if there were something between you and Mendax, I would actually have to fight for my chance. Kinda like how you're trying now."

Off in the corner, I spot Dakolas tugging his brother and mine back in the direction they came. Sighing, I bend and kiss Davina softly.

"I'll be right back."

"You've said that before," she says with narrowed eyes.

Trudging closer to Elara, I smile at Davina, who toys with her fingers while watching me.

"Do you really want this marriage? Loveless and unfulfilling?"

Elara huffs and rubs her brow.

"You won't marry me, even with my offer?" Elara paces across the paved path that leads back to the house or further into the courtyard, where a small maze sits forgotten.

"You know I won't, especially with that offer. I would never hurt Davina like that. We both know this marriage would be only to clean up images."

"What if I agree to let you have a child with her? After we have one?" she folds her arms over her chest, sparing me a glance before continuing to pace.

Davina lets out a gasp and says through clenched teeth, "I think the fuck not. Do you not have any respect for yourself?"

"I stand to lose everything if I don't agree to this, Mendax."

"Or you have everything to gain. A fresh start might be good for your image. Separate and reinvent yourself," Davina speaks softly, almost as if she is merely thinking out loud.

Elara lets out a bitter laugh. "I wouldn't even know how to start."

"I could help with that," Davina says with determination. "I know a thing or two about PR and risk management. Maybe we can work something out?"

Noise from the party begins to filter outside. Elara needs to accept that a relationship between us will never happen and move on. I have plans for tonight, and they in no way shape or form involve her.

"How did you two meet? You seem so different and unlikely." Elara bites her lip, spinning the ring around her finger.

"If you ask anyone else, they'll say it was during a pub crawl." Davina smiles up at me. "But I like to think it all started over a cup of tea."

"Black tea, to be exact." I smile back fondly, recalling that night. "Black tea and a special story." My fingers skate down Davina's cheek, and every single heartstring tugs as she leans into my touch.

"I hope I can find something like what you two have." A small, sad smile grows on Elara's face.

"Maybe you need someone unlikely, too." Davina smiles.

Without another word, Elara turns on her heel and walks back towards the house.

"Does that mean there's no engagement?" Davina whispers.

I look down at her. "Are you sad or suspicious?"

"I mean, I feel bad for her. She's a pawn in a terrible game. But—" she turns that doe-eyed gaze up at me. "—She didn't give you the ring back."

"I don't care about the ring. My mother gave it to her, not me. When I do propose to you, it won't be with that tainted rock."

Before Davina can say anything else, I bend down and kiss her again.

"I care about you." Another kiss. "I only want you." I kiss her again. "I will only ever love you."

The party is in full swing, but whispers follow us as we make our way through the crowd. My brother gives me a knowing smirk before pulling Wren to dance in the middle of the floor. Dakolas and Rolvak are off, charming a group of women.

My mother wears a scowl that could scare away a murderer in a dark alley. The staccato clicking from her heels swallows the chatter and music as she storms up to us, cutting off our exit.

"Mendax, you need to think about what you're doing," Megai whispers harshly. "Elara looked so heartbroken. And for what?"

Her tight smile is all she offers to those who venture closer to us. Her hand darts out, wrapping her fingers in an iron grip around my arm.

"She's good for you. Good for our *family*. Please don't do this. Really think about what you are giving up."

"I have thought about it, Mother. I've decided the woman I want is Davina. Davina has the heart I care about. She is who is good for me. As for our family, I've done more than enough. You need to decide, as well; if you care about me, you'll figure this out and actually be a mother to me."

She looks at me with glassy eyes. Maybe behind that sheen, she is replaying the lack of a part she and my father had in my upbringing. My entire childhood was filled with a revolving door of nannies and tutors. At least she had a vested interest in who taught Orroth.

Turning away from my mother, I frame Davina's face in my hands.

"Are you ready to go, Darling?"

"Pookie, I've *been* ready. But you owe me a dance or three. I got dressed up and I'm in heels and a push up bra with underwire."

"Dance with me, Princess."

I hold my hand out to her. Her fingers fit in perfectly with mine. Lifting them to my face, I kiss her knuckles and hold her stare.

Oh, my sweet Davina, let's see how ready you are for me. Guiding her to the center of the dance floor, I guide her in a gentle sway, feeling the rhythm of the music beneath our feet. Each song that plays adds to the magic of this night, which has turned out even better than I could have imagined. Even lost in our own bubble, others come up to talk to shop with us, much to my distaste. Davina, however, took every single one of the opportunities to try a new drink, or dance with her friends.

The little minx is leaving me to fend for myself. I guess it's only fair seeing how she had to do the same earlier.

The conversation I'm in now has me bored to tears. I can only hear about hedge funds for so long. Davina's laughter cuts into the conversation from behind me. Orr is laughing with her while he escorts her back towards me, pushing through the crowd, who doesn't seem to want to go home.

"Vi, don't you dare tell him what I said," Orroth pleads.

She folds one arm around her waist and taps her lip with her other hand.

"I promise I won't tell him, Orr. I get it, they have to figure it out themselves. But I'm telling your brother."

Orroth gasps. "I swore you to secrecy!"

She taps his chest, snags a shot glass from a passing server, and gives it to him.

"I know. So, obviously, I'm going to tell my boyfriend. If I know, he knows. Don't act like it's different between you and Wren."

Tossing the drink back, he laughs, "You got me there.

"Yo, Dax. Brought back your woman. Thank you for not hogging her all night." He winks and passes her hand to me.

Excusing myself from the hedge fund manager—who is still talking investments and trying to convince me to move my portfolio to him—I drag Davina to my side. Her breasts threaten to spill from the top of her dress with her shallow breathing.

"Are you ready to leave now, Princess?"

Her hand trails up and down my chest as she looks at me from under her lashes. "Very much so. My feet are starting to hurt."

My arms go behind her back and under her legs, as I pick her up and head outside.

While we wait for our car to come around, her arms wrap tighter around my neck. "Mendax?"

"Hmm?" I stare down at her, and I know for a fact I'm a goner for her.

She kisses me. It isn't rushed or frenzied, but it's the most intimate kiss I've ever had. Snuggling into my neck, her breath evens out, and she's drifted off into a light sleep.

I'll see to picking up where that kiss left off after she's woken up. She's going to need all the energy she can get.

Chapter 31
Ladder

Davina

HALFWAY THROUGH THE CAR ride, I woke up from my cat nap. I didn't even realize I had fallen asleep. I blame those drinks; they hit me hard, but the good news is there's no hangover feeling.

The car ride back to the apartment, after I woke, was a blurred, passionate makeout session with wandering hands. It was like we were hormonal teenagers keeping everything over our clothes. Thank goodness for privacy screens.

The night was long and emotional. I still can't fully wrap my mind around how everything happened, but one thing I know for sure is that Mendax is mine.

Now, standing in the living room, all I can do is stare at him while he walks around his kitchen gathering food and dishes.

"I figured you'd be hungry after tonight. Especially knowing you probably picked at the plate, I left you in the fridge."

"You're not wrong." I nod, trying to stifle a laugh.

Even though I ate the appetizers floating around trays tonight, it wasn't enough. I notice two plates of lasagna and smile.

"When did you get lasagna?"

"I'll tell you if you come closer. You don't have to stand there." Mendax chuckles.

I want to move but can't seem to get my feet to cooperate. How does all this feel so normal and new at the same time? Maybe I should take a picture of this—Mendax without a suit jacket, tie, or vest. No shoes or socks, the top three buttons on his shirt are undone, and his perfectly styled hair is a mess from my fingers running through it too many times.

Just him working in the kitchen with the sleeves rolled up and suspenders is an entirely different kind of turn on I didn't even know I was attracted to. It's certainly something I can get used to.

"Davina?"

"Yeah, what's up?"

That handsome smile spreads across his lips as he rounds the counter and saunters closer to me. With each step, my heart rate spikes.

"We should get you comfortable."

His large hand wraps around mine, tugging me to the couch. With a soft touch on my shoulders, Mendax pushes me to sit on the insanely comfortable cushions.

Kneeling in front of me, he delicately takes one foot into his hand and undoes the ankle strap of my heel. A small moan flies from my mouth as his thumb digs into the sole of my foot before his fingers disappear up my skirt and continue to massage my foot, ankle, and calf in slow, deliberate motions. As soon as he hears the moan, his eyes lock on to mine and I am transfixed. There's a hunger burning under his gaze that has me squirming in my seat, and I'm curious to see what he has planned.

Mendax's fingers are leaving a trail of gooseflesh with every delicate stroke. A heavy sigh and a furrow in his brow have me leaning, just waiting to hear what he's thinking.

"This may come as a surprise to you, but I've never been with a human before," he says.

"Well, how do I compare with everyone else?"

"You don't," he says with a simple shrug.

I almost pull my foot away, but there's a smirk on his face. He places my foot on the ground and picks up the other, repeating the process.

"No one holds a candle to you. You're divine."

I bite my lip, trying to hide the schoolgirl's smile, but keeping a blush a secret will never happen around this man. As his fingers leave an inch of skin, his warm lips are quick to replace them. Up and down my leg, kisses are planted.

"I should get some food in you," Mendax rumbles against my knee.

"You can get something in me." My eyes widen.

That was meant to be an inside thought.

A dark chuckle from Mendax sends a jolt straight to my core.

"Your stomach was growling like a feral beast in the car, Davina."

His fingers tighten around my thigh. The silkiness of my dress caresses my thighs the more I squirm from his heated gaze.

"That was past Davina. She was hungry. Present Davina is not. Did you know Rolvak kept passing me these little sandwich things? I don't know what was in them, but I ate a bunch of them. Oh, and there were these quiche-looking things. I was going to eat one, but it puffed hot air in my face, which turned me off. Also, when did you get lasagna? Did you make it?"

I don't know if I'm nervous or excited, but my mouth is forming more words than I want it to.

He teases the sensitive skin on my inner thigh through the slit of my skirt before flipping the fabric up to expose more of me. Mendax's beard scratches a path up the inside of my leg while more kisses are placed, and it makes me wonder how it would feel elsewhere.

"Davina, I love your voice, but you're rambling. If you need something to do with that pretty mouth of yours, I'll stuff it with my cock."

I am equal parts shocked and turned on. Who is this sexy monster and what happened to my gentleman?

"Oh, you like that idea, don't you?"

Witnessing this other side of my demon in his apartment and dressed how he is … I'd have to be a saint to resist him. Looking at him kneeling in front of me, I can only take shallow breaths and lick my suddenly dry lips.

All I can do is nod my head in agreement because, yes. Why yes, I do like that idea. I like it very much.

He stands to his full height, towering over me.

"In that case…"

My hands itch to touch him, but just as I snake my hands up his thighs, he snatches both wrists in one hand and pulls his suspenders down with his other, only letting my hands go to switch his grasp.

Hot damn. I'm completely enthralled with his show, and he knows he has my full attention when he unzips his pants.

His finger hooks under my chin while the other hand still clutches my wrists. "You tell me to stop, we stop."

I eagerly nod in understanding because my tongue still won't release words. A shiver rolls through me as his thumb rubs my lips before he bends and kisses me breathless. There isn't even a chance for disappointment when he steps away from me. My eyes zero in on how his ruby hand disappears into his black boxer briefs to pull out his hardened cock, jutting out from a trimmed mound of dark curls.

I'm not saying I'm porn star-level familiar with cocks, but I've seen my fair share—including my dick pic vault. What I'm looking at is by far the most glorious one I've ever seen. I thought a dick like this only existed in silicone. A scarlet shaft with a slight curve upward, while the crown is maroon, the sides protrude outward while prominent veins cover the top.

The moment he lets go of my hands I finally scratch the itch of touching him. He's long, thick and heavy. But I was not ready for the magnificent surprise I receive when I run my fingers underneath.

Mendax's eyes close and he hisses with pleasure.

"Holy crap. You have a Jacob's ladder."

"A what?"

"A Jacob's ladder."

My fingers skimmed the underside of his cock, feeling all nine rungs. I lick my lips as moisture pools between my legs, loving the feel of each ridge on my palm. Slowly stroking him, I have to ask, "Is this natural?"

"It is." He chuckles a deep, throaty laugh, grabbing my hand, moving it faster, showing me how he likes to be jerked off. "Probably because I'm part incubus."

"Part incubus? Is that like saying part 'Spanish from my mother's side?'"

His shoulders shake with silent laughter as an answer. Precum begins to bead on the tip, and I dart my tongue to taste him. The salty taste and the pure masculine scent of him are a heady combination. The tip of his cock presses to my lips.

"Show me how much you want to suck my cock."

Slickness runs down my legs by his words alone. Grabbing him more firmly, I kiss his crown and wink up at him. My tongue slides up from base to tip, feeling each rung roll before swirling my tongue over the crown. I give his cock another long swipe of my tongue, nibbling and sucking on the sides before getting back to the tip.

"Pull your dress down, Princess. Let me see your tits while you swallow me whole."

Pulling away from him, I reach behind and loosen my dress just enough to pull my breasts out of the cups of my bra. Looking at him from under my lashes, I smile and proceed to take him inch by inch until he touches the back of my throat. Bobbing my head up and down, I moan at how thick he is. I am growing wetter by the second, thinking of how his ladder will feel inside me.

"Fuck."

Hearing Mendax lose his gentlemanly manner of speaking adds another layer of excitement.

"You're so good with that pretty little mouth."

His praise makes my heart beat faster. Tingles shoot through me as his fingers thread through my hair, tightening at the root. Pushing him a little further into my throat, willing myself to breathe through my nose, I can't help the small gag reflex. The sound spurs him on more. My hand finds my already hard nipple, and my fingers pull and tug on it.

Fuck, this amazing.

His lower abdomen presses against my forehead as he pushes further down, making me gag around his girth again. I pull off him, not bothering to wipe the drool from my lips and chin. I spit on his cock and continue to stroke him while sucking on his balls.

"You're a little cock tease, aren't you, Davina?"

Knowing now how much he likes to hear me gag, a devious idea grew in my mind. The more I think about it, the hungrier I am for him.

"Mendax." My needy whisper is a sound foreign to my own ears. "Fuck my face."

His response is a groan that's a mixture of arousal and appreciation. The fingers in my hair tighten as he tilts my face up. He strokes my jaw,

"As you wish, princess."

Mendax shoves his cock hard and fast down my throat tears prick my eyes. His pace is relentless, and I'm helpless to keep up. All I can do is place my hands on his strong thighs and enjoy the feel of him using me for his pleasure. He is doing exactly what I asked for, and tears stream down my face while I gag and moan.

My pussy drips, making my thighs slick. Never have I been so turned on from a blow job. My nails scratch across his firm ass and down the back of his legs. I cup his balls, feeling them tighten as his hips slap against me. His cock is thicker and twitches against my tongue, and I'm more than ready to swallow every last drop of him.

To my dismay and surprise, he pulls out my mouth. Leaning closer to me, he wraps my legs around his waist and kisses me, stroking my tongue with his.

"You may make me feral, but I'm still a gentleman. You'll always come first with me."

"Do you want me? All of me?"

Where was this shyness creeping up from? This sex god just fucked my face after I asked for it.

"Davina, I want you. Always. You're in control here. If this is what you want, I will gladly spend the night exploring every inch of you. If you only want to sit down and talk about everything, we can spend the entire night doing that instead."

"Damn, you're a smooth talker," I say, biting my swollen bottom lip.

This man has my heart racing on any given day. But right now? Now he's sent it into overdrive.

"I do want to talk later. I also want to get out of this dress completely. It's digging into my ribs."

I kiss him. His hold tightens around me as I try to wriggle down closer to his thick cock. "And I'll absolutely lose my mind if I don't feel your hands on me."

"Well, we can't have that." Mendax eyes my breasts and licks his lips.

He's barely touched me, and my thighs are pressed together, trying to find some kind of relief from the ache building. Holding my breath, I wait and watch his knuckles trail up my sides and tease the underside of my heavy breasts. Just when I think he's going to rip this gorgeous dress off me, Mendax rights my dress, putting everything back in place. Everything in me wants to scream or cry because this is torture, and the knowing smirk only heightens it.

"There. No more digging."

Tingles erupt as his hand slides up the back of my head, weaving fingers into my hair. His hold is firm and sure as the grip tightens in my hair before a passionate kiss is left on my lips. I've never felt so wanted and cared for in my life.

He pulls me closer, trailing his lips down my neck and walking me back to the bedroom. With every press of his lips, the flames of desire burn hotter in the pit of my stomach. The room spins as he twirls me away from him, bending me over the side of the footboard. He sweeps my hair off my shoulder.

"Hands on the mattress, Princess." The whisper rakes a shiver down my spine.

I inhale sharply at the nickname I earned at some point during the night. My back arches at the sensation of his teeth nipping my ear, and a breathy moan escapes as he sucks on the soft flesh of my neck. Firm hands keep me in place, despite my desperate attempts to find more friction.

Seemingly endless kisses trail down the nape of my neck and the top of my spine. This is either the world's longest zipper, or he's torturing me on purpose. With every centimeter the zipper opens, his warm lips leave a searing kiss. I'm a needy mess, and his mouth alone has the power to ruin me. Mendax curls a hand around my throat, lightly squeezing as he stands me up straight. A rush of cool air sweeps over my heated skin as the dress pools around my feet. The roughness of his thick beard skims my shoulder as he peered down the front of my body. Leaning against the lean muscle of his chest I revel in rubbing my back against his cock. Spinning me and stepping away, he leaves me worked up and wanting.

With a snap of his fingers, the ivory, lace, push up bra and matching thong disappear off me and end up on a bench by the closet.

"Could you always do that too?"

I look up and clench my thighs. There is Mendax naked and stroking his cock.

"I only do that when I'm tired or in this case, impatient." He shrugs. "It's the type of spell I use when I conjured that bear earlier."

God, he did pull a teddy bear from thin air only hours ago. It feels like it was days, even months ago now. It seems my handsome demon was keeping a lot of useful and wonderful tricks from me.

I grin, watching his cock bounce with every measured step as he stalks forward. Lowering himself in front of me, my fingers slide into his dark hair. Mendax inhales when he gets to my mound, his tongue and nose running a line up and down, teasing me from my navel to clit. Widening my stance, his hot breath skims over my folds before he groans at seeing how wet he has made me.

"One thing should be made clear, Davina," he speaks with fingers squeezing the back of my thighs. "We will be equals in this relationship." He pulls my pussy closer to his lips and kisses my clit. "I fucked your face. Now you're going to fuck mine."

I squeal at the swift and sudden height change. Lifting me and placing both of my thighs over his shoulders he stands straight up like I weigh no more than a feather. My right hand clutches his hair pulling his face closer to my pussy while my left holds his horn and stroking the curve of it.

He breaks away from my core, his beard glistening with my arousal. "Ride my face, Davina."

Mendax licks a long firm line through my lower lips, unfolding me.

Up until this point in my life, I thought I was a moaner. Mendax wrapping his lips around my clit and sucking has turned me into a certified screamer. Alternating between sucking and licking, my hips bucked on their own accord chasing a release I know he can give me. Cold hardness presses against my back and ass, forcing me to arch further into Mendax.

Holy shit, he's pressed me against the floor-to-ceiling window overlooking the city. I don't even have it in me to care if these are tinted or not. If anyone can see the mess he's making of me, they're welcome for the show.

Using the window for purchase, I move my hips faster and harder, riding his face like the slut I am for him. My fingers brush against the tip of his pointed ear, and the vibration from his moan against me sends me even higher.

Mendax breaks away from me and parts my folds with the flat of his tongue. "I've never told you this—" he licks again, lapping up all my juices. "—the points on my ears are extremely sensitive." His tongue thrusts in me, causing me to drip even more. "In fact, it's a very intimate gesture to touch, play, and caress that part of my ears."

He makes it a point to rub the side of his face against my thigh. My heated skin meets his, and I'm all too excited to play with his pointy ears as he continues to eat me like his favorite meal.

His hands move from squeezing my ass and running up the length of my torso until they find my breasts. He growls and squeezes them. The vibration of his approval against my clit hurls me to the edge of my orgasm. His tongue prods in and out of my core while his fingers pull and twist my nipples. I am lost in a haze of passion and don't know what I'm doing anymore, but Mendax seems to have a plan, and I'll let him lead the way.

One thing I do plan on? I will be climbing that ladder.

Chapter 32
Heaven
Mendax

Davina has successfully invaded all of my senses, and I still need more. Her pussy dripping down my face and throat with each buck of her hips makes me feel like a man dying of thirst, and she's my oasis.

"Fuck," I inhale and thrust my tongue faster, savoring every crevice of her core. "You smell so good and taste even better."

"Mendax," she moans my name like a prayer, and while I'm no god, I'll answer her plea.

Wrapping my hand around her throat, I hold her in place against the window, squeezing softly before releasing over and over. While my tongue traces sharp circles over her swollen clit I run my left hand down her ribs, hips, and thighs before thrusting my middle finger into her dripping opening. Even though the sight before me is a work of art, I pull my face away to see the rest of her. I'm rewarded with seeing her face beautifully flushed, hair clinging to her damp forehead, and her hands playing with her breasts, tweaking each nipple. Adding my ring finger, I curl them upward, keeping her folds open with my index finger and pinky while my thumb strokes her lips. Her thick, toned thighs tighten around my head and horns before I replace my tongue with my thumb.

Her lips part. "You're going—going to. Yes. Yes. Fuck, I'm going to cum."

"Cum on my tongue."

Biting down on her clit, I graze my teeth over the sensitive nub, and she screams my name.

Running my hands up and down her creamy skin, her body begs for more with every tremor that subsides. She slides down my body, and I crash my lips on hers in a soft, dominating kiss. Her pouty lips open, allowing my tongue in to meet hers. She sucks my tongue clean of her taste, making my dick painfully harder. Precum is already beading at the tip.

The feel of her small body with plentiful curves and tight muscles is intoxicating. My hands wander freely, wanting to carve every dip, curve, and valley into memory. With a feather-light stroke, my fingers skate the side of her ribs while my left hand massages her scalp, drawing a moan from both of us. Davina melts into my embrace, and I'm eager to hold her closer until we've lost track of where one of us starts and the other ends.

Pulling away from her lips for a breath, I whisper against her lips, "Get on the bed, Davina." I follow it with a sharp slap to her ass.

Her eyes widen as her smile grows. Apparently, she likes this dominant side of me. This side of me must have been dormant, waiting for her because no one has ever gotten this treatment.

I can't help but admire my handprint as she swings her hips seductively towards the bed, tossing a wink over her shoulder. *Such a cock tease. I love it.*

The mattress dips as she settles on her hands and knees instead of laying down. My teeth plunge into my bottom lip, watching her press her face to the sheets, lifting her heart-shaped ass higher in the air.

I chuckle to myself; if she thought getting rid of clothing was fun, she was in for a real surprise. I never bothered to use my telekinetic abilities much, finding it rather lazy, but now I see it has a better use. Like now, to flip her on her back and hold her in place while taking my time to walk over and drink in the sight of her sweet, glistening pussy, and sweat-slicked skin.

"We can stop here if you don't want to go further," I say, sweeping the sweaty strands of hair off her face and cupping her cheek.

She leans her face into my hand and sighs with contentment. She really perfect.

"I promise you, I will cry if we stop now. I'm talking tears like I'm watching dogs in the animal shelter commercial cry level."

"We can't have that now. I'm not sure I have the necessary amount of tissues for that."

"Probably not." She places a kiss on my palm. "You probably have the right amount of pocket squares." She giggles.

I knew I shouldn't have told her about my collection of squares.

"You shush before I gag you with one."

She quirks her brow and bites her lip. "I'm making a mental note to mouth off for next time, so that happens."

You and me both, Princess. You and me both.

Having Davina naked, panting for me, on my bed is a feast for my eyes and pride. This beautiful woman is all mine, and I intend to make sure she knows it by ruining her for any other man who tries to take her.

So many things are irrelevant to me now. It doesn't matter what happened at the party; it doesn't matter that we come from two different realms or that I technically shouldn't be in hers. What matters is finding every spot on her body, inside and out, that will make her make those sexy moans and screams again.

No time like the present to start kissing a line from her feet up to her clit and enjoying her squirms and pants from the attention her needy nub draws from her. Continuing upward, her large, heavy breasts are begging for my attention. Cupping both of them, I squeeze and bury my face in between licking, sucking, and kissing each breast and nipple. I'm going to worship this goddess the way she deserves.

Her hands trace every line of muscle on my body she can reach while kissing my neck, shoulders, and chest. She unknowingly is searing herself into my soul. Her fingers weave into my chest hair, and she scratches the skin beneath before biting my nipple, causing my cock to jump between us. She wiggles and groans impatiently.

Reaching between us, my hand lands a heavy spank on her clit, causing her to gasp.

"Don't rush me, Davina. This is our first time together, and I refuse to speed through this like fumbling horny teenagers."

She huffs. "I thought you were impatient."

"I am, but I also know good things come to those who wait."

Lacing our fingers together, I secure her hands above her head. Pinning her thighs open with my knees, I let my weight settle over her.

Rocking my hips, the crown of my cock strokes her clit before I push into her tight center.

I'm mesmerized by how her eyes flutter close, and her head lulls to the side in pleasure. I crave to see how her face changes.

"Eyes on me, Princess."

She forces herself to look at me. *God, she is a masterpiece.* Slowly, I push further in, and her eyes roll back as each rung rolls onto her, making her arch and press her breasts into my chest.

"Oh, my god!" she screams, raising her hips and taking me deeper.

"You like that, don't you?" I moved myself out a bit before thrusting in all the way. "I can tell."

She cries out my name. Sliding in and out of her tight pussy is pure heaven. She grips me perfectly, like she was made for me.

"Please move faster. More. Please, Mendax."

Whatever my princess wants, she will get. If she wants more, more is exactly what I'll give her. A yellow fog curls around us until it lifts her off the bed, levitating her. I release her hands, and they fly to my waist, touching, scratching, and feeling every contracting muscle.

Her eyes widen as she realizes what's happening.

"You're full of surprises." She smiles, and knowing how much she trusts me completely in this moment has me even harder than I've ever been before. Hooking her legs over my arms, I sit back on my haunches, tilting her hips up, and ram into her relentlessly at the new angle.

"You feel so damn good."

Every word was accentuated with a deep thrust.

"Don't stop. Fuck, don't stop." She tosses her head side to side and clenches down on my cock.

Just as her orgasm is coming to claim her, I stop, letting my magic slowly settle her back on the mattress.

"Oh, you son of a bitch."

"Such crude language, Ms. Myles," I chide while starting a slow thrust.

Feeling each rung under my cock stroke her walls is the greatest feeling, and there is no comparison. I don't want us to finish yet. I want to play with her a little more.

Pulling out of her, I throw some pillows out of the way and sit back against the headboard, pulling her on top of me facing away. She leans her back against my chest, rubbing herself against my cock while my hands teased her nipples.

"Now, Ms. Myles, if I remember correctly." I mummer against her shoulder, licking and sucking all the areas I can reach. "When we first met, you told me there wasn't anything you wanted from me. Is that still the case?"

Her breath hitches, and her body stills, but my hands continue moving up her throat and back down her body, spreading her legs wider over my thighs.

"I think I changed my mind." Her voice is husky and needy, and I'd be a liar if I said it didn't turn me on even more. Davina's hand grabs mine, pressing my fingers against her clit.

"I want you."

She takes hold of my dick and slides it into her opening with a deep moan.

"And, I want you to make me cum."

The game I started is beginning to get away from me. This woman frazzles my brain, and I love every second of it.

"Nothing is free, Davina," I say sternly, grabbing her hips and stopping her from chasing her release. There's nothing I want more in this moment than to kiss that pout off her lips and give her what she desperately wants.

"You want me, and you want me to make you cum. It's going to cost you."

"Name your price." She rocks back and forth as much as she can.

"It would cost you nothing and everything. Some would say," I kiss behind her ear. "The price would be equivalent to your soul."

Davina stops, leaning forward a little to look over her shoulder.

"My soul? I was told to run away from someone who wanted that."

The confusion on her face is adorable. I can't help but laugh.

"I want your time, attention, devotion, love, and loyalty in return. I want you, Davina, all of you. I want you for now and always." It comes out as a whisper. It was too heavy of a proclamation to say any louder, or else it might shatter our moment.

Her heartbeat is so fast I could feel it pound against my own as she settles back, leaning into me. "And by getting me, would I get the same from you?"

I pull her off me and turn her so I can gaze into those brown eyes I love so much.

"I promise you all that and more, Davina. But I'll tell you a secret." My hand swipes a few stray hairs away from her eyes. "You've had that from me for a long time now."

She slides herself back down my length, both of us groaning at the sensation. Her lips brush against mine.

"Then we have a deal, Mr. Draxton." She smiles against my lips.

I claim her lips, body, and soul with a searing kiss. My fingers dig into her wide hips while hers press into my shoulders. I slowly lower onto my cock. We both groan at the same time before I bounce her up and down, hard and fast. Davina's hair cascades down her back, exposing her neck and chest to me as she arches back.

"Look at me, Davina. I want to watch you cum with me."

Her head snaps back, and she leans forward. Our foreheads touch, and our noses press together as we stare into each other's eyes. The feeling of being seen, wanted, and loved mixes with our carnal desire for each other, sending us tumbling over the edge. She clamps down on my cock as an orgasm rips through her, squirting on me and soaking the sheets.

Rolling her onto her back, I pull out of her while my thumb strums her clit, allowing her to come down off her high while my other hand strokes my cock furiously, splashing cum across her stomach and breasts.

Other than the rain pelting the window, our heavy, mingled breathing is the only other sound.

"Are you okay?"

Slinging her arm over her face, she laughs. "I can't feel my legs. I need a minute."

If my ego wasn't already big, it certainly is now. I move her arm and kiss her with all I have.

"I'll be right back. I'm going to get a towel to clean us up."

"I'll be here," She sighs with a thumbs up.

I'm pretty sure I've died, and she's my heaven.

Chapter 33
Religious Experience
Davina

LAYING ON THE EQUIVALENT of a cloud, in a mess I made with a sexy, handsome, and charming demon was not on this year's bingo card. Pushing my fingertips against my lips to stifle a bubble of giddy laughter, I listen to Mendax running the water in the bathroom. Watching him walk out, in all his naked glory, is enough to squeeze my thighs. There's no way I will ever get enough of this man, especially since I can still feel him and all nine rungs in me.

Damn, is this what it is to be God's favorite?

A snort comes out at the thought, and Mendax raises a brow in question.

"I'm just happy."

His suave laughter wraps me up better than my favorite blanket. "You really didn't move."

I smile and shrug. "I told you I'd be right here. Plus, I didn't want to risk dripping anywhere else."

He leans down and kisses me softly, and that kiss alone sends my heart soaring to new heights. It is different from the other kisses we shared tonight.

"I'm happy I get to kiss you now," he says before wiping my stomach with a warm, wet towel.

His hands are steady, and he is so focused on cleaning every inch I start to smile and hum.

"What song is that? It sounds chipper," Mendax chuckles while wiping between my legs.

Inhaling sharply, I try to fight the blush rising on my chest and cheeks.

"I don't know," I say. Even I didn't believe it with that high pitched tone.

This is going down in history as the worst time for my memory to retrieve Madonna's 'Like a Prayer' from archives.

"It just popped into my head. Like I said, I'm happy. Deliriously happy."

Well, maybe not the worst time; having him was the equivalent of a profound religious experience.

He smiles back and begins humming along with me after hearing it a second time. I break out in laughter to the point that it became hard to breathe.

"Did I break you?"

I snort at that. "You might have."

Mendax smiles and cards his fingers through his hair, pushing back the lock that always refuses to stay in place before scooping me up.

"Well, maybe we can fix that with the bath I drew you. You relax while I change the sheets, then I'll join you." He kisses my forehead.

At this rate of forehead kisses, I will be beyond stupid, but at least I'll be happy.

The bath took longer than it really should have. We're both to blame, though. We couldn't keep our hands to ourselves. Once the water was cold, we ended up in the shower and then dried off.

Mendax offers me a black silk button-down sleep shirt that grazes my knees while he wears the matching bottoms. It shouldn't surprise me that he doesn't have a regular T-shirt or sweatpants. I wonder what he would do if I got him some.

"No more distracting me, Davina," Mendax says, sliding a plate on the counter. "You need to eat."

The fork clanks against the counter as I fake my outrage. "Me? I did nothing to distract you."

He grabs a decanter from the fridge and two wine glasses, pouring a dark liquid into both glasses before setting them next to our plates.

"You're sitting there looking gorgeous."

"Somethings just can't be helped," I reply, cutting a piece of my lasagna off.

We both sit on the padded leather stools, silently eating the warm, layered, cheesy pasta with only the scrape of a fork against the plate to fill the silence. Usually, this kind of silence would drive me up a wall, but with Mendax, it feels right. We don't have to scramble to find any dreaded small talk; we can sit and enjoy each other's company.

It's as if he is thinking the same thing because he laces our fingers together and gives me a wink while he keeps eating.

The chilled glass rim presses against my lips while I take a sip of the liquid.

"Oh my god. This is delicious. What is it?" I take another sip, savoring the silky tannins of a wine with hints of cinnamon, chocolate, and…was that tea? "Is this wine or tea?"

Mendax lifts his glass, swirling the liquid before inhaling the scent.

"It's both. It's a cacao infused wine with an English Breakfast Tea." He takes an elegant sip before speaking again. "Personally, I think these are better than mimosas."

"First off, this is fantastic. Secondly, you can't compare this to mimosas. That's apples and oranges."

His lips tip up at the corners, the glass hovering mid sip, "if you say so." There's a smile that makes my insides turn to mush before he takes a long pull of the wine concoction.

With plates cleared, glasses empty, and our stomachs full, Mendax leads the way to a separate sitting room on the other side of his large apartment, which was more of a penthouse. He settles me on his lap after he sits in an elegant plum-colored wide wingback chair.

Snuggling deeper into him, I let out a content sigh.

"You know," I begin, "your place is amazing. It's beautiful, has a great view. It has everything finished and looks like it's out of Architectural Digest. You're putting my Pinterest boards to shame."

His fingers skim my bare legs while his shoulders shake in silent laughter.

"Why on earth do you spend so much time at my house?"

"Because you're there." His answer is swift and sure, and I'd be a liar if I said it didn't make me feel warm and fuzzy inside.

We watch the gray rain pelting against the window and the city below. According to Mendax, it was a rainy year, meaning every day it would rain all day with a few breaks every now and then. So, not much different from the Pac Northwest.

"Can you tell me about your tattoos?" Mendax asks.

It was such an odd question in the moment. There were a whole hell of a lot of other questions that we need to ask and answer.

"That's what you want to talk about? My tattoos?"

His finger traces the flora and fauna shapes on my hip before skimming under the hem of my shirt and tracing the ink on my ribs.

"For right now." There's a vulnerable edge to his voice I've never heard before. "I noticed little drawings in between some flowers while others have large gaps."

Knowing he was studying my body unleashes a legion of butterflies in my stomach.

"The tattoos started as a way to rebel against Mother Dearest." I chuckle at the memories. "She would always say, *'Your body is a temple, Davina. You shouldn't ruin it.'* But then I would say, *'Name the last time you saw a temple that wasn't adorned with art.'* My father steered clear of that conversation. Whenever I was sad or felt bored or lonely, I would add another flora or fauna, but I kept them in places where they wouldn't be easily seen. I guess part of me didn't want to fully disappoint my mom."

His hand settles back on my hip while I nestle my head between his collar and jaw.

"And the small drawings?"

"Those are so stupid, and I love them," I say. My fingers weave into his chest hair, scratching his skin lightly. A hairy chest has always been such a turn-on for me; it screams manly to me.

"They're little symbolic reminders of events or things that are important to me."

"The teddy bear peeking out from a leaf is a reminder of the first camping trip I took with both of my parents when we came across a mom and her cub. Mom freaked and never went on another trip again, even though Dad and I went back any time he could get away from the hospital."

Sitting on Mendax's lap, I think of all the little doodles: teddy bear, teapot, books, ghost, and—

"What about the pumpkin?"

I groan, "If I tell you, you have to promise never to bring it up or make fun of me."

"I promise to do my best."

I lean away, narrowing my eyes at the handsome devil who had the audacity to laugh.

"It's a nickname my dad gave me, and now they both call me that."

He grins, running his fingers through my hair. "It's a cute nickname."

"You didn't hear how I got it."

He shifts us, props his legs up on an ottoman, and motions for me to continue.

"Back when I was maybe five, I really wanted to be a pumpkin for Halloween. Why? That's a great question; the only answer I have is yes. Well, Mom promised she would be home in time to help me with face paint, but her flight from New York was delayed. Dad was running late with an emergency at the hospital, so he asked my Uncle to help since he was there baby sitting me. Neither of us knew the first thing about costumes, let alone face paint. I drew the best pumpkin face my 5-year-old self had ever done, with the paint Uncle Alex bought last minute from a craft store."

"That doesn't sound bad," he says, massaging my scalp. "I bet you made an adorable pumpkin."

Rolling my tongue over my bottom lip, I take a sharp inhale. "After Uncle Alex took me trick or treating, it was bath time. Mom got home just in time for that, but he stayed instead of going home like he planned since it was late, and there was always a spare room for him. Well, after a full pack of baby wipes, no tears shampoo—which is total bull shit by the way those caused all the tears—and mom's expensive face wash, the paint wouldn't come off all the way. I spent days. *Days!* Looking like a pumpkin. My dad and Uncle Alex were beside themselves with laughter while Mom was pissed and scolded my uncle about chemicals or toxins or something."

The best deep, velvet laugh vibrates into my chest. Mendax is full belly laughing, and if this is the reaction to my embarrassing stories, I'd gladly share more with him.

"Since then, my parents call me pumpkin. I pretend to hate it, but I secretly love it. It makes me feel special." I laugh.

Once he composes himself, Mendax kisses my temple. "Do they know about the pumpkin you have on your ribs?"

"Absolutely not. Dad doesn't need any more ammunition to roast or tease me. He's already told me about the file he has saved on things to embarrass me with for a wedding toast."

Crap-o-la. I said the wrong thing. I know I did because the silence isn't comfortable anymore. It feels like we're waiting for the other shoe to drop.

"Davina?" Mendax whispers into my hair.

I am too nervous to speak. I didn't mean to mention weddings or anything like that. "Hmm?"

He turns me, so I am straddling him. The buttons on his shirt seem particularly fascinating right now. Fingers stroke my jaw before tilting my chin up. I am met with an intense violet gaze.

"I know we said a lot of things in the heat of the moment," he pauses, searching my face.

Oh, frick, he's going to take it all back, isn't he? I know he is. Once again, I put myself out there only to get burned. This is why I don't date. I can't even hold a relationship with a human man; why did I think I could with a charming demon?

"But, I really did mean what I said. I want your everything. I want you." His large hands hold my face, and the look in his eyes softened. "Are you really mine?"

Wait. What?

"Cheezus Rice! Lead with that next time." I huff. "You were about to give me a heart attack. I thought you were going to say you didn't mean it."

This man must have bought audacity in bulk because he's looking at me like I'm crazy.

"Cheezus Rice?" He laughs.

I swat his chest. "Don't start with me, Mendax."

He fights a losing battle with a smile on his face.

"I'm yours for as long as you're mine." The smile he gives me would have dropped my panties if I had any on.

"We'll have to figure out how to make this work. I'm supposed to be on lockdown, and I can't take you out on dates in your town like you deserve. Now that I think about it, you didn't come here through the gateways either. Our portal is in a grey area of illegal activities."

"You've turned me into a criminal." I laugh, forgetting that I was technically harboring a fugitive. "Well, there are only a few places in Earvle worth going to. Anything else is a trip to the city. Plus, we can take this opportunity for you to show me around your world—realm, home. You know what I mean."

His lips meet mine.

"Sounds wonderful."

Clutching me tighter, he rises and tosses me over his shoulders, giving me a great view of his tight ass. *Who knew he was hiding these muscles under those suits?*

"Where are we going?" I laugh, enjoying my view.

"Home," is all he says before running into the kitchen and through the portal.

Chapter 34

Surprise?

Mendax

THREE MONTHS OF fiNALLY being with Davina has been amazing. One surprise I had were the windows and curtains. Apparently, the curtains hadn't been drawn so neighbors wouldn't see me; it was because there was a glare on the television. She actually put a film on the windows that made them a one-way mirror. We could look out all we wanted while the world stayed out there.

What isn't amazing is the heat here during the summer months. Silverling, though, Davina wears next to nothing while at home, like now. The fluorescent green cropped tank-top and denim shorts showcase every glorious curve and doodled tattoo. For once, I had to put away my suits and opt for linen shorts and short-sleeve button-downs. This is the most casual I've ever been, and it's honestly nice.

"Nancy, I am fully aware you're here to monitor conversations and make sure fair treatment is established. However, it's been months. Is this necessary?"

The padding of Davina's bare feet against the floor while she paces has been quickening over the past twenty minutes. In those twenty minutes, a vein in her neck has been making a slow appearance.

I already finished my work of finding buyers for Orroth to take a few items to; making those calls were the hardest calls of my life. Davina was taking a break before this call and decided while I was on the phone was the best time for a blow job. The evil little woman she is left me hard and slapped my balls so I wouldn't finish. How unfortunate for her, I find myself with a lack of things to do now.

Slowly closing the book, I take my reading glasses off, set them on the coffee table, and stand. With a flick of my fingers, I push a dining chair behind her knees, forcing her to sit on it.

"Don't you dare," she mouths, and I laugh. "N-Nancy, at this point, I think it's best if I file an HR complaint about Tony and your clear favoritism and overstepping." She sucks in a sharp breath as I kneel in front of her.

Maybe it's cheating to use a little demon magic, but I levitate her just enough to yank the shorts down her legs, but not all the way off. Lifting her legs, I pushed my face against her opening, which is already wet and ready for me. Draping her thighs over my shoulders, I begin licking and sucking. I look up at her and become unrelenting in my pace. Her mouth hangs open, and I chuckle against her, making her try to squirm away from me.

"Uh-huh. Yeah. I-I'm listening."

She breathes heavily, digging her fingers into my hair, pulling me even closer. Sucking harder, I slip one, then two fingers into her.

"I would like to exercise my right to have another advocate oversee—"

She tugs my hair hard, fighting back the moan threatening to tumble free. Her walls clenched around my fingers. Pulling my mouth away, I spit on her clit and rub it up and down slowly while pushing my tongue into her. Her legs quake around my horns while her thighs squeeze my head. Right when my favorite meal is about to gush on my tongue, I pull away and bite her nipple through her shirt.

Oh, she looked murderous and sexy.

"Nancy." Davina's voice is harder than the current state of my cock. "Until there is another advocate, this conversation is over."

She doesn't even bother saying goodbye before tossing her phone. It clatters somewhere on the ground. Where it ended up is anyone's guess. *I'll search for it later.*

"Those weren't very good manners, Princess," I chide, pulling her shorts back in place.

"Manners. *Manners?* Manners! I'll show you manners."

She pinches my nipple hard and runs around the corner. The back door slams open; her laughter hangs in the air.

"Woman, you started it," I laugh and give chase.

We've wasted away sitting on the living room floor, sharing a tub of strawberry cheesecake ice cream while playing video games all afternoon. The sun is beginning to set and I am getting anxious and excited. I have planned an entire date for us with the help of Wren. Those two have become thick as thieves, so much so that they have to team up on game nights. I've never seen two people so competitive over charades. All this time together, and we still haven't gone on a proper date.

"Are you ready for tonight?" I ask while button-smashing the controller, hoping it'll help me earn points in the battle.

She throws a grenade into an enemy hideout.

"Gotcha bitches!"

Davina pins me with her gaze. "I'm so excited for tonight. I wish you would tell me what you have planned."

Her teeth gnaw the corner of her lip. Movement on the screen captures her attention.

"You sneaky mother fuuu—"

Some sniper took out my guy—not that it was hard. I was out in the open but leave it to Davina to avenge my on-screen death. There's no way I could ever be bored around Davina; there are too many facets to her personality to keep me on my toes.

"Oh, my goodness, Mendax!" The controller dropped to the floor. "Are you going to propose? Because I'll tell you right now, I don't know how I feel about public proposals, you also have to ask my father. He's traditional in that sense." She gives a playful grin.

"I will propose, just not tonight." It's an easy statement because it is the truth. It seems to have shocked her, though. "I told you when we first met, you're stuck with me. I also told you I do intend to marry you eventually. But now I'm curious. What kind of ring would you like?"

Her character goes on to win the round and do a victory dance.

"Well, most women want something big and flashy. But me? You could give me any ring pop, and I'd be thrilled. It's not about what it looks like or how much you spent on it. It's about the promise behind it."

"You deserve more than any ring pop."

She sighs and leans her head on my shoulder. "You're right, it should be a cherry-flavored ring pop. Everyone knows red is always the best flavor no matter what."

"Is it now?" I say seductively.

She tosses her head back, laughing. "You would go there."

"Again, you started it." I stand, holding my hand out to help her up. The feel of her hand in mine is still perfect. "I'll help you clean up; then I have to go get ready and make sure everything is set."

She peers over her shoulder, an extra sway in her hips. "Are you trying to impress me tonight?"

Walking behind her, I wrap her in my arms. "My skill must be lacking because I'm always trying to impress you."

I swat her ass and make my way to the stairs as Gotha comes flying like, well, a bat out of hell. Her wings flap in a frenzy around my head before weaving in and out of my legs. Davina seizes the moment to slap my ass harder.

"Ouch! What was that for? Gotha, what has gotten into you?" *These ladies in my life, I swear.*

The doorbell ringing cuts through our chaos.

"I'll get that; you get all pretty for me." Davina giggles before pecking my lips. "Gotha, leave him alone. I picked some fresh berries for you."

Gotha hovers before darting to Davina and then to the door. She watches as I go up the stairs. I turn, and this wild woman lifts her shirt and flashes me.

"Don't keep me waiting, Handsome."

"Maybe we should have a date at home again?"

She laughs, and the doorbell rings again. "Go! I'm excited to see where you're taking me."

She gingerly skips down the stairs and opens the door.

"Oh, hey, Blake."

This guy. She's turned him down and he still can't take a hint.

"Wow," the bastard chuckles. "I mean, hey. Sorry, you look amazing. Not that you don't always look amazing. Did you do something different with your hair?"

"Thanks, um, nope. Hair is still the same. It must be that happy relationship glow."

I should leave; my ego isn't going to fit in this house if I hear her happily talk about us.

"Relationship?" His voice sounds thick.

Poor guy, I think gleefully.

The door creaks as she plays with the knob, swinging it open a little more.

"Yeah. He's amazing. Smart, funny, charming…"

I can squeeze my ego in here. I decide to stay and listen.

Davina laughs. "What can I do for you, Blake?"

She knows I am listening. *I love her.*

Their muffled conversation about boxes getting delivered wrong fades as I enter our room. The bed is still a mess from when I caught her, and we finished what she started. Taking a few minutes, I fix the sheets and dry off the vibrator we played with before tucking it back into the nightstand. *I should get her more of those.* Once everything is back in place, I walk through the portal, letting the magic buzz and crackle around me. There's an extra pep in my step as I step outside the pantry but it quickly dies.

"Explain the meaning of this," a male voice says furiously.

My heart drops at the voice and sight before me. My mother, Elara, and her father, Elsher Brelle, are in my kitchen.

"Mendax, please tell me that isn't what I think it is." My mother's fingers skim her neck.

How do I explain this when I've been caught?

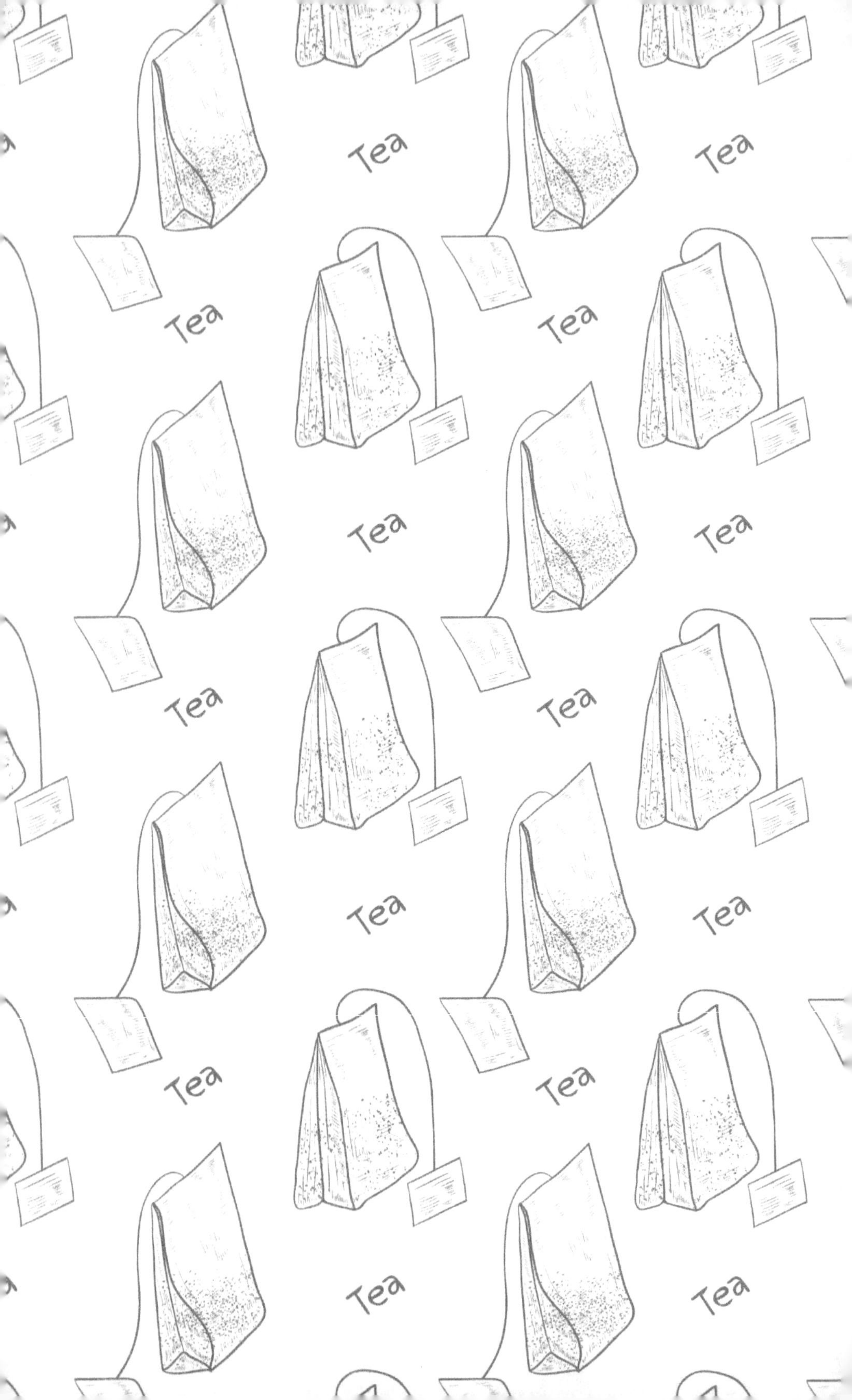
Tea
Tea
Tea
Tea
Tea
Tea
Tea
Tea

Chapter 35

Bruised

Davina

"RELATIONSHIP?" BLAKE ASKS WITH a bit of a crestfallen look.

After the party and everything that transpired, I texted Blake back, saying I appreciated him and his wanting to take me somewhere I would enjoy, but it wasn't in the cards. I thought I had let him down easy. He's my neighbor and a good guy and I didn't want any weird or hard feelings. Mendax saw the text and wanted me to reply with "no." That's it, just "no."

Mendax's footsteps have stopped at the top of the stairs, just outside our room which has me grinning like an idiot. He thinks he's slick. I could play coy or hype his ego some more.

"Yeah. He's amazing. Smart, funny, charming," I say, knowing full and well I just inflated his ego to the size of Texas. "What can I do for you, Blake?"

His fingers card through his blonde hair.

"Well, he's a lucky guy," he says with a tight smile. "Two of your boxes got delivered to my house. If I didn't know any better, I'd say you were doing it just to give me an excuse to come over and see you."

There was a weird, forced laugh at the end, and I give an equally awkward laugh.

"You could have texted me, and I would have gotten them. I wouldn't want to disturb your day."

"And let you lug this massive box across the street? I don't think so. These aren't just show muscles, Davina," he says with a wink. "And there's another tea delivery. I'm getting better at recognizing that box. I gotta admit you now have me curious about all this tea stuff."

I really hope he isn't trying to wait me out and see if he still has a shot.

"I'd suggest lemon, or chamomile, or even a fruit tea like cherry to start with." I lean against the door jamb, and the door opens a little wider. Gotha seizes the opportunity to swoop out from behind me and attack Blake the same way she attacked me.

"Is this really a damn bat?" he asks, quickly dodging while observing the small creature's wings frantically flapping near his face. "Ouch, that hurts!" Gritting his teeth, he frantically swats his hands around his head, trying to ward off the persistent bat.

Gotha is still on the attack. I'd bet good money she sharpened her talons in the kitchen because from here it looks like she got him pretty good.

"Gotha! Get back here." I hold my arm out, and she perches on top of it. "You're such a little trouble maker." I scold, gently rubbing my nose against her velvety head, feeling the warmth and texture of her fur.

"You have a pet bat? Aren't bats nocturnal?"

"I sure do. She's a designer breed, kind of rare, and doesn't really conform to bat expectations. Gotha is not fond of new people. It's usually a slow immersion thing with introductions." My fingers stroke her long, pointy ears.

"Anyway, thank you for bringing these over, Blake."

He stands there looking at me, rubbing the back of his neck. I stand here watching him in gym shorts and a tank top that has a joke about the periodic table on it: *I might be N Er Dy, but only Periodically*

Pushing my fingers against my lips, I stifle my laugh.

"Your shirt is funny," I say with a smile.

"Thanks. Not many people like science humor." He perks up a bit and smiles. "I don't want this to be weird between us. Um, can we be friends?"

"Friends." I smile back. "I have to get going; I gotta get ready for a date tonight. Again, thanks for bringing me my packages."

He nods. "I'll see you around, Davina."

I still have hours before Mendax will come to get me for our date, but hours means I don't have much time. Everything has been going fantastic with us, it's almost too good to be true. I can't help the impending feeling of doom, but I refuse to let the feeling fester. I believe in manifestation and I'm going to manifest a happy future with Mendax while dragging this oversized box into the house.

The ticking from Gotha's talons on the kitchen table is starting to cause a twitch in my eye. Normally, she nestles in between the bowls I set out for her and gorges on berries until she goes into a food coma. I should probably feed her something other than berries.

Mental note:

- Try to get Gotha to eat veggies, maybe meat?

Can she eat that? I'll have to ask Mendax.

The sun setting alerts me to the tiny fact that I should be putting the final touches on my makeup. Instead, I hyper-focused and rearranged my closet and dresser so that there's extra space in case Mendax wants to leave some things here. Maybe I'll suggest it tonight. Who knew I could fold shirts this tiny and neat? Not me.

Gotha was behaving oddly all evening; she flew from the attic to our bedroom in laps. Do bats get zoomies? This feels like she has zoomies. Having worn herself out, she flew into the cat tree house in the corner of our room about twenty minutes ago. Mendax laughed when I set it up two weeks ago, saying she would never use it. He was wrong. She loves it and sleeps in there and refuses the fancy cage he has. *I win.*

Looking in the mirror I adjust the sleeves on the mini yellow peasant dress.

"I should wear dresses more often, shouldn't I, Gotha?"

I look over to the bat.

"Why do you look so sad?" I pet her head.

She turns and dismisses me.

"Okay then."

The sun has fully set, and Mendax still hasn't shown up. I straightened up the attic, putting more of the colorful pens Mendax likes in the holders, then brought up some files of my own. The laundry is switched out and I even began running an analysis for a client who had just signed on with the firm yesterday.

The dark screen on my phone mirrors a dark pit in my stomach. What could be taking him this long? There's a small flame of hope simply that I've simply missed a call or text from Mendax. The flame is extinguished when there are no new notifications, at least none I care for.

Padding into the kitchen to start the kettle in hopes some hibiscus, peach, and white tea blend from this month will help settle my nerves. The click from the kettle boiling water goes off in tandem with my phone. Leaping for the phone on the table, the cool glass meets my thumb. It's a group chat message, but it's the family group chat.

Why Therapy Is A Thing

Mother Dearest

Do you still want this?

Dad

She better keep it! The amount we paid for it she needs to wear when she gets married.

Laughing while looking at my old prom dress, I begin to type.

Depends...

why are you asking???

Mother Dearest

One of my clients is looking for donation gowns to build a community closet for underprivileged youths.

Dad

But it cost so much

Sorry dad, charity wins this one. Not even my size any more.

Dad

Fine. Are you still going out with Mendax tonight?

I think so. He's late picking me up.

Mother Dearest

fifty dollars says his mother is holding him up. Isn't that what happened last time?

I swear, Davina

She's more meddlesome than I am. I've had a lot of stress from work, and I'm ready to fight someone.

Say the word, and I'll fight her.

Dad

Can I watch? Also this fight must have proper attire. Bikini bottoms, white t-shirt and it's only fair if it's in a pool.

Mother Dearest

Oh you would like that…

Dad

Come to the garage and see how much

FOR THE LOVE OF GOD I'M STILL IN THIS CHAT!!!!!!

Rubbing the bridge of my nose and then adjusting my glasses, I decide to forget all about the tea I was making. My parents, I love them, but damn, they might be worse than Mendax and me. Walking up the stairs, skipping the second one from the top—the one that always squeaks—I call up the attic once more. My old friend, silence, greets me.

"Okay, that's it."

I'm going to go myself, even though I'm still nervous to walk through the portal alone. Pulling up the group chat with my friends, I decide to type while giving myself a running start.

Cultured Miscreants

Has anyone heard from Mendax?

Instead of bouncing dots on the screen, dots of light flashed behind my eyes. Wincing, I stand rubbing my tailbone. Great, I am going to have a bruise on either my nose or ass, maybe both.

"Where the hell did the portal go?"

There's no reason why I should have run face-first into the wall. This should be a pantry filled with labeled jars organized by size and category of food. What the hell just happened? He wouldn't leave me, would he?

No. No. He wouldn't. He was happy.

We were happy.

So why does my heart feel more bruised than my ass?

Chapter 36
CUT-OFF
Mendax

S HEER AND UTTER CHAOS. Elsher, Elara's father, is turning an unsightly shade of purple from his blood boiling and rising beneath his blue skin. If he holds his anger and breath any longer, we may get lucky and see steam shoot out his ears.

My mother is hurling one question after another, and I am hopeful she'll faint within the next several minutes from lack of inhaling. Elara is desperately trying to calm both of our parents and failing miserably.

My apartment is in chaos. It's not even the good, fun, chaos that I've grown fond of with Davina.

Like the many times we'll sit to watch a show she picked, and halfway through, we're rearranging the room or researching a random question like "Do bees fart?" *She's perfect, and I love her.*

Maybe I could slip back home to where it's controlled chaos. Sure, there are a bunch of trinkets everywhere, and Davina couldn't tell you where the house keys are or what cabinet the extra dryer sheets are in in the laundry room, but she could tell you that there's a paperclip on the floor in the dining room in the back corner where the floorboards have the one dark spot by the snake plant.

Controlled and organized chaos is what I have come to appreciate. I should put more effort into convincing her to make use of the attic office instead of the dining room. It's really why I organized it all, but according to Davina, the dining room makes more sense because she's closer to the kitchen. If she's closer to the kitchen, she won't forget to eat. *That is a complete lie.*

Maybe I should set up a spare room in the back of the apartment as an office for her. Whatever we decide, I know one thing for certain; I can't go back now. They can never know this portal leads directly to her bedroom. *Damn.*

"Well? Have you nothing to say?!" Elsher seethes.

Smoothing my beard, I raise a brow. "Which question are you referring to? They all got jumbled."

Turning, I march into the study, looking for the slim, green phone Davina made me buy. Right after I purchased it, Rolvak, bless him, did the same tech wizardry he did to Davina's phone. Now, it works literally everywhere.

The trespassing inquisitorial squad is hot on my heels. My mother gasps.

"Mendax! What happened to your neck?" she scurries around me, holding my shoulders and pulling the collar of my shirt down. "Where did all these bruises come from? Where have you been?"

Davina certainly left her mark on me the past few nights. While I may have several small hickeys, these are nothing compared to the two I left on both her upper, inner thighs. She cursed me up and down because they rub together whenever she walks.

"It's my fault!" Elara hastily shouts.

Oh, this I have to hear.

Elsher's brows slant down. His chest puffs out, trying to claim as much space in my home as possible.

"Explain yourself."

"Let me speak with Mendax first, Daddy, then we will talk to you both. Do you not always tell me cooler minds prevail?"

The plastered smile must appease him. His chest deflates while his feet stomp across the wall of books, grumbling something I can't make out.

I sigh, tossing a yellow cushion Davina smuggled into this room from one of her spare rooms onto the black chaise lounge.

"Excuse us, Mother." *Where the hell is my phone?*

My mother's silhouette in the window holds a stillness to rival statues. The sun is low in the sky despite it not being close to sunset yet. That can only mean a torrential downpour is coming soon. The arcade would have been the perfect spot for our date tonight.

Mother's voice cuts into my spiraling thoughts of this date being ruined and how I'm going to manage to sneak back out to see my woman.

"Does this mean the engagement is happening?" she asks with hopeful eyes.

Honestly? Of all the things she could ask, that was her best option?

All I can do is scowl as a response. My lack of words is the response she was dreading. With a shake of her head, she pushes away from the window, disapproval painted on her face, walking slowly towards the door. The soft click from the door sounds more like a final nail in the coffin.

"I would ask how you've been but judging from the growth of hair and hickeys." Elara gives a small smile. "How's Davina?"

Resting my hip against an armchair and shoving my hands in my pockets, I try to think of how to get out of this situation.

"She's wonderful. The real question is how she will be after this. It's our date night. Why are you and your father here?"

Elara's long blue fingers toy with the engagement band on her hand. Unease settles around us thick, cold, and heavy like an unwanted snowstorm.

"I've thought about the offer you and Davina gave me. I've been trying to tell you that I accept, but no one can get a hold of you. Orroth isn't much help as a messenger. He calls me 'you' with a scowl on his face and ignores me." She chuckles at the last part. "I called off the engagement."

Moving to the writing desk to continue my search for the errant phone, my foot pauses midair. My eyes volley from her face to her hand where the ring is still placed. *Sure, called it off.* Huffing, my shoes tap against the highly polished floor landing in me in front of the desk.

"My father is pissed to put it mildly; he demanded answers from your mother and she had none to give. So, surprise." Her fingers wiggle at her sides.

Pulling out the top drawer there's nothing but a rainbow of highlighters and pens. The second drawer houses my ruler, labels, and tape. Except for the new addition, a pair of pink lace underwear I took from Davina last week before we had our game night here. Who would have thought Candy Land would be so intense? I blame Orroth, the idiot, decided to steal the lollipop to win. He was caught by Davina. The next round, Rolvak stole the cinnamon roll, better choice for a card, wrong choice overall. Wren found it in his sleeve when he passed her the popcorn bowl. Good times.

Elara continues to speak, pacing the width of the room, "Megai, thought it was a grand idea to come here. Heaven forbid I call off something and just hand the ring back."

Sighing heavily, my eyes pinch shut until little dots explode behind my lids. "You know, if you really want out of this you could just start dating someone. I could have Davina introduce you to her neighbor. He's very single."

It would solve her problem, and it would also keep Blake away from my woman.

"You know they wouldn't care."

There's so much defeat in her tone I actually start to feel bad for Elara.

"I would love to tell Davina the good news of you calling this off."

Clenching my jaw, I look away, so I don't have to see the hesitation written clear as day on her face. Of course it wouldn't be this easy. *Why would something be easy when we were finally happy?*

A warm, soft hand wraps around my wrist.

"I can fix this, but you'll owe me. Because if I do this," Elara's thin voice barely breaks above a whisper, "I will lose everything."

"You better tread carefully, Elsher. I agreed to this engagement as long as both parties agreed. You will not threaten my son. He didn't break it off; Elara did. Mendax fulfilled his obligations to date her; that was all he had to do. I read the contract letter by letter." My mother speaks through clenched teeth.

Elsher stands toe-to-toe with my mother, which is more comical than it had any right being. He takes three steps back and tilts his head back to look her in the eye, and she isn't even in her heels.

"I still hold the seat of power in the high courts. I may not be able to tack on more time, but I can still take everything. Or did you not read the fine print in the clauses?"

My mother scoffs as she sits on the sofa, smoothing the wrinkles in her skirt. "Oh, please. We both know you've been after me for years. Now you're after my family. You wouldn't dare abuse your power."

"Are you willing to risk your secret being known? It would destroy you."

Elara gazes up at me from the hall. Her teeth have all but scraped the pink lipstick off her bottom lip.

Placing my hand on her shoulder, I ask, "Are you sure about this? I promise Davina and I will do everything we can. But if you do this, there is no going back."

She pats my hand, nods and begins walking away. Sharp clicking from her heels stops as she turns to look at me.

"It's time I stopped chasing after his approval. He behaves like a rabid dog because everyone is too afraid to be bitten. Plus, I managed to move some of my trust fund, so I won't be completely destitute."

I follow her wordlessly with my hands in my pockets. Finally, I remember where I left my phone. It's on the couch back home. It's probably on vibrate, too.

"Daddy!"

Elsher immediately stops his tirade, blowing out a harsh breath.

"Elara, honey. I'm doing this for you. You're too soft."

"I think you mean you're doing this for yourself and your son. I told you I don't want to marry Mendax, but I also didn't want his girlfriend to have him, so after an argument, I sent him away." She shuffles closer to her father, skirting the end table next to the sofa. "It was childish but done in the heat of the moment. For that, I apologize."

"Oh really?"

Elsher is calling her bluff. Not that I can blame him. Even from where I'm standing, her lie is easy to spot.

"You have to drop all the charges Mendax has and count his time as served, Daddy."

Her voice is small and fragile. Is this still part of her act, or does she always sound that way around him? It wouldn't surprise me if she learned to make herself small around him. Many girls are taught at a young age to be demure, quiet, and agreeable in our social circles. The perfect society wife should be small. The notion always rubbed me wrong. If Davina and I ever have a daughter, small is the last thing I will teach her to be. No daughter of mine would ever be made to feel she needs to be lesser.

Elsher snorts. His pants strain as his meaty fists shove into his pockets.

"Why would I do that? I—We wouldn't get anything out of that."

"Because I'll expose the truth. You're not the only one with secrets to share. Forget about this forced marriage. You and your precious son get to keep your name and image. No one else outside of this room will ever have to know what you really did."

Elara juts her chin in defiance. Even in the study, she refused to tell me what card she had to play. All she would say was it was the "nuclear option."

The atmosphere is more intense than a game night with Davina and Wren on opposing teams. My mother shifts in her seat before fixing the nonexistent flyaways in her slicked ponytail; only the soft tap of her shoes breaks the stillness. This is my apartment, and I feel like an awkward stranger twiddling his thumbs during a family dispute.

Elsher's dark chuckle grows louder, sparking a tinge of worry in the pit of my stomach. Narrowing his eyes, he surveys all of us; calculating his next move. Heavy, methodical steps echo menacingly towards Elara. She gulps. I edge closer to her, ready to intervene if needed.

Clasping his hands behind his back, he speaks with an eerie smile plastered on his square face, "And what truth would that be? Hmm?"

"How you orchestrated the theft of the witch's ladder Mendax was charged for."

Elara's small voice cracks toward the end. Her face is downcast, not able to meet mine. The whispered statement is ricocheting in my mind.

If that blow wasn't enough, Elara keeps talking, "All so you could collect the insurance on it and sell it on the black market after receiving the appraisal from Mrs. Draxton all those years ago."

This, son of a bitch! I ruined my good name, my family's good name, for a supposedly anonymous buyer through a third party. I found a buyer for the witch's ladder; it was stolen from me, I couldn't prove it, and I was charged with theft of a mystical item.

I am seething. My black nails imprinted tiny crescents into my palm.

Elsher's composure slips momentarily. "You can't prove that."

Elara laughs. "But I can."

She walks around the living room, eyeing the artwork on the walls.

"Your son, my stepbrother, itemized it, and you know how dense he is. His two brain cells constantly compete for third place. I saw it and kept it in my back pocket for a rainy day. You didn't think he did the work himself, did you? No, all that came through me."

Elsher staggers backwards. "You ungrateful brat. If you do that, you'll ruin the entire family."

"A family I was never welcomed in. A family who only ever wanted sons. Plus, I don't work for your firm anymore. I handed in my resignation letter weeks ago. I need to break free from you, from our family." She takes a shuddering breath.

"Drop the charges, cancel the engagement, and no one has to know. I refuse to marry Mendax. He's happy with Davina, and honestly, they belong together. I have no interest in marrying someone who is me in a male form. I want what they have."

A newfound respect for Elara takes over. I still want to murder her father, but the last thing I need is another charge for choosing violence. The respect quickly dissipates as I realize she has knowingly sat on this information all these years; I could have been a free man. Would I still have met Davina if that had been the case, though? My mother's jaw is agape, and she looks like could keel over at any given moment.

The look on Elsher's face makes my skin crawl.

"I need assurances then." He rounds the back of the sofa, knuckles turning white with every dig of his fingers into the cushions.

It is my turn to speak.

"What could you possibly need?" I ask, flexing my fingers to control my breathing.

"You." Is all he says with that same creepy smile again. "You stay while I get you cleared of all charges. It doesn't happen overnight, you know."

He stands to his full height—which isn't exactly tall— and fixes his suit.

"He won't be needing that portal anymore since he found his way back from what appears to be a wonderful vacation despite being confined to this realm." Spittle collects in the corners of his mouth before flying through the air.

"Get rid of the portal, or I'll have the guardsman's wizard come and ward this entire place with the three of you in it."

Megai shoots out of her seat. "Elsher, are you out of your mind!?"

The shock has finally worn off, and I haven't seen this side of my mother in a long time. Her willowy frame vibrates with rage, and the cursed painting by the door crashes to the floor. Wooden splinters sail through the air upon impact.

If destroying my apartment made my mother feel better in her fury, she can have at it. My concerns are much bigger. I need that portal to get to Davina. I need to be with her. I need her. Despite trying to beg her not to go along with it with my eyes, Elara isn't looking at me. Her focus was firmly on her father.

"Daddy?" Her watery voice breaks my heart.

At this moment, she seems like a broken little girl, desperate for a parent's approval. I shouldn't feel anything towards her, but Davina has changed me and made me sympathetic.

His response is to dig the phone out of his breast pocket and sneer. "Don't you 'Daddy' me. You want to play big girl games; you win big girl prizes. You can also kiss your trust fund goodbye. Also, you'll be struck from my will unless you close that portal now."

She gives me an imploring look riddled with guilt.

Can she really do it? Opening and closing portals is rare amongst our kind. Even if she can, will she?

Holding her arm out and rotating her palm, she calls the magic of the portal to her. I run as fast as my feet will carry me to the kitchen, hoping to jump through the portal with whatever magic is left.

"Davina!" My heart races as I leap through the air, feeling a brief moment of weightlessness before crashing into the shelves in my pantry, sending a cascade of items tumbling to the floor. "No!"

I am officially cut off from Davina, and I have no idea how long it will take to get back to her.

Chapter 37
PETTY
Davina

SUMMER CAME AND WENT, and soon, the crisp fall air fills my home as I leave the windows open. Gotha is swooping in and out of each window while I wait for the apple, cardamom, and cinnamon tea to finish steeping.

I haven't heard from Mendax or any of my friends since the day he went missing. The only text I got in the group chat said, *"Sorry, everything is going to be just fine."*

Then, they all left the chat and blocked me. Well, all the guys did. Wren still hasn't responded.

With a heavy sigh, I shut the green book full of stories and rhymes. Another day, repeating that nursery rhyme hasn't worked. I've wracked my brain trying to figure out if I'm doing something wrong or different. I have tried saying the stupid nursery rhyme to summon Mendax every day for the past three months. I even tried drinking tea from that cup again, just like last time, to no avail.

"Hey, Pumpkin, do you have a ladder?" My dad pokes his head around the corner, smiling, holding up the ghost decorations he brought over.

Mom was over the moon to get rid of what she deemed "tacky" Halloween decorations. Harvest decorations were always more her thing. These were some of my favorites: the zipline ghosts, floating witch hats, and the giant cauldron, with green LED lights and smoke that currently took up most of my front yard with a few scattered gravestones.

Heat from the oven fogs my glasses.

"I think it's in the garage," I say while pulling out the tray of sugar cookies. "Wait, no, it's not. I think Blake has it. He's hanging spiderwebs and giant spiders around his porch. I can text him to see if he's done with it."

Gotha swoops towards the cookies, but I chase her away before she gets close.

"Don't you dare."

Plucking the white and brown spatula from the utensil drawer, I transfer the cookies from the sheet to the cooling rack. So far, there are three dozen cookies in a mixture of pumpkins, witch hats, and ghosts ready to be decorated. I intended on making one dozen but apparently I forgot to cut Uncle Alex's recipe. *I'm sure these will freeze fine.*

My dad inhales the warm vanilla aroma, rubbing and patting his stomach.

"I'm not a huge fan of that guy. He's waiting to swoop in. Before you say anything, I'm a man, and I have eyes." He juggles two cookies in his hands. "Oh shit, ass, that's hot."

"Dad," I chide. "One, he's not waiting. Blake and I are just friends and neighbors. He knows I'm currently in a long-distance relationship. Second, you saw me take the cookies out just now, they don't even have frosting or sprinkles on yet."

"Gotha and I are hungry. We've been hanging decorations all morning. This house will absolutely win the town competition once I'm done with it. Oh, and he's *absolutely* waiting. Mendax needs to marry you and take you off the market. Throw in a few grandbabies, too, really seal the deal."

He shoves one cookie into his mouth before holding out a piece for the spoiled bat.

"Now, finish up those cookies; you've made more than enough. Once your mom gets back from Target, we'll go out to dinner. We need to leave early to be back in the city tomorrow to help with the Halloween gala for the children's hospital."

"I still can't believe you agreed to sit on the committee for the hospital."

My dad feeds the last piece of cookie to a now over-sugared Gotha and shrugs. "Well, it was the right thing to do. Plus, Simmons is an idiot and would have run that committee along with the funding into the ground."

"He's also Mom's college ex-boyfriend." I give him a pointed look wiping my hands on my flour dusted apron.

My dad gives me a boyish grin. "I gotta remind her of what she's got, every now and then."

I laugh so I won't cry. But my face can't hide it.

My dad wraps me in a giant hug, rocking me softly. "What's wrong, Pumpkin?"

I sniffle a little. "I just don't know when Mendax is coming back. I feel like a whiny baby. I was never like this before."

I had come clean about everything to both my parents over the summer, from the accidental summoning and the fake dating to actually falling for the handsome demon. At first, my mother was pissed because I lied and also practiced magic, and my dad cried with me; then, my dad was pissed because his little girl got her heart broken, and mom went into fix-it mode. They stayed with me for a week helping me to recite the spell that brought Mendax here in the first place. Then, Mom tried to figure out if there was a way to change the wording to get his mother or brother instead. Dad was so optimistic at one point he stated, "There are three college degrees between us. We're smart enough for that; we're smart enough for this."

Needless to say, we didn't figure it out.

"You're like this because love scrambles your brain and makes you act funny. Look at your mother and me. When we were dating, I actually convinced her to get a tattoo on her butt on a dare." He snorts.

My jaw drops. Extricating myself from his bear hug, I stare.

"All the crap she gave me about mine, and she has one?" I snatch a tester cookie, AKA, a misshapen cookie, off the cooling rack and shove it in my mouth.

He smiles and tosses his head back, blindly swatting the air. "She made me get a matching one on the opposite butt cheek. I have Pac Man with a few dots, and she has a ghost with a few dots."

His hand smacks my arm. I've always managed to get in the crosshairs of his laugh smacks.

Leave it to my dad to brighten my mood. I wonder if I could convince Mendax to get a tattoo?

Grabbing a few strooples off the shelf, my eye caught a stack of letters.

"Oh, I got a letter from the law firm Uncle Alex used."

"I thought all his affairs had been settled."

Dad's eyebrows lift in surprise as he settles himself in a kitchen chair, not batting an eye at the sudden subject change. Gotha flaps wildly around him until he opens his flannel, and she settles herself inside as he buttons it back up.

"Think Mom would get jealous if I tell her I got a little lady sleeping on my chest?"

I laugh and snap a picture. *I should frame this one.*

"Um, probably. Do it. I dare you."

He leans to the left, pulling out his phone and chuckling as his finger taps at the screen. "I'm going to ignore it for a bit if she responds. I may need to sleep in the other guest room."

I snort. "Always welcome here, Dad."

Standing on my tiptoes, the floorboards creak while I put another tin can of tea on the nearly full shelf that is entirely too high for me to reach, but perfect for Mendax. I swear he did that on purpose. The lids have all been made into coasters; the cans, I'm saving. I promised to make them into little flowerpots. *I'll get to it eventually.*

"Almost everything was settled. They finally managed to track down those antique cars. The Series 10 Cadillac is up in Canada, and customs is being a pain, but the red Coupe DeVille is in a climate-controlled car storage facility in Portland. I have to go up there and sign some papers."

My dad looks wistful. His thumb strokes his bottom lip.

"The Series 10 is probably only good for selling to a collector who isn't afraid of a lot of work. The last time I saw it, the floor was rusted out, and the backseat was nothing more than a home for mice. Now, the Coupe DeVille; that is worth getting back."

Blowing the steam from my cup and sitting across from him, curiosity gets the better of me. "Why is that worth getting back? I mean, I am going to get it back, but why do you care?"

"That is the car I took your mom in on our first official date."

Oh well, that's sweet. I scoot further back into the chair, tucking one leg underneath me, getting ready for the story I know is about to come.

"You were also made in the backseat."

"Oh, come on, Dad. Really? In front of my sugar cookies!?" I regret asking him now.

Dad has devolved into a fit of laughter and tears as he blindly swats the air again. *Thank goodness I'm on the other side of the table.*

Another day, another spreadsheet, another meeting. The house is starting to feel stuffy, so I take myself, my laptop, earbuds, and a few notebooks down to the coffee shop. Thankfully, the seating outside the shop is pretty empty for a Wednesday morning. Drumming my fingers on the wooden table, my eyes scan all the Halloween decorations. The town has mounted jack-o'-lanterns on street lights, fake cobwebs drape the windows of local boutiques, and signs for the pumpkin patch and hayrides are plastered on every available surface. I swear they're pumping pumpkin spice into the air to complete the motif.

My screen flickers as someone joins the meeting.

"Good morning, Davina," Faith, my HR advocate, greets me.

This meeting has been a long time coming. Tony, that little bitch, finally pushed me over the edge. He pushed every one of my buttons like a toddler in an elevator. He has refused to use Slack, even though everyone on our team uses it; there's a better communication flow there. Then there's the mixed-up research results and botched presentations. How he's still working here is anyone's guess. My team's productivity has gone down to the point where our clients are being transferred to other teams, and we're being told we're on probation. If things don't improve, we'll be forced to be in the office and not have the choice of hybrid or telework anymore.

"Morning, Faith."

I nod a thank you to the barista who brought out my Halloween-themed tea, the "poisoned apple." The name was off-putting, but I have to give 'em points for effort. Shockingly, it tastes like a caramel candy apple with a hint of licorice.

Faith clears her throat while tucking a microbraid behind her ear. Her deep brown eyes narrow behind her blue-rimmed glasses before sliding them on her head.

"So, the goal for today is to stick to the plot and file your grievances. I reviewed the file, and I can tell you I have no idea what Nancy was talking about. Your correspondence with Tony is strictly professional.

"Also, thank you for granting us access to the Slack channel to review, as well. Obviously, we can't account for the phone calls since those aren't recorded, but he has a nice stack of complaints about you, and I quote, 'being demeaning and emasculating.' I do have to ask: what would you like to see come from this meeting?"

The cold air nips at my cheeks and neck. It only it works to cool the hot anger thrumming in my veins.

"I'm not even sure, to be honest. I never thought telling him he needed to do better and pointing out his lack of knowledge and how badly he messed up every project would result in this. Those phone calls were me telling him to send the work to Gina to double-check his numbers and then to fact-check with Tina in research for updated information on market trends. Someone with his lack of experience should be interning and learning, not working on the most integral parts of projects for clients of the caliber I and the rest of my team handle."

She gives a deep chuckle that sounds like she has a laugh that would get an entire room to laugh with her.

"So, you want him off your team and would recommend he go back to training. Got it. If that doesn't happen?"

Now, that's the million-dollar question.

"Ten years I've worked for this company; working my way up from the intern pool to the senior position I'm in now. Being the 'yes man'—for lack of a better term—agreeing to take on extra work and responsibilities, Training other employees and everything in between. There are clients who come to this firm to work specifically with me and my team. If me and my work are not valued at a higher level, then I really don't see a future with this company. I know my worth along with the value of my work."

Faith nodded while scribbling away on a notepad. "Okay. Let's see what we can do."

More faces pop up into little boxes, and so begins the HR meeting that could very well be its own level in Dante's Inferno.

For months Mendax had asked me what I wanted. He always said nothing was too big or too small. I always had the same answer, "nothing. I don't want anything from you."

If I was going to be honest with myself, what I wanted scared the crap outta me, especially after running the risk numbers. During Easter, after the egg hunt I made him do—which he will never admit he enjoyed—he sprung the question again—telling him that starting my own consulting firm seemed so outlandish at the time. But now? Why shouldn't I? There's nothing to stop me, especially with the hefty severance package I was given to keep my mouth shut after it was revealed by freaking Tony himself, after he poorly timed a cough to cover up a fart, that he's the owner's nephew.

Echelon Nexus Consulting is no longer a dream. Despite the risk analysis telling me there's an eighty-five percent chance of failure, I'm leaping into the fifteen percent armed to the teeth with years of knowledge, experience, ambition, and, hopefully, a clientele that is still untapped. Plus, I can always poach my clients and clientele waitlist to start my firm and raise my chance of success to ninety percent. It's not sleazy; most, if not all, the current clients were persuaded by a magical ring to begin with.

There are so many forms now, plus insurance and everything in between, that I was not prepared for. I definitely need to do more research.

"I should call my mother." She'd help me with all this.

With that thought in mind, I sent an email to my team explaining my departure and scheduling out my final two weeks of redistributing products and offering meetings and introductions to new project leads to my current clients.

At the end of the day, no one can say I'm not a professional. I am petty, though. Which is why I hope Mr. Jason Walker loses that charm ring. I hope Nacy's phone never charges unless her charging cable is wrapped so many times and set at a certain angle. As for Tony, I hope he stubs his pinky toe on every corner of his home and that he always steps in a wet spot while wearing socks.

Chapter 38
CALL HER
Mendax

THERE'S BEEN A TUG in my chest every day for the past year. It's been both comforting and maddening. Knowing Davina hasn't given up trying to summon me back is the greatest feeling; knowing I can't get to her because of the magic blocker currently strapped to my ankle makes me hate everything.

Even though my life has turned into an absolute dumpster fire, I'm trying to think like Davina and see the silver lining. When I do get back, it'll be the same time of year, and we can pick up where we left off. At least, that's the lie I keep telling myself. Truth is, I'm afraid she'll be too angry at me for disappearing to actually still want me.

It's killing me not being able to see, talk to, or touch her. After Elsher left that day, my mother got into an all-out fight with Elara about holding information that could have seen to my innocent verdict then, never mentioning it while we had our "dates"—and I use that term lightly.

To her benefit, Elara actually looked guilty and apologized profusely, but the damage was already done. The unfortunate events didn't stop there.

Elsher went back on his word, and the apple apparently doesn't fall far from the tree. Elara didn't want to release the information she had. Rolvak, being the tech genius he is, ended up hacking into her work and home network and found multiple files of blackmail and money laundering.

He said he didn't do it for me, he did it for Menvina.

There was also a request to name our first-born child after him. His suggestions were, obviously, Rolvak—or Rolvac with a C—Roland, or Rowen.

There have been countless meetings with our new counselor. With all the new cases being opened, she advised us to cut contact with Davina since she technically caused me to break my arrest and harbored me, and there are also zero records of her traveling through any realm gate. We didn't need or want to implicate her in anything, so that's exactly what we did after a few heated exchanges between my brother, our mother, and me.

Orroth was the first to sidestep that warning and sent her a message asking her not to worry. I knew for a fact a message like that would do the exact opposite. We were also banned from realm travel for the time being since they were all complicit in my escape.

Luckily, Rolvak wiped every message thread. We probably should name our first-born after him. It's been absolute hell until now.

I've waited months for this day. Anxiety wriggles its way through my veins as I stand in front of a new panel of judiciaries. All of them were replaced ahead of term once the scandal about Elsher broke, and it turned out two others were just as dirty.

The hum of the cold, harsh, white overhead lights nurtures the anxiety in anyone standing beneath them. Taupe walls close in on the desks in the circular room, strangling any hushed conversations anyone may want or need to have.

"Mr. Draxton." A small woman with wrinkly, pale white skin and three orange eyes peers down at me. "We have reopened your trial and reviewed all statements and new evidence put forth. This panel humbly requests your acceptance of our apologies as we redact and erase all false charges from your record. You are a free man, Mr. Draxton." She offers me a smile.

"Please let us know if there is anything the court can do for your forgiveness and compliance."

Anxiety turns to pure excitement and electricity. I'm free to finally go home. There's a media circus outside waiting for any scrap of a sound bite they can run for days on end. It's no surprise the judiciary panel wants my forgiveness and compliance. It's in their best interest to make me happy and sweep this under the rug.

"As a matter of fact, there is something you can do."

Rolling my shoulders, I allow myself to exude a fraction of my charm to waft freely around the room. I'm going to need a grand apology for Davina, and I have an idea how this panel can help me with that.

"I humbly request a motion of citizenship to be granted to Davina Nicole Myles as well as approval for a business license named to the same person."

From where I stand, it looks like heads might explode.

"I'm not asking for much." I'm asking for a lot; we all know that. "Years of my life were taken unjustly; my name and business tarnished. These two *minor* requests are simple and easy."

"You're asking us to circumvent a lot here, Mr. Draxton." An orange man with four horns and large, bat-like wings states.

Plastering on a smile and releasing a bit more of my charm, while fixing my cufflinks. "Correct me if I'm wrong, but is it not easier to circumvent this rather than the press?"

"Dax, you really should call her," Orroth says, leaning against a light post.

The realm gate is quiet at this hour, and it's perfect. I had debated on calling Davina after the hearing, but I wanted to surprise her and show up on her doorstep.

Wren wraps her arms around Orroth and smiles at me. "Leave Lover Boy alone. I think it's romantic. Sure, she'll probably have a heart attack, but it'll be worth it. Now go, I'm dying to talk to her again and have another game night."

A new sensation blossoms in my chest. "Game night sounds fun. *After* I've had time with her." I'm giddy just thinking about her. Knowing I can be with her again.

A throat clears behind me, and the soles of shoes squeak against the polished stone tile.

"Here you go." Mother holds out a small black gift bag. "There's some transformation pills for you in there and a few for Davina so she can see through the glamour. There's also a gift for her, as an apology from me. Please tell her I'm sorry for my behavior, and I hope we can have a more appropriate conversation in the near future."

An apology from her is a rarity and isn't easy for her to issue. Even with the sour look on her face from swallowing the bitter pill of apology, I find myself walking closer to her. This means more to me than she will ever know. The awkwardness of our strained relationship has built up years worth of walls between us, but I might as well start chipping away at it now.

Plucking the bag from her fingers, I wrap my arms around her shoulders and hug her tightly. It's a few seconds before she returns the hug with a warmth I thought was only possible as a figment of my imagination. This entire time, something has been nagging at me and if I ask now, it could ruin the progress we've made. But I'd rather take one step forward and ten back.

"Mother," I begin, angling my body so we have some semblance of privacy as my hands grab hers, "What secret did Elsher threaten you with?"

Her head hangs, her and shoulders slump like she's tired of carrying the weight of the secret.

"I never wanted you to find out, not like this." The age of her voice sits heavy on every word.

She tips her head towards a bench, and we make our way over. Orroth begins to move but stills at Wren's touch to his chest and her whispers in his ear.

Now I'm not sure I want to hear the truth. The stone bench is cold and unwelcoming, but I push past my comfort and give my mother my full focus.

Clicking from the strand of pearls under her long nails fills the conversational void while she gathers her thoughts and the right words to use.

"Before I entered my arranged marriage, I was supposed to marry someone else. He was my everything, but I wasn't his. I found that out when I read the paper and saw a formal engagement announcement to another. It shouldn't have bothered me, but it did. At the end of the day, I was nothing more than a business traction between families, and a better option presented itself."

Her brows crease while taking a shuddering breath. The soft cotton from her skirt meets my palm as I try to give her a reassuring squeeze.

"I was already pregnant with you when I entered the new marriage. We didn't know until after everything was said and done. The dates didn't match up, and I was accused of trapping my husband. That's why he has never really been around. It has everything to do with me."

Her watery voice seeps through her eyes. My thumb catches the heartache running down her face.

It all makes sense: the nannies, the tutors, why everything always felt forced with my father. It also explains why I came out a bit different. My horns are larger; my height towers over everyone in my family, and they all have some type of pink hue to their eyes, while I'm left with violet.

How did I not notice it before? I'm left reeling and unsure how to process all of it.

"I take it Orroth doesn't know?"

She answers with a shake of her head. "I'm so sorry, Mendax. You deserved so much better growing up."

"It wasn't your fault. You were used and thrown away. But if you know what it feels like to have to lose the one you considered your everything, why subject me to it."

She stands and smooths her skirt. Her small, warm hand cups my cheek. "Apparently, I'm no better than my parents. Good thing you're already better than I could ever be."

Nodding, I stand and gather my thoughts with each step toward the gate. There's one final round of farewells and promises to call soon. Tucking the official paperwork for Davina into the gift back into the gift bag, I grab my bag, and step away from my family towards the gate. Towards Davina. Towards home.

I know I'm free to come and go as I please, but when I think about it, I don't know when I'll come back. Going home is far more appealing.

The sleek black town car that drove me from the Portland gate drives away from the corner house on Trilley Road. The sun beats down on me and my three-piece navy pinstripe suit. All this time, this is the first time my eyes have been in front of the house. The grass is slightly overgrown, but the rosemary and lavender bushes dotting the porch are full and well-maintained. Planter boxes hang off the porch full of purple and yellow daisies. Smooth teal paint coats the entirety of the outside. *She's certainly kept herself busy.*

Guilt threatens to creep up into my heart, but I decide it's better to shove it back down. Rolling my shoulders and walking across the level brick pathway, my heart knocks against my ribs before my fist can meet the door.

"It's just Davina. No need to be nervous," I tell myself, but it only makes me more nervous.

What will I even say to her? Should I kiss her with reckless abandon? Let my actions do all the talking? Will she yell at me for being gone without a word?

Staring at my reflection in the mirrored window, a bark of a laugh escapes me. There's no possibility of kissing her at first sight. She'd knee me in the balls. I don't even look like the Mendax she knows. While I still have my height, my raven black hair is cut shorter, and my beard is trimmed closer to my face. The horns are gone under the cloak of magic and my garnet skin now appears as a sandy beige. The only thing that physically resembles the man she knows is the violet and pink eyes staring back at me.

"Maybe I should have called."

I roll my shoulders back, taking a deep breath before striding towards the door. With determination, I raise my hand to knock.

"Can I help you?" a deep voice calls from behind me, leaving my fist hovering inches from the wood that separates me and my forever.

Turning on my heel, I'm faced with a tall man with sandy blonde hair resting his hip on the handle of a lawnmower.

He looks too comfortable on our front lawn.

"I don't believe I know who you are," I say, stepping around my luggage and adjusting the onyx and sterling silver cufflinks.

His chest puffs out under his plain white shirt, causing the material to strain.

"That's because you never asked." He gives a cocky grin. "I'm Blake."

So, this is Blake. The same Blake that went out with my Davina and asked her out again. I wonder if he's attempted to take my woman out on another date. Blood simmers in my veins, bubbling into jealousy and possessiveness.

He's a good looking man. The kind of handsome that always gets leading roles in the romance movies Davina watches while eating ice cream with a heating pad on her stomach. What makes me irrational is thinking how they would look like a beautiful couple if she were standing next to him.

Strolling down the stairs, I smooth my skinny silk black tie.

"So, can I help you?" Blake says, eyeing me with suspicion.

Only Davina can bring this side out of me.

"Knowing that you don't own this house or live here, I doubt you can." I step closer to him, towering over him by several inches.

A classic, all-red convertible Coupe DeVille pulls into the driveway. My little oxygen thief slides out of the driver's seat. Her legs look longer while her body seems more defined and tanned in a white strapless sundress with pale blue clouds scattered across the fabric. The neon yellow in her hair looks brighter than I remember in a sleek, high ponytail.

"Hey," she draws out the greeting, her eyes darting between me and Blake. "Everything okay?"

I'm rooted to the spot, too stunned by her beauty to move a muscle. Her voice is a balm to my soul. Then, her thighs take center stage as she leans into the back seat, grabbing a few canvas bags. Blake jogs over to her, snatching the bags from her delicate hands. *Crap, I should be doing that.* He leans in and whispers something in her ear. She looks so happy and I'm dying inside. *Am I too late?*

I make my way over as her face scrunches in confusion as she eyes me warily. If I was dying before, someone should dig my grave now. She doesn't move closer to me; if anything, she inches towards *him.*

"I'll take those."

I move to pull the bags from Blake, but he turns his body, hiding the bags and Davina behind him.

He chuckles. "Yeah, I don't think so, Buddy."

Part of me wants to be mad and jealous at how he protects her, but the other part of me knows I don't have a right to feel that way. *I abandoned her.*

"Davina?"

I peer over his shoulder. She's looking at me with those wide brown eyes. She's right there; I can smell her perfume mixing with the summer breeze. I'm going to go mad if I don't have her in my arms in the next few seconds. For being outside during the summer, the tension and awkwardness are heavier than the humidity clinging to our skin.

"You know him?" Blake asks over his shoulder.

Shock, joy, and rage dance across her face in an endless loop. Shoving past Blake with a force that makes him stumble, she unleashes on me.

"Where have you been?" Fury laces her voice.

I know this is not the time for me to get turned on, but some things can't be helped.

"Do you have any idea how long I've been trying to get a hold of you?"

In the blink of an eye, she snatches a grapefruit from a bag and hurls it towards my face. Dodging to the left just in time, it whizzes past my ear, landing with a thud on the grass.

"Any of you! Not a single call, letter, email, smoke signal!" She shoves my chest, but I don't budge, which seems to anger her further. "Mendax, I want answers."

"Oh, you're the long-distance boyfriend." Blake laughs. "You come on strong, man."

Shuffling the bags into one hand, he holds the other up in a wave.

"Nice to meet you, I guess. Davina, give the guy a chance to talk."

Maybe Blake isn't so bad.

"Yeah, Davina. Give me a chance to talk," I say with a smile, which only seems to enrage her more.

She whirls on him, fists down by her hips, back pulled taut like a bow string.

"Thank you for fixing my mower, Blake." She grabs all but one bag full of groceries from him. "Here's what you asked for; I'll message you later to figure out that new run schedule. My *boyfriend* and I need to have a long talk."

He readjusts his grips on the brightly tinted bags and leans my way.

"Dude, I hope you brought her some nice antique or something as an apology. She. Is. Pissed." He strolls away whistling.

"Good luck!" he yells from across the street.

I should have called her.

Chapter 39
WELCOME HOME

Davina

IT'S BEEN ONE HELL of a year. I've missed Mendax every single day, and now that he's here, I'm mad. This isn't what I thought seeing him would be like.

If it weren't for his eyes, I wouldn't recognize him. Even though his voice registered, it was like watching a dubbed movie that wasn't synched.

"Are you coming?" I ask from my porch, watching him stand next to my car.

That's when it hits me. This isn't what I had in mind because he looks like a stranger. It's funny how the car is the same shade I'm used to seeing on his skin. He's still devilishly handsome. In this form, he's the picture of tall, dark, and handsome. This Mendax is who I would picture as a default book boyfriend in a mafia romance.

His long, measured steps tap lightly against the newly paved walkway. Bending, he grabs his luggage in one hand and all the grocery bags in the other, before pulling up to his full height and leaving a searing kiss on my forehead.

This man, I swear. It took a full year to get my brain cells back, and he's already starting to kiss me stupid again. Every thought and emotion I had is wiped clean. Charming bastard.

"I missed you," Mendax whispers in my ear, but it sounds louder than a clap of thunder in my heart.

A stupid smile grows on my face, I bounce on my toes, turning to unlock the door. Sinking my teeth into my bottom lip I gaze at him from over my shoulder.

"I missed you too."

The cool brass knob turns in my palm.

"Oh, don't freak out when you meet Ghoul. He's a really sweet boy."

Nerves have taken up residence in my veins. The house has had a drastic interior change. The walls in each room are dark, moody colors: forest green, eggplant, navy, and onyx with pops of vibrance. The dining room is an actual dining room now and not my makeshift office; I finally made use of the attic office.

The antique frames are still on the wall, but the pictures have been replaced with faces I actually know and care about. There are even a few of me and our group of friends. I still need pictures of me and Mendax. It's not to say that I don't have any. We've taken pictures, but it's a little hard to explain why he looks the way he does in every picture when it isn't Halloween.

His luggage settles on the floor next to the tan leather couch. Mendax's eyes scan every new detail. I wonder if he can spot all the trinkets and artwork he brought into our home displayed on the bookshelves and walls.

"How's Gotha?" He quirks a brow while flexing his fingers at his sides. "I imagine you two grew close."

His fingers undo the buttons on his jacket before he shrugs it off and places it on the back of a yellow velvet armchair I thrifted from a yard sale. The vest is the next to go before he loosens his tie.

Twiddling my thumbs in front of my hips, I gingerly walk over to him. Where did our familiarity go? We're behaving like this is the first time we've ever met. Unable to help myself, my fingers skate over the suspenders and across his shoulders.

"She's great. Spoiled rotten by my dad," I chuckle. "He built her a bat house for the backyard that looks like a Disney castle. If he hadn't built me a badass treehouse when I was little, I would be jealous."

A bolt of lightning strikes us, zapping all inhibitions from us; his hand wraps around my hip, pulling me closer while the other skims my neck before cupping my jaw. My hands squeeze his biceps while my eyelids flutter closed. Darkness consumes my sight before familiar fireworks spark and ignite in the pit of my stomach, exploding behind my lids.

His lips are still a conundrum to me, firm and soft. I've missed this. I've missed him.

Goosebumps rise on my skin as his grip tightens on me, digging into my flesh. The kiss is dizzying, all-consuming. The world fades away until there is only us.

Mendax breaks the kiss, giving us a chance to gulp in the air while he rests his forehead on mine. "I couldn't wait any longer. I was going to go crazy if I couldn't kiss you."

Tracing the sharp angles of his face, I giggle. "Took you long enough. I thought you would pounce on me the second the door closed."

"I intended to knock and surprise you with a kiss at first." He grins. "Then I saw what I looked like."

Mendax's large hand travels up and down my spine, ghosting over the top of my ass. Settling his hand on my lower back, his thumb sweeps back and forth, making me feel alive.

My hands cup his face. "You're so handsome like this. You could be on the cover of GQ. It's certainly a surprise."

He's right; if he had knocked and kissed me sans explanation, I would have one hundred percent kneed his balls.

He gives me another long kiss. Mischief sparkles in his eyes. "Where is Gotha and who is Ghoul?"

My body is vibrating with excitement and joy.

"Gotha, Ghoul! Come here."

From the gothic princess bat castle, Gotha shoots out like a rocket, followed by deep rumbles of barking that would make a grown man cry in the dark. Charging out like a spartan warrior from his bougie doghouse—also built by dad—is my good boy, Ghoul. The black and tan Doberman is larger than average, with a large scar running down the right side of his body.

"You named him Ghoul?" Mendax asks with a lopsided grin, but his body is stiff.

Gotha is flapping around his head, smacking his face with her wings. Probably giving him a piece of her mind, which is fair. Ghoul has his snout buried in Mendax's crotch.

I shrug. "It wasn't me." My nails scratch at my palms. "Whoever owned him before named him that. He won't respond to anything else."

I got Ghoul a few months ago after seeing him at an adoption drive at the pet store. Hearing how he was going to be placed back in the high kill shelter if he wasn't adopted that day made the decision for me. Gotha adapted to him quickly. Now, she flies around, grabbing scraps of food off the counter and tables for him, and he guards her while she's sleeping during the day.

They even have zoomie competitions and bicker like siblings. Now he's my running buddy, and I gotta say, I've never felt safer while running. Ten outta ten, highly recommend getting a running dog. Having them to curl up with on the couch and watch movies has been comforting for months now; it's honestly the only way I haven't felt lonely at night.

Once my boy starts licking Mendax's hand, he takes it as an invitation to crouch down and pet the loveable dog. With Gotha flitting around Mendax and Ghoul, plucking berries every thirty seconds to bring back to them, my heart feels ready to explode out of my skin like in classic cartoons.

A handsome man in a suit sitting in the grass, while a powerful black dog who came bounding out of his miniature log cabin of a doghouse and wiggles around in the green blades looking for belly scratches, is something I never knew I wanted. Apparently, I'm chopped liver because Ghoul has decided he likes Mendax more, declaring me the "spare" human despite giving him a life of luxury. Traitor.

The entire afternoon seems like a dream come true. Grabbing my phone off the patio table, I snap a quick picture. Sending it to my family group chat, followed by another quick text of "He's back!" This is a picture worth framing; the scenery is only made more perfect with the three beings who take up residence in my heart and home.

I finally fixed the garden beds and replanted the berry bushes and flowers. Dad helped me replace a few rotting fence posts and slats. Well, more like I helped him, but not really. I passed the tools and made sure he had something to drink. I'm not built for manual labor.

"Sooo," I clasp my hands behind my back because I don't know what to do with them while I toe some grass with my white Converse. "Feel like telling me what happened?"

There I said it, and I should be sorry about the edge to my voice, but I'm not. I deserve answers. A ball of tangled emotions rolls around my stomach as I watch Mendax pat Ghoul's side before standing and wiping his pants free of grass and dirt.

Tucking his chin into his chest, the same unruly lock of midnight black hair falls into his eyes.

"There is so much for us to catch up on."

The way his eyes scan my body, and his tongue darts out to lick his bottom lip has my thighs clenching. The urge to jump his bones like a cat in heat is almost unbearable. Instead, I revert back to the familiar nerves that have me in an icy choke hold.

"Can I get you anything? Water, tea. I'm still outta blood of a virgin." I softly laugh, remembering our first encounter.

The sun shines behind him outlining his edges in an almost ethereal glow. That smirk, the slight crinkles around his eyes that sparkle with amusement; damn, even in this glamour, he's still a handsome devil in a suit.

"Tea would be lovely." He steps closer to me, tilting my chin up with a single finger. Violet eyes bounce between mine. "Any kind you have is fine."

It's just like déjà vu.

The soft click of the kettle alerts me the water is done boiling, again, for the third time. For some reason, I can't bring myself to make the tea. He kissed me, and it was wonderful. I want to do more, but there's something holding me back.

"It's so stupid," I chuckle to myself, filling a glass with water.

Cool metal from the sink presses through the fabric of my dress and against my lower abdomen as I lean forward, trying to find Mendax in the backyard. The soles of my sneakers squeak against the newly waxed wood floors with every inch I stand closer to the window on my tiptoes. All I can see is Gotha plucking more berries to drop them into Ghoul's outdoor water bowl while he barks at the birds who dare to enter the backyard.

"Oh!" I gasp.

Warm breath fans the shell of my ear, I feel a pair of gentle fingers wrapping around my shoulders, sending shivers down my spine. His deep velvet chuckle makes my pussy weep sinfully. *God, it's been so long.*

"You scared me. I didn't hear you come in."

"I know, Davina."

A feather light kiss brushes my cheek, and I can feel his smile which sends my heart into overdrive.

"I've been standing in the doorway watching you for almost ten minutes now. Are you okay?"

"I'm good, great, grand. Are you okay?" I stammer as goosebumps rise in the wake of the path of kisses, he leaves down my neck. "Are we okay?"

"I'm fantastic now. I was horrible without you." He kisses my neck. "Let me show you how okay we are."

A single finger pulls down the strap of my dress before his hand skims down my chest, beneath my dress, and gently cups my breast. His warm fingers brush my hardening nipple, pulling a soft moan from me as my head lulls backward, resting on his chest. I have never been happier than I am now that I can't wear a bra with this outfit.

"Let me get something for you first." He mumbles against my neck.

"I already know what you can get me." I call out to him while turning. *An orgasm, he can get me an orgasm, or three.*

My knuckles are white from gripping the sink to steady myself, while my lust sends my head into a tizzy.

As fast as he leaves the kitchen, he comes back.

"For you. It's not exactly romantic teddy bears, candy, or jewelry, but I think you'll appreciate this."

Holy heck, was his voice always this deep and husky? Why does it always get hot around him?

I look down and see the familiar pearlescent pill waiting in the palm of his hand. A smile breaks out across my face.

"This is absolutely perfect." My hand hovers over the teacup, until I remember I didn't even brew the tea yea. "I forgot the tea."

His natural campfire scent surrounds me as he cages me against the counter. Hands braced on either side of my hips.

"I don't want to drink tea right now, Davina." In the blink of an eye, the pill is pressed against my lips. "I want to drink every drop of you dripping down those beautiful thighs of yours. Then, I'm going to relearn every curve of your delectable body and retrace every tattoo while you scream my name for all your neighbors to hear. I'm going to fuck you in every room of this house. Then we can have tea and talk." His hand wraps around my ponytail, tugging my head back. "Swallow it, Princess."

All moisture has left my mouth and is pooling in my panties.

"My mouth is dry," I rasp. "I need water."

There's a dangerous glint in Mendax's eyes, matching his dark chuckle. "Water, huh?"

I'm hypnotized as he brings the glass from around me and in between us. He lifts it to his own lips, sipping it like we're not in the middle of something. His thumb drags my bottom lip before pushing past my teeth and pulling my mouth open. Claiming my mouth, he passes the water from his lips past mine.

"Swallow."

It isn't a request; it's a dark demand. So long, Gentleman; hello, Beast.

Like the obedient girl I am—who is an unashamed whore for this man—I swallow and stick my tongue out to show him.

"Grab the sink, Princess."

He kisses me passionately, wedging his knee between my legs. Darting my hands behind me to grab the rim of the sink, anticipation builds with bated breath.

The pill is fizzing in my veins while I clutch the sink behind me and watch as Mendax sinks to the ground and disappears under my skirt. His deft fingers curl around the top of my lace thong, pulling it down at a pace that could make me give up the nuclear codes. Stepping out of them as quickly as I can, colors swirl in the corner of my eyes, and I have to blink to fight off a growing haze.

Excitement thrums through me when a crimson hand tucks the nude colored thong into his back pocket.

Before I can say anything, Mendax inhales and groans.

"Oh, princess. You're drenched."

The flat of his tongue presses against my slit, parting my folds as he makes his way to my clit. A moan flies from my lips, followed by a gasp. Horns press against my thighs, and the face I remember stares up at me. This man winks at me seconds before he sucks on my clit while thrusting two fingers in me.

My head falls back, and I grip the sink tighter.

"Mendax!" I scream his name as his skillful digits curl into my G-spot, stoking a fire in me.

With each prod of his fingers and swirl of his tongue, I'm coaxed to the edge of bliss. Rising on the balls of my feet, my hand finds his horn, and I use it to bring his face closer. Grinding my hips shamelessly against his mouth, chasing my orgasm.

"Mendax, I- I'm so close. Don't stop," I beg, somewhere between a moan and a whisper.

A whimper leaves me when cool air rushes against my damp skin.

Standing to his full height, he grins while slipping the straps off my shoulders, letting the top fall to my waist. Mendax's lips find my hardened nipples as he pushes my breasts together. He licks, sucks, and bites at one, then the other, going back and forth until they're both painfully hard.

"Every part of you is so damn sweet."

His fingers dig into my thighs, lifting me so I wrap my legs around his waist. His pants are ruined forever, but I can't bring myself to care as I rub myself against his cock, tenting in his pants.

"I can't hear you, Davina; I need you to be louder if you want to cum. I told you the neighbors will hear you."

The textured peach wallpaper I decided to keep scratches my back, and my fingers fumble with his zipper.

"Please."

"'Please' what, Princess?" His nose brushes my neck.

The ridges of the underside of his cock roll in my hand as I stroke him. A deep groan comes from his throat while he sucks and bites my neck.

"Let me cum. Please, Mendax. Make me cum."

I'm panting, shoving his pants and boxer briefs down his narrow hips. My eyes flutter closed at feeling him prodding at my entrance. One of his large hands adjusts mine around his neck.

"Look at me," he groans and rocks a little in my hand.

My eyes fly open at the command. He pulls his hips away just enough to have my hold on his cock drop and places that hand around his neck, too.

"I love you. I'm not letting anyone, or anything, take me from you again," he rasps out before entering me in one brutal thrust. "God, you feel so good." He pushes in and out of me at a wild pace my hips desperately try to match.

I'm clawing at any part of him I can reach. Pulling him even closer to taste the salt on his sweaty skin with my lips and tongue.

"Fuck, Mendax, you feel so good. So. Good."

My back arches, pressing my breasts into his chest. Skating my fingers between us, I find my clit, circling it faster and faster. His forehead presses against mine, our gazes flickering between each other and down to where he disappears in me. His pace is brutal, demanding, relentless, and perfect.

In one swift motion, I'm pulled away from the wall. My legs tighten around him while he stays inside me, moving me to the little kitchen table. With one swipe of his arm, placemats and random items careen towards the ground. The searing kiss he plants on my lips causes my pussy to clench around him.

"You're so beautiful." His voice is husky and strained. "Eyes on me when you cum. Cum for me, Davina. Cum all over my cock."

The table bangs against the wall with each thrust. Vascular arms frame my head as he closes the distance between our bodies.

His words are enough to send me soaring over the edge. If there is an art form to looking gorgeous during an orgasm, it's certainly not a talent I possess. Forcing my eyes to stay open, I gasp locking my eyes on his face full of unbridled pleasure.

"Mendax!" I scream, squirting so hard I soak his shirt.

He kisses the hollow of my throat and spills himself inside of me while my pussy milks his cock for every last drop.

My hair is halfway out of the ponytail, my dress completely off my chest and gathered in the middle of my waist. Sweat clings to my flush skin.

"Better than I remember," I laugh, resting my head on his chest.

That sinful chuckle floats in my ear as Mendax slips out of me and gently sets me down. There's only enough space for me to gaze up at him while he removes his shirt, discarding it on the floor.

"Well, let's see if I can give you a permanent reminder of how good we are together."

A high pitched yelp escapes me as he tosses me over his shoulder.

"What are you doing?" I chuckle.

His heavy hand strikes my ass cheek, making my pussy quiver.

"I told you I was going to fuck you in every room of this house. The kitchen is only one: we still have nine more, not counting the garage."

Heat rises up my chest, painting my cheeks a hue close to Mendax's ruby skin. In a blink of an eye, I'm tossed on the bed.

"I love watching your tits bounce." He smiles, discarding his pants. "You should take that dress off if you don't want me to tear it off you."

He doesn't have to tell me twice. As soon as the cotton dress hits the ground, he's on me again, rolling us to guide me on top of him. His hands roam up and down my body, leaving a trail of goose flesh in their wake. My left hand finds its way into the dark chest hair covering his lean chest. Rubbing my slit along his thick length, my right hand slowly massages his balls.

Leaning closer, I kiss him and whisper, "I've missed you, and I'm so fucking happy you're home."

Then I sink down on his cock. My toes curl, and my head tips back.

He sits up, holding me closer. We're consumed by each other's kisses, touches, and moans. Feeling every ridge of him slide in and out of me is getting me closer to my next orgasm faster than I thought possible.

"Keep going, Davina, ride me until you can't anymore, then I'll take over."

Mendax continues to bounce me on his cock, thrusting upwards.

He is entirely too handsome right now, bordering the cusp of beauty. His dark hair is mused, sweat beading on his skin, and thick dark brows furrowing in concentration.

"You're mine, Davina. All mine. And I'm all yours," he grunts out.

A moan flies from my lips. "All mine. All yours."

Digging my fingers into his defined shoulders, I bounce faster.

"Come with me, Mendax."

He shakes his head. "You first. You'll always be first if I can help it."

And I am; I come first and hard. Another orgasm rips through me before the waves of the last are over with, his skillful finger working in tandem with his cock until he's past the edge and empties into me again.

Thank god I'm still on birth control because the amount of him dripping out of has to be a personal record.

Tea has been exchanged for electrolytes because we just went five rounds, counting the kitchen and the bedroom. A pile of dark chocolate and Oreo wrappers litter the coffee table. He finally told me everything that happened, and I didn't know if I was more angry or disgusted that someone could hold that kind of information. I can't believe Elara and Elsher would do something so horrible.

I got mad again when he told me the reason they couldn't say anything to me. Like, I get it, but damn, someone could have sent me something. *That* revelation led to angry sex and round four. Laying on his chest in the living room, his fingers draw lazy shapes on my back.

"I noticed you added a few new doodles to your collection."

Running my fingers up and down his arm, I laugh. "Yeah, I got them the last time I was in Portland for a business meeting, and my artist had a last-minute opening."

I sigh contently as his fingers run through my hair, massaging my scalp.

"Did I notice sneakers and a teacup?"

I snort. "So, you noticed the horns behind the teacup, then, too, huh?"

"Mhhm." He sounds smug, but I'll allow it. "I like it."

"Well, I ran my first and only marathon two months ago in Portland. Blake actually ran that with me. I also got the line chart to mark the start of my firm, which is growing faster than I anticipated, and I'm sure you can guess the teacup."

His fingers brush against my cheek as he tucks a stray strand of hair behind my ear, his fingers lingering for a brief moment. "You ran with

Blake?" His brows raise in surprise, and his voice betraying a touch of jealousy that he tries to mask.

My shoulders shake as I try to fight my laughter. "Yes, he was in the marathon, too. We did a few buddy-runs. The longer ones, actually, since Ghoul isn't a fan of more than ten miles, and I didn't want to run trails by myself."

With a slight frown, he purses his lips, deep in thought. "I can't blame you for wanting someone to keep you company. I still don't like him. But if you're happy, than I'm happy."

Mendax wraps his fingers behind my neck bringing my face closer to his. He kisses me with his full lips, moves on to the next topic. "Tell me about your business."

Sitting up, I bounce with pure glee. "Echelon Nexus. It's my own consulting firm."

He swallows roughly. "Davina, I'm trying to be a good and attentive boyfriend here, but if you keep bouncing like that, I'm going to slip back inside of you, and you won't be able to walk tomorrow."

"Walking is overrated. I can tell you about the firm when dinner gets here."

He licks his lips. "We didn't order dinner."

I lick my lips. "I guess we have time."

This is a welcome home he won't forget.

Chapter 40
Family

Mendax

THE SUMMER BUSTLE OF children laughing and chasing each other on electric bikes and a different genre of music playing in every backyard is all background noise for our walk. It's a miracle we made it out of the house, but, as Davina put it, the entire house was "smelling like whore's tea house." She said it like it was a bad thing. I guess four days of making up for lost time calls for a break, new sheets, and more clothing than a robe.

There was a time when Davina and I had the urge to fill the conversational void, but now? With our fingers laced and a gentle summer breeze, the silence between us while we walk is comfortable, easy, and perfect. She sighs and rests her head on my arm while curling her hand around my forearm until we end up at a park across the street from a graveyard.

"Let's go over there." She points to a shady spot under a white oak tree.

Setting down the red checkered picnic blanket, I move to grab everything out of the small basket Davina packed for our lunch at the park.

"Get comfortable, I'll set everything out."

She bites her lips like she's trying to not laugh, and I finally get it when I open the basket. I sigh. "Davina."

"It's girl lunch!"

"That's not a real thing."

She bursts into laughter, seeing my face. I feel the laugh in my chest build as I pull out pickles, goat cheese, carrot sticks, almonds, rolled salami, and snack bags of popcorn.

"Remind me to cook you a decent dinner tonight."

I lean in, smiling, before I kiss her.

Children's laughter mingles with the chirping of birds above us and fades into background noise. Davina sighs with the warm summer breeze, popping the last almond in her mouth. I kiss the top of her head. This level of happiness and contentment is a foreign feeling I don't think I'll ever get used to. Staring down at our entwined legs, resting my chin on her head, I hold her a little tighter.

"I don't know if I told you, but I'm proud of you," I say, watching her wiggle down my body, her head landing in my lap. "You built a successful and thriving firm from the ground up all on your own. Without the help of a magical oddity."

Her shoulders shake as she laughs. "Not gonna lie, a ring like my old boss had would certainly have made things a hell of a lot easier. Lucky for me, he's just as much of an idiot as Tony. He put Tony in my place, and everything started to fall apart. My old team asked if they could work for me, and news spread pretty quickly. The clients trickled in after that. It's still new and not exactly large. Gina and Tina are calling it a 'boutique firm' because we have high-profile clients but not very many. It looks like we're super selective, which isn't bad." She lifts one shoulder and laughs through her nose. "Looking selective makes us appear exclusive and desirable."

Her purple crop top slides up a bit higher as she stretches before sitting up. The way her nose scrunches and fingers pick at her denim short shorts stirs something in me. My fingers itch to touch her all the time, so I give in to the urge, tuck a strand of hair behind her ear, and watch her sort through her thoughts.

I love being able to do things like this with her. It's not fancy, but it's perfect. It's us getting to be together out in the open. Being with her at home is wonderful; curled up on the couch watching a scary movie followed by a cartoon is amazing. But this? This is new for us, and I'm just happy there's still an *us* after everything.

"Mendax?" Davina breathes.

The blanket crumples as I pull her closer to me to rest her back against my chest. "Hmm?"

Closing my eyes, the summer breeze blows strands of her into my face. Pressing my nose into Davina's silky strands, I inhale deeply, letting her lavender scent consume me. Maybe it's creepy, but I can't bring myself to care.

Her voice is soft and tentative. "Can we open another portal to your apartment?"

Her question causes me to open my eyes and peer down at her. She nibbles the corner of her lip, pulling away just enough to look up at me.

That wasn't a question I was expecting. I thought she was going to ask for another pet, maybe a cat, so we can grow our family more.

"Why would you want to do that? It's not a no. I'm curious." The silence stretches comfortably between us while she leans back to nestle further into my arms and play with my fingers. I must say, I'm not in a rush for anything. Not only is this comfortable and makes me stupidly happy, but the view down her shirt is fantastic.

"Well, it would be easier for you to visit your family. I'm sure Gotha would like to go back, too. I also don't want you to feel like you're stuck here." My brows pinch when she whispers the last part.

Extracting her from my embrace, I turn her and cup her face in my palms. I need her to focus on me and only me right now.

"Davina, look at me."

Her eyes peek up from under the dark curtain of her lashes. The sun slots through the leaves of the trees, highlighting the flecks of amber in her large brown eyes. For a moment, I'm sucked into a deep chestnut vortex, and I have no intention to try and escape, at least not until she resumes nervously biting her plump, pink bottom lip waiting for me to continue.

"I'm not stuck here. I'm choosing to be here because you're here. Where you are, I am. But I think we can find a way to open a new portal to *our* apartment. We can think of it as a vacation home."

A breathtaking grin spreads across her lightly freckled face. *God, this woman is a work of art.*

She purses her lips to the side in thought. "Can we not have it leading into our bedroom? Maybe the backyard or the garage if we want to factor in the weather."

"That sounds perfect. The easiest way would probably be for me to go back and have you summon me again. I should set up the other end of the portal in the living room next to the door. The kitchen pantry wasn't exactly ideal." I laugh. "We can also ask Wren to help you, just in case."

A bright blue ball rolls towards us. Reaching across me, she picks it up and spots the wobbly toddler on a mission to get the ball back. A grin splits her face and I find myself smiling with her. Scooting off my lap, I allow my fingers to graze the strip of exposed skin around her waist. Her thigh muscles flex as she squats in front of the mop of curly blonde hair on chubby legs.

"Is this yours?"

The child claps and laughs, and she laughs along with them. It is like a glimpse into a future I could possibly want. Perhaps a little girl with black hair, like mine, but a spitting image of Davina. If she ends up with any demon traits of mine, the horns won't sprout until she reaches puberty. Two or three would be nice. Who am I kidding? Davina could say eight, and I'd agree because I'm that in love with her.

She flops back next to me, tucking her legs underneath herself, picking up our conversation as though I didn't just watch the next few years of our lives play out in my head.

"Goodness, Wren has been texting me nonstop, asking for juicy details."

It's my turn to lay on her lap. I smile up at her.

"What did you tell her?"

A playful glint in her eye accompanies the mischievous smirk. "I don't kiss and tell. Except I did mention how I couldn't walk the day after you came back."

Pride swells in my chest, and my ego gets a little bigger.

A full belly laugh leaves her. "Careful there; I'm not sure there's enough space in this park for all that humility you got."

Her hand swats at my chest and I ensnare it in mine leaving a kiss on her fingertips.

Yeah, this is perfect.

Days have come and gone, and life has never been better.

"There." I toss the screwdriver up in the air and catch it in my palm; I stand back to admire my handiwork.

Rick claps a meaty hand on my shoulder. "Great work, Mendax. I knew you could do it."

He came over with Paloma today to help us install a new lock for the garage door, along with a video doorbell. I have never claimed to be Mr. DIY, so I have zero issues asking for help.

Davina suggested asking Blake since he's handy. Before she could walk across the street and ask, I was already calling her father instead. He was more than willing to help, especially since he said, and I quote, "Any man my daughter chooses should know the basics of tools and building furniture."

Like hell I'll let Blake anywhere near our house to fix things while I'm here. Sure, she considers him a friend, and I respect that. But as her man, it's my job to take care of her, even if that means learning how to use tools, even though I've always just paid people to do this sort of thing before.

"Thank you, Rick." I holster the tool in the toolbelt he got me…the one that matches his exactly.

He also forced me into a pair of jeans and a simple T-shirt. I feel completely out of my element, but the way Davina stared at me and slapped my ass any time I walked past her today, makes me think I'll wear them more often.

"Davina?" I call out from the garage into the backyard.

The brown sandals, followed by her tan legs, swing into the door first, followed by the rest of her. Even in this simple grey T-shirt dress, with no makeup and a floppy bun on top of her head, she's breathtaking.

"Yes, Pookie?" She grins.

Rick chuckles behind me, "*Pookie.*"

Rolling my eyes, I return her smile. "Can you text Orroth or Wren to try the portal now?"

Last week, I went back so we could establish the portal again. Wren was more than happy to help us, except she refused to leave for two days because she needed girl time with Davina. Then my brother came, followed by Dakolas and Rolvak. They became instant cock blockers.

The portal didn't stay open as long; apparently, there is a usage limit to the spell her uncle created. With Wren's help, we managed to tweak it…I hope. The portal itself is a grey area when it comes to legal gates. I had to get a permit for it, and with the help of Dakolas, he redrew the blueprints to our apartment and called it an entrance into a panic room.

"They should already be here," she grins. "I texted them, like, fifteen minutes ago."

The sound of heavy boots reverberates through the cramped garage.

"Yo!" Orroth makes his presence known with his typical loud and attention-grabbing entrance.

Rick clutches his chest and leans against the red vintage car.

"Fucking hell." His cheeks puff with an exhale. "I wasn't as ready as I thought I would be."

We gave Rick and Paloma the anti-transformation pill so they could see past the magic as well. Rick took it like it was a shot from his party days in college. Paloma is still deciding if she wants to take it or not.

"Now, family game night can begin!" Orroth announces himself and the rest of them. "Where's my niece and nephew?"

He runs past me with a clap on my back and a quick introduction to Rick before skipping over to Davina. After twirling her in a hug, he yells out for his *niece* and *nephew*.

"Gotha! Ghoul!"

The rest of the group files out of the garage, introducing themselves to Davina's father and over to her with hugs and kisses. It's like we're one giant, dysfunctional family.

Ghoul is running out his zoomies and taking everyone out in the process—almost everyone. Rick snatched Paloma up in the knick of time, and there was a charged exchange between them. They tried to scamper off unseen but bumped right into me. I told them my lips were sealed and went to distract Davina before she asked where her parents had gone.

Ten minutes later, Paloma's usually neat and tidy appearance is gone. Her lipstick is wiped clean, her sleek bun forgotten, with her hair tossed in wild waves. Rick sported the largest shit-eating grin I've ever seen.

Paloma stands next to me, jutting one hip out while sliding her hands into the back pockets of her jeans. She looks like an older version of my Davina.

"You're a good man, Mendax. You make my little pumpkin happy, and that makes me happy." A glassy sheen coats her eyes as she stares off at her daughter and husband who are busy playing with Gotha.

"I can only hope I'm making her as happy as she makes me. She's everything I never knew I wanted or needed."

She inhales sharply and quickly swipes a well-manicured hand under eye, before rubbing my arm and walking back into the house. A minute later, there's a vibration in my pocket. Fishing out my phone, I swipe it open, smiling at the photo of Davina curled on the couch with Gotha and Ghoul while she's gaming, which I set as my wallpaper.

I'm praying it isn't my mother asking me to start working the front end of the business again. She's been on me for days about meeting with buyers and sellers. My heart stops beating when I see a thread of messages between Davina and two unknown numbers to me. It isn't the previous messages that caught my attention; it's the new one addressed to me.

The slam of the back door reminds me to breathe and clear the overwhelming emotions clogging my throat and burning the back of my eyes. Paloma walks by me and smiles. I watch as she whispers into Davina's ear. Whatever she told her has my princess grinning ear-to-ear, hugging her mother, and running over to me.

Rick is spinning his wife to the music playing on the outdoor speakers. Orroth is playing tug-of-war with Ghoul, both of whom have the orange rope in their mouths, and Wren is videoing everything. Rolvak and Dakolas are tossing berries into the air for Gotha to catch and into each other's mouths. *This is my family.*

"Hey, Pookie." Davina wraps her arms around chest. "Mom drank the pill, so now we wait for her reaction."

I stare down at Davina, brushing my thumb along her cheek.

"Are you happy?"

While reflecting on her question, I tenderly tug her hand, bringing her nearer to me. Our bodies gracefully follow the beat of the music.

She giggles, standing on her tiptoes to peck my lips.

"Happy is an understatement."

The only noises tonight are the crickets in the backyard, and Ghoul snoring like a chainsaw on the couch with Gotha curled into his side. Everyone's upstairs sleeping. Davina's parents are in one room, and the rest are in the smallest room, even though they could have gone back to the apartment. The promise of breakfast burritos lured them into staying.

It was fun seeing Davina squirm beneath me, trying to stay quiet while I took her over and over again until she tapped out and begged for sleep. Now, her hair fans across my chest, the ivory blanket drapes over her waist, and the moon kisses her skin while my eyes roam over her because sleep keeps evading me. Maybe I'm too high on happiness and love, but I don't think I'll ever come down. Sliding out of the bed, I move my pillow in my place and watch as she yanks it closer to her face.

Tiptoeing downstairs, I skip the one step that squeaks.

"I should ask Rick if he knows how to fix that," I whisper.

Standing at the counter, I watch the blue light of the kettle flicker off when delicate hands skate across my abdomen and up into my chest hair.

"What are you doing, Handsome?" Her soft, full lips kiss down my spine.

I turn and hoist Davina up onto the counter and step between her legs. She's wearing my shirt from earlier while I'm only in a pair of grey sweatpants she bought for me. According to her, grey sweatpants and black boxer briefs are male lingerie. My fingers skim her thighs in soft circles.

"I couldn't sleep. I thought maybe some tea would help." Leaning down, I press a quick kiss on her forehead.

"I have chamomile in the yellow container on the shelf," she yawns. "Mind making me a cup?"

The sleepy smile curling her lips pulls a smile from me. I'm obsessed with my girlfriend.

"Of course not. Tea, just like everything, is better with you."

I can't help but chuckle when I see the soft blush rising to her cheeks.

"You're beautiful."

"You're charming."

"Obviously, I'm charming." I playfully roll my eyes. "These are new." I put the unicorn and axolotl steeper's into the mugs before pouring the hot water in.

The ceramic slides along the counter as I pass her a rose-pink mug with the letter "D" and puppies all over it, and reach for a muted green mug with an "M" and bears on it. My thumb traces the letter of the jade-colored ceramic.

"I thought they were cute." Davina grins, blowing the steam in my direction. "Plus, with our home becoming the hangout house, we needed more cups, plates, mugs."

"Snacks, too."

Resting my hip against the counter, I stare at her under the warm orange lights; the only lights on in the entire house. This kitchen has become our own personal bubble, I'd even call it a sanctuary from the rest of the world.

"My brother and his friends eat like they're going through a growth spurt."

A soft smile graces her lips while she hums in agreement. Her warm fingertips brush across my forehead. "I saw the message Mother Dearest sent you."

Try as she might, her grin can't hide behind the ceramic in her hands.

"It was pleasantly unexpected." There's a happiness I don't even bother hiding in my voice.

Comfortable silence settles between us for a few moments.

Light scraping from the mug on the counter breaks the silence before she does.

"Hey, Mendax?"

Her legs hypnotically swing back and forth while I trace the long lines of them up to her hips. Touching her is my new favorite hobby.

"Yes, Davina?"

"Can you do the levitation thingy and get the strooples off the top of the fridge? I hid them behind the picnic basket." Her eyes are wide with excitement.

I bark out a laugh before she slaps my chest and shushes me. Looking over to the fridge, I snap my fingers, and the waffled cookies float over on a hazy cloud of yellow. Plucking the box, I grin, and she wiggles with glee.

"Here you go, Princess." I hand her the box and kiss her cheek.

She sighs happily. "I love you, Mendax."

"And I," cupping the side of her neck, the steady beat of her pulse matches mine, "I love you."

She leans in to kiss my lips, then my nose, and, finally, her soft lips linger on my forehead. *So that's how that feels.* It's like she's kissed away every thought in my mind.

"Can I request more forehead kisses?" I quirk my brows.

After placing a cookie over each of our mugs, she pulls me back between her legs and kisses my forehead again.

"Absolutely. Didn't you know? Anything you could want or need; I can get for you?"

We spent the long, quiet hours of the night sipping our tea and talking about absolutely nothing. To think all this love and happiness because she invited a demon to tea.

EPILOGUE Part 1

Holy Halloween

Davina

"**I** SAID 'GOTHA!'" I refuse to lose by one point, especially on something like this.

Dakolas chucks the blue erasable marker toward me. "Well, that's wrong! The answer is 'bat!'" His eyes narrow at me.

Gotha flies around the living room, pelting the rest of us with fun-sized chocolate from the trick-or-treating bowl.

Rolvak dives off the back of the couch, floundering for a gold wrapper. His hand shoots up from the floor, where he landed with a thud.

"Finally, she gives me a caramel."

Mendax comes into view and lifts me off the couch to settle me on his lap before I continue my tirade.

"Gotha and bat are the same fucking thing."

This guy has the audacity-like he got it on sale for a bulk buy- to look me right in the eyes and say, "No, it isn't."

"We're supposed to be on the same damn team, Dakolas."

"Not if you don't follow the rules, Vi."

"Hey, only I call her 'Vi,'" Orroth calls up from his pillow and blanket fort that he made of Gotha and Ghoul to snuggle with him in.

Wren makes her way down the stairs in her Halloween costume.

"You shush, Orr, you drew a penis instead of a trombone," she laughs, smoothing the black cat ears over her goddess braids.

Gotta admit, her costume is amazing. As it should be, apparently, she had it custom-made. Lucky for me, she had a costume made for me, too, but I wasn't allowed to know what it is until tonight.

"I stand by what I said; my trombone was a work of art, like my dick." He slides out from his overstuffed fortress. "Plus, you can blow both of them. Especially in that."

"This is why I can't take you anywhere."

She tries to look embarrassed, but we all know better, which is why we all laugh. Everyone is crowded around the whiteboard propped up against a potted plant on a shelf. "Oh, Davina, it's your turn to get changed. I laid everything out for you."

I can't remember the last time I dressed up for Halloween; well, actually, it might have been a drunken Halloween college party. To this day, the scent of vodka churns my stomach, and I dry heave just a little. As if it's perfect timing, the doorbell rings to signal the first wave of sugar-hungry children.

"I'll get it."

I slide off Mendax's lap. He stands behind me, and his large hand lands on my waist guide me towards the stairs.

"No, one of us will get it. You go change."

Dakolas and Rolvak are fighting to get to the door first, and Orr throws himself into the mix for good measure.

Wren snags the candy bowl off the couch, which looks suspiciously less full since Rolvak took charge of it, muttering about them being childish. She opens the door to a chorus of children trick-or-treating.

Crossing my arms under my chest, I pout.

"You know, it's not fair; you four don't have to wear costumes."

I eye each demon in my living room. They all opted for the bitch way out of Halloween and took the anti-transformation pill to look like themselves for tonight. Instead of wearing a full suit, though, Mendax opted for black slacks and a black silk button-down shirt. He looks like sin incarnate.

He lifts my left hand, running his thumb over the knuckles before kissing them. "You're adorable when you're jealous."

I roll my eyes and turn to hide my smile when a sharp smack cracks across my ass cheek.

"Don't roll your eyes at me, Princess."

"You can't even prove I did."

I turn and roll my eyes again so he can see it, and high tail it up the stairs when he playfully lunges for me.

Wren, God bless her, she has some kind of dark and twisted sense of humor. This is what I get when I confessed to her, I called Mendax "Satan" when I first saw him.

I'm standing in the mirror, admiring how the white feathers on the angel costume seem to emit a golden halo around me every time I move. The white gown has a corset, milkmaid top that presses my girls almost up to my chin, while the skirt is sheer with feather appliques to cover up my lady bits. Let's not even talk about the slit on both sides that goes up to my hip bones.

Holy mother of cheesus, I'm gonna catch a charge tonight because I may accidentally flash someone.

The house is oddly quiet during my careful descent down the staircase.

Everyone probably went outside to celebrate and cause mayhem. I love them.

A warm orange flickers on followed by another, and another, and another.

"Oh, crap. Did I leave a candle on?"

My modesty is all but forgotten as I run down the stairs, hoping my house isn't starting to set a blaze. I come to a grinding halt, seeing floating candles dancing around my living room and leading into the kitchen.

Mendax stands from the small kitchen table, where two teacups sit steaming. Gotha comes sweeping in from the open kitchen window and drops something in his hand before nestling into a shelf watching us.

"Mendax? What is all this?"

I nearly faint at the sight of him dropping to one knee.

"Holy Halloween."

EPILOGUE Part 2

Say yes

MENDAX

I F HEAVEN IS A real place, then Davina looks as though she's been plucked straight from there. This is the only woman I will ever get down on my knees, or rather knee for. Gotha did her part of dropping the ring off, even if it was a bit early. Ghoul wanted no part in this once he saw the floating candles.

"Holy Halloween."

That's a new one. I chuckle and smile.

"Davina, you accidentally summoning me was the best thing that has ever happened. I love spending every day with you. I love everything about you. From that beautiful brain of yours to the dusting of freckles on your nose that crinkles when you laugh. The doodle tattoos on your skin to the small scar on your leg. You're controlled chaos set my life in a whirlwind where I changed for the better. I grew into a man despite thinking I was already one. I want more game nights, you teaching me how to play video games, and more late-night tea in this kitchen. I want you as much as I love you. Will you, Davina Nicole Myles, make me the happiest man in all the realms and marry me?"

I swallow down the lingering nerves and hold the ring-pop-shaped box in shaking hands. Slowly, I flick open the red faux diamond to show the ring I had made especially for her. The 14k gold band is nestled in black cushioned velvet, making the elongated, hexagon, moss agate stone with three diamond accents on either side stand out.

Months ago, when my mother said she had put a special gift in the bag for Davina, I never in a million years would have guessed it was the family ring. While I appreciate her wanting me to give it to Davina, the ring felt tainted, and Davina deserves something that isn't laced with bad history.

Tears are falling freely from her eyes as they dart from my face to the ring. Her smile outshines all the candles floating around us as she bounces on her toes, but the silence stretches.

"Ow, shit. You stepped on my toe with your boots, you asswipe," Dakolas hisses from under the open kitchen window.

"Shut up, I'm trying to hear," Orroth whispers.

Wren pipes up next, "She didn't say anything yet. Why didn't she say anything?"

Valid question, but I'm prepared to stay in this exact spot all night if I have to.

"Say yes!" Rolvak's yell is followed by a series of smacking sounds from the others.

Davina laughs and wipes her eyes. "Oh God, I answered in my head and was wondering why you weren't putting the ring on. Yes! Yes! Yes! I'll marry you."

"Oh, thank God. You had me nervous."

I slide the ring on her finger and watch as the magic-infused band resizes to fit her finger.

Standing and leaning closer to her, I cradle her face in both hands and kiss her. Pouring every ounce of love and adoration I have for this woman, my woman, into the kiss. I never want this kiss to end. Her arms snake around my neck, pulling herself even closer to deepen the kiss. I could get a case of amnesia and never forget the taste of this kiss. It's a perfect mixture of her naturally sweet lips and a hint of the salt of her tears. Just like her, this kiss is perpetual bliss.

Eventually, we break away from each other to breathe and give our swollen lips a break. Holding her closer to my chest, she lifts her hand to admire the ring.

Cold white light and flashes go off at the window. Four phones peek out from the window, capturing this moment before one of them starts playing some soft pop love song. Ghoul howls with the music, which causes a grin and laughter to erupt between us. Our bodies sway to the music, enjoying the here and now.

"I told your parents about this. Your mother threatened me within an inch of my life when I told her about the ring pop. Your dad dared me to do it. Paloma terrifies me, so I had the ring box made instead."

"Even with a ring pop, I would have said yes."

"Just another reason why I love you."

The soft glow of the candles dances around her costumed wings, creating an ethereal spotlight around her. I should ask if Syn will make a wedding dress for Davina.

"The fact that you remembered what I said about a ring pop and it being red." She sniffles and kisses my hand. "I love you, too."

The music changes to something more upbeat.

"Can we come in now?" Orroth whines.

"Yes!" Davina laughs.

I hold her closer as the stampede of friends comes barreling through.

Surprisingly, Wren elbows everyone out of the way with a ferocity I've only seen in sports. She stands in front of Davina, eyes wide and a huge smile on her face. Davina pulls away from my arms and stares at Wren.

Ear-piercing screams and squeals of excitement consume the entire house as both women jump up and down in a circle. The guys are still shoving each other as they make their way over. For a moment, I stiffen as my brother hugs me. We've never been touchy with each other, but this is nice, so I hug him back. The twins take it as an invitation to hug me as well before jumping up and down with Davina and Wren.

There's a knock on the door, and since my fiancé is busy showing off the ring, I move to answer it. *Fiancé. I like how it sounds. Wife will sound even better.*

Just shy out of earshot, I hear her say, "I gotta say, this ring, just like that man, is perfect for me."

God, I love this woman.

Grabbing the candy bowl that's almost empty after the fifth refill, I swing the door open.

"Trick-or-treat, whoa! Your costume is soooo cool!" a little girl in a Red Riding Hood costume squeaks.

There's a shuffle behind her, and I notice a man dressed as a wolf behind her.

"Uncle Blake, do you see his costume?"

Blake shuffles close, and his eyes widen, "Wow, you go all out, huh?"

"You have no idea."

I bend down in front of the little girl. "Would you like the rest of what's in this bowl?"

Her eyes widen, and she furiously nods her head.

"That's too much," Blake interrupts his niece's excitement.

"I insist." I stand to my full height. "We'll be too busy to answer the door because we're having a little celebration party."

I smile. I know what I'm doing; it's the equivalent of a dog marking his territory.

"Mendax? Oh, there you are, I was wondering if you—"

I don't miss the way Blake's breath hitches at the sight of her. He swallows roughly.

"Hey, Blake."

He blinks several times and releases a harsh breath through his nose.

"Davina, wow. That's a fantastic costume." He's staring at her a little too long and hard. "Beautiful." It's a rough whisper, but I heard it nonetheless.

"They match like we do, Uncle Blake," the little girl pipes up, shaking her uncle out of his dreamy haze.

Just for that, I dump the rest of the bowl into the pillowcase she's holding and wink. She stifles a giggle while her hands clutch the bag closed so her uncle can't see.

"I heard you're celebrating something."

He's still eyeing her up and down until he tracks her hand on my chest. I wrap my arm around her shoulder to give her a peck before dropping it to her almost exposed hip.

Davina gives a happy sigh before offering me a beaming smile. "Mendax proposed. We're engaged!"

The crestfallen look on his face shouldn't make me happy. I'm a bigger man than that, but I can't bring myself to feel anything but happy about how everything turned out.

"Con—congratulations."

His smile is forced and a little painful. I do feel a little bad for him. She's probably going to be the one that got away from him, and unless he decides to move, he's going to see her every day. He'll see how happy we are; he'll see her pregnant with our babies—maybe—which is sad for him. For me, this is our happily ever after.

"Thank you," I say, even though he wasn't talking to me. "We shouldn't keep you and your niece from the night. Have fun."

I make sure to smile before swinging the door closed.

"Mendax," Davina starts, probably to tell me how that was rude, but her chiding turns into a moan as I press her against me and kiss her senseless.

"I love you. I'm deliriously happy." She beams.

"I love you too. Don't worry; I'm only getting started on making you happy for the rest of our lives."

ACKNOWLEDGEMENTS

First, thank you to my husband for supporting my dreams and goals and cheering me on while I make them a reality. Thank you to my team of beta readers who kept asking for one more chapter, especially Shay and Riley who helped shape this story into what it is, and pulled quotes for me. Also a big thank you to Reina for designing such an amazing cover. To my fellow author and friend E.C Garret, thank you for your support, your friendship and dedication to all things bookish is truly inspiring.

Thank you to Darling Author Services for handling the ARC portion of publishing allowing me to focus on all the other aspects. Also, a big thanks to Happily Booked PR and Management for helping me create some stunning images for my social media.

Shout out to my kick ass editor K.F. Starfell for doing amazing work on this book. Your comments were top tier and gave me the motivation to tackle the edits and that's saying something because editing is not fun for us authors.

To all the ARC readers who read this and left reviews, thanks. You leaving reviews is so valuable to authors especially those of us in the Indie Author community.

Lastly, I want to thank past me who needed a world to escape into and for being brave enough to write something she had never written before.

ABOUT THE AUTHOR

Marilu Moser is the sensational scribe behind fiery female leads in fantasy, monster romance, and paranormal romance stories. She hails from the land of chocolate, crayons, and American history, also known as Pennsylvania. Marilu is a proud mother and wife with a degree in Psychology, which is used not only to shape characters, but also illuminates her path towards nurturing the hearts of her cherished ones.

Her dad joke game is top-tier, and she's a tireless optimist who's powerless to resist root beer floats and pizza. Legends speak of her snort-laugh, a sound of pure delight. When she's not busy conjuring tales of enchanting characters and worlds, you can find her snuggled up with her furry companions, lost in the pages of a gripping novel, indulging in crime shows, or racing the orange roads of Hot Wheels with her children. And when the board games are brought forth, her fierce spirit leads her to triumph over her husband with a smile, every time.

AFTERWORD

Dear Reader,

I hope you enjoyed reading "Who Invited The Demon To Tea?" as much as I enjoyed writing. Don't forget to subscribe to my newsletter for updates on all my stories and even surprise bonus chapters and epilogues. You may even get surprised with an announcemnt of a spin-off involving different characters from the same world.

https://landing.mailerlite.com/webforms/landing/y9z7y6
Or scan here:

Until next time,
Happy Reading!